# TRANSFORMING HELEN

## Morgan Blair

Book Publishers Network

Book Publishers Network
P.O. Box 2256
Bothell • WA • 98041
Ph • 425-483-3040
www.bookpublishersnetwork.com

10 9 8 7 6 5 4 3 2 1

Printed in the United States of America

LCCN   2013944837
ISBN   978-1-937454-92-0

*Editor: Julie Scandora*
*Cover design: Laura Zugzda*
*Interior design: Stephanie Martindale*

FOR

BILL , LEAH, ESTHER, AND JONAH

# CONTENTS

# ACKNOWLEDGMENTS

S ome important people listened to me read portions of this book or read it for themselves or discussed aspects of it with me. Some did all three. They provided both encouragement and information. I gratefully acknowledge the assistance of all of them: Leslie and Justin, Bill, Richard and Betty Heaton, and Bev Harrington.

# PART I

❧

# OCTOBER

"Tell me something about how and when you met your husband," said Helen, sitting forward and putting her small notebook on the coffee table so she could take notes.

"About five years ago, I was working in a medical clinic in Woodinville. I'd been there since high school. James was a deliveryman. He came to the clinic about twice a week to bring us medical supplies and stuff. I was the one who checked them in, so I saw him all the time. I sort of started flirting with him. After a couple of months, I asked if he wanted to meet for coffee sometime, and he said yes."

"It sounds as if you had to take the first step …," Helen trailed off, leaving the question hanging between the women.

"I did. He was really shy. I'm shy too, but he's much worse," she said. "Maybe because even then he was too heavy. Not as much as now, but still …"

Pam Butler was overweight to the point of obesity, and if she talked about her husband James as overweight, Helen believed it was more likely an understatement than the reverse. Helen moved forward in the interview slowly, asking next, "Tell me about the birth of the girls."

"Susie was born three months after we got married, which we had to do because James's parents said they would only help us if we were legal. Neither of us really wanted to get married, I don't think. Then Janie came along not quite two years later. After she was born, I had my tubes tied because I sure didn't need any more kids."

"Let's talk about the girls, Pam. Tell me all about them, what they like and don't like, how you make them behave when they act up, when they get up and go to bed … all that sort of thing."

The interview continued for an hour with Helen writing down a good deal of what Pam Butler had to say. Pam was reticent and, Helen thought, a little fragile. Helen avoided some issues that she knew were important, such as alcohol use, because she did not want to push Pam too far at a first meeting. When she had been at Pam's house for about an hour, Helen stood and began putting on her coat and gathering up her umbrella and purse. She left the notebook and pen out, suspecting that she would hear something important as she left.

"I've left my card with my cell phone number here," Helen said. "You can call me at any time; leave a message if I don't answer. I'll be in touch with you again after I've had a chance to conduct more interviews. And I'll need to observe you for an hour interacting with the girls. I'll arrange that later. For now, you think about who else you might want me to interview, maybe your best friend or a relative … someone who you think can give me another view of the situation." She said this as she moved toward the door.

"I can tell you how this will turn out," Pam said. "James's parents have been after the kids since the beginning, and they won't be happy 'til I'm out of the picture and they can raise the girls however they want."

When Helen stopped and turned to look at Pam, she was not surprised by the tears in Pam's eyes running down her cheeks to drop on the stained pink sweatshirt. "They'll tell you I can't do anything, and I can't take care of the girls. They'll say I'm a drunk and didn't go to college, and I'm not a fit mom. I don't know how to clean the house or cook. They hate me, and they'll do anything to get rid of me. And they keep trying to turn the girls against me too." Pam was talking fast, gulping and hiccupping, spilling out the words as fast as the tears spilled out of her eyes.

Helen stood still and nodded. "I think you're right. I think I'll hear that. Your job is to concentrate on taking care of the girls and yourself. I need to talk to everybody and to listen to all of the stories. Until then, I can't make any judgments about what's best for Susie and Janie. I'll give you a chance to answer back to everything I hear. OK? This is just the beginning. We'll be talking more."

When Helen got to her car, she wrote up notes on the last part of the conversation with Pam. She wanted to get as much detail as possible while it was still fresh. She had suspected, from her preliminary reading of the statements in the file, that the in-laws were mounting a full-on effort to move Pam to the sidelines and become the stand-in parents of the two little girls. They had the money, the time, and the lawyer and were probably accustomed to getting their way.

❧ ❧ ❧

It was after eight that same evening when Helen sat in front of her computer to write an e-mail to Edward Pierce, her attorney. She had a number of instructions for him and referred to various files to provide details he would need to do his work. Helen had a fried egg sandwich, a raw cabbage salad, and a large glass of water and ate as she worked, paying little attention to the food next to her other than to make sure it went into her mouth rather than on her clothes or the keyboard. A Sinatra CD played softly in the background. Helen's small office was basically a Parson's table for the computer, a small stand next to it for the printer, a simple wood chair, and a bookcase with boxes to hold files and basic supplies. The furniture and equipment took up one corner of her dining room. It was situated so she could look out the apartment window and down to the street four floors below. She spent as much time watching the evening foot traffic in and out of the bars and restaurants on both sides of the street as she did typing. Her lights were dim so she would not be noticeable to the people below her if they happened to glance upward as they strolled. Two hours later, she stopped working and put her files away.

She undressed and put on loose cotton pajamas. Then she sat on a small rug in her bedroom, legs crossed in front of her. She sat quietly for a half-hour, meditating. Then she chanted for ten minutes, rose, and went to bed. As she lay staring up at the dark ceiling, her almost-fifty-year-old body gradually relaxed into the mattress. She sighed, closed her eyes, and drifted into sleep.

At midmorning the next day, Helen was on her computer when the phone rang.

"Helen, it's Michelle from CASA. I know you just started the Butler case, and I hate to ask you to do this, but I have another case I'm in a real bind with. The volunteer assigned to it is leaving town because her husband got a new job. She was late getting the case started, had it for almost two months before she made the first contact. All she's completed is the first interview with the mother. I thought of you because it's a third-party custody case, and you have more experience with those than our other volunteers." The court appointed special advocate supervisor, Michelle Sullivan, was talking fast so Helen would not be able to interrupt before getting hooked. "I know you don't like working on more than one case at a time, but I need this report done fast … The court date is in a month."

"Tell me more about the case. I'm not promising anything, and I don't think I want another case right now, but I'll listen." Helen felt guilty whenever she turned down a case, even though she was a volunteer. She knew Michelle played on that guilt. It was not so bad if the case was one that Helen felt any other CASA could handle just as well as she could. On the other hand, if it was one of her "special cases," she had no choice; she could not turn it down. Promises and vows she had made to herself were all that held her life together.

"Great, I was hoping you'd say that. The child is a three-year-old girl. The grandmother petitioned for primary custody. The judge granted her temporary custody until he sees a CASA report. The grandmother says in her deposition that the mother is unable to care for the child because of drug use and homelessness. The mother moved out of the grandmother's house, left the child there, and only visits the child for a couple of hours once a week."

"What does the mother say?"

"Mother says grandmother is denying her access to the child. Says she is going to a work-study program to try to get a job so she can support child. Also says she went to a drug rehab program and is clean." Helen heard the ruffling of paper as Michelle was talking. "Oh, I see now the grandmother also petitioned the court for child support from the mother."

"How long ago did the mother move out, and does the CASA say why?"

"Just a minute …" Helen sipped her tea as she waited for Michelle to look through the file some more. "OK, grandmother said mother moved out because they had a fight and mom didn't want to follow grandma's rules. That was just over two months ago, a week before she filed the papers for custody." Helen heard papers rattling as Michelle rifled through the paperwork some more. Then, "The mother, in the interview, stated her mom threw her out. She said she came home late one night. Her mother wouldn't let her in and had thrown all of her clothes out on the porch. She stayed with various friends for a couple of weeks, then moved in with her father on Vashon Island. That's where she is now."

"The grandmother didn't waste any time going to court," Helen said.

"No, and her statement in support of the motion is full of legalese … It almost reads like a professional did it. But Grandmother filed it herself; there's no lawyer involved."

"How old is the mother?"

"She's twenty, had the child when she was seventeen."

"Where's the father?"

"Not in the picture. He's in jail in Arizona. Has never seen the child, has no money, has never paid child support."

"Well, at least it cuts down on the number of people to interview. You can go ahead and send me the file. I'll work on it alongside the Butler case."

Helen could hear the relief in Michelle's voice. It was never easy to get a volunteer to take a case on short notice, especially one that another volunteer had bailed on. Many CASAs were retired and traveled a lot, often for several months at a time. The others, those still working, just did not have the free time to take a case unless they had a four-month lead before the trial date. Constant recruitment of CASAs was necessary, and turnover was high. People who wanted a responsible volunteer job found out in a hurry that the work was harder emotionally and more time-consuming than they had anticipated. Many worked only one case before quitting.

After Helen hung up, she changed clothes for a noon yoga class, grabbed her grocery list from the door of the refrigerator, left her apartment, locking two separate locks with two separate keys, and then walked down the hall. The door to the apartment across from the elevator opened, and an older woman peered out.

"Hello, Helen," she said. "I'm so glad I caught you. I wonder if you would like to come over this evening for wine and snacks. I've invited several friends I'd like to introduce you to." The woman smiled warmly, and Helen could see she was anxious for a positive response.

"I am *so* sorry," Helen said. "I've just taken on a big commitment, and I need to work this evening. But thank you for asking; it was very nice of you." Helen hoped she did not offend Mrs. Mayhew, who had moved into the apartment building about two months earlier. Mrs. Mayhew was in her early sixties and did not work. The building was home to mostly young, affluent, single people. Mrs. Mayhew was lonely, Helen suspected, and wanted to form a friendship with the only other older woman in the building. Helen, on the other hand, had picked the apartment building, in large part because of the demographics of the residents. She wanted to avoid entering into any relationships. Mrs. Mayhew seemed to listen for Helen to lock her door whenever she went out as, every two or three days, the older woman accosted Helen near the elevator. Helen wondered how many polite refusals she would need to issue before Mrs. Mayhew would give up. Her experience over the years had taught her she could never waver and accept even the smallest token or offer as it only prolonged the time required to snuff out all overtures toward friendship. Helen was not suited to, and did not want, friends. They asked questions and wanted to share confidences, and Helen could tolerate neither.

❧ ❧ ❧

Monday morning, Helen received a FedEx package with the file for the new client. She sat at her small chrome-and-cherry-red Formica dining table, a mid-century find from an antique store, and started on the file. She would be the advocate for Sedona Kirk, aged three. Sedona's grandmother, Judith Flack, aged forty-four, claimed that her daughter Merida Kirk was unfit to parent Sedona. After reading the entire file, Helen mapped out her strategy. She would talk first to Judith, allowing the grandmother to tell as many stories as she wanted. She would ask a number of random questions after Judith finished building her case against Merida. And, most important, she would take copious notes that would include a lot of verbatim quotes. It would be the second interview where she would get tough, after she had had a chance to get versions of stories from other people. She also planned to evaluate the child interacting with Judith, and she hoped to see the child alone at some point, if the child appeared willing. After listing the basic information she wanted, she prepared a small notebook for her interviews. She developed the initial set of questions she wanted to ask of both Judith and Merida. Then she made her phone calls.

"Hello, Mrs. Flack? My name is Helen Paige, and I've just been assigned as the new CASA for your granddaughter. The previous CASA had to move out of state so I'll be completing the case. I want to give you a brief overview of what I'll be doing. It will take about three minutes. Is this a good time to do that?" Helen had learned that any time she said it would be less than five minutes she was never refused. This time was no exception. "I represent Sedona, and I have her best interests in mind in everything I do. I'll start by talking to everyone involved, plus I'll talk to others who know all of you. My job is to gather information and then make recommendations. No one is paying me; I'm a volunteer so I don't have any agenda of my own here. I can't promise anyone what the outcome will be as that will be up to the judge if the case goes to trial. I believe it's always best if you all work together to come up with a solution to the issue on your own. The parties involved have the best information, and since they need to work together in the best interests of the child, it's good practice to start off working together on the parenting plan or custody and visitation issues or anything else that comes up.

After I've talked to everybody, I'll write a report for the judge. You will get a copy of the report. Do you have any questions so far?" She waited.

"Well, how long will all of this take? I want it settled." Mrs. Flack had a raspy voice with a sharp, take-charge tone.

"I can start as soon as you can make time to see me. How about tomorrow, Tuesday?" Helen had learned to reflect back the attitude and temperament of those who tried to control the agenda. She heard the intake of breath as Mrs. Flack reacted.

"Well … I guess I can make time. Where do you want me to be?"

"Since I have to see the house where Sedona lives, I'll go to your home. Do you prefer morning or afternoon?" She heard another intake, this time surprised and maybe even angry.

"Um, I'm not … well, the afternoon would be best."

Helen was amused at Judith Flack's dilemma. She suspected Judith would need the morning to make the house look its best as she would not want to have Helen see how she really lived. But she could not put the meeting off since she had already pushed for quick action.

"Excellent, I'll be there at two." Helen hung up and made notes on the call, then got on Google Maps and located the home and noted the time it would take to get there. Then she looked up a number in the file and started again.

"Hello, my name is Helen Paige … Is this Merida Kirk?" Helen went through the same preliminaries as before.

Merida's voice was soft and wavering. "Can you tell me how Sedona is? My mom hasn't let me see her in two weeks. Last time, Sedona cried and cried. She kept asking me to bring her home. Mom won't even let me talk to her, except for a few minutes. I went over there about six times, and she keeps saying Sedona's sleeping or out with my sister or something."

"I haven't seen Sedona yet," said Helen. "I hope to see her tomorrow when I go to interview your mother. So there isn't much I can tell you." She could hear Merida trying not to cry. "Will I be able to see you this Wednesday? I can go to Vashon Island to your father's house if you give me the address, or I could meet you in downtown Seattle somewhere if that fits your schedule. I think you're in a program or something there, right?"

"I'm in WorkSource, south Seattle, down past the arenas. Could I meet you there at my lunchtime, about noon?"

"Great, that works for me," said Helen. She got the address, and they exchanged enough personal information to recognize one another and then ended the call.

That evening, Helen ate a small dinner of pea soup she had made earlier in the day and a banana. She dressed in a long-sleeved shirt with a quilted vest and twill pants. Pulling on a light raincoat, walking shoes, and a hat, she left the apartment about six-thirty. The fall evenings were not cold, but she often did not get home until after nine, and by then, the cool air off the Puget Sound was chilly enough to bother her. She walked about a mile to a small church between the Queen Anne neighborhood where she lived and the area of South Lake Union that had not been totally renovated by Paul Allen's Vulcan company when Amazon decided to relocate there in 2012. The church had a vestibule with stairs leading to the basement. Helen went down and entered a meeting room, taking a chair near the back. A few minutes later, she rose to say, "I'm Helen, and I'm an alcoholic."

It was over an hour later when she left the meeting. She walked down to the Seattle Center and wandered through the paved pathways, stopping for some minutes to watch the water at the International Fountain. It was getting dark, and families that had been there for some time were gathering their things to leave. The children were complaining about having to leave "so soon, we just got here." The parents were either scolding or cajoling them into helping clean up the picnic debris. She watched them, wondering if the parents knew how lucky they were. Then she started the walk up the steep part of the hill and turned left onto Highland to take the long circuit that overlooked the city and sound. Kerry Park was full of the typical tourists getting the typical photo shots of the skyline with the Space Needle lit up. She walked for another hour before heading back to her apartment and the evening of work she had before her.

Wednesday afternoon, Helen parked her twelve-year-old Acura in front of a modest bungalow with peeling paint in a poorer part of Burien. The front yard, which was mostly dirt with some random paving stones, was enclosed with cyclone fencing. Helen went up to the front door, noting the rotten wood on the steps leading up to it. She looked for a bell or doorknocker and then rapped on the door itself.

"Coming, be right there," she heard the rasping voice yell out. The door opened. Mrs. Judith Flack was an overweight woman with thin brown hair pulled into a ponytail. She wore the sweat pants and top favored by many women of her stature. "Come on in," she said, stepping back and opening the door wide. "Have any trouble finding it?"

"No, no problems. Much as I hate to say it, technology these days can save a lot of headaches when it comes to that."

They went through a mostly empty living room into the dining area located between the kitchen and living room. As they walked through the first room, Judith pointed to the small girl sitting on the floor with her back to them, watching a small television that sat on an up-ended milk crate. The television was turned low with cartoons on, and the girl was totally absorbed in it. She did not turn to look at them when her grandmother said, "That's Sedona. She'll stay like that for quite a while so we can talk."

The dining room was overfull of furniture. The table and six wood chairs took up much of the room, and an overflowing bookcase, a desk with a computer and printer, a large buffet piled with manila files, and two tall file cabinets all competed for the remaining floor space. The table itself was clear on one-half and covered with files and paperwork on the other. Judith sat in a large ergonomic office chair with a high back at the end of the table closest to the computer set-up. She motioned for Helen to sit at the table and cleared a space for her. Helen took off her coat and gloves, got her notebook and pen from her purse, and settled into a chair.

"What do you want to know about first?" asked Judith. She had a half-smile on her face and appeared open and friendly. "Oh, and would you like coffee or tea? It's no trouble."

"Thank you, but I just finished a coffee while I was driving, so I'm good to go. How about we start with Merida's early life. I'd like to know about what she was like as a child, her role in the family, where she lived and went to school … that sort of basic biographical detail."

"OK. She was born in Everett. We lived in quite a few places. I may not even remember them all in order. I think we were in Shoreline when she started school, and then we were over in Poulsbo for her middle school years. She started high school in Seattle, then we moved to Arizona, and that's where she met Scott. She got pregnant and dropped out her junior year. We moved back here about two years ago." Judith was relaxed and spoke slowly enough so that Helen could get all of the details written down. In fact, Judith watched her writing and paused whenever she saw that Helen needed more time.

"What sort of child was Merida?"

"She was real easy, good student, no trouble at all until she hit her teens. Then she sort of went wild. I tried hard to manage her, but she's pretty stubborn. I warned her not to get mixed up with Scott, told her he was bad news, but she never listened to me once she met him. Then, after she had Sedona, she just started hanging out with whoever had pot or pills. I think she was addicted to uppers and downers. I had the cops pick her up once, and we put her in an in-patient rehab center for drugs. That was a couple of years ago, when we were still in Arizona. Just a second, I think I can find you some paperwork on that."

Judith wheeled her chair around to the bookcase behind her. She ran her fingers over several binders on a lower shelf and pulled one out. "I think this might be it." She opened the binder, checked an index in the front, and turned to a page marked with a blue tab. "Here it is; I thought I'd kept it. She was at Mesa View Ranch, outside Phoenix. Fancy name, but a pretty basic teen rehab clinic. I have the intake form here. Do you want a copy? It's no trouble; I have a printer/copier right here."

"Yes, thank you, I might want it for the contact info. I usually get a few releases signed so I can access records on school and medical or mental health issues. I won't know what I might want until later, but it never hurts to have a head start. Maybe I should have you sign a release, in case they want it from you as well as Merida if your name is on the case as her guardian at that time."

"No problem," said Judith, making the copy as she spoke. "I was the one who signed her in there. She was still seventeen, so you might need my signature. She was there a couple of months. I don't know how many counselors she saw, but you can probably get case notes from them if you want. Not that they did such a terrific job 'cause I think she went right back to the drugs when she got out. I know she's still using. And she lies all the time. You can't believe a word she says. Then she started fighting with all of us. Every time she came in the house, she'd start a fight with her sisters. And she expected all of us to take care of Sedona so she could go out and cat around. I never knew if she was going to be here or not, couldn't count on her for anything. She had a job, but I think she lost that, probably because of the drugs. She was paying the rent on the couch and chairs for the living room, but then she stopped making the payments, and they came two weeks ago and took the furniture back. That's why the living room is empty. She just can't be trusted. And she sure as hell can't be a mother for Sedona. She doesn't even bother to see her. She's too immature to be a mother. She never paid any attention to whether Sedona was fed or bathed or put to bed or anything."

Helen noticed that even though Judith appeared totally open and natural in telling the story, she was making sure Helen got everything down in the notebook. Helen glanced back and forth between her writing and Judith's face during the story, nodding and encouraging Judith.

"OK, I have that. Now tell me about the rest of the family. Who lives here with you?"

Judith sat back in her chair and rocked slightly before answering. "Well, my daughter Angie; she's twenty-four. Merida's younger sister Moira; she's nineteen. Kenya, my son, is fourteen. And Callie is twelve. Just a second … I want to check on Sedona and give her some apple juice."

Helen waited while Judith went into the kitchen, passed back through the dining room with a small plastic cup, and went into the living room. "Hey, sweetie, Grandma brought you some juice. You havin' fun with the movie?" She heard bits of murmuring but couldn't make anything else out. Then Judith came back and took her place in her chair.

"Are we about done here? I'm going to need to fix Sedona's snack and put her down for a nap soon."

"Just some more background. Tell me about Merida's father. Is he in the picture?"

"No, he and I divorced right after Moira was born. Merida was about eighteen months old. He paid child support, but he moved, and we never saw much of him. Maybe once a month he'd come to see the girls."

"Is he the father of the other children?"

"He is of Moira."

"And the others?"

"Well … I've been married a couple of times. Is that all relevant? I've been divorced and alone raising the kids for the past ten years. Is that what you want to know? If there's a man in the house?" Judith's smooth veneer was showing some wear. She raised her voice and talked fast at this point.

Helen nodded some more, kept her eyes on her pen, and wrote. She let the last question hang in the air for over a minute while she continued writing.

"I'm trying to get a sense of Merida's background and the influences on her when she was growing up. So yes, it is relevant who was in the home where she was raised and what role they played in her life. For example, did Angie's father spend time in the home when he came to see Angie?"

"He never came. He didn't want to have anything to do with being a father."

"How about Kenya, does he see his father?"

"He knows his dad. They see each other about every other month when his dad comes to town from out in Aberdeen. But Merida hasn't been around him, so he has no influence on her."

"And Callie?"

Judith was becoming noticeably cooler. Her hands were gripping the arms of her large chair, and she was leaning forward, her head jutting out over the table. "I don't think any of this has anything to do with your case," she said.

"I'm sure it seems that way. But if you want primary custody of Sedona, then I have to check out who will be around her. In fact, I still need to collect the date of birth and legal name of all of the children over the age of eighteen who reside in the home. We're required to do background checks on everybody who lives with or has significant contact with the child." Helen maintained a calm and matter-of-fact voice and tone. She smiled at Judith. "I'm sure you understand the need for us to verify that Sedona is safe and cared for."

Judith sat back again and took some deep breaths. "OK, I get it. So, Callie's dad lives in Detroit. He's a long-haul trucker and always on the road. Callie went to live with him and his second wife for about three months last year, but she hated it. She called me all upset, and I drove to Detroit and brought her back. So, no, she doesn't see him, and he's not around Merida and won't be around Sedona."

"Your last name, which of the children share it?"

"Is it important?"

"Well, I need to name them in the report, since they live in the house."

"Flack is my maiden name. When I was married, I always kept it. So Angie's is the same as mine, and Merida and Moira have their dad's name, which is Kirk, same as Sedona. Callie's dad is named Roloff. Kenya has my last name. I told you I'd been married a few times." Judith sounded both angry and defensive.

Helen then moved to a less sensitive area, and the interview continued for another twenty minutes as Helen asked about Sedona's favorite foods and activities and her schedule. Then Helen asked, "May I meet Sedona now?"

Judith went into the living room and turned off the television. She came back into the dining room with Sedona. The child was very attractive, with tangled brown hair and eyes, beautiful olive skin, and dimples when she smiled.

"Hi, Sedona, I'm Helen. I have been wanting to meet you. I've heard all about you." Helen put out her hand as though to shake, and Sedona walked up to her and held out her arms to be picked up. Helen obliged and put the child on her lap.

"Do you know my mommy?" asked Sedona.

"I almost do. I talked to her on the phone, and I will meet her tomorrow."

"Will you tell her to take me home? I miss her."

"I know she misses you, too. Where is your home?"

"My home is where Mommy lives. Will you take me?" Sedona starting crying and put her head on Helen's chest. Helen put her arms around the child and held her. She looked up at Judith.

Judith looked angry. She shook her head. "Sedona's just tired. When she cries, it's always because she needs a nap or some food. I'll take her." She took the child away from Helen and went into a short hallway off the living room. She opened a door and shouted up some stairs. "Callie … come down here and get Sedona!" A girl came down the stairs, took the still-crying child, and went back up. Judith closed the door and returned to the dining room. "She's fine. She'll settle right down with Callie." They could both hear Sedona still crying and Callie trying to quiet her.

"Well, I've probably taken enough of your time today," Helen said. "I can follow up with more questions on the phone. Then I'll come back again to do an observation of you and Sedona, and I'll look at the house then. That should take about an hour."

Helen turned to the back of her small notebook and took a folded piece of paper from under a paperclip. "Here's the release form. Let me just fill in the top, and you can sign it. Then I have it ready in case I need to process it to call the clinic in Phoenix." The women took care of the form, and Helen clipped it back in the notebook. "Is there anything else you want to tell me today? You can always call if you think of things later, and I'll give you a card with my cell phone."

"That's about it," said Judith. "I think you have pretty much what you need for your report. When do you think it will be done?"

"I'm not sure yet. This is my first interview. I'll want you to give me the names of one or two people you want me to talk to as collaterals." It was interesting to Helen that Judith never asked what that meant.

"No problem, I already have that for you." Judith gave Helen a slip of paper with the names and contact information for three people. "That's my mom, my sister, and one of my best friends. They can tell you all about Merida and her problems with the family."

"Excellent, I'm glad you're so prepared. I'll be talking to them within a week to ten days, depending on how the other interviews progress." Helen gathered her things and left.

❧ ❧ ❧

The office belonging to Edward Pierce, Esq., was located in a small art deco building on Queen Anne Avenue, just blocks from Helen's apartment building. Mr. Pierce had only three rooms, his lobby/reception area, a private office, and a small conference room. When Helen arrived, Mr. Pierce was in the conference room, arranging a series of papers over the table. Helen said hello to the paralegal at the desk in the reception area, a man of about her own age, and walked into the conference room. "Good morning, Mr. Pierce," she said, taking off her coat and hanging it on the back of a chair. She would never call him Edward.

"Good morning, Ms. Prescott. I'm just about ready. Can Mr. Osborne get you some tea? You know he loves the excuse to get all of the paraphernalia out when you come to see us."

Helen smiled. This was the one office she valued for its own sake. The two men who formed the complete law practice were not only kind and competent; they were also the most discreet people Helen knew. She recognized from the first meeting that they were a long-term gay couple and could tell that they knew she knew, but it was something none of them referred to. It was to them alone that she had disclosed her legal name, her business affairs, and a part of her history. She relied on them for a number of services that made her life and her work possible. Best of all, they seemed to like and approve of her. Normally, Helen did not care whether others liked or approved of anything she did or was, but these men were the exception in her life.

"I have some new red bush tea," said Kenneth Osborne, moving around the tea cart and cabinet set into a corner of the reception room. "It's from Botswana, flavored with vanilla. I think it's worth a try. Then I'll make some PG Tips to follow it up and give you a lift. What do you think?"

"Sounds wonderful. I knew you'd have something special so I skipped my second cup this morning. I'm parched." Helen sat at the polished wooden conference table, and Mr. Pierce joined her. "I can't believe you got all of this done so fast," Helen said. "I expected it to take at least two weeks, even for you."

Mr. Pierce smiled. "It would have, except the Morrison couple who own the duplex turned out to be in the middle of a nasty divorce and were so glad finally to get an offer they demanded a quick settlement so the buyer couldn't back out. I talked to Frank Brewer; then he went back to them with no inspection and no loan on our offer and got us a great price. I also have some paperwork for the institute for you to sign and some tax and accounting items you'll want to see." He placed one small set of papers in front of Helen just as Mr. Osborne entered, rolling the tea cart carefully to Helen's right side. He pulled out a chair next to it and sat, waiting quietly for the others to be ready. They both stopped and turned to him, giving him their full attention.

Mr. Osborne was clearly in his element. He had a kettle with hot water, two ceramic tea pots, two elaborately decorated tins with lids, a small wooden scoop, bone-china cups and saucers, two strainers, a small bowl for dregs, linen napkins, small china plates, and thin lemon cookies. No sugar, no milk, no lemon. He opened a blue-patterned tin and added two scoops of tea leaves to the first pot, then added the water and looked at his watch. "We'll give the red bush five minutes, I think. It needs about that long to get the full medicinal benefit, from what I've read. No cookies with it; save those for the Tips. I'm going to give the Tips only two minutes; we could use it a little weak after the red bush."

Helen smiled at him. She was reminded of Felix Unger from *The Odd Couple*. Mr. Osborne (she would never call him Ken) was on the thin side, always dressed totally unlike anyone else Helen had seen on the streets of Seattle. He wore three-piece suits, and his ties were always beautifully matched to the suits and shirts. Even when he was working at his desk on the computer, the only concession he made was to remove the suit coat and substitute a cashmere cardigan, which invariably matched the suit pants. His hands were those of a pianist, and she suspected he actually was a piano player, given the music he selected for the office.

"The construction on the street is so loud," said Mr. Pierce as they waited for the tea to steep. "Whenever I go out, I think about putting on those ear things all of the young people walk around with and playing music. I'll be so glad when they finish this new building."

"Do you think they'll just start another right away? Two years ago, it was the one with the bank on the bottom floor, and before that it, was mine, with the drug store on the bottom." Helen kept up her end of the conversation, understanding that no business could be discussed during Mr. Osborne's tea-serving period.

"I'm not sure how many apartments Upper Queen Anne can fill up," said Mr. Pierce. "We went for ten or twelve years with no changes at all up here; now it's all bustle, bustle, bustle. I grant you the buildings they tore down to put these up were old and not in good repair, but I think renovation instead of demolition could have been tried. Three new buildings in five years seems excessive to me, especially since they all have apartments from the second to the fourth floors. Does your building stay pretty full?"

"I think so," said Helen. "I've only noticed six or seven move-ins in the two years I've been there, and I doubt anybody could move in without me seeing it."

Both men nodded, both suspecting she was right. Helen probably not only knew how many people were there but also who they were, what sort of work they did, how long they planned to stay, and what their income was.

"Oh, this is fabulous," Helen said, taking her first sip from the cup Mr. Osborne finally handed to her. "Tell me more about it."

This was exactly what Mr. Osborne was hoping for, and he launched immediately into a discussion of the history of the plant, its fermentation into tea, the medicinal properties, and the studies that supported them—anything and everything that could be learned in two or three hours of Internet search. He was an excellent teacher and lecturer, and Mr. Pierce and Helen were the perfect audience, both interested and appreciative of the information. By the time Mr. Osborne had finished talking and answered a few questions, they were all drinking the second tea and munching on the lemon cookies.

"Mr. Osborne, you never fail me. I came here today wishing it wasn't always business that brought me to you. And here you've given me a terrific shot of information mixed with entertainment, not to mention two wonderful cups of tea." Helen noticed the flush of pleasure that rose from Mr. Osborne's neck up to his cheeks. She wondered what it would feel like to be so pleased with so little.

"I'm so glad you enjoyed the tea. I've packaged up some for you to take along when you leave. Think of it like a vitamin pill, just a cup a day for all of those health benefits. You can use that little one-cup strainer we gave you for your birthday, no trouble at all." While he talked, Mr. Osborne gathered up the teacups and plates, put everything neatly on the tea cart, and started walking backward toward the door, pulling the cart gently along with him.

"Let's get down to business," Mr. Pierce said. "First the duplex. We need to sign the closing documents and get the payment settled. Bottom line here is three hundred ninety-two thousand plus change. Where do you want that money to come from?"

"The Prescott family. But I plan to fix up the duplex, so I want to add a hundred thousand for that. Make a call to Boston. Tell the Prescott lawyer I want a donation of five hundred thousand to the foundation, tomorrow at the latest. Then transfer the funds from there to your escrow account. Will that work?"

"Yes, let me make the call right now. It's already past noon in Boston, and I want to make sure it happens overnight. You can read the institute minutes while I'm gone." He handed her a binder turned to a page titled New Life Institute Minutes and left her alone while he went into his own office. "This is Mr. Pierce calling from Seattle. I'd like to speak to Spencer Hancock directly, please." Mr. Pierce stood very straight with his back to his desk and his gaze on a picture of Mt. Rainier. He breathed deeply and slowly into his diaphragm, imagining himself to be addressing a senior judge. He wanted to convey gravitas and authority to a man he had never met personally but whom he knew to be a formidable legal opponent. As he expected, his call was put through immediately.

"Good afternoon, Mr. Pierce. Mr. Hancock here." The voice was deep, and heavy with authority.

"Good afternoon, Mr. Hancock," Mr. Pierce said with what he hoped was an equal voice. "I'm calling to make a request that you transfer funds to the Claudius Foundation this evening. We would like a donation of five hundred thousand dollars. I assume this will not be a problem?"

"Mr. Pierce, that makes well over two million this year, and it is only October. Can you tell us if this is the last donation this year you expect to request?" The voice was heavy with sarcasm this time and very dry.

"I can only assure you the foundation is making excellent progress on its goals for the year, and your clients' funds are making a difference in the lives of very deserving individuals, as always. We do not anticipate requiring additional funding this year and have not budgeted for it. On the other hand, as you know, unexpected situations do arise, so of course we cannot make any assurances."

"I'm sure," said Mr. Hancock, "that your work is most worthy and that the Prescott family will be only too happy to support your endeavors." There was a pause, but Mr. Pierce sensed that the conversation was not over. "I should mention, Mr. Pierce," continued Mr. Hancock, "that to a neutral and disinterested party this request could appear a bit … shall we say, confiscatory?"

Mr. Pierce thought for a minute before answering. "I have only limited information, of course, about the specifics of the underlying situation, Mr. Hancock. However, the small amount I do know leads me to understand the donations, which I believe were freely suggested by your own clients, could actually be considered not only reasonable but well below what one would think your clients would be moved to give, considering that the donations are used to further a cause in which they have a powerful and abiding interest." Mr. Pierce felt quite proud of himself for this bit of careful prose.

"I see," said Mr. Hancock in the same dry voice as before. "I will have those funds transferred before I leave the office. But I do think you might advise your client that my clients may want to discuss the matter further in the future."

"Thank you for your prompt action on our request," said Mr. Pierce, ignoring the last comment. "And I hope you have a nice day. Goodbye, Mr. Hancock." He hung up, breathed in and out deeply and rolled his head slowly from side to side. When he turned back toward his desk, he noticed Kenneth watching him from the other room. Kenneth raised his eyebrows in a question. Edward gave a small nod and an equally small smile. Kenneth grinned and went back to his own desk.

"That's done. The money will be available tomorrow, and I can move on with the closing. Do you want to sign those papers now or talk about the institute minutes first?" Mr. Pierce moved to his own chair in the conference room as he spoke to Helen.

"Let's talk about these minutes. I see you and the institute leaders are going to have a conference in March in Sun Valley. But the minutes don't say what's on the agenda for the conference."

"Doctors Schofield and Collins thought it was time to broaden the work of the institute. They are talking about moving to the regional level and inviting professors of psychology, sociology, economics, and criminal justice from all of the Western state universities to discuss setting up a multi-disciplinary program for graduate work focused on women moving from dependency to self-sufficiency. That's the general thrust of the conference, which would be exploratory more than anything. They want a wide range of opinions and input so they decided on an attractive setting with some lower rates for non-peak season. They thought that might bring out a broader audience."

"I agree with most of that. But if they want it for an extended four-day weekend, they should make it someplace you can get to easier. To go to Sun Valley will require everyone to rent a car and drive from the airport in Boise, most likely, and that time of year, the weather could be iffy. Why not make it Denver or Boise or even Reno or Santa Fe? Or else move it to April or May when the weather will be a little better?"

"Good points. I'll take them up with the others. Anything else on that?"

"Well, I should wait for the results of the conference, but my first thought when I look at the list of disciplines is that you left out the education or training angle. If women are moving into self-sufficiency, they probably need training of some kind."

"OK, I'll add that to my conversation with them." Mr. Pierce was impressed, as usual, with Helen's quick grasp of the essentials of a subject. He had been her lawyer for just over two years, and the sheer breadth of her affairs and interests still amazed him. He did not know any women her age, and he guessed her to be in her low- to mid-fifties, who had the energy and stamina she possessed, especially with what she had been through in her early and middle years and the toll those earlier tragedies had to have taken on her.

They signed the papers for the purchase of a duplex for the Claudius Foundation, looked over the financial statements for three of the foundation projects already in operation, and talked about some renovations to the new duplex. "I want one unit, the one in the best shape, still available for a tenant. Then I want to start right away on the second one. I want hardwood floors, a laundry, a shower added in the bathroom, either in addition to the current set-up or else put a new showerhead over the bathtub—we'll see which works best. I want the yard fenced, too. If we have kids in there, the mother needs those things as a minimum. Once we have the first side done, we'll move the tenant into that unit while we do the same to the other unit. Can you work on that?"

"Certainly. I'll call Mr. Patten, give him instructions, and have him bring in some bids." Mr. Pierce had been taking notes while Helen talked. "Will you want to see it all before we start, the drawings and specs?"

"Yes, and I want to visit the property, too. I haven't seen it, except for the virtual tour thing, and that never gives me a good-enough feel. The neighborhood is good, though. I checked on the crime rates in the area and the availability of parks and childcare options. All of that looks really good, so we just need to get the place up to speed, and I think it will work out well. Oh ... I forgot about the security ..."

"I know," interrupted Mr. Pierce. "I already put that on my list. I know that's always a top priority. We'll have lights that go from the front gate to the door and come on automatically with movement. There are some bushes up near the door so I'm going to have those trimmed back and then movement-activated lights put in and around them. Then we'll install a couple of lights pointed out toward the street a bit. That way, when the woman comes home she feels safe from the minute she gets out of the car. Then we'll beef up the locks on both front and back doors. In fact, we could use steel doors clad with wood."

"Excellent, you're really on top of all of this. I appreciate it to no end."

They talked over some other details. Then Helen left the office and headed back to her apartment. On the way, she stopped at a corner deli and got a sandwich and some chips for lunch. Mr. Pierce and Mr. Osborne suddenly came to her mind as she waited for her sandwich, and she wished she had invited them to lunch with her. Oh well, maybe some other time, she thought. But then, on second thought, that might be just a bit too much. If she took them to lunch, there was always the danger the conversation would turn to things she did not want brought up.

❧ ❧ ❧

Helen completed yoga practice before starting her phone work for the afternoon. After forty minutes of working on a series of poses, she took a warm shower. Still feeling unprepared to take on the tough work ahead, she sat on the floor and engaged in breathing practice until she felt a deeper calm. Then, renewed, she got out her files on the two CASA cases and reviewed them. These were going to be tough calls, and they were critical to her overall handling of the cases. She took notes on a legal pad and mapped out her strategy and questions for each call with different options that depended upon the answers she would get and the direction each call might logically take. She knew it was impossible to plan for everything as people had a tendency both to ramble and to take off on tangents. Sometimes the tangents were the most important clues so she needed to be ready to follow them. Feeling finally prepared, she settled into her living room chair, feet on a footstool, tea at her side, notebook and pen at the ready, and punched numbers into her cell phone.

"Hello, Mrs. Meredith Butler? I'm Helen Paige, the CASA assigned to Susie and Janie. I've talked to Pam and will be talking to your son James next week, as he probably told you. From my reading of the file, it would appear that you and your husband are quite active in the lives of the girls so I feel your input would also be important in my investigation

We could do it over the phone or in person or even a combination, whichever you prefer."

"Well, let's start with the phone, and then we can meet in person if you think that would be helpful. I'm so glad you called. I wanted to call you anyway since I think my husband and I have a lot to add to the whole thing. We've been helping Pam and James since they got married, and we're very close to the girls. We've been worried sick about them for the past year since Pam starting drinking. She even drives when she's been drinking, and if there was an accident with the girls in the car … well, we'd just never forgive ourselves. We've tried not to interfere or anything, but when the safety of the children is involved … well, that's another matter altogether. And Pam has just gone downhill. The house is a mess all of the time. The girls aren't being fed properly. Pam just gives them pizza or toast or cereal, no proper nutrition. And Pam is heavy herself, as you saw, and she is feeding those kids on nothing but fat and sugar. She's ruining their health. And she's drunk at night and never puts the girls to bed at a decent hour. Sometimes they all just lie on the couch watching junk on television until midnight. The girls aren't getting the sleep they need. We can't let it go on like this."

"It sounds like a real crisis," Helen said when she could finally get in a word. "Can you tell me when things started downhill and maybe why it happened?" Helen decided to give Meredith Butler plenty of time to state her case before getting to any of the more sensitive issues.

"We think it started after Janie was born. Pam probably had postpartum depression and never got treated for it. I don't think it ever really went away. The drinking started about a year ago; maybe she's self-medicating with alcohol for the depression. But she was never what you'd call a really good mother before that. When it was just Susie, Pam still couldn't keep the house clean or prepare a decent meal. And her weight! That's been a problem all along, but it has gotten a lot worse. I paid for her membership at a health club and told her I'd pay for Weight Watchers if she would go, but she never wanted to do that. We bought her a treadmill right after they moved into the house, and it still sits in the basement, not used. Sometimes I drop off bags of fruit just so they'll all have some healthy snacks around. I offered to get her a whole new wardrobe if she could get down to size ten. But I don't think she really cares about clothes so that never happened. I've done everything I could think of to help her lose weight, but nothing has worked. We tried to get James involved, too. But he never seemed to care. He works nights, you probably know that, and so he needs to sleep in the daytime. He just doesn't seem to notice that the house is a mess and the girls aren't being taken care of. I was over this past weekend, and the laundry was lying all over the floor in front of the washer, but the washer wasn't on. Crazy. And I couldn't find any clean clothes for the girls. They were wearing dirty clothes, for heaven's sake. I took them to the mall and got them some new things and just left the dirty clothes in the dressing room. We really are at our wit's end."

"I can hear that this has been very difficult for you," Helen sympathized. "Sometimes it really is hard to know how to help someone."

"You're telling me," Meredith continued. "We have bent over backwards for James and Pam. And we love those girls to death; we'd do anything for them. We're talking about moving into the house so we can help James with the girls when Pam moves out. Right now, we live in a lovely neighborhood. I play tennis twice a week at the clubhouse here, and our home is right on the golf course. We have lots of friends here, but we just feel we need to be there for Susie and Janie."

"That would be a big change for you," said Helen. "Do you think James would rather stay in the house or move to something smaller after the divorce?"

"James will stay in the house. My husband and I own it. We bought it for James and Pam right after they got married since Pam was already pregnant and we knew they'd need a place to live. But it needs work now. James just hasn't been able to keep up with the yard, given his work hours and then needing to fill in for Pam. He's just got too much on his plate. My husband has been going over twice a week to garden. He put in new plants, and he's started on a new slate patio out back with a fire pit and gas grill. We've arranged to have the basement spare room made into a bedroom and bath for James. That way it will be quieter for him to sleep when he gets home from work. Then we'll stay on the main floor in the master bedroom so we'll be closer to the girls."

"It sounds as if you've been busy planning for this," Helen said with a neutral voice.

"Well, we've seen it coming for some time. We couldn't let things go on as they are, and we knew we'd need to step in." Meredith sounded slightly defensive but sure of herself.

"I appreciate the time you've given me today. May I call you again if I have further questions? I never know in the beginning what kinds of things will need follow-up later."

"Yes, call me any time. We're anxious to help. Our lawyer said you'll be writing a report soon, and we'll get a copy of that."

"Yes, I have about three months yet before it's due, but you will see it as soon as it's complete. My supervisor at the CASA office needs to review it, and then she'll have me go back to fill in anything she feels I may have missed. That's probably when I would need to call you. Then her boss, the CASA director, goes over it as well, so the whole process takes some time."

"I understand you're meeting with James next week?"

"That's right, he and I plan to meet next Wednesday morning when he gets off work."

"I should tell you, then," said Meredith, "that he's pretty quiet. You may not get much out of him. And he might try to defend Pam. He's old-fashioned and thinks the role of the husband is to take the side of the wife. So you need to take what he says with a grain of salt. He may gloss over how bad the situation really is."

"Thank you for sharing that," said Helen, pushing one fingernail into the other palm until it hurt. She tried hard to keep any emotion out of her voice. "I'll keep that in mind during the interview." She said a polite goodbye and hung up and then went over her notes, adding and enlarging on the existing material. She filled her teacup and calmed herself with deep breathing before she returned to the chair for the next call.

"Hello, my name is Helen Paige, and I'm trying to reach Earl Roloff. Is he available?"

"I don't know. What's this about?" The woman's voice did not give much away, but at least she had not hung up yet.

"It's about a child custody case in Seattle, not involving Mr. Roloff directly, but I could use a little background information."

"Does this involve Judith Flack?" The voice suddenly sounded hard and cold.

"It does, and a petition for custody."

"Which kid this time? That woman's crazy, you know." Helen was even more grateful the woman had not hung up on her and anxious to keep her on the line.

"I'm trying to collect some facts, checking on stories I've been told. There seem to be some differences of opinion on things, and I'm trying to get a handle on it." The woman laughed, or snorted; it was hard to tell. Helen could tell the woman knew something of value and hoped she would be willing to share.

"Differences of opinion? That's an understatement. I bet there're so many lies in there nobody can see through them all."

"You seem to know about the family," said Helen. "Are you related to Mr. Roloff?" She was interested in this woman and wanted to see if it was possible to use her as a collateral in the case if she could not get to Earl Roloff.

"Yeah, I'm his wife. We took Callie last year, thought we were getting her for good, but then Judith came and kidnapped her, and we finally just said the hell with it."

"Kidnapped her? Were the police involved?"

"Sure, there's a case file on her here in Detroit. She drove in, called Callie, they met up at a McDonald's, and drove off back to Seattle. We thought Callie was in school, but she and her mom had planned this, and Callie skipped out after her first class and went to meet her mom."

"How did the case end up?"

"The police put out a warrant for Judith's arrest. Then Judith called us and put Callie on the line, and Callie said she didn't want to live with us anymore and asked us to let her go back to Judith. We talked it over, decided we didn't need the hassle. We have two kids of our own, really great kids. Callie was jealous of them and fought with them a lot. So we told the prosecutor we wanted it dropped. That was it. The only good thing was Judith said she'd send us back the child support every month in return for us getting the case dropped. The child support goes straight to the state, then they pass it on to her. So now she's been sending it back to us. So that's good; eleven years of those damn payments have stopped."

"Were Earl and Judith ever married?"

"Hell no, he hardly knew her. They had sex at truck stops near Seattle when he drove through the area. Then she got herself pregnant. She told the state who the father was, and they made him take a DNA test. Then he had to start paying. He never hardly met the child. This was all before I met him, but he told me all about it. He sure don't have sex with strangers any more, I'll tell you that. He's a good man."

"May I ask your name? You've been really helpful, and I can't tell you how much I appreciate this."

"My name's Jeanette. Jeanette Roloff. Do you still want to talk to Earl? He's out back building a storage shed."

"Yes, please. Maybe when he comes in, you could give him my cell phone number, and he could call me. I'll only need seven minutes or so. You've given me so much. All I really need to do is confirm it with him." Helen was humming inside. This was just what she needed, and getting Jeanette, who loved to talk, had been better than she could have asked for.

After she hung up and wrote up her case notes, Helen thought over what she now knew about the case. She had spent some time the previous day with Merida, and it had gone well. Merida admitted that she had abused her mother's pain medication, but not without her mother's knowledge and consent. She claimed her mother gave her the medication when she was only sixteen, starting after a bad fall from the balance beam in gymnastics. Her mother already had the prescription and kept encouraging Merida to "take just a little dose" whenever Merida was feeling bad about something or having cramps or was moody. That had been the beginning of a spiral downward that Merida had only pulled out of after the birth of Sedona. She volunteered to go to the in-patient rehab program to help with withdrawal. But she claimed it was her high school counselor, not her mother, who had encouraged her to go. She went to the counselor just after learning she was pregnant with Sedona. She still wrote to the counselor, who was the only adult to really befriend her at that time in her life. Merida gave Helen the counselor's contact information.

Merida confided that her mother used the children for a source of income;. "At least, that's how it looks to me," Merida had said. She then detailed the history of her half-siblings. Angie, the older daughter, had been sent to a mental health clinic as an in-patient at age fifteen for rebellion and being aggressive. After four months, her mother had pulled her out, then had her in and out of school for the next three years. Angie got tested for learning disabilities and put in special classes. At Angie's eighteenth birthday, Judith had applied for Angie to get SSI with the Social Security office, and Angie had been getting a check from them since then. Now she worked in a sheltered workshop six hours a day, which gave her something to do but did not endanger the welfare payment.

"My mom is really smart," Merida had told Helen. "She reads all of these regulations and books about welfare programs, and she took online courses to be a paralegal. She spends most of her time figuring out how to game the system. We got food stamps and WIC checks and disability payments. Mom would even get grants from churches and non-profit places. And we moved a lot. Mom would get Goodwill or the Salvation Army to give us the deposit and first month's rent, and we'd just up and move from one town to another. Burien, Port Townsend, Shoreline, Bremerton, Issaquah, you name it. We had a whole box full of the post office change-of-address cards, and Mom would make me and Angie and Moira fill them out each time. Mom even got herself on Worker's Comp from when she had a job as a 911 dispatcher in Arizona. It just goes on and on." Merida turned out to be an observant, intelligent young woman, smart enough to understand the disadvantages her background had given her and determined to do better by her own child.

Helen had immediately followed up with the counselor from Merida's high school in Arizona, Ms. Hardesty, who confirmed what Merida had related. Ms. Hardesty admitted she was, as she said, "more than a little prejudiced" against Judith Flack, largely because she felt Judith was a neglectful and uncaring parent. She reported that she thought Judith had "cowed" both Angie and Moira, who Ms. Hardesty also knew, and that Judith was unable to do the same to Merida because Merida was "too strong," in her words. "Mrs. Flack always said Merida was stubborn," Ms. Hardesty had commented. "And that may be true, but Merida was standing up for her rights in the only way she knew how, and when Mrs. Flack couldn't handle it, she manipulated Merida onto the pain meds. That was just wrong."

Helen felt she was in a place now where, if she played it right, she could get a total resolution in a fairly short period of time, and it would be the best of the available options for the child. A lot would depend on the outcome of her talk with Merida's father, scheduled for the following day. Helen was totally drained after the intense phone calls. She had hoped to make one more call but knew better than to push on when she had reached this point.

The day was drawing toward dusk so she decided to go for walk and then to a meeting. She first ate a cheese-and-tomato sandwich in the living room while watching the evening news at five. Then she dressed warmly and walked to South Lake Union. She went into the same small church and downstairs to the same meeting room. At the appropriate time, she rose and said, "My name is Helen, and I'm an alcoholic."

Several people, after the meeting, indicated they would like her to stay for coffee (that and cigarettes being the approved substitutes for alcohol at this meeting spot), but she gave a small smile and said she had another appointment for the evening. That was the worst thing about attending the same meeting too many times. Regulars started noticing, and you never knew when they would want to become more than a fellow traveler with a problem. She thought it might be time to look for a new location, though she really liked this one. The distance from her apartment on Queen Anne was just far enough to be good exercise when she needed a walk. And she liked the little church. She would have to think about it.

❧ ❧ ❧

Monday morning, Helen got up at six, did a half-hour of yoga in the living room, had breakfast, and packed a lunch. She was due to meet with Merida's father, Richard Kirk, on Vashon Island at eleven and was not sure enough about the ferry system to the island to take any chances of missing one and being late. The Washington State Ferry fleet, biggest in the country, had years of experience in running ferries on time, but the vagaries of weather and tidal action on the Puget Sound sometimes created problems. Helen had a real aversion to being late and preferred to arrive on the island early and poke around a bit, rather than take a risk of being off schedule. It was a long habit of hers, perhaps stemming from her five years of institutionalization, never to be late to anything.

Helen drove to West Seattle and found that the line for the ferry was only about ten cars. She knew she would have a spot on the next ferry, so she was able to relax and read over her case notes while she waited in line. The ferry went from West Seattle to Southworth and stopped midway to drop off passengers for Vashon Island. She made sure she drove onto the ferry in the lane designated for the cars departing the ferry at the island, rather than continuing on to the mainland.

Helen stayed in her car on the ferry. She watched a grandfather with two grade-school children standing at the roped-off area near the front of the ferry. They were throwing hunks of bread to the seagulls that always flew around the ferries and laughing at the ability of the birds to hover and then time their dive to grab the bread before it could drop to the water. The grandfather was obviously enjoying the spectacle as much as the children, and they all were laughing and shouting as they called out to the birds. Helen started to smile at the sight, but the sudden pain in her stomach made her grimace instead. She felt her throat tighten, and tears formed in her eyes. Inhaling deeply, she lowered her shoulders and relaxed her body until the feeling passed and a calm came over her. She was grateful, not for the first time, that her Indian yoga teacher had given her the tools to deal with the pain of her personal history.

Once Helen disembarked, she drove to the restaurant near the ferry landing and went in. Taking her iPad with her so she could use the map application to locate Mr. Kirk's home, she sat in a booth near the windows overlooking the water and had tea and toast while she studied the map and oriented herself to the island. When she realized how large it was, she decided to drive to what looked like a small commercial area several miles down the island. That would get her closer to Mr. Kirk's home yet still allow her to wander around until it was time to show up at the house.

Richard Kirk's driveway was a long, unpaved track with grass in the middle. At the end of the drive, there was a large area for parking and turning around. Two large trucks and a car were already in the space, and Helen pulled her Acura in among them. When she got out of the car, she saw two dogs loping toward her, tails wagging and tongues hanging out. They did not bark at her but stopped and sat about ten feet from her car, watching her.

A man appeared on the second-story balcony and called, "Prince, Dragon, down." The dogs put their bellies on the ground but remained alert. "They won't bother you. They're just checking things out. Come on up," the man hollered to Helen.

She noticed a staircase on the side of the house that led to the large balcony running the length of the house. She went up the stairs and held out her hand. "I'm Helen Paige, the CASA."

"Richard Kirk. Good to meet you. I tell you, I've been lookin' forward to this." He was a tall man with a broad chest, dressed in a flannel shirt and jeans and wearing work boots. He reminded Helen of a lumberjack, though she could not remember if she had ever actually met a lumberjack. He looked like what a lumberjack *should* look like. His hair was thick and brown and not especially well groomed, but he had a rugged air about him that Helen thought made him look attractive and friendly. He was in his mid-forties, by Helen's estimation. She noted that he was looking her over as well, and she wondered what he was thinking. Her gray hair was cut to collar length and hung straight down. Her face was round, with a long thin nose, straight brows, and gray eyes. She thought she looked every bit her age and never wore much make-up to change that look. She was approaching fifty, fast.

"That's a good beginning," she said. "It's always better to have somebody who doesn't mind seeing me."

They had shaken hands and moved toward the open door behind them. They entered a large room with one wall dominated by a stone fireplace that had a fire burning low. The furniture was large, leather, and well lived-in. It reminded Helen of a lodge in a Western national park. Richard pointed her toward a corner away from the fire where two chairs flanked a small table. She sat in one of the chairs and took her notebook and pen from her purse before settling in.

"Merida and Sedona went to check out a day-care center a couple of miles from here. Then Merida will take Sedona to McDonald's to play on that climbing thing they have there. She'll call to ask me when to come back."

Helen was surprised. "I didn't know Sedona was here. How did that happen?"

"Judith called Merida last night about eight and said Merida could have Sedona for three days. Don't know why. Merida just grabbed my car keys and drove off to get her right then, before anything changed. I have no idea what that's about. I'm not askin' any questions."

"I'll check that with Merida later. For now, I'd like to hear your story. When you met Judith, how long you were married, what caused the divorce … anything you want to tell me."

"Right. Like I said, I been waitin' for this. I was too young and stupid back then to just get a lawyer and let him fight it out. Judith was way ahead of me." Richard sat forward with his forearms on his thighs and clasped his hands together. He stared at the floor for a minute, collecting his thoughts and then started. While he talked, he glanced up now and again to make sure Helen was still with him. He talked for about twenty minutes without pause.

Richard said he met Judith when he was twenty-two. She was his first girlfriend. She already had a child, Angie, and Richard thought she was a good mother. They moved in together, married a short time later, and had the two girls, Merida and Moira, in two years. Then, he said, things "went to hell in a hand basket." Judith complained and nagged at Richard, wanting him to bring in more money. He was a carpenter then and was working overtime and weekends. There was a building boom going on. He thought he was making plenty, and he had very little time to see his girls as it was. Things got ugly, and Judith kicked him out. He tried to see the kids, but Judith made it hard for him. He paid the rent for her to stay in their house. Paid the utilities, gave her money for food and clothes for the kids. Plus he bought her a car and paid for the insurance and gas. "I kept on supporting them just like we lived together. That went on for about five years. Then I found out she was pregnant with Kenya. That did it. She was lettin' me spend one day a month with the girls, that's all. I told her no more; I was gettin' a divorce.

"After that, after the divorce, I actually got to see the girls more. I had them from Friday night until Sunday night every third week. It was great. I brought them here, and my parents helped me take care of them. That lasted maybe a year or so. Then she started moving all over the place. I tried keeping track, but she didn't make it easy. I was talking to Kenya's dad, his name's Bob Henderson, and he was havin' the same problems. We both paid child support the whole time—I guess he's still doin' it—but we had to fight to see the kids. Sometimes, it was just too hard, and I guess I was wrong to let it slip, but that's water under the bridge."

"What is your relationship to your daughters and to Sedona now?" Helen was intrigued by the idea that Richard knew Bob Henderson, Kenya's father. She wanted to ask more about that but was not sure it was relevant to her case. Sometimes, she knew, her curiosity caused her to go beyond what could be called her reasonable responsibilities. On the other hand, she had learned that wandering into fields that appeared non-essential often led to a better picture of the truth than sticking to the more obvious paths.

"Moira has pretty much written me off for now. She's turning into her mother. But Merida's different. She always had a mind of her own, and she and I get along real well now. She moved in with us after her mom kicked her out, and I'm fixing up the lower level for her and Sedona. We all love Sedona. Who wouldn't? She's a great kid. Loves it here."

"Who shares the house with you?"

"This was my parents' house. My dad died, and I bought it from my mother. She still lives here. Her health isn't so good, but she gets around OK. She has two rooms in the back, so she has her own space. Then my sister Elsa, she never married and always lived here. Then I have the upstairs. There's my office and bedroom suite up there. Lots of time, the nephews are here, my married sister's kids. They come over to help out and watch TV." He nodded toward a huge television built into a shelving system on the wall that contained the fireplace. "This is sort of sports central on weekends, and maybe ten people will be here for the games. Elsa cooks for everybody. She's a nurse but only has to work during the weekdays so she's here all weekend. And she sure likes to cook. And we have two extra bedrooms on this floor in case anybody wants to crash here after the games or has too many beers or something. You want to look around? I'll give you a tour."

They walked around the house, looking at everything except Elsa's room and his mother's suite, as both doors were closed and Richard wanted to respect their privacy. Richard's cell phone rang at one point. He answered it and, after checking with Helen, told Merida it was fine for her to return to the house. Then Richard took Helen downstairs to the floor below the main living area.

"This is what I'm fixing up for Merida. It was all a big storage room first, kept woodworking tools, table saws, even appliances we'd get on sale and save for when we built a house that needed them. Then my dad sort of made it into a hang-out room for us kids when we were teenagers. It's just been sittin' empty for years now. You can see I'm still workin' on it."

Helen looked around the area. There was a fully finished bathroom with both a shower area and a bathtub. It was large and had excellent lighting. The floor and walls were tiled. Adjacent to the bathroom was a large bedroom. It had windows on two sides that overlooked the spacious yard. The bed was neat, but there were several full bags lying on the floor. Richard explained that Merida was still moving in, and they had yet to buy her a new chest of drawers. A small room adjoined the bedroom. "This is Sedona's bedroom while she's still small. I haven't finished it yet. This week, we're puttin' in wood floors and replacin' that old window with a new one that's insulated better so it stays warmer. I'm goin' to install a wall heater too, but up high so she can't reach it. Then when Sedona's older, this can be an office area for Merida, and we'll make a bigger bedroom on the other side of the bathroom for Sedona. And I'll put in a little galley kitchen with some eating space so if Merida wants to do her own cooking and be totally independent of us, that's fine, too."

"It looks like you plan to have both Merida and Sedona here for a while." Helen was concerned about Richard's investment in time and money. It was still up to the court what to do about custody of Sedona, and Merida might not want to live on Vashon Island for the long haul.

"We talked a lot, me and Merida. Elsa and I want her and Sedona here, but that's up to Merida. She can work for me part time. I have a remodeling and construction business, and there's always paperwork. She can pay bills and type up estimates and send invoices. I have an accountant, but she can do the weekly bookkeeping things. She can use child care when she needs to; I can pony up for that as an employee benefit. So for now, at least, she plans to stay here long enough to get some training. She needs to finish her GED, and she might even want to go to college. I want this whole level of the house fixed up so she can do that if she wants. If she doesn't, well … we can always find a way to use this space. Maybe a nephew will want it for a while. Or maybe we'll be needin' some live-in help when my mom gets older. Can't hurt to have the space."

"Sounds as if you think Merida will get primary custody of Sedona."

"I sure do. I'm not so young and stupid any more. I told Merida to go to a lawyer and fight back. I'm payin'. She went two days ago to a guy here on the island. So yeah, I think she'll get her daughter back." Again, Helen was surprised by the news about the lawyer. She wanted to get that information to her supervisor at CASA as they would need to be aware of it. She made a mental note to get the attorney's name from Merida.

Merida and Sedona were just getting out of a Prius when Richard and Helen left the lower level and started toward the outside steps leading to the main upper floor. Sedona ran to the waiting dogs and starting playing with them. She picked up a ball from the ground and threw it, though it only went a few feet, and the dogs were not impressed. "Mommy, you throw," said Sedona, when the larger dog gave her the ball. Merida took the ball and threw it almost halfway to the end of the large yard that sloped toward a stand of trees almost a hundred yards away. The dogs took off, racing each other to the ball while Merida turned to join Helen and Richard.

"Hi, Helen," said Merida. "I thought you could use this trip to do the observation of me and Sedona, if you have time. I remember you said we'd need to do it before you wrote your report, and this is a great place for it. Sedona needs some outdoor time, and you could see and hear us from the balcony."

"That's a great idea, and I can do it now. I thought I'd have to make another trip, so this is a real bonus for me. You can go join Sedona, and I'll just observe for maybe fifty minutes to an hour, if that's OK."

Merida went back down the stairs and joined Sedona in the yard. For the next half-hour, they took turns throwing the ball and some sticks for the dogs. When the dogs got tired, Merida took Sedona out to a large tree that had a tire swing attached, and she pushed and twirled Sedona on the tire. They laughed and talked a lot while they played. Then they got a basket from an outbuilding and picked up pinecones. Helen wrote notes while observing them.

At one point, Richard came out of the house and gave Helen a large glass of water; then he went back in. Sedona said she was hungry, and Merida suggested they go in the house and make peanut butter and banana sandwiches.

"Yummy! my favorite!" squealed Sedona and ran to the stairs ahead of her mother and started climbing. "Hold the railing," she said to herself as she grabbed a railing installed at her height and climbed to the top.

"My dad and I installed that two days ago," Merida said as she climbed behind Sedona. "I'm teaching her to get in the habit of always putting a hand on it, just in case. Sometimes, with the rain, the steps get a little slick." She joined Helen on the balcony. "Want to come and watch us make sandwiches?"

"No, I think this is enough on the observation. Your dad tells me you consulted an attorney."

"Yeah, and I told my mom that yesterday morning. Then, after dark last night, she called to say I could have Sedona. Three days every week. You can bet those two things are related. I also told her that I'd given you Earl Roloff's phone number. That made you-know-what hit the fan." Merida had a distinct glee in her voice. "I think I may beat her this time, especially since my dad is helping me."

"How is he helping?"

"Well, he's paying for the lawyer; that was his idea. And he's letting me live here so that gives me a chance to get on my own two feet, I can

work for him and still get an education. I'm really glad I called him
when Mom kicked me out. Did he show you how he's fixing up the
lower level for me?"

"Yes, he did. It looks wonderful. I think he's really excited to have
you in his life."

Merida blushed and look at her feet. "Yeah. It's kind of nice to have
people who really want you just because they do, not for what they can
get. And I have a super grandma and a super aunt and some cousins.
It's like a whole new family. And they're all really nice to Sedona."

"What about WorkSource? Aren't you supposed to be there today?"

"Yeah, but I called them this morning and told them I had Sedona.
I explained that I'd be working for my dad, so I didn't need their help
anymore. I'm going to South Seattle Community College tomorrow to
find out about taking some classes and getting my GED finished. I found
a great child-care place near here, and Grandma or Dad or Aunt Elsa
can help with picking Sedona up and dropping her off when I need it,
depending on my schedule."

"Looks as if you've landed in a good place," said Helen with a smile.
"Make the best of it. I'd like your attorney's name; then I need to go. I
have quite a bit of work ahead of me. I probably have all I need from your
end, but I'll call if I have questions before I finish the report." Sedona
handed Helen the attorney's name and phone number, and then Helen
rose, gathered her things, and left.

❧ ❧ ❧

It was late afternoon when Helen returned to the apartment. She had
eaten her lunch at a small park overlooking the western edge of the Puget
Sound. Then she took a walk along the bluff, enjoying the solitude before
returning to the ferry. Traffic had been heavy in West Seattle and on
into the city on Highway 99, and it had taken her almost an hour to get
back to Queen Anne. As she exited the elevator, Mrs. Mayhew stepped
out of the facing apartment. Helen nodded to her, looked down, and
started to move around her in an evasive maneuver. But Mrs. Mayhew
held up her hand, palm facing Helen.

"Don't brush me off. I know you want to, but just hear me out. I have a serious problem. I can't talk to family, friend, lawyer, or police. I need an outside opinion. I won't offer cookies or friendship; I just want an opinion. Say you'll listen to me. I need it." She stood firmly planted, making it difficult for Helen to sidle around her. Mrs. Mayhew was a soft, round, short woman. If you asked ten amateur Caucasian artists to paint a portrait of a grandmother, Mrs. Mayhew would be the result.

Helen had successfully avoided the woman thus far but now found herself forced to engage. It was difficult to give in gracefully. In fact, Helen did not know how to do anything gracefully.

Helen sighed and stared into Mrs. Mayhew's soft green eyes. "OK," she said. "But I can't spare much time." She was as cool and forbidding as she could be, but Mrs. Mayhew was not dissuaded and would not be ignored.

"Good. Shall I call you Helen or Ms. Smith or something else? I may have to call you something, and I don't want to be offensive about it. My name is Alicia, if you didn't already know."

"Helen is fine."

"OK, just sit down a minute, Helen, and I'll get the letter." Helen entered the apartment, which had about the same layout as her own, and went into the living room. Mrs. Mayhew's apartment was a study in black, white, and gray, sophisticated and streamlined, not at all what Helen had anticipated. On the wall behind the sofa was a large graphic of bright red poppies, and there were bright red pillows around the room. A red blown-glass vase on a side table was the only other ornament. Mrs. Mayhew returned from her bedroom with a plain envelope in her hand.

"First, I need to give you some background. I became a widow almost two years ago. I was married for forty years to the founder and CEO of a successful company, headquartered in Bellevue. We weren't at the level of the Gates or anything, but we had the big house on Mercer Island and the private plane and the rest of it. Our children had every advantage, and all three of them are financially successful and socially prominent. They're well known for philanthropy in the arts. I'm not bragging; you just need to know this. Their lives would be destroyed by scandal; they'd be outcasts. I'm sixty-four. Some of my friends would disappear, but I'd survive. All that said, I received this letter today. I need you to read it and tell me what you'd do in my place." Alicia put the letter in Helen's hand and sat in a chair opposite, hands in her lap.

The letter was hand-written, and Helen thought the ink looked like the old-fashioned ink-pen kind, not a ballpoint or anything similar. The paper was a heavy ivory stock, plain but expensive. Helen read:

Dear Mrs. Mayhew,

It is not pleasant for me to relate the following, but I find myself in a most embarrassing position. Your husband, Timothy, and I shared a "particular friendship" from when we met in college at Georgetown right up until his death. Being gay when we were young was not only outside the pale socially; it was also illegal. We were always discreet, and no one ever suspected the nature of our friendship.

Your husband was far more financially capable than I, and he was very generous to me. He provided me with a comfortable living situation, far more than I would have had on my own. I have always lived alone, except for him, in the house I still have today. He originally paid for the house in full, but I obtained a mortgage on it without his knowledge some years ago. I won't bore you with what I needed the money for or what happened to it.

At this point, I face foreclosure, and I have no resources to fall back on if I lose my home. I am the same age as Timothy, so I cannot start over. It is too late for me. I am writing to prevail upon you to help me, not just for my sake, but for the sake of Timothy's memory.

You may reach me at the address below. I know this must be a shock to you, as Timothy told me you were completely unaware of the situation. I hope, however, that after you have given careful consideration to what I have related you will see your way clear to coming to my rescue.

Sincerely,

The letter was signed with a simple "George." The address was a P.O. box in Shoreline, with just the name "Mr. George." Helen read the letter through twice before handing it back to Alicia with the words, "Looks like blackmail or extortion or something. Why not take it to your lawyer?"

"I don't want this out there. These days, even a law office isn't secure. Everything's on a computer. And with technical workers, paralegals, secretaries, and who knows who else, it's just too dangerous. This would be a juicy scandal if it got out, and with the Internet and blogs … well … I just can't risk it. My children would be totally humiliated."

Helen looked at Alicia. She was totally dry eyed, which Helen thought a little off, given the harsh facts in the letter.

"Do you think this could be true?"

"That's just it. I've been thinking back over the marriage. This sounds strange, I know, but our marriage was a really happy one. Our friends envied us for how solid it was. But now I'm thinking more critically. And the truth is, I just can't say with total honesty that I think the letter is a lie. That shocks me, but I just have to wonder." Alicia looked more confused than saddened at her admission.

Helen thought for a few minutes, staring off into space. "I'm not the best person to advise you," she started. "Why don't you let me think about this for a day or so. You do the same. Then maybe we could talk again." Helen mentally kicked herself for saying this. It forced her into yet another conversation with Alicia Mayhew, something she desperately wanted to avoid.

Alicia let out her breath with such a loud sound they were both startled. Alicia hadn't even been aware she was holding her breath. She laughed a little. "I guess I was awful nervous about this. I'm so glad you're willing to think about it. I know how much you want to avoid me. I'm not a dunce, you know. So it means a lot that you're willing to give me an opinion. I'll wait for you to knock on my door. Promise. No hall-pouncing."

Helen laughed. "Fair enough. Day after tomorrow at the absolute latest." Without another word, she rose, left Alicia sitting in the elegant living room, and saw herself out.

The cell phone in Helen's purse was ringing as Helen walked into her own apartment. With her mind in a confusing muddle over her encounter with Alicia Mayhew, she did not even bother to look at the number. She just opened it up and said, "Hello, Helen here," the way she always answered her calls.

"This is Marjorie Flack. My daughter said you were going to call me, but you haven't. So I decided to call you instead. You're supposed to interview me." Marjorie Flack sounded simultaneously angry and nervous.

"Yes, I do have you on a list to call. I'm sorry it has taken so long, but I've several things going at the same time, and it has been difficult. I'm so glad you called. If you give me just a minute to get my notebook and pen, I'll be able to start. Your interview is important, and I want to make sure I get it all down. This is a good time for you, right?" Helen was trying to mollify Marjorie so the interview would not be confrontational. While she talked, she took off her coat and got out her notebook and a pen, moving toward a chair at the small dining table at the same time.

"Yes, I've been wanting to get this over with. Judith needs to get this business settled so she can protect Sedona." Her words left little doubt about which side she was taking in the custody fight over the child.

"I'm ready now," Helen said. "Maybe you would like to start with telling me whatever you feel is most important." Helen suspected Marjorie had a list or some notes about the issues or stories that she wanted on the record.

"First thing is you've got to understand that Merida is a terrible mother. She feeds Sedona pure junk, candy and crackers, that's about it. And she has no schedule for her. Sedona gets up and goes to bed whenever it suits Merida. She'll drag Sedona out of the house at nine or ten at night and go next door to smoke pot or get high on drugs with the neighbor. Sometimes she won't even make it home. Sedona just sleeps on the floor or in a chair or something."

"I've got that down," Helen said and thought about following up with a question about how Marjorie might know this. Her next thought, however, was that confrontation should wait a bit.

"Next, you need to know that Merida can't support Sedona. She had a job at a Taco Bell, but she quit that job about two months ago. She expects Judith to provide board and room for both her and Sedona, and that's not right. Without a job, where is she going to live? She just stays here and there with friends, bumming off them. That's not good for Sedona. It was Judith that got food stamps for them; Merida didn't even think of doing it. Merida stopped paying rent to Judith and stopped making the payments for the furniture. So Judith had no choice but to kick her out."

"Just a minute. I'm still writing that down." Helen knew Marjorie was anxious that everything she said would be written, and she'd be reassured by the confirmation. "You said Merida stopped paying rent to Judith, right? Let me make a note of that."

"OK. Now I need to tell you about how Merida is treating the rest of the family. She fights and argues about everything. She refused to take Kenya to his basketball practice the other day, even though she wasn't working or anything. And she picks on Callie, so Callie's in tears every time they're around each other. She got in a fight with Angie and shoved Angie against the kitchen wall. It just got so bad Judith had no choice. So Judith told Merida she had to leave. Merida yelled at Judith, cussed at her right in front of the others. It was ugly. Then Merida stomped out of the house and didn't come home. Judith's worried that if the fighting keeps up it could get physical. She had to kick Merida out so the rest of the kids would feel safe." Marjorie stopped. She seemed to have reached the end of her list.

"I've got all that down. I'd like to ask a few questions, if you still have some time." Helen exhaled slowly and lowered her shoulders so her voice would take on a mellow, relaxed tone. When Marjorie agreed that she had time for questions, Helen started slowly.

"First, can you tell me how often you visit with Judith and her children?"

"Well, I live a couple of miles away, and don't have a car. So I don't see them as much as I'd like."

"Maybe once a week?"

"Yeah, about that. Judith usually comes over to see me every week. We have coffee together, sometimes go out for lunch. My other daughter that lives next door comes over too, and we have a good visit together."

"When she comes, does she bring the children?"

"Not usually. She needs to get out of the house sometimes, just to get a break, you know. It's not easy to have that many kids all the time. So she comes here for a little relief."

"Can you tell me about the last time you were in Judith's house visiting with your grandchildren?"

"Well … let me think … maybe about a month ago. Yeah, it was Kenya's birthday, and my other daughter and I went over for cake that evening."

"So you don't spend too much time at Judith's when all the children are around?" Helen bit her lip, trying hard to keep her voice even and neutral.

"Not so much. It can be kind of wild over there. And now, there's not even anyplace to sit. And you can't watch television; there's too much noise with all the kids."

"So, then, a lot of what you know about the situation is what you heard from others, not what you saw yourself, is that right?"

"Well, I …" Marjorie stopped. Helen could hear her breathing. "I used to be there a lot more …" She re-grouped. "And I talk on the phone to them all the time. Callie and Angie and Moira tell me things. They confide in me a lot. It's not just from Judith. I know what's going on."

"OK." Helen started closing down the conversation. "You've been helpful to me, and I've got it all down. I appreciate that you called." There was no need to push Marjorie further. "I want you to call me any time you have something else you want to add, OK?" Helen mentally patted herself on her back for how sweet she thought she sounded.

"Sure. I hope I helped you get a better idea about this. Judith's a wonderful mother, and she'll take real good care of Sedona." Marjorie provided the final comment as though it was something she was supposed to say, but had forgotten earlier. Helen wrapped up the conversation and got off the telephone with a huge sigh.

Exhausted and drooping visibly, Helen dragged herself to her bedroom, took off her clothes, and went into the bathroom for a long shower. Warm and refreshed afterward, she put on a flannel lounge suit. Then she went to the kitchen and poked around, trying to decide what she could eat. She put a bowl of leftover pea soup in the microwave and rummaged through the refrigerator and cabinets while it was heating. Then, putting the soup on a tray with a plate of nuts, cheese, and crackers, Helen carried the dinner into her dining room, put it on the table, and sat down with a pen and notebook. While she ate, she looked over the notes from the Vashon Island trip as well as the phone call with Marjorie Flack. She filled in some details she recalled hearing but not recording earlier. About to type the notes into the computer, she thought better of it and decided some yoga and meditation would do more good than working.

After her practices, she crawled into bed and closed her eyes. Then she remembered the letter Alicia Mayhew had shown her, and she mulled it over it as she fell asleep.

ॐ ॐ ॐ

At eight the next morning, Helen called the CASA office. "Is Michelle in yet?" she asked the woman who answered the phone. "Darn, I was hoping for her. How about the director. Is she in yet? Great, put me through to her. Tell her it's Helen Paige Smith." Helen didn't like going straight to Hilary Armistead, the executive director of CASA. Hilary was an attorney and represented the volunteers in court, together with another staff attorney. She was overburdened with the typical tasks associated with being in charge of a large volunteer organization in addition to the legal work it entailed. Helen never bothered her as a rule, but she knew the office would want a heads-up in this case so they wouldn't be blind-sided.

"Hi, Helen, what's up?" asked Hilary.

"Hi, Hilary. I think you may get a request to have me removed from a case Michelle gave me last week. It's the Flack case, third-party custody request from the maternal grandmother."

"You're right on that one. She called yesterday. Judith Flack. She was lit up like the Fourth of July. Sounded as if she wants your head on a stick. I thought I'd wait a day or two … Figured you'd call."

"Yeah. I think this case is going to go away, maybe real soon. Grandmother Flack has just found out a couple of things that have her worried. First, the mother has an attorney. Second, Grandmother found out I was in touch with at least two of the four men who are the fathers of her children. One is the paternal grandfather in our case. And the whole drug thing she accused the mother of blew up on her. Then I found out she was once charged with kidnapping one of the kids. That happened in Detroit. She's probably figured out I heard about that. So I suspect she's getting really nervous about the report. She probably thinks if she can get rid of me and get another CASA maybe she can start fresh."

"How do you want to handle this?" Hilary asked.

"Well, as I said, I think she's running scared. She has to know by now that she doesn't have a snowball in hell's chance of getting custody. We need to let her simmer a day and get used to the idea. She's a smart woman; I think she'll figure it out for herself. I doubt she wants me nosing around any further in her business. I'll call her tomorrow, act as if I haven't heard about the request to have me removed, and see where we stand. Does that work for you?"

"Sure, sounds good to me. Saves us all some work if we can get it settled right now. How about the mother and the kid? Is that going to work out? "

"No problems. The mother moved in with the grandfather. There's a great-aunt and a great-grandmother there as well. Looks like plenty of resources, plus everybody is happy to have both of them. Mother will work part-time for the grandfather. I think they're going to be fine. Mother is also going back to school."

"Good outcome. Will you need anything from me?"

"Not yet. Since Ms. Flack knows how to do the paperwork and knows her way around court procedures, I'll just suggest she do it herself. That's if she's in a reasonable mood when I call. I'll shoot an e-mail to Michelle after I make the call and give an update."

"Good, nice job, Helen. Thanks for taking this on, short notice and all. Wish all of my CASAs made my life so simple."

They both laughed and hung up. Helen put the file to one side. She ate breakfast, donned yoga clothes, and walked three blocks for her regular Tuesday morning class.

The classes were held in a large room in the local community center. Helen usually went two days a week, each day with a different instructor. Both her Tuesday and Friday classes, held during typical workday times, were designed for people over the age of fifty-five. Most students, like Helen, were women who did not work, either because they were retired or did not need to work. A few men attended, usually married to another person in the class. The classes were large, over thirty people.

Helen went straight to the closet, collected a yoga mat, a pillow, and a blanket, and took her usual place in the corner furthest from the door, the instructor, and the front of the room. She did not care if she could see the instructor or not since she tended to modify the poses to suit herself. Having attended five years of daily classes from a swami in an ashram, she felt more comfortable and competent with the discipline than either the instructor or the other students and did not want to distract others or have them distract her. She found that she needed classes as a way to force herself to continue the work, or she would not even bother to attend. It had taken several months after her move to Seattle to find a place she could tolerate so she was grateful to have found one so close by. She found the community-sponsored classes far less irritating than the typical gym-based programs that considered yoga some type of exercise rather than a spiritual path.

The class proceeded in the usual way. The instructor had the students do some warm-up work, then about forty minutes of poses, and a final relaxation period. The students were quiet, except for the period just before and after class. At those times, they chatted as if they were at a cocktail party. Helen avoided all of the other students and tried to slip in and out of the class without being noticed.

As she was leaving on this day, however, she overhead a group of women talking in the front of the room. This was normal, but Helen recognized one of the voices and turned to look more closely at the group. She was startled to see Alicia Mayhew in the middle of a conversation with three other women. Helen put her head down and walked quickly to the door. At first, she wondered if Alicia could have heard her leave her apartment and followed her here. But she realized how paranoid that was. Alicia was obviously well known to the other students. She must have been in the class all along, and Helen had just never paid any attention. She decided she might have to consider switching her early class to a different day if she noticed Alicia in the future.

Back home, Helen fixed a cup of tea and settled at her computer. She had several hours of work in front of her, writing up her notes from the previous day. She also started the first draft of the Flack/Kirk report, even though she suspected no completed product would be needed. She found it easier and faster to work on the reports as she worked the case, rather than waiting until all the interviews were complete.

After two hours, Helen stopped for lunch. She looked around the kitchen for some minutes before realizing that she did not have much. Crackers, no cheese. No soup. No bread for a sandwich. Not even a couple of pieces of fruit. She was irritated on two counts. First, she had to stop important work for something as meaningless as eating. Second, she had not thought ahead enough to get food while she was out anyway. She put on her coat and walking shoes, grabbed a re-useable grocery bag (Seattle had recently passed a law specifying no plastic bags and pay for paper ones), and checked her wallet for money. She went across the street and down a block to a local grocery and got enough food for two or three days and then returned home. She made a salad while she boiled an egg to put on top of it. Then she carried the lunch to the dining table and read through her file on the Butler case.

A few days without actively working on a case, Helen found, and it just seeped out of her brain. Age, maybe. Or other things taking up the space and pushing it out, she wasn't sure. As she reviewed the file, she realized it was time to arrange for observations of each parent with the children. She wanted to space everything out, though. The trial was still six months away, so she had time to dawdle on the report while she put other plans in place.

The interview with James had been revealing. She learned that the elder Butlers, Ted and Meredith, had been pushing James toward a relationship for some time prior to James dating Pam. They wanted grandchildren, and James had no siblings. James told her, "They were disappointed in me, I think, and wanted a chance for a do-over." He reported that he "never did anything right" in that he was always overweight, uncoordinated, and shy. His parents, on the other hand, were athletic, social, and popular. "I was not exactly a prize for them," he had said. He liked Pam because she made him feel that he could make something of himself. She never made fun of him. "I loved her, and I still love her," he had said, and he had tears in his eyes when he said it.

Ted and Meredith were happy when Pam got pregnant. They pushed the couple to marry before James and Pam felt financially prepared for a marriage. Ted and Meredith picked out the house and took James to see it, promising that if he married Pam they could live in the house for one hundred dollars a month. Given that incentive, plus the pregnancy, the young couple got married. James worked nights the entire marriage while Pam worked days as the office manager of a medical clinic. She quit working for four months after the birth of Susie, returned to work, and quit again shortly thereafter because of her pregnancy with Janie. James said, "Pam and I never had enough time alone, what with my night job and the two babies. We never really had a chance to bond as a married couple. There was just too much stress."

James did not want to divorce Pam, but he felt pushed into it by his parents. The couple continued to live in the house together, even though the divorce was in the works. James returned home from work at three or four in the morning and went straight to bed in the basement. When he got up, usually between ten and noon, he would take over as parent while Pam left the house. Then she would return in the evening and put the children to bed, and sleep in the master bedroom. She then had the children until James got up, and then she would leave. James had no idea where Pam spent the day. When asked how they wanted to handle custody and visitation, James was perplexed. "I guess the kids should stay here. Pam doesn't have a job or a place to live. If she gets the kids, like, two or three days a week, then I can live at my folks' house, and she can be here with them." It sounded to Helen as though Pam and James had not really gotten that far in their longer-range planning.

At this point, Helen added her recent notes to the earlier draft report. Then she considered her next steps. She wanted to conduct her observation of Pam and the girls first, as she could use the time with Pam to ferret out Pam's current thinking and follow up with the drinking problem Meredith had told her about. She decided to set that up next. First, however, she consulted her calendar to see which days were clear.

"Helen Paige here. Is this Pam?" she asked. "Good, how are you doing today?" She listened patiently as Pam actually answered the question. The girls were sick with colds, the dishwasher was broken, and she was trying to arrange interviews to find a job. She could only interview in the afternoons when James was available to take care of the children, and the last two personnel officers wanted morning appointments. Pam ended her litany with "It's so irritating that I have to leave the house at noon every day. It's hard to schedule the dishwasher repairman for a certain time, and I know James doesn't want to deal with it. And I hate asking Meredith to be here for that kind of thing. And then I have to do the laundry either early in the morning so it's all done and folded before I leave the house, or else at night."

"Would it be possible for me to do the observation next week?" Helen asked. "The girls will probably be well by then. I have Tuesday or Thursday in the morning, or Wednesday in the afternoon. Would any of those times fit? I need about an hour."

"Where would you want this to happen?" asked Pam. "We could do it at the house, but I need to tell James. He gets up before lunch, and if he would be willing to leave the house, I could stay there and we could do it in the afternoon. If we do it in the morning, it should be somewhere else, so we don't wake him up or anything."

Helen was surprised at Pam's concern. It would seem to her that James was sleeping every morning when Pam had the girls at the house, so Helen's presence as an observer, not talking, should not be an issue. She mentioned this to Pam.

"Well, lots of mornings Meredith comes and takes the girls so they don't wake James up. Or I take them to the park or the zoo if it isn't raining or the mall or the Science Center if it is."

"I see," said Helen. "Well, I could follow you around the zoo or park, but I don't think the mall thing would work so well. Why don't you check with James and see if the afternoon on Wednesday will work, and we'll plan on that. Otherwise, if the weather looks good, we'll do a morning in the park or zoo, and you can pick whichever day looks least like rain." At this time of year there was about an even chance of some rain at some point on any given day.

"OK. I'll call you back later after I talk to James."

"Just leave a message on my cell if I don't answer. Whatever you choose, I can make it work on my end." They both said goodbye. Helen made a note on each of the possible days in pencil on her calendar so she would not schedule anything else until it was settled.

With the CASA tasks for the day completed, Helen turned to the problem of Alicia Mayhew's letter. At first, she just sat and thought about it but found other things intruded. She needed to clear her mind first. She went into the bedroom, sat on the small rug on the floor, and went into her meditation routine. After twenty minutes, she returned to her living room and sat in her favorite chair with a pen and notebook. She tried to be Alicia in her mind. That part she did not find difficult, but when she tried to be Timothy, she had real problems. Never having met him, or even seen a picture, she decided, was a huge disadvantage. So she turned to George. She found that his letter made it possible to imagine him. The primary element here, however, was whether or not the facts in the letter were genuine. If they were, that implied one sort of person and situation. If it was all a hoax to extort money, that was a whole separate kettle of kippers. She decided to go with the idea that his story was exactly as presented. She made some notes and formulated some options on paper. When she was satisfied she had done her best, she closed her notebook.

Now she needed to decide whether she wanted to face Alicia today or save it until tomorrow. It was already after four in the afternoon. She decided to call Mr. Pierce and then decide.

"Mr. Osborne, hello. This is Helen Prescott. I wonder if it would be possible for me to meet with someone at the duplex tomorrow and do a walk-through?"

"Good afternoon, Ms. Prescott. Mr. Pierce is in a conference right now, but I think I can arrange this. Let me just look at a couple of things." He was off the phone for about three minutes. "OK, I know the contractor, Drew Patten, is going over there tomorrow. It's on Mr. Pierce's calendar. Let me call him and see what time he'll be there, and maybe you can meet him. Shall I call you back, or do you want to hold while I use the other line?"

"I'll wait," said Helen. She listened to some sort of piano music while she stared out the window. A few minutes later, Mr. Osborne was back. "Mr. Patten will be there at ten in the morning. Would that suit you?"

"Yes, tell him I'll be there at ten. Thank you, Mr. Osborne. And I wanted to thank you for the tea you gave me the other day, the red bush with vanilla. I drink a cup every day and enjoy it so much."

"I'm glad; that's just what I wanted to hear. And I have a new tea to share next time you come in." They said polite goodbyes and hung up.

Helen knew she needed to talk with Judith Flack the next day, and she would want to spend the afternoon dealing with the renovation project as well as checking on another building the foundation owned. She decided, therefore, that it was better to talk with Alicia Mayhew about the letter right away, rather than putting it off.

Helen knocked on her neighbor's door. "Hi, Alicia, is this a good time for you?" she asked when the woman answered the door.

"Yes, come in. This is a perfect time. I've been anxious about the whole thing and I'm so glad you're here to help me with it. . Can I fix you something to drink before we start?"

"If you have some tea, that would be nice," responded Helen. She spoke as she moved toward the living room.

"I have Earl Gray, Constant Comment, a peppermint, green, and some PG Tips. Which do you prefer?"

Helen raised her eyebrows. She seldom met someone who had a selection of tea on hand that was similar to her own. "I'll go with Earl Gray."

"Me too," said Alicia. "I think Earl Gray is the perfect later afternoon tea, especially in the fall. Mint is my go-to early afternoon, and Constant Comment is for rainy days, late morning." Alicia busied herself in the kitchen, where she already had a teakettle full of hot water. She quickly prepared the tea, three teabags in a china pot. "I guess you don't want lemon or sugar, is that correct?"

Helen agreed.

Alicia carried the teapot and two cups with saucers into the living room on a wooden tray, placed the tray on a low coffee table, and took a chair near Helen's. She settled into her chair and waited.

"Well, my first take on reading the letter was that it was probably a hoax to get money out of you. But when I thought it over later, I had doubts. Now I'm leaning toward the idea that it's sincere."

"That mirrors my own opinion," Alicia responded. "Each time I read it, I become more convinced that it's honest. So what should I do next?"

"You have a couple of choices, as I see it. You can decide to ignore it. I think you would be safe with that choice. He would either get in touch again, probably with another letter, or he would not. If he does, you could deal with it then. If he doesn't, I don't think he would do anything. He doesn't directly threaten to expose the secret in his letter. If he were going to do that, he would give you at least one more chance, and he'd be more explicit with a threat of some kind. That's just an opinion, you understand."

"What's the other choice you have in mind?"

"Answer it. Ask to meet in person so you can judge him for yourself. See then if you actually believe the story. Decide if you want to ask him for proof of some type. This choice is a bit riskier. You have no idea what you would be setting yourself up for. It could be really unpleasant. Maybe he's so desperate he would threaten you personally or something. He might bring someone scary to the meeting. It's totally unpredictable. I'm not sure I could recommend that, given the chance you'd be taking."

"Is the first choice what you would do? Ignore it and see if he gets in touch again?"

Helen looked straight into Alicia's eyes. "What I *would* do and what you *should* do are probably not the same."

"Right. So it's settled. I'll answer the letter and meet with him. Now, are you willing to go with me to that meeting or not?"

Helen's mouth opened in surprise. She was speechless. She just stared at Alicia, who stared right back. Then Helen burst into laughter, and Alicia joined her. Helen hastily put the cup back on the coffee table as she shook with laughter. Every time she glanced at Alicia, she laughed harder. Tears welled up and ran down her cheeks. Alicia laughed just as hard. Helen bent over and clutched her stomach, trying unsuccessfully to gain control of herself. She took a very deep breath, then another, and felt she was over the fit. Then she looked at Alicia and started laughing again.

"What in the world …" she was finally able to sputter. It took several minutes for Helen to regain her composure. When she felt calm, she said, "I can't believe this. I'm a total stranger. First, you share this letter. Now, you want me along when you confront the man. What's that about?"

"It's about trust, Helen," said Alicia. "I need someone I can totally rely on. Someone discreet. Someone with no dog in the fight. I need you."

"But you don't even know me."

"You're wrong. I know everything I need to know. You've been in yoga on Tuesdays with me for two months. I've seen you on the street, in the grocery store, in the bank. You've never noticed me, but don't presume I haven't noticed you. I'm an expert at noticing people. And you forget that one day last month when you were out I accepted a package for you and signed for it. It was from the CASA office. When I lived on Mercer Island, I was on the board for CASA. I called Hilary as soon as I got the letter. I didn't tell her about the letter; I called her about you. I said I was looking for a person of the highest integrity, someone with a first-class brain, and someone who could maintain strict confidence. I told her I had heard of someone named Helen Smith who went by the CASA name of Helen Paige and asked her if you would fit the bill. She, by the way, said I couldn't have picked a better person. So you see, I *do* know you, at least everything about you that's important to me."

Helen was, again, speechless. She was not sure what she even thought about what Alicia had said. First, she was upset that Alicia would notice her. Then she was angry that Alicia would talk to Hilary about her. Then she was embarrassed at the compliments from both Hilary and from Alicia herself. She was too confused to respond and knew enough simply to remain silent. She picked up her cup, finished her tea, poured another cup from the pot, and sipped some more. Alicia sipped her own tea and waited. Helen noted that Alicia, too, knew something about silence.

"OK." Helen broke the silence. "I give in. I'll go, but only if we do it on my terms."

"I'll try not to show I'm gloating. Thank you, Helen. I can't tell you how grateful I am. I accept whatever terms you choose."

"We want a public place. We need everybody sitting down. Hands have to be visible. So, I think we need to suggest lunch. Let's leave it to him where; just give a reasonable radius to here, say within two miles of downtown Seattle, something like that. He already knows where you live so—"

"No, he doesn't know. The letter was addressed to the house on Mercer Island and forwarded by the post office. I moved out two months ago when I came here."

"That's good … Actually, that's really good. You'd think someone wanting to blackmail you would check your place out or something. If he did that, he should've noticed you weren't there. So maybe that means we're not dealing with sophisticated con artists or something."

"I want to write back now," said Alicia. "It's already been something like five or six days since he wrote it so he's bound to be looking for a response. Why don't I get some paper, and we can draft a letter right now. I may even run out and drop it at the post office this evening."

"Let's use the same kind of language," Helen said. Alicia got some paper, and they worked on the letter together until both were satisfied. It read:

Dear (Mr.?) George,

I was shocked and dismayed to receive your letter. I find the contents difficult to believe. Certainly, I cannot provide you with funds while I am somewhat mistrustful of the whole narrative you have related. If all that you say is true, then perhaps I have some obligation to Timothy in terms of fulfilling his wishes. Also, of course, I prefer not to see this sort of suspicion about Timothy made public. May I suggest we meet for lunch so we can talk personally about the best course of action to resolve this matter? I prefer to stay within a reasonable distance, perhaps two miles, of downtown Seattle, and I prefer as well that we lunch at a very public place. Other than that, I leave it to you to select the date and precise time for us to meet. I will wear a red coat and hat so that you may recognize me. Please let me know something similar about yourself.

Sincerely,
Mrs. Alicia Mayhew.

"This is perfect, Helen. I'm going to write it up on some personal notepaper and mail it right away. Thank you so much. I already feel a lot better. I think I'll finally get a good night's sleep."

"You're welcome," Helen said. She was uncomfortable now that the reason for her visit was over, and she wanted to be alone again. She rose and went to the door. Alicia followed. Still walking, Helen turned slightly and said, "Let me know when the lunch is as soon as you hear back. I may have to cancel something else to go with you so the sooner I know the better." By now, she was standing at the door. Opening it, she said goodbye and walked out.

Alicia smiled as she said her goodbye to Helen's back.

When Helen got home, she went to her bedroom and sat on the rug in her meditation corner. She reviewed the entire encounter she had just endured at Alicia's. She tried to relive the feelings she had had. First, there was the tea thing, and the feeling there was mostly just surprise. The whole laughing business was at a different level altogether. She remembered feeling several things during the laughing itself. It felt really good, plus it was embarrassing, plus she had no control over it. The latter feeling, no control, made her feel powerless. But there was no fear connected to the loss of control or power. She *should* have felt fear, but she really did not. Helen pondered this. Using tools from step four of her AA training, she tried to analyze the larger meaning of the feelings. Finally, she concluded that her over-arching feeling would be called "accepted." She felt that Alicia totally accepted her. Not just the behavior, the laughing, but her as a person.

Her thoughts went next to the "confession" Alicia had made. She recalled her anger about being watched, heightened by learning Alicia had asked the CASA director about her. Helen's first thought was such actions were tantamount to spying. But Alicia had admitted to being the kind of person who just noticed people. So maybe it was not spying. And she could not fault Alicia for calling Hilary. That was just smart when you looked at it from Alicia's point of view.

Helen continued the difficult process of examining her emotional responses to Alicia as she had been taught through her therapy and the AA program. She knew it was important work, more important than anything else she did. If she could not stay sober, she could not accomplish anything else. Then she realized that she had no desire to take a drink. And she had had no such desire while she was in the middle of the encounter with Alicia. In addition, she found she could contemplate the lunch she would go to with Alicia, again, without wishing she could have a drink. She could handle this. No problem. Just to be safe, however, she decided to go to a meeting. She checked her schedule of meetings, got her coat, and went out.

❧ ❧ ❧

Helen rose early the next day and did some exercises before eating breakfast. Then she reviewed the Flack/Kirk case file and prepared for her call to Judith Flack. If she had pegged Judith right, this could be the end of the case. She read the paper until after eight and then placed the call.

"Hello, Mrs. Flack. It's Helen, Sedona's CASA. I know it's early, but is this a good time for you to talk?"

"Yeah, it is. I hear you've been a busy beaver." Judith's voice was heavy with sarcasm.

"That's right. I have definitely been working the case. I conducted the observation of Sedona with her mother. And I've talked to your mother and Merida's father. Merida gave me Mr. Roloff as a collateral, so I've made a call to Detroit. I also talked to Merida's high school counselor in Arizona. I still need to talk with your sister. And I haven't completed the observation of you with Sedona. I've made this a top priority since I knew you wanted fast action on your request." Helen talked as though everything was moving along as normal. She knew she did not have to tell Judith any of the content of the out-of-state calls. "Merida told me you had consented to letting her have visitation three days a week. That's excellent, as I believe it's best to have Merida very much in Sedona's life."

"So, what will your recommendation be?" Judith sounded hostile as well as curious.

"I've learned that handling a case is like peeling an onion. I just learn more and more as I go along, and I don't know where it will end. I try to keep an open mind until I've finished gathering all of the information. Right now, what I have is mostly from Merida's side, other than my interview with you. I can't really use much of what I got from your mother, since it was mostly hearsay. You might want to give me a couple of more collaterals."

"Actually," Judith drawled, "I've been thinking about the whole thing. I tried to save Sedona. But I'm gettin' too old to want to raise another kid. It takes more energy and money than I have. I'm thinkin' it's time to let someone else worry about it all."

Helen said nothing for a while. "So … are you saying you want me to stop working on this?" she finally asked.

"Yeah, I think maybe I don't want custody. It's too much responsibility, and my health's suffering."

"I can understand that," Helen said. "Children can be a lot of work. If you tell the court now, I can stop the interviews and not write a report at all. Otherwise, if we just wait for the trial date, I'm going to need to get my report in because there'll be a settlement conference before trial, and the report needs to be part of that."

"There's no reason to make you do that report," Judith said. Helen smiled to herself. "I can write up a request for dismissal and take it to the court. There's time for me to do it today. You could get on to something else."

"That's great. I'm more than happy to just hold off and let it happen. I'm busy enough with other things anyway, so this takes a real burden off me." Helen hoped to sound both encouraging and grateful, leaving Judith some space to keep her pride.

"Right. I'll get on it. Thanks for calling." Judith sounded relieved as they said their goodbyes.

When Helen hung up she went straight to her computer and e-mailed Michelle at CASA with a copy to Hilary. Then she printed out everything she had written on the case and deleted all of the case-related files from her computer. She put the printouts, her notebook from the interviews, and the file given to her by CASA into a large envelope. It would all be returned to the CASA office once Michelle notified her the paperwork at the court was accepted. Helen's role in the life of Sedona Kirk, age three, was over.

Helen made one more call before preparing for her visit to the duplex. "Hello, Brendan, Helen Smith calling."

"Hi, Helen, I've been meaning to call you, too. I have something I need to talk to you about."

"I plan to go to the building today so maybe we can talk then. I think it will be after lunch. Maybe around one? Would that work?"

"Yeah, Dakota'll be in kindergarten, so I'll be totally free. Lookin' forward to it."

Helen next pulled out her file on the duplex. There were lists she had made and data on items from websites. She also had some pictures from magazines that she had cut out. She spread everything out on the table and made notes. Once she felt prepared for her meeting with the contractor, she put the papers in a thin leather briefcase, added a notebook and pen, and hung the case over the doorknob so she'd remember to take it with her. Then she showered and dressed.

As she arrived at the duplex, Helen noticed Drew Patten's green truck. He had been her contractor on several other projects. She went up the sidewalk of a very wide two-story house with a full-length covered porch that had two doors. The duplex was similar to several others in the same block in a reasonably well-cared-for area in the northern part of the city. She spotted her contractor through the open door of the left-hand side of the duplex. "Hey, Drew. How are things with you? What do you think of this place?"

"Well, it's dated. You have to get a look at the bathroom. But the bones are good. There's no rot; the roof's in good shape. Plumbing and electrical meet code so that helps. I think we can make something of it. You have a tenant in the other unit, you know. I met him earlier; seems like a nice guy. Lives alone. He let me look at the condition of his unit. Looks like he takes pretty good care of it. The best news I have is the floors. I pulled up some of that carpet, and we have solid oak floors. After we pull it all up, we'll know if we need to refinish them. But what I saw, I swear, they've never been walked on. Beautiful. It'll save us a lot of money right there."

By now, Helen had reached Drew and was standing on the porch near him. He was a large man, over six feet and barrel-chested. He had a full red beard and smile-crinkles around his green eyes.

"That all sounds like terrific news. Is there any bad news I need to hear?"

"Not so much. The guy next door said he's been having trouble with slow drains, and his toilet stops up too much. So I need to check out the sewer lines. That tree there may have roots giving us problems. I already called a guy to come out and check it." He pointed to a large fig tree in the front left corner of the property.

"Great tree, wonder if the figs are good. I don't want to lose that tree if we don't have to," Helen said.

"I hear you. I like figs myself. Want to come in and start? I put a board over a couple of sawhorses we can use as a table."

Helen put her briefcase on the makeshift table. She noted that Drew had already used graph paper to draw the basic plan of each of the two floors. He had entered the measurements of each room. "Let's walk around first so I can get a feel of the place," Helen said.

She went out of the living room, through the small dining room behind it, and through a door to the kitchen. "You know the first thing I'll want, don't you?" she said as she looked at Drew.

"Sure do. You want me to knock out this wall and connect the kitchen to the dining area."

"Right. How can we do it without losing too much cabinet space? There isn't much in here to begin with."

"I been thinking about that. I think we should take the whole wall out. Then take the counter from this wall and bring it out into the room as a bar, with the kitchen side of the bar where the wall was. That gives us another two or three feet inside the kitchen area. We could either make the bar the same height as the counter or step it up to the height for tall barstools. Then we'll put cabinets under the bar to replace what we lose. Make the bar wide enough for kids to do homework or art or something while Mom's cooking."

"Sounds right. Let's see if that still leaves room for a table. If not, we could make the bar start at cabinet height and then drop lower to use it as the table. Maybe one foot width for the top part and two-foot width for the lower part. Then she could use the rest of the room for a play area for the kids. That way, she could put a small TV in there with an easy chair. Get more use from the space." Helen stood in the doorway between the two rooms, looking back and forth at each. "In fact, I like that idea better, even if there is room for a table."

"Great. I like it too. Let me go make a note so I don't forget." He went to the drawing on his table and made notes right on the plan. Then he used a yellow legal pad to write a more detailed description of the cabinet and bar area. By then, Helen had moved back into the living area and started up the stairs to the second floor. Drew joined her.

"Oh my God, I see what you mean about the bathroom." It had 1950s pink tile, pink toilet, pink sink, pink bathtub. It even had dirty pink walls and a pink curtain. "This reminds me of Pepto-Bismol," Helen said. "Even a woman can take only so much pink."

"Thought you'd like it," Drew said with a grin. "There's a way around this. We can have all the tiles and fixtures painted. I'd get professionals to do it. They use good bonding agents and acrylic paint. It comes in several colors if you're interested in something other than white. Lot cheaper than taking all of this stuff out and replacing it."

"Great idea; let's do it. I want the white. What I really like is that this old sink is fabulous, so we can keep that. And the tub is so big. You could fit two or three little kids in there with rubber ducks and plastic cups and keep them entertained for an hour."

"And I have another idea," Drew added. "Come look at these two bedrooms. They're huge."

They went into the first one, and Helen agreed.

"I wonder how this happened. I thought in the 1950s the bedrooms were all small. I don't think most people had even heard about queen-sized beds back then."

"Yeah, most bedrooms were small. I've been thinking about it. Maybe they wanted to save on materials, cut cost that way. Could easily have been a three-bedroom unit, but they saved money with just two larger bedrooms. Since it was a duplex instead of a single-family, maybe they figured people would move when they had more than one or two kids."

"It makes it easy for us to improve," commented Helen. "The closets are small. We could build in a whole wall unit on the bathroom wall in this room. Make part of it a closet with rods, then some drawers in various sizes. Maybe even a shoe rack thing. And on the bottom, some big deep drawers for storage of things like winter coats and extra bedding and stuff."

"That's good. The other room is the same size. Let's say it's for kids. They don't need a lot of space. They can use bunk beds if there're two of them. So we can use some of the space in there, add it into the bathroom, and put in a shower. I think that's a real plus."

"Fabulous, Drew. I had in my notes to put in a shower if we could manage it. Perfect solution. And that reminds me; I want a laundry. Should we try to fit that in here as well?"

"We could, but we have choices. First, right here, we have a linen closet." He opened a door in the hall that ran from one bedroom door to the other. "This is big enough for an apartment-sized stackable unit. Then we can squeeze a linen closet into the bath when we build in the shower. The other option would use a sort of mudroom cum storage area downstairs. Let's go check it out and see what you think."

They went downstairs to see the mudroom. For the next hour, Helen went over the unit with Drew, pointing out things she wanted changed. "If we come in way under budget," she said, "let's think about what we could add that would take this place up a notch, make the tenants feel really special."

They shook hands, and Helen got into her car.

After a quick lunch at a fast-food outlet, she drove to the Capitol Hill section of Seattle. She arrived at the Lenora Apartments, a large three-story building two blocks from the main commercial avenue, and parked around the corner from the main entrance to the building. Then she placed a call on her cell phone. "Hi, Brendan, it's Helen. Will you meet me at the door in the alley?" She reached into the back seat and grabbed a large hat with a wide floppy brim. She put it on, left her car, and went into a narrow alley, lined with dumpsters, storage sheds, and covered spaces meant for parking cars but often used for bikes and miscellaneous items. She saw Brendan Riska, the building manager, standing in an open door and walked quickly to him and then into the building. They went up two stairs, Brendan leading the way.

As they entered the first-floor apartment, Brendan turned to Helen to take her coat. Smiling at her, he said, "We did it; no one saw you. And even if anyone did, he didn't see your face." She smiled back at him. Brendan had lived in the building for two years, since the day Helen had bought it for the Claudius Foundation. Brendan's son, Dakota, was then a lively three-year-old.

Dakota's mother was a drug addict. She and Brendan had dated for only a few weeks before Brendan learned of her drug use and stopped seeing her. It was only when Dakota was three months old and Brendan was required by the state of Washington to take a paternity test that he learned he was a father. He immediately asked the court for visitation rights with his son. The court, based in part upon the recommendations of an advocate, awarded Brendan primary custody. Minimal visitation, always under professional supervision, was granted to the mother. She saw the child only twice and then disappeared from their lives.

Brendan wanted to be a full-time parent for his child. He gave up his job as a junior-level accountant at a young bio-tech company. The need for a job that would allow him to remain at home had led him to the option of apartment-complex management. He started at a large residential complex in Southcenter but did not like the location. When he saw the ad for a position in the Lenora Apartment Building on Capitol Hill, he applied immediately. He was hired at the interview. A real bonus for him was that he received both a larger apartment and a higher salary. He had been treated well and was uncomfortable with what he was going to say in this meeting with Helen.

"Do you want to go first, or shall I?" she asked. They sat in the living room. There would have been a lot of space in the room, but much of it was taken up with the toys of a small boy—a train set, a castle-like structure made with Lego materials, trucks and cars, a small chair with a table covered with paper, colored markers, glue, and other art supplies.

"Unless you need more than the regular report, maybe I should," said Brendan, in reply to Helen's question. She nodded, and he continued. "You know I appreciate everything you've done for me. And I've been happy here. But Dakota started all-day kindergarten last month. The school has a before-and-after-school care option. He loves it. I think it's time I go back to work. I should've told you sooner because I already sent résumés out. I just wasn't sure I'd find anything with the economy so bad. One job was a facilities manager position at a headquarters building in South Lake Union. It seemed a fit so I applied. Long story short, I got the job."

"I know," said Helen. "They called me for a reference. Mr. Pierce took their call and sent them to me."

"Oh, no. Now I feel like a jerk. I should've thought of that. I should've called you right when I applied."

Helen laughed at Brendan's woebegone expression. "It's fine," she said. "We knew we wouldn't have you for long. This job is not a career for someone like you. You're young and smart. You need to be out in the world. We're just grateful you gave us the two years. The building is in good shape. We won't have any trouble getting someone to keep it going now that you've got everything sorted."

"Oh, good. I felt as if I was letting you down. That's a relief. Do you want me to stay a couple of weeks or a month to train someone?"

"Only if you want to. What's your starting date?"

"I gave them a definite for November 15 and said I'd let them know if I could come earlier. They'll take me whenever I show up. So that gives us almost a month to get someone in here."

"Do you have a place lined up to live?"

"I've been checking around. There're a couple of places free right now, and the management company for one place said there were three more coming up at one building in two weeks. So I won't have any problems with that side of things."

"Excellent. Let me talk to the board. We could probably handle things ourselves for a couple of weeks if we had to. You go ahead and make your plans. We'll start looking right away on our end. I'll have one or two board members meet with you to find out whatever they'll need to know to take over until we install a new person."

The discussion then moved to Brendan's monthly report on the building. They covered everything from general maintenance and landscaping issues to tenant complaints and problems. "One good idea came up at our last tenant meeting," Brendan said. "Two of the women suggested we use a storage locker on the main floor for strollers. We could have six or seven or however many we think we need, and everybody could share them. It saves keeping them in their own places, bringing dirt and mud up the stairs, and having to lug them up and down all the time. We have five women who already own them and would like to donate them to the common good. A couple of the women can't afford strollers and already borrow from neighbors so they said they'd be responsible for keeping them clean."

"That's a great idea!" Helen was enthusiastic. "Why didn't we think of that? Do it tomorrow. That can be your last official contribution to the group."

"Right, I'll get the space cleaned up and collect the strollers, then buy a padlock, and have keys made up, ready for anybody who needs one. Right now, of the twenty-three apartments, I think about 40 percent still use strollers, so that's quite a few keys. I'll get one of the women to take charge of it and report in to the manager. No sense us having to get involved unless there's a problem. We'll post it on the bulletin board to let everybody know whom to contact."

"If I don't see you before you leave, I want to tell you how much we'll miss you, Brendan," Helen said as she stood. "I hope you keep in touch. I know the tenants have loved having you as their manager. And best of luck with the new job." She shook his hand, collected her coat, and left.

ॐ ॐ ॐ

It was a sunny Tuesday shortly after noon when Helen arrived at the home of James and Pam Butler for her observation of Pam and the two little girls. She parked on the street. The house was in Magnolia, an upper-class neighborhood just north of downtown. The Butlers were not in the best part of the neighborhood, the part that overlooked the sound and city. They were on the lower east side, where the houses, though still expensive, were a bit more modest. The house was a ranch-style brick affair, built on a downward slope that allowed for a full walk-out basement. As Helen walked up the driveway to the house, she could see someone working in the back on a patio that abutted the lower-level sliding glass doors.

"Good afternoon, Pam," Helen said as she stepped into the home. "I see you're having some yard work done."

"That's my father-in-law. He put in a patio. Now he's getting ready to build a big cooking area, something my mother-in-law calls an outdoor kitchen. She saw the idea on some HGTV design show or other. They own the house so they pretty much decide everything that happens around here." Helen heard the undertones of bitterness and dislike.

"James knew you were coming, and he went to his parents' home. I think Meredith, my mother-in-law, sent Ted here to work so he could keep an eye on me. Not that he'll see anything from back there. I figured if we wanted to go outside we could do it in the front yard."

By now, the women had moved into the living room where two little blond girls were busy with a dollhouse on the floor. Helen got her pen and notebook from her purse and took a chair in a corner away from the children. Pam sat on the floor and started interacting with the girls. Helen noted that Pam would sometimes make suggestions but mostly allowed the girls to decide things, and then Pam would help carry out the plans. They arranged and rearranged furniture and little dolls in the house for about twenty minutes.

"Let's go outside. The sun's shining," said Susie. She was five. "I want to skate."

"Me too," said three-year-old Janie. "I have skates too."

Pam agreed, and they all moved to the front yard. Pam helped the girls put on roller skates. The sidewalk and the driveway were both flat, and the girls skated about, falling at intervals.

At one point, Janie fell hard and started crying. Pam picked her up and gave her a hug and then put her back down with the words, "I'm sorry you got hurt. Learning new things is always like that, isn't it?" Janie agreed, stopped crying, and started skating again. The hour passed quickly. Pam had as much as she needed for the observation part of her report.

"I need to talk to you some more," she said to Pam. "Should we try to do that now or on the phone later?"

"Ted would be happy to watch the girls in back," Pam said. "There's a swing set back there so they won't be any trouble for him." She took the girls' skates off, and they ran around the house to their grandfather while the women returned to the living room.

When they were settled, Helen began. "I have to talk about the alcohol issue. The court order assigning me lists it as a topic that needs to be addressed in my report."

"I know," replied Pam. "I didn't want to write about it in my sworn statement earlier because I knew Meredith and Ted's lawyer would use whatever I said against me. So, here goes. We go to dinner at the Butlers' once a month. They pay for us to have a sitter, and they're pretty insistent we always show up. We hate it. They have a fancy house and always invite at least one or two other couples, friends of theirs the same age. There's a long elaborate dinner, with a cook and a maid hired for the evening. It starts with champagne or cocktails in the living room. Then at dinner, we have about four wines. Usually I'd just take a sip of each and leave the rest. But for about a year, or maybe two, Meredith has been really pressing me, and Ted does it too. They fill my glass and then urge me to drink it all. I'm so stupid. I never wanted to make a scene, and I hated the attention if I tried to ignore it. Meredith would keep talking about it and making jokes about how I was rejecting wines she especially selected to go with this or that food. James never backed me up, not once. He's, like, almost scared of his parents, I think. I got so drunk once I went into the bathroom and vomited halfway through the meal. Another time, I started to get up from my chair and fell over backward. I was leaving the house so drunk I could hardly walk to the car, and James would have to help me. Twice, I vomited in the bushes once I got outside and the cold air hit me. The next day, I was always sick as a dog."

"What have you done about this?" asked Helen.

"I knew they'd use it against me, just as Meredith wrote in the statement you have. So I called an alcohol rehab place and asked them to evaluate me. Now I go there whenever they call me and get random testing. And I go talk to a counselor every other week."

Helen was amazed. "I was going to ask you to do just that. How did you know to do it on your own?"

"Because something like this happened to a woman where I worked, before I met James. She was accused by our supervisor of drinking, and the human resources people set it up for her to get treatment and testing. I called her and asked her about it, and she told me what to do."

"Well, you're way ahead of the game, then. I'll want you to sign releases for me so I can talk to the rehab counselor and get testing results. You also need to tell me about your drinking in general, not just these dinner parties."

"Right. I have a beer maybe three times a week, in the evening after dinner. That's about it. James and I used to go out sometimes, and I'd have wine with dinner. But we haven't gone out alone in a long time."

"Tell me where you stand now with James. I notice you still share the house."

"We do. James is good to me. If it were just him, we could get a divorce and still live here. We even talked about it. I'd be able to work part-time in the day when he was here, and I'd be here at nights when he worked. The only difference would be that we wouldn't sleep in the same bed. We always liked each other, so we could have done that. But his parents don't want me in the house, and it's their house. If James doesn't do what they say, they'll kick him out too."

"May I ask why you're getting a divorce?" Helen wanted to be careful around the topic, as she did not think an answer would be required for the report.

"We need something to change. We're thirty-five. We're just sort of sad most of the time, both of us. I don't think that's good for the girls. We agree on that. And the pressure from his parents is driving me batty. After five years of always holding my words in, I might just lose it and take after that bitch." Pam gasped and put her hand over her mouth. "Oh God! I can't believe I said that."

Helen had a half-smile and was biting the inside of her lip not to laugh. "Maybe you needed to say it," she observed coolly.

"I shouldn't say it, whether I need to or not. The girls come first, and if they heard me say something like that about their grandmother …

well, it would not be a good thing, that's for sure. I want the girls to have a relationship with Meredith and Ted. It's good for the girls. Meredith is devoted to them. The girls mean everything to Meredith and Ted."

"Fair enough. Now I want you to think about the ideal outcome for you. By this, I mean what you want to happen after the divorce. Tell me where you will live, how much time you'll have with the girls, whether you will work outside the home."

"My first choice is to stay in the house and even to share it, as James and I talked about. I wouldn't work. But I know that can't happen. So my next choice is to get an apartment and have the girls live with me. To do that, I'd need a job, and the girls would have to go to day care. Maybe James could have visitation every day from something like noon until I get off work. That way, the girls would only have morning day care. That would be great. Then we could somehow share the weekends."

"Do you think you could earn enough to pay for day care and the apartment and still have enough for a car, food, utilities, and things?"

"I don't see how. I've been out of work quite a few years. Maybe I'd need some child support. But then again, James doesn't make much. We couldn't live here, except his parents let us pay almost no rent." She sat for a minute, thinking it over. Helen waited. "You know, I'm going to be in trouble …" She started to cry. "I won't get the girls, will I?"

"Let's not go there right now," Helen said. "The judge will decide, based on the needs of the children, but that won't happen for five months yet. So you have time to try to line something up. That's what you should be concentrating on. That and keeping up with the rehab thing."

Pam was trying to pull herself together. "Maybe if I get a job and just a studio apartment, and work really hard, I could increase my salary enough. I did pretty well when I was in my twenties. I could do it again. Would I be able to get the girls back once I made more, if I lose them now?"

"I can't answer that. But you're not going to lose the children. You'll be very much in their lives, even if you don't have primary custody. I *can* promise you that much. Remember, my job is to represent the girls. I've seen nothing that makes me think you're not a good mother. And every child needs a close relationship with her parents unless there's something very wrong with the parents. So don't spend time worrying that anyone will take them totally away from you. That just won't happen."

"Right, I knew that, I think. I just want to make sure I get as much time with them as I can."

"Understood. I've got about all I need from you for now, other than collaterals. Whom do you want me to talk to? It should be people who can tell me about you, the girls, how you are as a mother, that sort of thing." Pam gave Helen the contact information for two friends she once worked with, as well as a sister.

When Helen returned home, she decided to follow up with calls to Pam's collaterals. Before she could start, however, Alicia knocked on her door.

"I have a reply from George" was the first thing Alicia said when Helen opened the door. Helen stepped into the hall.

"What did he say?"

"He wants to meet me tomorrow for lunch. Do you want to read the letter? I left it home."

"Yes, I think I do." Helen closed her door, and they walked down to Alicia's apartment.

"Read this while I get you some tea. I know you just got home," Alicia said as she moved into her kitchen. "The letter is there on the dining table." Helen noted the letter was written on the same type of paper with the same type of ink as the first one. Helen picked it up, sat at the table, and read:

Dear Mrs. Mayhew,

Thank you so much for the reply to my earlier note. As you might imagine, I am under a great deal of pressure from the mortgage holder regarding my late payments. I don't want to burden you with that, but I hope you can understand why I wish to meet with you as quickly as we might arrange it.

My preference is that we have lunch next Wednesday. I would like to suggest the Green Lake Bar and Grill on East Green Lake Drive North. We could meet there at eleven-thirty. This early arrival provides the opportunity to select a table in a quiet corner as we would precede the customers who work and would be on a later lunch hour. My clothing will be a dark sage cardigan over a pale sage shirt and a burgundy tie with a paisley print. My hair is thinning and grey, with a part on the left. I do not wear glasses. That, I hope, is a sufficient description so that you might identify me without difficulty.

I hope this meets with your approval. My telephone number is written below. You may reach me to confirm this appointment. Again, I am most grateful for your willingness to consider my plight.

Sincerely,
George Pendergast

"This is good," Helen said as she sipped her tea.

"The letter or the tea?"

"Well, both. I meant the letter, actually. It sounds genuine—he's signed with his last name, and he gave a phone number. We could easily check him out on the Internet to verify, but I believe him. I can go tomorrow if you can."

"Yes, it's no problem. I'm anxious to do this."

"Good. Why don't you go ahead and call him now. Then we'll talk about how we'll handle it."

Alicia went to the kitchen telephone and looked over the bar into the dining room so Helen could see and hear her end of the conversation. "Hello, this is Alicia Mayhew. Am I speaking with Mr. Pendergast?" She listened for a moment. "Yes, the time and place are good. I look forward to meeting you as well. Thank you. Goodbye."

"That was short and sweet. How did he sound?" Helen asked.

"I think he sounded embarrassed. Maybe even a little shy. But his voice is like his letter, sort of an old-fashioned formality. If I had to guess, I'd say he's from New England. And he sounds like old family, if you know what I mean by that."

"I know exactly what you mean by that," Helen said dryly.

"So, what's our plan?" Alicia resumed her seat at the table.

"Well, we might *think* this sounds legitimate, but we still need to be careful. I'll drive there and arrive at 11:15. I'll go in and get a table and watch for him. I expect he'll be on time. You get a taxi and get there about on time. But have the taxi driver stop a block or so away and park. Wait for a call so make sure you take your cell phone and have it turned on. I'll call you when he gets there; you have the taxi drive up and let you off. Don't leave the taxi until after I call you. I'll meet you at the door."

"What are we afraid will happen?"

"I have no idea, but this just makes me feel better. If he brings someone, and I don't like the look of either of them, I'll walk out and call you, and we'll talk about it. At least this way, we're playing it smarter than just walking into a situation with no warning." Alicia thought it was a bit paranoiac, but since she had agreed to do it Helen's way, she did not say so.

When Helen got back to her apartment, she pulled out the notebook on the Butler case and found the contact numbers for Pam's collaterals. She decided first to call one of the women who had worked with Pam five years ago.

"My name is Helen Paige, and I was given your number by Pam Butler. Are you aware of Pam's situation regarding her marriage and child-custody issues?" Helen had learned earlier that some of the collaterals given to her were not helpful at all. Sometimes they did not remember the client or had never seen the client with the children or had been out of touch for too long to comment on the current situation. She could save herself a lot of time addressing those problems up front.

"Yes, I know about Pam's divorce," replied Laura Redfield. "In fact, I'm probably one of the people who caused it."

That caused Helen to say, "Tell me about that, if you don't mind."

"I've known Pam over ten years. We met at the Woodinville Medical Clinic. When she got pregnant, I told her to get an abortion, but she wouldn't do that. So then, I suggested she raise the kid herself rather than get married. No dice to that either. She figured she and James could get along pretty well, and James wanted the baby. At least he told her he did. Anyway, she and James never had a chance to make a go of it. His parents interfered from the very beginning, and James is a class-A wimp. I could see Pam just sort of deflate over the years. She used to be fun. She was full of life. And ambitious. She had a good job at the clinic and had gone up the ranks to a responsible managerial job really fast. Since her marriage, she gained weight and got depressed. That's all she got, except for the girls, of course. They're great. So I've been after her to get out of the marriage for years now."

Once Laura started, Helen found, it was hard to stop her or get a word in. Luckily, she could write fast enough to get most of Laura's words down on paper.

"How often do you see her?"

"I go over there about two or three times a month. I only work part-time now so sometimes I'll go in the morning and have coffee with her when James is sleeping. We go to a movie one weekend a month when James and the girls are with the Butlers. And we talk on the phone every week at least once. Sometimes we'll talk two or three times a week at night after the girls are in bed."

"It sounds as if you know her pretty well. What can you tell me about Pam as a mother?"

"She's great with the girls. She plays with them, takes them to the children's museum and the zoo. She and I take them to the park a lot of mornings when the weather's good so they can play with other kids."

"How about discipline?"

"She doesn't need to do much. I remember when Janie pushed another girl at the playground about two weeks ago. Pam got straight up and went over to her. She told her that was *unacceptable.*" Laura laughed. "That sounded funny to me, like will a three-year-old really know what unacceptable means. But I think Janie did. Then she told Janie to tell the other girl she was sorry. And Janie did it. No backtalk or nothing. I've never seen Pam do more than just talk to them, maybe hold their arm while she does it. But that's all they need. They pay attention to her."

"Have you ever been around them during mealtime?"

"Oh, sure. With kids that age, it's almost always time for some little meal or other. Mornings when I'm there, she usually gives them a snack around ten or so. It's something like apple slices with peanut butter to dip them in or maybe an orange and yogurt or maybe crackers and cheese. I've seen them eat all of those things. Sometimes toast with jam. Oh, and they eat sardines on crackers. I've never seen that before, little kids eating sardines."

"Do you know anything about Pam's drinking?"

"She doesn't, to speak of. After the movie sometimes, we'll stop for a beer, but neither of us has more than one. She used to drink wine, but I don't know if she still does. She told me about getting drunk at the Butlers', so I know about that. But there's nothing to it, really."

"Well, I thank you for talking to me. I don't have any other specific questions. Is there anything else you think I should know?"

"Just that Pam's afraid her in-laws are trying to gain control of the girls through James. She's afraid they'll force her out of the house any time, and she doesn't know what will happen. She's welcome to crash with me, but I have a husband and four kids, two of them teenagers, so we're sort of cramped. I think she hopes to go back to work so she can afford an apartment. But then she can't be with the girls. So she's really pretty scared."

"Yes, I noticed how worried she is. These can be difficult situations in terms of re-building a life." Helen continued with a few more platitudes before hanging up.

Helen typed the notes in her computer. Then she fixed a grilled tuna-and-cheese sandwich and ate an apple with peanut butter to dip it in. Dark fell, and she went out to walk and go to a meeting. She felt good, she decided. She was not sure why; she just knew she felt good.

❧ ❧ ❧

Wednesday dawned rainy and overcast, a typical day for late fall in Seattle. The sun made an appearance about eleven, and the city glittered under the clear blue sky, also typical of Seattle. Helen noticed the Cascades, topped with snow much of the year, gleaming in the clear air as she drove to Green Lake. She entered the restaurant and asked for a seat at the window, from which she could see the door. Within ten minutes, she spotted George Pendergast. He was just as he had written. He looked in his seventies and was of medium height. His posture was excellent, as though he had been a gymnast or soldier earlier in life. And he was alone. While he asked for and was given a table in the far corner, Helen called Alicia.

"All clear. This looks good to me," she reported. When the taxi pulled up, Helen went to the door, met Alicia, and led her to the table. George stood as they approached. He almost smiled, then did not. He started to hold out his hand and then withdrew it. He looked very uncomfortable.

Alicia put out her hand to lessen his tension, and he shook it gratefully. He pulled out a chair and seated her and then did the same for Helen. "This is Helen, a dear friend," Alicia said. "She is totally reliable. We can trust her implicitly."

George smiled at Helen, nodded to her, and resumed his seat. "Shall we order before we talk?" he asked. When they agreed, he suggested a few things he especially enjoyed as they looked at the menu. Once the order had been given and the drinks delivered, he began. "I really don't know how to start this conversation. Is there anything you would like me to address first?"

Alicia thought for a few minutes. "I'm curious about a lot of things, of course. I guess I'd like to hear about you and Timothy. Nothing intimate, of course," she hastily interjected. "Maybe how you met and something about when and how you kept up through the years or something."

"Yes, I understand. Timothy and I were roommates in our second year at Georgetown. Before that, we had noticed one another in various classes we had in common. We're the same age; I'll be seventy-eight in December. We got along so well, right from the start, and roomed together until we graduated. We fell in love, but we thought it was platonic. We were both naive about a multitude of things regarding human relationships. And we were both good Catholics, of course. I'm originally from Philadelphia. My family has been established there for some time. I went back after college and tried to fit into the family business. But my heart wasn't in it. Then Timothy moved to Seattle to go to graduate school, and I decided to move here as well. I qualified to teach and taught in a private high school from then until I was sixty. Timothy and I roomed together my first year here. That's when we finally admitted it wasn't just platonic." He looked at Alicia. "This is difficult, I know. I wish there were an easier way." She nodded, and he continued. "We knew we couldn't keep rooming together. We were getting older, and it could cause some talk. So we rented two apartments in the same building. That went on until after his company was successful. He married you just before that, of course. Then, about twenty-five years ago, he bought the house for us." George relaxed as he talked. It seemed to get easier for him.

"How often did you see him?" Alicia asked.

"Quite a bit. I rose within the school hierarchy and didn't spend so much time in the classroom. On Tuesdays, I took off from eleven until two to walk the Green Lake circuit. Timothy joined me as often as he could. He tried to plan business travel so he'd be in town on Tuesdays."

"I remember," said Alicia. "He often mentioned he'd met some Georgetown alumni during his lunch."

"Yes, we both stayed active in the alumni association. It provided us some cover. He tried to come over for dinner with me once a week, usually when you had book club or a board meeting.

Then, when he traveled on business, he'd get me a ticket, and I'd fly in ahead of time and stay in a room in the same hotel. He often stayed over a day or two, and we had that time together and the times you spent a week with your girlfriends. That was twice a year when you were in either San Francisco or New York. He and I would travel then as well. We would visit Hawaii or Costa Rica or something. And later, there was the annual fishing trip to Alaska."

"You loved each other all those years, didn't you?" Alicia said it with some wonder but no rancor. "Do you know if he loved me?"

"Yes, he did. He was devoted to you and to the children. And very proud of all of you. But he loved me, too. It was hard for him. He tried to give me up once, but after a month, he was so unhappy he said you noticed it, and he was afraid he'd end up telling you. He really didn't want you hurt."

"I remember that," Alicia said. "I caught him crying in the bedroom. He'd never cried before. I asked what was wrong, and he sobbed like a child. He really was heartbroken. He would never say why. It worried me, and I remember watching him closely after that for a while. But then, it seemed to pass. That must be when he went back to you."

"Yes, he told me about that. As I said, it was all very difficult for him."

"I guess I've heard enough," said Alicia. "Now tell me about your financial situation."

"Yes, that. When Timothy had his first heart attack, when we were sixty-five, I was frightened. First, I was already retired. Second, my pension isn't overly generous. Even then, with social security, I could manage. Remember, I had no rent payment. I worried that if something happened to Timothy, it could happen to me. An expensive health issue could create problems, especially if something happened to Timothy as well. I might end up on pretty thin ice. If you recall, we were at the beginning of that crazy housing bubble. Somehow, it occurred to me that I could get a loan on the house and use it to purchase a small condo. It would provide an extra stream of income. Perhaps that strategy had been outlined in a newspaper column or something, I can't recall. However, I do recall that it seemed like a grand idea at the time. So I borrowed two hundred thousand dollars, using my house as the collateral for the loan. The house is worth much more than that, even now. Then I employed those funds as a down payment on a condo and received a loan on the new condo of another one hundred thousand dollars. I thought I was being a responsible steward of my money. I never told Timothy because I was afraid he'd worry. I already knew he couldn't leave me any money if he died, or it would all need to be explained to his heirs, so I thought I'd sort of fend for myself.

"You can guess what happened. First, I lost the condo. It went down in value as soon as I bought it. I sold it for enough to pay off the loan on it and half the loan on my house. That still represented a loss to me of over one hundred thousand dollars. More, really, as I had all of the costs associated with the sales on both ends. At present, I have a loan of one hundred thousand dollars left. When I did all of this, I was given one of those interest-only adjustable rate loans that were so popular. Well, it adjusted all right. Then the payment went up because I had to start paying on principal. I tried to keep up and spent half my emergency savings to do it. I realized that was foolish, so I started making only half a payment each month, hoping things would somehow change or I'd get lucky or something. I really don't know what I was thinking, to tell the truth. Then, when I got so desperate I was almost suicidal, I wrote that note to you. And here we are." He sagged in his chair and, suddenly, to Helen, looked older than his years.

"I see," said Alicia. "I need some time to think this over. And I'll have to talk to my own financial advisors. I prefer that the children don't learn about your relationship with Timothy so I need to be careful whom I turn to for this."

"I understand," George responded. "I, too, wish this kept from your children. One of Timothy's greatest fears was that they would learn of my existence. I believe he felt you could somehow bear it. He had great faith in you, you know. And great respect for you."

"Yes, I believe he did. He always treated me well and encouraged me in whatever I wanted to do." Helen thought Alicia looked happy and sad at the same time, a very odd thing in her book.

"I would not want to presume or anything, but … well, would you be at all interested in seeing the house?" George was hesitant.

"You know, I do believe I'd love to see it," Alicia responded. "Where is it?"

"Very close. I walked here. You ladies look young and spry. Shall we walk there now?"

That settled, they paid the check, each putting in about one third of the total plus tip, and gathered their belongings. They walked one block on Green Lake Drive, turned, and walked three more blocks in the quiet residential neighborhood of small to mid-sized homes. George talked about the neighborhood and its history as they walked. "It dates from the end of the 1800s. Certainly there are houses now that date from about 1904. I believe the neighborhood was quite popular during the time of the Arts and Crafts movement."

It was apparent the area was as desirable a neighborhood now as it was then. After ten minutes of walking, George led them up the slate walk of one of the larger homes. It was pale gray with stained glass windows beside the door, all of it original to the house.

"This was built in 1921. It's not very big, maybe eight hundred square feet on the main floor and the same on the upper floor. But you can see the roofline, which makes the usable space up there a bit less." As he talked, he unlocked the front door and led the women into the foyer. Immediately in front of them was the staircase. It was wide with gleaming reddish-gold fir treads and risers. There was a substantial thick handrail and balusters. About ten steps led straight up, then a landing turned to the right, and finally a few more stairs went to an upper railed balcony.

"This is a beautiful staircase," said Alicia. "I love the way they did those curved banisters of wood. What skilled builders they were back then." To their left off the foyer was the living room, seen through a partially open fir pocket door. To the right was the dining room, again with a pocket door. A hall running next to the staircase led to yet another door, with a fourth door off the hall into what Alicia suspected was the kitchen. All of the rooms on this floor were oak, and she knew the upper rooms had fir floors, given the period in which the house was built. She noticed that much of the flooring was covered with what she knew were old and valuable Persian rugs, mostly in deep reds with intricate multicolored patterns.

"I can see why it's so important for you to keep this house. It's beautiful."

"I've always called it the gem. I think of it as a jewel, you see, full of gleaming facets. I want to show you the dining room, but I'm a little afraid. It won't be easy for you to see, Alicia." He looked at her for a reaction, but she just nodded. He pulled the pocket door open all of the way and motioned for her to precede him.

Directly facing them was the original, fir, built-in buffet along the entire length of the wall. There were drawers in the middle section and leaded-glass-fronted cabinets on either side of the drawers. The top, about four feet up from the floor, was backed by a framed mirror running the entire breadth of the buffet, from one wall to the other. Above that was an equally long row of leaded-glass windows.

The remaining three walls were hung with thin silk tapestries, all in warm colors. They covered almost every bit of the wall space and lent an Asian elegance to the room. George pushed a button just inside the door. Suddenly the tapestries rolled upward, like window blinds, and the women watched them disappear into rounded tube-like structures they had not noticed earlier. Hanging on the three walls were black and white photos that had been hiding behind the tapestries. The pictures were mounted inside thin black frames. With the patterned textiles gone, the photos were the only decoration in the room, discounting the beautiful rug under the round mahogany table, the six chairs, and the original Arts and Crafts chandelier. All of the pictures were of George Pendergast and Timothy Mayhew.

Alicia walked further into the room. She turned slowly, looking at each wall, just standing quietly for some time, looking. Tears rolled down her cheeks and ruined her perfect make-up, but she did not even wipe them away or try to stop them. She just blinked her eyes clear and looked from one area to another, eyes moving up and down the walls.

The pictures had been taken through the years, from college at Georgetown (Alicia recognized the buildings in the background) to the recent past. Many were taken outdoors—in the woods, on beaches, at the edge of the Grand Canyon, in boats and canoes. Others were at dining tables, often at sidewalk cafes in what looked like foreign cities. In some, George and Timothy were smiling at each other, holding wine glasses in a toast. A few were taken inside what looked like hotel rooms, with one or the other of them sitting on a balcony or in a chair in the room. What struck Alicia was the expression on the faces. Timothy had never looked at her with such a relaxed smile and such happiness as he did in these pictures. George's look in the dining-al-fresco pictures could only be described as devotional. It was like religious pictures from the Renaissance where such adoration was regularly captured in the pictures of saints or the holy family.

Helen had followed Alicia partway into the room, then stopped and took a step back. She and George stayed near the entrance to the room and never uttered a word. When the tears started, they quietly turned and left Alicia on her own. George motioned for Helen to go with him into the kitchen. He plugged in a teakettle and started getting a tray ready. When the water was almost boiling, he poured it into a prepared pot, covered the pot with a cozy, and picked up the tray. He and Helen walked out of the kitchen, through a small mud entrance from the back of the house, and into the large living room, which extended from the front to the rear of the house. The room had windows, large ones, in the front wall, the long east wall, and the back wall. Light flooded into the room. Helen sat on the sofa while George put the tray on the coffee table and sat in the chair nearest her.

"Was that a mistake?" George finally broke their long silence.

"No, she just needs time, I think. At least you won't have to wonder if she believed you earlier." George and Helen sat quietly for another minute. Then George got up and put music in the CD player on a nearby shelf. It was cool jazz, soothing to their nerves.

"Is the restroom upstairs?" Alicia called from the pocket door without looking in at them.

"Yes, right at the top," answered George.

After another few minutes, they heard Alicia come down the stairs. She entered the living room and joined them. Helen noticed that her eyes, though slightly red, had new make-up.

"Sorry, it was a bit of a shock," Alicia said. "I guess the whole thing just still hasn't penetrated my mind. It's a bit surreal."

"I wish I knew what to say to make it better," George said. "I can't say I wish it hadn't happened or that Timothy had given me up for you. But he was my life, you know, so I can't regret anything. Except how much it hurts you, of course. I regret that very much indeed."

"Thank you, George. Anything I say now will probably be wrong, so I just won't say anything. Except for this: I don't want you to lose the house. I have to figure out the best way to handle it so it will take a while. But right now we need to get the foreclosure threat off your back. How much will it take to make you current, do you know?"

"It's hard not to know when they send me a letter every week and call at least that often. It's just under five thousand."

Alicia opened her purse and pulled out a checkbook. "Fine. I'll give you a check right now. Let's make it six thousand so we have some lead time. You send it in right away. Then I'll call you when I've had a chance to take some advice." She wrote out the check and handed it to George. There were tears in his eyes, and his hand shook.

"I don't know how to thank you. Timothy always said you should be a model for a painting he would call 'The Generous Spirit,' and I see now what he meant. He really did love you, you know."

"I know he did. There's a lot of ways to love, George, as we both know. Now let's just enjoy a cup of tea, and you can tell us all about this lovely room. I'm admiring your wonderful antique tables, which look as if they came from all over the world. Must be a lot of memories stored here."

They walked back to Helen's car an hour later. Alicia was lost in her thoughts on the walk, and Helen remained quiet. They got into the car and had driven for several minutes when Alicia started talking in a somewhat low, subdued voice.

"I met Timothy when I was in college at Seattle University. He was at the University of Washington then, doing some part-time teaching. He had invented some technical medical applications using software he had created. And he was starting his company, still lining up funding for it. I met him at a mixer thing for Catholic singles. We started dating right after I met him, though we only went out one night a week. He was a lot older than I. I'd just turned twenty-one, and he was thirty-three. I was a virgin and not worldly at all. My parents kept me all wrapped up in cotton wool or bubble wrap or something. I was never exposed to anything. When I met Timothy, I just respected him enormously and was really flattered that he was interested in me. I didn't know what he found interesting about me, but I was so grateful *someone* did."

At this point Alicia slowed down. She fiddled with the clasp on her purse. "Something dreadful happened to me one night at an apartment near my dorm at Seattle University." She stopped talking for a minute. She swallowed a couple of times. "I've put it pretty well behind me, but it comes back sometimes, sorry."

"Take your time. I'm not going anywhere. Only tell what you want to. The way I keep my own secrets, you know you can keep yours." Helen was trying to figure out whether she should encourage Alicia to unburden whatever it was or to get her to keep her private life private.

"You can say that again. You could teach clams to clam up." She hesitated only a few seconds. "I got pregnant, no idea by whom … it was a group, and they'd gotten me drunk." She shuddered, then shook it off, and continued. "The only person I could think to tell was Timothy. I was so ashamed; I couldn't tell my priest or family or anybody. Timothy was great. He'd never done much more than kiss me to that point, but he just put his arms around me and said not to worry. He told me he would marry me right away, and everybody would assume it was his child. We'd never tell anybody different. That's the kind of man he was. What could I say? Other women were having abortions by then, but that was no option for me. I thought about having the baby and giving it up. That's what good Catholic girls did back then. I couldn't. The marriage was the perfect solution. So that's what we did."

As so often in talking to Alicia, Helen was dumbfounded. She'd heard plenty of stories in her CASA work, but this was a different thing altogether. In less than three minutes, she'd heard about a gang rape, a pregnancy, an engagement to a relative stranger, and a secret held for a lifetime. She had no idea what she should say in response. She took her usual route out and said nothing at all.

Very soon, they were back in their parking garage. They both went upstairs and into their own apartments without further conversation.

Helen was too unsettled to work so she resorted to her calming routine of breathing exercises and yoga for an hour. Then she settled at her dining table with her old-fashioned Rolodex. She flipped through cards, pausing over one or two before moving on, final stopping on one that suited her. She called the Community Mental Health office in Ballard.

"Good afternoon, I'd like to speak to Elsa Dutton, if she's available." She waited. "Elsa, hello, it's Helen Smith. I need ten minutes of your time. Is this good? Great, I'll talk fast. First, let me give you some names and numbers so if I take too long and you need to run you'll have that." Helen looked at her file and gave out Pam Butler's name and phone number. "Now, here's the situation. I want Pam to apply for a job as manager of the Lenora Apartments on Capitol Hill. She currently goes to a counselor for alcohol addiction. It's called A Positive Alternative, and her therapist is Margaret Suskind. Maybe you could talk to Ms. Suskind and figure out a way to slip the idea to her and get her to pass it on to Pam. The deal is the same as always. My name can't come up. Pam can't have any way to trace this back to me. So ... there you are. This is the best way I can think of, but if you have another idea, let me know."

This was not the first time Elsa, a social worker, had received what she thought of as a *special secret helper* task from Helen. However, a lot of what Helen asked her to do worked out extremely well. More important, it all fit into Elsa's idea of what a good social worker *should* be doing. "Right, Helen. Let me come up with an approach and give it a try I'll let you know my results within a week."

"Good show, Elsa. You're a trooper. I appreciate everything you do. I'll wait for your call."

Helen looked in her file for the number for Meredith and Ted Butler. She started to dial and then stopped, too drained for a conversation with the senior Butlers. After closing the file and putting it away, she sat in her chair in the living room and listened to NPR for an hour.

Then she changed, put on a coat, and went to a meeting. "My name is Helen, and I'm an alcoholic," she said at one point.

Two hours later, she arrived home in the dark, carrying a bag of groceries she had picked up on her way back to the apartment. She spent some time in the kitchen, preparing a dinner of fish, sweet potatoes, and Greek salad. Eating at the red table, she concentrated on the taste of the food itself. Then she took a long shower, meditated, and went to bed. As she lay in bed, she thought about the meeting between Alicia and George Pendergast. She knew there was something in that meeting that held special meaning for her. She wished she could discern what that meaning might be.

❧ ❧ ❧

"James, this is Helen Paige, the CASA on your case. I hope I didn't wake you."

"No, this is fine. I got up about an hour ago. Did you want to talk to me or Pam? She's out with the girls. I think they're at the zoo, but I expect her back by one."

"I wanted to talk to you. I still need to arrange an observation time so let's set that up. What's the best for you?"

"Maybe Sunday morning? By then I've had all day Saturday to rest, and I have Mondays off. We could do it here at the house if that's OK."

"Yes, that's fine. Let's make it at noon. Perhaps I can watch while you feed them lunch. Let me make a note of it," Helen said, pausing to write on her calendar. "I also want to talk about your longer-range plans. When we talked earlier, you said the children would remain in the house, and you and Pam would sort of be in and out, depending on whose turn it was to have residential time with them. But I've since talked to Pam about it, and she seems to believe your parents want her out of the house altogether." Helen stopped and waited for James to comment. She could almost hear him getting upset. His breathing was rapid. Finally he broke the silence.

"Yeah, she may be right. And they do have a case to make, since it's their house. I can see their side of it. But Pam and I would like to share the house."

"Do you see any way to reconcile the two options?"

"Well … maybe not. Will the judge decide?"

"No, the judge can't tell people where to live. Well, that's not exactly true. The judge can say the children cannot move out of a certain jurisdiction without getting the court's approval. For example, if you wanted to take the children and go to California, the judge could say the children had to stay here until a hearing on the matter. But none of that applies to you. So … I need you to tell me what you want. I'll be making recommendations, and I want to recommend something that both of you can live with, if possible. Your input is important."

"I don't know … maybe you could give me more time to think about it?"

"Yes, I can do that. But sooner or later, I'm going to need your decision on what you want. For now, we'll just let it ride a bit. And I'll see you on Sunday."

Helen pressed the button to cut the connection and then immediately dialed a new number. "Hi, Mr. Osborne, it's Helen Prescott … Yes, I'm fine too, thank you. Could you ask Mr. Pierce to call a meeting of the foundation board of directors? I'd like the quarterly meeting as soon as possible rather than waiting until the end of the month. I want the agenda to include discussion of a new manager for the Lenora Apartments." She held the phone and pulled the calendar in front of her. "Yes … next Wednesday at three works for me. I'll put it in pencil until you call to change or confirm. Thank you, Mr. Osborne."

Helen decided she had done enough work. She was sufficiently on top of everything to give herself a break. She searched the Internet until she found a weekend yoga retreat near Bellingham starting Friday evening. If she left at nine o'clock on Sunday, she would have plenty of time to make it back for the observation with James Butler. She called the number listed and made a reservation.

❧ ❧ ❧

The trip to Bellingham was calming, even though I-5 was congested. Helen had given herself a full hour extra and relaxed with the flow of traffic as she listened to Barbara Streisand on her CD player. She arrived at the retreat center with a half-hour to spare. The center was a large building, surrounded by eight or ten small cabins, which were connected to the mother building via wooden walkways, slightly elevated from the ground. Each cabin had a wooden porch across the front, with doors for two rooms.

Helen checked in at the main lobby area, got her room key, and walked to her assigned cabin. Her room was small. It had a double bed with a small dresser, a table and chair, and one bedside table with a lamp. A small bathroom was attached. This was the most luxurious of the accommodations, as most rooms had two beds and no bath. Yoga retreats, Helen had found, were typically Spartan affairs. After she put her few belongings away, she picked up her yoga mat and went to the meeting room in the main building for a two-hour yoga practice, followed by dinner. The meal, like the center itself, was Spartan, vegetarian, of course, but beautifully seasoned.

Helen had been resident at this center before. She especially liked it because the swami in charge preferred no talking in the large building. He also discouraged talking while walking on the grounds. All cell phones had to be turned off and left in the bedrooms. There were no televisions or radios on the premises, no newspapers or magazines. Further, it was made clear to participants that no computers or other electronic devices were to be brought to the grounds. In spite of all that, Helen found the retreats here were very well attended. She considered herself lucky to have gotten in at such short notice.

By Saturday afternoon, Helen was well into the peace of the retreat. She had completed over six hours of yoga and three of guided meditation. She was now in her room for a two-hour break before dinner. She lay in the corpse pose on her mat and let her mind relax. It was time to examine her reactions to the meeting between Alicia Mayhew and George Pendergast. This was the main private work she wanted to accomplish on the retreat, and she felt she had achieved the right mental attitude to do it.

She was confused by three separate issues. First, why would George even *think* about getting in touch with Alicia? After all, he had been part of the biggest betrayal of her life. Alicia would very rightly think of him as an enemy, at the very least. How could he risk such a rebuff?

Second, why would Alicia even consider meeting him? The threat of exposure of the life-long affair had been barely hinted at. No evidence had been given or even alluded to. Alicia should have ignored the first letter altogether.

And third, why did they seem to get along so well? This question was most disturbing to Helen. How could they have come to the point that George would ask for, and receive, money? Why did Alicia offer it? And what lay behind George showing the photographs to Alicia? Wouldn't they be more likely to make her turn away from him rather than help him? After all, the photos made it very clear that Alicia's forty-year marriage was a sham.

Finally, why had Alicia told Helen about her background, including the fact that her oldest child was the product of a rape? Helen could not imagine telling a stranger such intimate details of her life. She was accustomed to hearing such details, of course, as a CASA, but that was an entirely different issue. At least it was to Helen.

By simply listing and pondering the questions, Helen realized how off-balance the issues made her. Her own emotions were very difficult to analyze. She tried to *feel* instead of *think about* what she experienced as she reviewed each set of questions. The first two issues involving the initial overture by George and the response by Alicia, Helen thought, involved a great deal of courage and trust on the part of both. The common thread, of course, was Timothy. His love for each of them must have been extraordinarily profound. It was his love that then gave each of them the confidence to be open to the other. Helen's feeling about that was, she decided, something akin to admiration for both Alicia and George. There was a warm fullness to how she felt when she recalled it. It required great trust for each of these two older people, one quite old, to reach outward. She also acknowledged that she felt envious. She knew she had never been loved in this way and was saddened by that knowledge.

That brought Helen to the third issue, the meeting itself. She distinctly recalled her feelings as they walked to the house. By then she was charmed by George and felt light and happy as she walked. Then the dining room. Her feeling was of reverence more than anything. She knew George felt the same. They could have been at the viewing before a funeral, leaving space for a grieving widow to say her goodbye or something. After leaving Alicia alone in the dining room, George and Helen had been reverential in maintaining silent until Alicia rejoined them. She had composed herself by then. As Helen turned it over and over, she simply could not conjure up a word to describe her feeling when Alicia joined them in the living room for tea. This was something that happened more often than Helen liked to admit to herself. She was not as good at knowing her feelings as she wanted to be. After years of hiding them or drowning them, it was difficult work to resurrect and accept feelings.

Then there was the ride home. Helen remembered her feeling at that point very well. She was appalled. But why was she so shocked? Because what Alicia did was something she would never do. Could not do. Had never seen or heard anyone do. It was simply beyond her ability to understand. She finally left it at that, knowing it was a lack within herself that created this unknowing.

Helen turned next to the issue of Pam and James Butler and their two little girls. When she had first moved to Seattle and become a CASA, she had had two cases that were somewhat similar and caused her to speed up the process of having the Claudius Foundation purchase housing opportunities in the local area. The Yeltsin case, immediately upon the heels of the Melton case, was the final impetus. Marie Yeltsin had not completed high school when she became a wife and mother. By the time Helen was assigned to the case, Marie was getting divorced and hoping to gain a ruling as primary residential parent for her son, Gavin, who was four years old. The father, Miguel Yeltsin, had never been involved in Gavin's life. The observation Helen conducted between the father and son indicated no bonding. Helen's interviews with collaterals further supported her own suspicions that Miguel's main interest in becoming the primary residential parent was to avoid paying child support. However, Marie could not provide a stable home environment as she had no family support to fall back on and little prospect of gaining employment sufficient to provide even a minimally acceptable apartment for herself and Gavin. Marie could not apply for a subsidized apartment unless she received primary residential custody, which she could not gain because she did not already have the apartment. A classic Catch-22 situation. Against her own wishes, Helen had to recommend Miguel be given primary residential time and Marie given visitation that did not include overnight stays until she had a stable housing situation. Helen's sense of failure in the Yeltsin case had been traumatic.

Now, in the Butler case, those same feelings of failure were looming over her. She hoped the outcome would be different in the Butler case, but that was not guaranteed. At least now, Helen was conscious of her own feelings—dread, fear, and anxiety, mixed with hope and determination to use the foundation to keep Pam Butler from going through what Marie Yeltsin had to endure.

As she examined her feelings, she felt lonely. Lonely for Swami Rameshrawananda, her own guru. His return to India from upstate New York had been the impetus for her to move to Connecticut, where she had gone to work for the investigative firm of Doyle Judd and Associates. She almost cried from the longing she felt for Rasmesh's wisdom and counsel. She also missed Doyle Judd, who had become a friend, the only one outside the ashram when she returned to the world. She knew she had gone as far on this road as she could on her own. She would need to get outside counsel or wait for the answers to come to her. The retreat could take her only so far.

ॐ ॐ ॐ

Sunday afternoon was rainy. Helen drove from the retreat straight to the Butler home, arriving just before noon. James met her at the door. Helen had forgotten how very heavy he was. She wondered if she should ask about his weight, trying to recall if it was appropriate to ask to see his medical records. Poor health might be a factor she should consider in making custody recommendations. She made a note in her book to check in with Michelle. Meanwhile, she followed James into the living room.

James mentioned that Pam had gone to a movie, and he was home alone with the children. Susie and Janie were playing with dolls on the living room floor. James sat in a chair near them and watched them play. Now and again, they would bring a doll to him for his help with dressing it. "Daddy, hold my baby. My other baby needs a bath. You hold this one," Susie said, handing her father one of the dolls.

"OK, I'll hold this baby. I'll take really good care of her." James entered into the play as though he were accustomed to it.

"Mine, too," said Janie, and she handed him another doll.

"No, Janie. He can't have two," Susie said and took Janie's doll away from James. Janie started crying. James put the doll he was holding on a side table and held out his arms for Janie.

"Come here, sweetie. Come to Daddy." She came to his side, and he picked her up and held her.

"Susie, you hurt Janie's feelings," he said softly while rocking and patting Janie on the back. "It makes me sad if you hurt Janie."

"I'm sorry, Daddy. I won't do it again." She came over to pat her father's knee and then went back to her play. Janie soon joined her on the floor again.

"I'm going to fix lunch now," James said, after about fifteen minutes. "Would you like peanut butter sandwiches or chicken nuggets?" They both wanted the sandwiches, and James went into the kitchen to fix them. He soon put small plates on the table and called the girls to eat. While they ate the sandwiches, he poured milk for them, then sat at the table, and read a book to them while they ate.

Helen made notes as she watched and listened to them interact. She wrote the words: "comfortable with each other, very natural" at one point and "responsive to questions" at another. She was diligent about getting the actual behaviors but felt the tone of the interaction was also important. After lunch, the girls said they wanted to make a puzzle. James cleared the table. He then helped the girls select a puzzle from a large basket of books and puzzles on a shelf in the living room.

As they were spreading out the pieces on the dining room table, Helen said, "I think that's plenty of time. James, I wonder if you can provide me with contact information on collaterals. I believe we talked about that at our first meeting."

"Oh, yeah, I forgot. How about my parents? Can I use them?"

"I already have them, and so far I've talked with your mother. I'd like someone who isn't related. Someone who has known you and Pam for a long time would be good. Maybe a friend or best man if he's still in your life or a neighbor you're friendly with and who knows you pretty well."

"I can't really think of anybody," James said. He hesitated. "There're some guys at work, but they only know me there."

"How about a minister or an old high school friend. Do you watch sports with anybody?"

"Just my dad. And we don't go to church."

Helen could see this was going to be a real problem. If James was so isolated he saw no one but his family, she would have to put it in the report. "Why don't you think about it?" she said. "Maybe Pam can help. I really do need to talk to someone." She did not want to let him off the hook too easily. She really wanted an outsider's view of the situation.

"OK, I'll ask Pam."

"Good, I'll look forward to your call. Do you still have my card?"

"Yes, I keep it in my wallet. I'll call you." With that, James went back to his daughters while Helen let herself out.

❧ ❧ ❧

The rain did not let up all day. Helen cooked a pot of bean soup and made a beef stew in a large Crock-Pot. She got out some glass containers sized for a one-person serving. Then she put a label on each lid to identify what would go into the container and the date it was prepared. While the food cooked, she took a shower, unpacked her clothes from the weekend, and did a load of laundry. Then she sat at the computer and typed the notes from her observation with James. She watched the rain from her window. The quiet of the apartment was broken only by the wind driving rain on the windows as darkness fell. By ten o'clock, she was in bed and drifting to sleep to the sound of the rain.

Monday morning, the rain continued. Helen went to an early yoga class. On the way home, she stopped at the bank and then at a small restaurant for tea and toast. Sitting at a table, she opened up a local paper she had bought, read it, and then did the crossword puzzle. She stared at the pictures next to the comics where it said, "Find six differences in these pictures." Glancing back and forth for five minutes, she gave up. She could find only four differences. As she finished her third cup of tea, she realized that she was unsettled and keeping herself busy to avoid dealing with whatever was causing the discomfort. She got up, paid, and walked back to her apartment.

In the lobby, Helen stopped to collect her mail from her box. She rifled through the envelopes as she entered the elevator and pushed the button. One letter had a return address in Boston. It was written in blue ink, not typed. Worse, it was addressed to "Helen Paige," a name she used only for her volunteer work with CASA. When she stepped out of the elevator, she almost bumped into Alicia.

"Sorry," she said with abstraction, not even looking at Alicia.

"No problem," Alicia said and stepped around Helen to enter the elevator.

Helen went into the dining room without removing her coat. She sat at the table and contemplated the envelope and considered just throwing it in the trash. In the end, she left it there and went into her bedroom to change out of her yoga clothes and shower. Then she went back to stare at the letter. Finally, she opened it. It was all hand-written in the neat penmanship taught at expensive private schools forty years ago.

Dear Helen,

Please hear me out. *Please, Helen. Please* read this. I cannot go through my life wondering if my sister will ever see me again. My children are growing up without knowing their wonderful aunt. The boys are thirteen and nine, and Renee is eleven. You've never even met them, and they're so great. What prompted this letter is Gregg turning into a teenager. Time is moving, Helen. It's too precious to waste this way.

I know I let you down. I've cried about it. I've prayed. I've asked for forgiveness a thousand times. No day goes by without thinking about you. Please don't punish me anymore. I need you in my life. No one has ever loved me as you did.

I was only twenty when it all happened. I was a self-centered bastard, I know that. I should have fought to get you out of Riggs Erickson. No excuses. I failed you. What else can I say? Please, Helen, please let me back in.

Love,
Derrick

Helen was crying when she finished the letter. She put her head down on her hands and sobbed, almost wailing in her anguish. After several minutes, she stumbled into her bedroom and threw herself on the bed, still crying. Eventually, worn out, she fell asleep.

When she awoke, it was mid-afternoon. The rain continued. It was already turning to dusk with low dark clouds pressing down on the city. Helen sat in her living room chair, wrapped in a blanket, drinking tea. She wanted a drink. More than she'd wanted anything in a long time, she just wanted a drink. She knew she should get up and go to a meeting. It was all too hard. The rain, the dark, the heaviness in her whole body. She could not move. An hour passed, and dark descended outside her window. She did not switch on the lamp. She sat. Then she fell asleep again, this time in the chair.

By Wednesday, the rain had finally stopped, and the sun was back. Helen sat at her table making calls and filling in her calendar. First, she arranged for another visit to the duplex. Some of the demolition work had been completed. Drew had samples of countertops and bathroom tile for her to see, and she wanted to look at the back yard, which she had forgotten to check on her first visit. The meeting arranged, she moved on to the next call on her list.

"Hello, Meredith, it's Helen Paige … Fine, thank you, and how are you and your husband? Good. I guess you know I had another meeting with James." She needed to wait for Meredith to talk before she could continue. "I have two things I want to discuss with you today. First,

James hasn't been able to come up with a collateral. That would be someone who knows him, both as a husband and a father, who would be willing to talk with me. Can you think of anyone? How about a cousin or other family member who has been around at family gatherings? Is there anyone like that?"

"We have a very small family," Meredith replied. "James is an only child, and my brother never married. My husband's only brother was killed in Vietnam. That's why our granddaughters are so precious to us."

"I see," said Helen. "I can certainly understand how important Susie and Janie are to you. Maybe Pam can help me out. I'll take it up with her. My other item is James's health. I wonder if it is adversely affected by his weight …" Helen's voice faded as she left the question hanging.

"I'm not sure what you mean," said Meredith. "He was never sickly as a child. His health is fine. Have you heard anything different?" Helen heard a defensiveness, mixed with the tiniest tinge of hostility.

"No, nothing. I was just concerned …" She faded again.

"Well, there's nothing to that. He's fine, strong as a horse. You know he works in a warehouse, don't you? He doesn't lift things anymore or anything; he's a manager. It's like a FedEx facility. He's on the night shift because it pays more, and he's been doing it so long he's used to the schedule. He never misses a day. You can check that out."

"Good, I'm glad to hear that. Thank you so much for telling me. Moving on, I will want to have a meeting with you and Mr. Butler, but I'd like to put it off until maybe January. By then I'll have gathered a lot of other material, and I'll be writing the report."

"Why leave it so long?" Meredith asked.

"Because James and Pam's lives are in such a state of flux. If I turn in the report too early in the proceedings, I just have to turn around and write an updated report. I'll already need to do an update about a month before the settlement hearing, whether I do one or two reports before then. So it reduces the time and paperwork if I send in the first one not more than two months ahead."

"Well, I guess that makes sense. We leave for Arizona every year in the middle of January, stay until Easter. So we'll need to be on your schedule soon after the new year." She paused. "Of course, this year, that could change. If Pam gets moved out, we may need to stay here to take care of the girls. I wish she'd hurry up and find a place. This dragging everything out is a real nuisance. Makes it hard to plan."

"Right, I'll make a note of your trip and call in mid-December to schedule a date, maybe the first week of January. And, of course, you're always free to call if something comes up before that." They concluded the call, and Helen wrote it up in her notebook for later entry into the computer.

Finally, she started a letter to Derrick. By the third draft, she felt she was getting close to what she wanted to say. She was rereading it, making minor corrections and changes, when the phone rang.

"Helen, it's Edward Pierce," he said quietly. "I've got Kenneth in the conference room having tea with a Mrs. Mayhew so I can talk to you."

"What? Why would Alicia Mayhew be in your office? Do you even know her? And why call me?"

"Because of what she wants. You know her? I never met her until ten minutes ago. She called earlier today and made an appointment. Said she saw the sign on the street and decided to use me for a situation she doesn't want her regular attorney to know about. Now I'm not sure I can disclose what she wants since you know her."

Helen thought for a minute. "I think I know. Is she trying to arrange to pay off a house loan for someone? And she wants to know how to structure it so there won't be an obvious connection between them? Maybe so her kids wouldn't wonder who the person was she's trying to help out? Something like that?"

"Something very like that. I thought of the foundation as a conduit."

"Oh boy, she is some woman. Can we do what she wants?"

"The foundation needs to know about it and be a part of it. But it's perfectly legal. And we have a lot of options. Can you come to the office and sit in when I make suggestions? We're working on it now."

Helen was torn. If she joined the meeting, it would mean letting Alicia know something about her business. She was not happy about that. On the other hand, she knew a lot about Alicia's business, too. She kept Edward Pierce waiting while she thought about it. Finally, because she trusted the feeling inside, she agreed. "I can be there in ten minutes," she said. Grabbing her coat and keys, she shoved the letter to her brother aside and left the apartment. As she waited for the elevator, she wondered if what she actually felt was relief at escaping from the difficult letter writing, rather than a pleasant anticipation at seeing Alicia.

When she arrived at the office, Mr. Osborne was back at his desk. "Hello, Helen. I've left a cup of tea in there for you." He pointed to the conference room while he took her coat to hang up in the small closet.

When she entered, Alicia looked at her in surprise.

"Helen? Why are you here?"

"I asked her to come," said Mr. Pierce. "She has a potential role in your transaction, which I will explain in a moment. I had to call her, but until then, I didn't know you two were acquainted. I told her nothing about what brought you in today, though she then told me she already knew."

Helen could see that Mr. Pierce wanted Alicia to know her confidence had been maintained. Alicia didn't look as though she especially cared one way or the other.

"So, can I join you?" Helen asked of Alicia.

"Of course, you know I'm delighted you'd want to be here, especially since you've been with me up to this point." Alicia turned to Mr. Pierce. "So, Edward, what's the best way for me to do this?"

"I want to introduce you to the idea of using a foundation. Helen is involved at a high level in one called the Claudius Foundation. The goal of the foundation is to purchase, sometimes renovate, various properties that are then put in service for women, or men, on occasion, who have housing problems. They usually have children as well. Now, you are thinking about paying off the loan on the house, but you want no direct paper trail from you to the owner. Have I stated your desires correctly?"

"Absolutely. Edward. You inspire confidence. You actually listened to me earlier. So refreshing. Many professionals think once a woman's over sixty she's so gaga she needs to be talked to like a kindergarten student."

"Yes, well," stammered Edward with a smile. "To continue, if you make a donation to a qualified foundation, you get a tax deduction. The foundation can use its funds for any purpose consistent with its charter or other governing documents. So the foundation can pay off the loan. However, the foundation needs to have a logical reason to do so. Now, if the gentleman in question would go along with this, there are several ways it could be structured. One way would be for us to create a charitable remainder trust. In this case, the foundation would buy the house outright and provide the homeowner with a stated monthly, or yearly perhaps, income stream. Upon the homeowner's death, the house would be occupied by the foundation, or even sold. In this case, the homeowner would immediately receive a tax benefit. A second option is simply for the homeowner to structure his will to have the foundation his beneficiary and hence be the recipient of the house upon his death. A third possibility would be for the homeowner to sell the home to the foundation, subject to what is termed a life estate, meaning he retains the right to remain in the home, rent free, until his death. Any of these would work equally well. All are totally legal."

"One problem I could foresee is that the house is worth a lot more than the loan," said Alicia. "It wouldn't be fair to George if the foundation gave him only one hundred thousand dollars."

"You're right, Alicia," added Helen. "The foundation would either have to pay more up front or else provide a generous payment over time, like two thousand dollars a month or something, as the income from the charitable remainder trust. George might like to receive a regular income. All of those details would need to be worked out."

"So we need to call George and get him to talk about this with us," added Alicia. "Edward, how long will all this take if we get George on board with it?"

"I can do all the work in-house so we could do it in something like ten hours maximum. Depends on whether I have to write a new will or create a charitable remainder trust or something. You also need to get the foundation on board. I suggest you do that at the board meeting later this month, Helen. Maybe you and Alicia could get together and make up a proposal."

"I can do that now, if you can," Alicia said to Helen. "At least get a start on it, if nothing else."

"Sure, we can go back to my place. I have minutes of other meetings where we've taken up purchase decisions in several ways. We can use those as a template for this. So, *Edward*, I guess we'll call you if we get stuck with anything." It was the first time Helen had used Mr. Pierce's first name, and she smiled at him when she did it. After all, if Alicia could use it the first time she met him, it was perhaps time Helen did so as well.

The women retrieved their coats and walked out of the office together, back to their building, and went up the elevator. Helen unlocked her apartment door and stepped back as Alicia entered. Then she led Alicia into the dining area.

"Oops, let me get another chair," she said as she sat Helen at the only small red vinyl-covered 1950s chair that matched the chrome-and-Formica table.

While she did so, Alicia looked into the adjacent living room. She was startled. The only furniture in the rather large room was a comfortable-looking stuffed chair with ottoman, a table on one side of the chair, and a floor lamp on the other. Alicia thought there might be a television on a stand across the room but could not see past the fireplace that jutted out from the wall and separated the living from the dining room. She said nothing.

Helen, meanwhile, carried her own wooden office chair from its place in front of her computer and put it on the opposite side of the table from Alicia. "I have the minutes right over here," she said, looking through some thick black binders on a bookshelf. She pulled one out and opened it on the table. "I forgot to offer you some tea. Let me fix it now before we go any further," Helen said.

"I'm going to the bathroom," said Alicia. "Your apartment's just like mine, so I know where it is." She went down the hall to the bathroom shared by visitors and the guest bedroom and found an unused bathroom with nothing in it that had not been installed by the builder. No toilet paper, no towel, no soap. Not even a shower curtain. "Helen," Alicia called out, "I can't use this bathroom. There's nothing here to wash my hands or anything."

"Oh, you're right. I don't use it. Go to the one in the master bedroom." Helen sounded perfectly normal in admitting that her guest bathroom had never seen a guest.

Alicia moved further down the hall and stepped into the master suite. She stopped at the door, appalled. The room was like a monk's cell. Alicia had never actually seen a monk's cell but assumed this was what it would look like. A small camp bed was pushed lengthwise against the far wall. The corner on the window wall had a small prayer rug, a very short wooden stool, a large cushion, and a folded shawl or blanket of some type. A small Asian table, about six inches off the floor, held some candles, small dishes, and a box of incense sticks. That was it, except for a lamp on a milk crate near the bed. It was clean and tidy, but empty. Alicia almost tiptoed through the room to the bathroom, went and washed, and walked back out.

She returned to the dining table and rejoined Helen, who now had the tea things placed on the table near the big black binder. "Helen, please don't answer if you don't want to. I'm not intruding; I'm just an insanely curious person. But why don't you have any furniture?"

Helen looked surprised. "I never thought about it. I guess I have what I need."

"Helen, this is a fourteen-hundred-square-foot apartment. It's the biggest apartment in one of the newest buildings on Queen Anne. Your rent, when you add in the utilities and parking space, is about four thousand dollars. Why would you want to spend that kind of money when you could just as easily put all of your stuff in a three-hundred-square-foot studio?"

"Oh, no Alicia. I love this place. It has everything I was looking for. The location, the windows overlooking the street, the security system. It has a lot of light. This is definitely where I want to be." Helen said it as though it all made perfect sense to her.

"But the cost, doesn't that mean anything?"

"No, it doesn't. Money's just money. You know that as well as I do. You're living well below your means by being here, I'm sure. I'm doing the same."

It had never occurred to Alicia that Helen had major resources. Her clothes, her car, her lack of jewelry, even her haircut and unpolished nails spoke of limited means, in Alicia's world. As, of course, did the lack of a proper bed or any other furniture.

"Do you want to talk about my furniture or what you came here for?" Helen said. She smiled when she said it.

"OK, I give." Alicia smiled back. "But some day, you know, you're going to have to explain a few things to me. Not any time soon, but when you're good and ready."

"Fair enough, and that's not today," Helen said, and they turned to the binder.

"Now, when we bought a place eighteen months ago, it was a bungalow, smaller than George's house. It was in the estate of the woman who had lived there forever, and her kids were selling it to clear up their mother's business affairs. None of them wanted to live in it. It needed updating before they could sell it at full price. So we got a pretty good deal. It's in Wallingford. We could use that one as a template because the kids didn't need the money. What they wanted more than cash was a tax advantage. So they sold it to the foundation for a hundred fifty thousand. The house was valued at four hundred thousand. Then they took the hundred fifty we gave them, used it to pay estate tax on their mom's total legacy, and deducted their share of the two-hundred-fifty-thousand difference as a charitable contribution, which they split among them. I think this would be a good case study to show George."

"Great, but I like the idea of giving him the income stream Edward talked about, too. Let's call him." She pulled out her cell phone. "Do you have his number written down somewhere?"

"I do indeed," said Helen. "I'm a little compulsive about that because I'm forever looking for contact info on people." She rummaged around some papers near her computer until she found the number and repeated it to Alicia.

"Good afternoon, George, this is Alicia. How is your day going?" Alicia listened, and Helen was then privy to a major conversation about people's activities. It ended with, "George, I've just come from a lawyer's office. He gave me lots of suggestions for how we can pay off that loan. But I don't want to decide the best way by myself. I want you to help me choose what's best for you. Can you meet with Helen and me to do that?" There was a pause. "Wonderful, do you want to meet at your place or mine? I live on Queen Anne. I have an extra parking place if you drive." Another long pause while Alicia listened to George. "I can understand that. You know, Timothy was getting to the point where he only wanted to drive between ten and two. Just too much traffic otherwise. We can go to you if you prefer." Another pause. "That sounds delicious. I did something similar a couple of times, only tomato instead of avocado and arugula under ... Oh no, yours sounds fantastic. I'll do mine sometime for you, and we can compare. Let me check with Helen. She's right here." Alicia put her phone inside her shirt and talked very quietly to Helen. "He'd like us to come to lunch. He wants to fix an avocado-stuffed-with-chicken salad on sautéed spinach. Shall I accept?"

Helen was dumbfounded. They were supposed to talk about a house sale and were caught up in recipe exchange. She glanced at her calendar to be sure it was clear before she spoke. "Tell him sure. I can make it any day in the next eight days."

"George, Helen says she's good this Friday and next Monday or Tuesday. Do any of those work for you? Perfect, let's make it Monday then. Say twelve thirty? Excellent. We both look forward to it." She paused. "And George, can we eat lunch in the dining room with the photographs? That would be so special for me ... Thank you, George. See you then." She closed her phone and put it back in her purse.

"You really want to eat with those photos of George and Timothy all around you?"

"Not especially, but I know how much it would mean to him. I'm getting used to it, believe it or not. And I like George. So this is something that I can do that would make him happy."

Helen shook her head, made a mental note to herself, and went back to the binder. "Right. Let's make a few notes about what we need to tell George. First, we need to find out what's important to him beyond just getting the loan paid off. He may have heirs he wants to protect. That would mean he will want some provision for them, like the extra payments to continue until a certain date in the future."

"I'm not sure I follow that," said Alicia. "Give me an example."

"Well, let's say the foundation pays two hundred thousand for the house, plus payments of two thousand a month for thirty-six months. That's only three years. Now say George has a great-nephew aged ten. He really wants to provide college funding for the child. We could write the deal so the foundation pays fifteen hundred a month instead of two thousand, but pays it for fifteen years and pays it to the child upon George's death. That takes the child to age twenty-five."

"Now I understand. We need to make up some different scenarios for George to consider, depending on his personal goals. You're good at this so you can probably do a lot of that while we talk with him, right?"

"I could do some of it, yes. But we should jot down some notes so we don't forget anything important." They spent the next half-hour going over what critical information they felt they should tell George.

When Alicia had gone, Helen put back the binder and picked up other papers they had used. In the process, she uncovered the drafts of the letter she had started to Derrick. She read over the draft she had written. It seemed heartless and somewhat cold. She thought she had done well but could see now that she was wrong. In trying to figure out how she could have failed so miserably at writing the letter, she thought of Alicia. She reviewed the conversation Alicia and George had shared. Even though she only heard one side, she could feel the warm quality of the call. Warm versus cold. She needed to think about that. She threw the drafts of the letter away.

❧ ❧ ❧

Helen arrived early for the meeting of the board of the Claudius Foundation. Mr. Osborne, who served as secretary for the board, had laid out the minutes and financial records on the table in the conference room and had rearranged the room so it could accommodate up to eight people. He took Helen's coat and asked if she would like tea while she looked over the papers.

"Yes, please." She sat at the table and made some notes as she read. Within five minutes, Mr. Osborne returned with a tray. Mr. Pierce came into the conference room to join them for tea.

"I can't wait for you to try this," Mr. Osborne said. "It's from an herbalist in Gig Harbor who mixes the teas herself. At least I think it must be a 'her.' It's sold at farmer's markets so I've never met the herbalist. Anyway, this is called Honeybush Spice. It's a red tea called honeybush, I think. Then it's mixed with ginger, cardamom, licorice, cinnamon, orange peel, and star anise. The package says it has vitamins and antioxidants. And it's good for digestion."

"Sounds like one of those old-fashioned tonic advertisements from about the 1920s and '30s we've all heard about," Mr. Pierce said with a half-smile on his face.

"It does, but it still sounds as if it would taste wonderful," said Helen. "I'm anxious to try it. How long does it steep?"

"Five to ten minutes. I want to go to the whole ten to get a strong taste of it." Mr. Osborne looked at Mr. Pierce. "Shall I tell her?"

"I think you have to tell her now. Otherwise you'll leave her too curious to be a good board member when the meeting starts."

"Whatever it is, you best tell me right now," Helen laughed. "My heart rate is increasing."

"It's so exciting. Well, at least for me, it's exciting. A friend of mine from my childhood is going to open a tea shop here on Queen Anne. Right next to the sewing shop just this side of McGraw. She's been talking about it for years but was always too busy with her children. They're older now, and she decided to go for it. She and I have been tea lovers for years. We go to high tea every year at the Fairmont. We go to tea shops together on weekends, buy each other books about tea, that kind of thing. Have done since forever. So … she asked me to invest in the shop and be her partner. Isn't that fabulous?" Mr. Osborne's face was pink with excitement. Helen had never seen him so animated. She glanced over at Mr. Pierce. He was smiling hugely, obviously as happy for Mr. Osborne as Mr. Osborne was for the tea shop.

"What will you do as partner besides invest?" asked Helen.

"I'll handle all the paperwork, apply for licensing, get the signage arranged, do the taxes and payroll, keep all the records, pay the bills. She'll be free to just order, blend, serve, and sell. We have it all worked out." Mr. Osborne looked almost smug, and it made Helen laugh.

"Mr. Osborne, this is fabulous news. No one will be a better partner for a tea shop than you. And it's so nice to be involved with something you care about so much."

"Yes, just like you with the foundation and institute," Mr. Osborne said. Then he covered his mouth. "Oh, I'm so sorry. I forgot myself. Please, please, pretend I never said it." He looked totally stricken.

"It's forgotten. Don't think a thing about it," Helen said. Inside, however, she felt a strange tightness. "Just tell me more about the tea shop. Will you have tables or just a sales counter? And what else will you sell there? And how will the shop look? Tell me everything." She smiled at Mr. Osborne, and he quickly launched into his story again. In only a minute or two, he was happily sharing all of the details. Helen listened with half an ear, still monitoring her emotions, trying to figure out what she was really feeling about Mr. Osborne's comment. Then she put it aside for later so she could rejoin the present.

"And we're talking now about what kind of theme we want. You know, sort of colonial British or maybe Asian. But Sonja's Norwegian, so maybe we'll go that direction. Then we'll get things for the walls and fabrics for the windows and cushions."

"How long before it opens?"

"We think maybe six weeks, but we'll have to work like crazy to make it happen by then." Mr. Osborne suddenly realized he was steeping tea. "Oh my, I think this is ready. Pardon me for getting carried away. Let's have tea and talk about something else." He strained, poured, passed around the cups, and settled back to be a listener rather than a talker.

Helen and Mr. Pierce discussed her goals for the board meeting. Since Mr. Pierce served in the capacity of legal counselor and not member, he did not attend the meetings unless Helen felt his advice would be needed and would not be participating in this session.

They were soon joined by Joe McGregor, the president of the board, and Harriet Kilcoyne. They lived near one another in Innis Arden and always drove to the meetings together. Within a few minutes, Frank Brewer, another member, arrived. It was Frank who kept an eye out for the sort of properties the foundation needed. He had years of experience in the sale of residential and apartment properties, was retired, and enjoyed driving around and looking at whatever came on the market.

Mr. Osborne reported that two other members, Nancy Osgood and Eric Murphy, would not be present so the meeting could be called to order. Mr. McGregor did so. Helen had picked Mr. McGregor to join the foundation at the suggestion of Edward Pierce. Joe McGregor was known personally to Mr. Pierce, who also knew of Joe's background as a developer. Both Mr. Pierce and Helen felt Joe's knowledge about building and zoning issues, as well as a general feel for the value of land and buildings, would be valuable assets to bring to the table. Later, as he learned more about the goals of the organization, he became even more valuable. He not only took on the presidency; he also decided to engage in what he called "fund development by arm-twisting." He started hosting parties, with his socially prominent wife, at which he would promote the organization and brazenly ask his guests to feel free to write tax-deductible checks to the Claudius Foundation. Helen, seeing how much he enjoyed it, did not demure, though she felt the foundation was funded well enough through her own sources. Joe insisted that his wife had been taking him to such events for years, and this was his chance to "do unto others," given the number of checks he had been encouraged to write.

Joe called upon Mr. Osborne to read the minutes of the previous meeting, which were then duly approved. Joe then asked for the treasurer's report.

Harriet stood to report, obviously feeling her role required a certain amount of formality. "The foundation received a donation of $500,000 this month. Interest income was $437.76. Outgo included a payment of $392,657.81. That expenditure is for the purchase of a duplex on Dibble Avenue. Helen will fill us in on that in a minute. We currently have a balance of $314, 907.26." She looked around and, satisfied there were no questions, resumed her seat.

"Let's move to new business," said Joe. "I need to report that Nancy Osgood's mother has cancer. She lives in Arizona, and Nancy will be spending a lot of time going back and forth for at least a year. She has given me a letter of resignation, but she hopes we'll accept her back when her mother's condition changes, one way or the other."

"Next, Eric Murphy has been offered a job in Washington, DC, at The World Bank." Joe McGregor did not sound at all unhappy about losing Eric from the board. Helen had noticed from the beginning that Eric seemed to get under Joe's skin, and she suspected it was because Eric was a negative person in general. It was true that Eric found objections to almost everything new or unusual that someone suggested, but

that trait seemed to bother Joe more than it did the other members of
the board. Handing a letter to Ken, Joe said, "Eric gave me this letter of
resignation. You'll want it for the files. Now, I need motions on accepting these."

"I move we accept Eric's resignation letter," said Frank. "I further
move we accept a temporary leave of absence from the board for Nancy,
pending her return to full board duties in two years. Then we can replace
Eric with someone and get another board member with a two-year term
to fill in until Nancy returns. And make sure Nancy knows we want
her to come back when she feels she's ready." Helen was interested that
it was Frank Brewer, a tough real estate agent, who would add such a
sensitive note to the issue.

"Good idea. I second both motions," added Harriett.

"Moved and seconded that we accept Eric Murphy's resignation.
Moved and seconded that we permit a leave of absence of two years
for Nancy Osgood. Voting on the first motion, show of hands in favor.
Let the record show unanimous. Voting on the second motion, show of
hands in favor. Let the record show unanimous. Ken, write a letter to each
of them. Put a personal note on Nancy's about how we want her back.

Helen was reminded what a great president Joe was. He moved the
meetings along at a brisk pace without ever making people feel pushed
around. He also had a sincere interest in everyone else and made sure
each one knew it.

"On to new business. Maybe we should talk about some replacements for the board. Who wants to go first?"

"I'd like to," said Kenneth Osborne. This was a surprise as Kenneth
tended to stay in the background and take notes rather than actively
participate. "I'd like to hear Helen's opinion about asking Alicia Mayhew
to take Eric's place."

Helen looked at Mr. Osborne. She had a hard time thinking of or
addressing him as Kenneth, even if everyone else did. She looked away.
She tried to assess her feelings about this development. Being unsure
about them, she started talking, hoping a discussion would bring some
clarity for her. "Well, I'm trying to think about what assets she would
bring ..."

"For one thing, she knows what we do. She was involved in adding the newest property to our foundation, which is the next item on the agenda. Second, she has supported us financially already. Third, she's in a position to help with fundraising if we ever need it."

Helen thought Mr. Osborne was making a strong case for Alicia.

"What's the downside? Is she hard to get along with? Will she be a pain in the ass?" Joe McGregor was nothing if not direct. He tended to go right to the point of whatever he wanted to know.

"No, quite the opposite," Helen was quick to interject. She wondered why she felt obliged to defend Alicia. After all, she was not the one who had put the name up for consideration.

"She's sensitive to people, but she's not a pushover," added Kenneth. "I think she has the time, too. She told me she was looking for something new in her life since she moved to Queen Anne from Mercer Island."

"Why'd she move?" asked Harriet. "Or is it any of my business?"

"She was open about it with me, so I don't think I would break any confidences if I answered," Kenneth replied. "The first time I met her, before she became a client of the law firm, she was talking to me over tea. She was widowed two years ago and moved here to build a new life. She wanted to jettison the image of herself as the wife of someone important and become more of just herself."

"So, we have some positives here," said Joe. "No negatives. Shall we invite her to a board meeting so everybody can meet her? Maybe ask her if she'd even like to be on the board? What action shall we take?" As usual, he wanted to move the board forward. The members looked at one another, each giving the others a chance to add something.

When no one spoke up right away, Kenneth continued. "If everyone is agreeable to having her on the board, I could call her right now and ask if she wants on. Then we'd have a new member by the next meeting. Otherwise, we'll be two short."

"I'm in favor of that," said Harriet. "The way the foundation is adding properties to the portfolio, we may be needing more help."

Kenneth stepped out to make the call while the board moved on to the next item.

"Harriet, will you take notes for Kenneth?" Joe asked. "And, Helen, do you want to present on the duplex?"

"Yes. We purchased a duplex located in the seventy-six-hundred block of Dibble Avenue Northwest. That's up Fifteenth Street on the way to Carkeek Park. You can get the exact number from Mr. Osborne. We paid just under four hundred and have budgeted one hundred for fixing it up. So it just about equals the donation we received this month. We hired Drew Patten to handle some renovations. We used him before, I'm sure you all recall. I have some before-and-after floor plans here; plus Drew sent me some photos so you can see what we inherited with the place. I especially want to draw your attention to the lovely pink bathroom. Drew is on-site every day, so I told him to expect any or all of you to show up for a personal tour."

"Do you have any tenants in mind?" asked Harriet.

"Not yet. We still have a tenant on one side. We're renovating the sides one at a time. We'll see if the tenant wants to move to the completed one when we start his. He's a good tenant from what I hear, and Drew thinks he'll want to stay."

"Will that be a problem if we move a woman and kids in? If she's been abused or something?" It was Joe who asked.

"Depends. We may have to select someone based on just that. But if we have a good tenant in place, paying market rent, I hate to throw him out."

"I can see how a woman might want the male tenant next door," put in Frank. "She might feel safer that way. Especially if she was abused."

"Yeah, we can't predict any of that. Let's just let it go until it comes up when we get a tenant, " added Joe. "We ready to move on to other business, or does anyone have more questions on the duplex?" Hearing no objection, Joe said, "Next item, Brendan Riska. Want to report on that, Helen?"

"Right. Brendan is the on-site manager of the Lenora Apartments on Capitol Hill. He has a new job and is moving on in his life. He's a real success story for the foundation. He can move any time, within two weeks probably, so he can get scttlcd in time to start his new job. I want a woman named Pam Butler as the new on-site manager. But I haven't gotten it lined up yet. I have a social worker trying to figure out how to get her to apply for the job. She's a CASA case client, so I need to keep arm's length. Meanwhile, until I can get it all in place, I need someone to take the baton from Brendan and then pass it off to Pam. Harriet, I thought you might want to take that on."

By this time, Kenneth had re-entered the room with a smile and a nod to everyone to indicate that Alicia had agreed to be a board member. He resumed taking notes.

"Tell me what's involved," Harriet said. "How complicated, how much time required."

"You need to find out all of his contacts," Helen told Harriet. "Make a list of the people he hires for everything. That would include people like a plumber, electrician, landscaper, roof repair, laundry facility repairman, the works. I suspect he has a book of this, or you may need to create one from whatever records he has. That's first. Then he probably has a scheduled maintenance system, like when to change furnace filters and check fire alarms in the units, shampoo the carpets in the halls. We need all of those items listed by month. A list of the apartment tenants, identifying each person who lives in each apartment, plus phone numbers for each person. I'd even like an emergency contact name and number for each apartment. Again, I think he has all of this; we just need to collect it."

"Does he do any of the work himself?" asked Harriet.

"He might," Helen responded. "You need to ask him that. If so, find out who he would hire if we had a manager who couldn't do it. He was working on a storage place to create a stroller-lending closet as an amenity. You need to check on that and see if it's working."

"How about rent collection and screening of new tenants?"

"I think he has the checks sent to the bookkeeper. Everybody pays a different rent, based on child-support payments, any part-time work, that sort of thing. He gets tenant referrals from me or sometimes from social agencies. He does some of the initial calls and background checks. Then he and I get together to make actual selections after we talk to the potential tenants personally. We don't have too much turnover, less than one every month or so. If it came up before Pam got in, you could refer it to me or Mr. Osborne."

"OK, count me in," said Harriet. "I'll call him later this week and go get the details. By the way, how about I ask Alicia to join in? If she's going to sit on the board, she should find out right up front that we're a working more than a sitting board."

"Ken, put that in the minutes," said Joe. "Harriet, as usual, stepped into the breach—and dragged Alicia in with her." He smiled at Harriet.

"Shall we vote now on adding Alicia Mayhew to the board? Do I hear a motion?" Joe asked.

"I move to elect Alicia Mayhew to the board," said Kenneth.

"I second," added Helen.

"Moved and seconded. Vote by raise of hands. It's unanimous. Moving on. Next item of new business is the possible addition of a new property. Helen, you ready to present it?"

"Yes. This is an unusual property and comes to us in an unusual way. The property is a beautifully preserved 1921 Craftsman in Green Lake. It is currently lived in by the owner, who is seventy-eight. He'll sell it to us, subject to a life interest, meaning he has the right to continue to live in the home until he dies, rent free. We would pay two hundred fifty thousand. There's a loan of one hundred thousand that we would pay off."

"What's it worth?" asked Frank, the retired Realtor. "In Green Lake, any kind of location at all, that's got to be north of five hundred grand."

"That's what we estimate, anywhere from five hundred to seven hundred. We get a good deal, and he's happy to have the extra cash now, plus be out from under the loan. He has no heirs to pass it on to, anyway. He's competent, and he could live for another ten years from the way he looked to me. The issue is I don't know quite how we'd use it. It has two bedrooms, but seems too big to me for one of our usual tenants."

"That's no problem," said Frank. "If it doesn't fit into the goals for our tenants, we just sell it and get something else at the time. Think of it as a great investment to add to our endowment for the future. You have to grab it at the price. In fact, I move now we buy it before the owner can think about it more."

"I second," said Joe. "Any more discussion on buying the Green Lake Craftsman? None noted. Moved and seconded. Show of hands. Unanimous. Any other new business?" Seeing no indication anyone else wished to talk, he continued, "Meeting adjourned. Ken, note the time."

Helen walked out of the meeting with Frank Brewer. Harriet was right behind them. "I plan to go to the duplex tomorrow afternoon, maybe about two. Either of you want to come along?" Harriet asked.

"Sure, I'm free. Call when you're ready. I'll do the driving," said Frank, adding, "Helen, you game?"

"I think I will tag along, thank you. Call when you're headed my way, and I'll be on the street."

"How about you ask Alicia? You're the one who knows her," Harriet said. "That way I can meet her and see how she feels about helping me with the Lenora Apartment deal."

"I'll check. If she wants to go, I'll have her with me on the street."

By then, they had left Mr. Pierce's office building and were talking on the sidewalk. They parted ways, and Helen went back to her apartment building. When she got out of the elevator, she knocked on Alicia's door.

"Hi, Helen," Alicia said as she opened the door. "I'm so grateful to you for putting me on the foundation's board. It's just the sort of thing I hoped to get involved in."

"Good, because you're going to get involved right fast if the rest of us have our way. Tomorrow, three of us are going to check on the renovations to a new place we bought, and we thought you might want to go along. It's in the afternoon, about two."

"Great, I'll do it. I was going to play bridge with friends on Mercer Island, but this is a much better offer. I'll tell them to get a substitute. Who's driving? I'll do it if no one else wants to."

"No, that's settled already. A man named Frank Brewer will pick us up. We just have to be out front on the sidewalk at the right time. So I'll knock on your door when I'm ready to head down. Bye." She turned and went into her own apartment without further comment, leaving Alicia's invitation to come in for a cup of tea unspoken.

Helen entered her apartment, put her purse and coat down in the entry, and went straight to her room. Meetings tended to exhaust her.

It was the presence of so many personalities and so much conversation. She sat cross-legged on the prayer rug in the bedroom. Her mind was too unsettled to meditate. It simply roamed, loose and undisciplined. Soon she was musing about Joe McGregor. She had been in Seattle for only a month or so and had spent much of that time in private meetings with Mr. Pierce. They had sorted through her affairs, and he had guided her in the process of purchasing her first local property. It was he who had suggested she establish a board, rather than running the foundation on her own, as she had in Connecticut. He had suggested Joe and told her to meet with him and see if they could work together.

Joe and Helen met in a coffee shop on Queen Anne, two blocks from Helen's apartment. She told him about the foundation and her goals for it. As she talked about putting children in safe housing, Joe became very solemn, even tense, Helen thought. He swallowed several times when she paused in her discussion. Then he began to talk, hesitantly. Uncomfortably. "You should know … well, I'm not sure you *should* know … but it's better you know …" He sounded as though he were debating with himself whether to disclose whatever it was. "Starting over. I'm a man of few words. Direct to the point of bluntness. If we work together, you'll notice. My dad was worse. Awful man. Drunk on Scotch every day. Terrorized all of us. Some of us survived. Others didn't. I couldn't stand to think I'd do that to anybody. So, my wife and I don't have kids. She can't. Probably why I married her."

Helen was quiet. Her lot in life seemed to be absorbing pain. Her own and others.

"But I like your goal. I'd fit well. I like children. Just couldn't raise them. Too afraid. So … if you want me, I'm on board."

Helen almost smiled at him. She liked him very much. That was the beginning of his involvement, and she had never regretted having him as the president.

≈ ≈ ≈

"Tell me again why the foundation buys property," Alicia said. It was two days later, and they were approaching the duplex.

"I can do that," Frank said as he parked. "We're actually in the kid-helping business. We believe we can help the community by helping kids grow up healthy. So, we start from the kid. Moving a rung up the ladder, we reach the parents. The kid, to get a good start, needs a healthy mom and dad. But the kids who end up in trouble often come from broken homes. We can't keep the parents from parting, but what we can do is help them land safely when they do part.

"One issue when the family breaks up is housing. The poorest parent, sometimes both, often ends up in housing that's either unsafe or in a neighborhood that puts the kids at risk. More often than not, it's the mother. She gets primary custody a lot of the time because the father works. So she moves into a crappy place, and the father pays child support, and the mother collects food stamps if she needs to. They all live hand to mouth. I'm not talking the families that are well off; we don't deal with them. We're talking about the ones that were scrimping by to start with. We buy property in good neighborhoods, fix it up if it needs it, and offer it free or at a low rent so the kids end up in a decent neighborhood."

By now, they had left the car and were on the porch. "So," Alicia said, "this place will eventually have two people with kids, probably women?"

"Right. So as we look at it, try to imagine them in here," added Frank. "Hey, Drew, good to see you." The two men shook hands. "This is Alicia; she's new on the board."

They all moved into the living room, where the makeshift table still stood, and Drew began, "Let me show you the drawings. I have some samples here too, so we can make some decisions." Drew went over the same plans with Harriet, Alicia, and Frank that Helen had already seen. She wandered into the dining room to look at the progress.

"Helen and I talked about three different locations for the laundry. We didn't make a decision, but I'm ready to get the plumbing in, so today's the day." He showed them the options.

"Upstairs in the hall closet," said Alicia. "She won't want to carry things up and down the stairs. She can collect it from the bath and children's room, which is where 90 percent of the laundry comes from when you have children, and save herself a lot of time and effort. And while we're at it, let's find space for a folding table. You can use any wall up there and put in one that folds down to fit flush with the wall, then swings up when you need it."

The others all stopped and looked at Alicia. "Damn, that's good!" said Drew. "Why didn't I think of that?"

"Because you're a man who doesn't do much laundry," said Alicia, and they all laughed.

Helen, coming back to join them, laughed as well. "I never noticed the fireplace in here," she said. "Does it work?"

"Don't know," said Drew. "It's been blocked up like that for quite a while, I suspect, so I need a mason in here to look at it. I have that on my list."

"I can't imagine a mother with small children wanting a real fire," said Harriet, "what with lugging in the wood and the mess of sweeping up all of the bark and dirt that falls off, then carrying out the ashes. It's a lot of work."

"Do we have gas here?" asked Alicia.

"Yeah. Good thinking. Drew, is there gas?" Frank was joining in with ideas at this point.

"There is. So, are you guys on board with a gas fireplace if I can get the mason to agree? I know your tenant would love it."

"Yeah, let's do it," said Frank, looking at the three women for confirmation.

"The hearth juts out into the room about twelve inches," Alicia said. "Do we have enough funds in the budget to make shelves on each side to match up with the fireplace and run both ways to the walls?"

"Actually, we're still under budget," said Drew. "I don't have to replace any floors except the bathroom upstairs. Most of the work up there is build-out. We have a new shower, and we need the tile for that, plus the laundry room and the built-in for the bedroom. I have drawings of that, which I'll show you in a minute. Then, the kitchen is demo of a wall, then build out the peninsular bar deal, which I have drawings on. I want to salvage the cabinets and just paint them and put on new hardware. A new sink and faucets, counter, and lighting in there. So I still have something close to ten thousand left over on this unit, I figure."

They all looked at the drawings Drew wanted to show them and then walked through the house together. "I love these arches," Helen said to Alicia. They were examining two small niches in what had been the dining room. "And look, the doorway that connects this room to the living room is arched. That's a nice detail."

"It is," said Alicia. "And it gives me an idea." She went back to the drawings. "Look at this built-in Drew is making for the bedroom. What if we did this?" She picked up a pencil and drew a header over the top of the unit with arches over each section. "Then, when he builds in the shelves on each side of the fireplace, we do something similar, like this." She turned a paper over and sketched the fireplace with arches over shelving on each side. "We need two arches each side, I think, to make it balance nicely with the entry arch and the dining area arches. What do you think?"

"Alicia, you're a constant surprise," said Helen with admiration. "Let's show the rest of them."

Drew came downstairs with Frank and Harriet in tow. "Show us what?" asked Harriet. Alicia showed them her drawings and explained her ideas.

"You sure have an eye," said Frank. "Drew, what do you think? Can you do it?"

"Sure, no problem. It doesn't cost anything, given we're building things anyway. And it sure looks great." He turned to Helen. "Remember when you said you wanted to add something to take it up a notch for the tenants? I think you've done it with the laundry-folding table, the gas fireplace, and the decorative arches."

They stayed another half-hour, looking at the countertop finishes, the paint swatches, bathroom floor covering, and appliance options. When they were going back to the car, Frank said, "Anybody want to stop for a beer and snack? Or dinner?"

Harriet and Helen both declined, but Alicia said, "I'd like that. You can tell me more about the foundation and what other properties it owns. If I'm part of it, I want to know more." That settled, Frank dropped off the other two and took Alicia to dinner.

The following morning, Helen went to yoga class and walked home in a steady rain. It was not a Seattle drizzle; it was a "hello, winter's coming" rain. The clouds hung low, steel gray, and unforgiving. Helen decided it was a perfect day to sit at home and read. She put a pot of steeped tea on her chair-side table, turned on her gas fireplace, and settled into her chair, wrapped in a batik-patterned blanket from her ashram days. She had three books next to her, a mystery novel by Jacqueline Winspeare, a history of the cracking of the enigma-code machine during World War II, and her tattered copy of *The Bhagavad-Gita*. She was set for the day.

When dark descended, which was early with such heavy cloud cover, she put on a raincoat and walked to the South Lake Union meeting.

Upon her return, she saw a package leaning against the apartment door. She picked it up, saw her name on it, and took it inside. The wrapping was plain brown paper, much like that from which paper bags at the grocery store were made. Helen cut the twine holding the wrapping together and took off the paper. Inside was a matted and framed pen-and-ink drawing. It had a date of 10/12/38 under the artist's signature, but Helen could not decipher who the artist was because the signature was not legible. There was a sticky note on the glass that said, "This makes me think of you. Hope you like it. Alicia." The drawing itself was of cloisters. The repeated arches of the cloisters receded into the distance, and a garden was visible to the left of the arches. There were bushes and flowers in the garden lining a path. Helen studied the drawing. The harmony of the repeated arches appealed to her. There was something calming about them—and more. Shadows cast by the arches on the stone wall beyond the cloister drew her eye to the light hitting the side of the arches that faced the garden. She liked the black and the white, the hidden and the revealed, the sunlit and the shadowed. So much implied color in nothing but black and white, she thought. She decided it was the perfect picture. She carried it into her bedroom and leaned it against the wall opposite her bed. It would be the first thing she would see when she woke up, the last thing she would see as she went to sleep.

The next morning, Helen was back in Mr. Pierce's office. She reported on the trip to the duplex and some of the changes they would be making. "The bills will probably be coming in at a fast clip, from what I saw.

Drew is moving right along. You best check to see that the tenant in the other unit knows where to send the checks, too. Maybe we should do something for him for having to put up with the noise and mess. What do you think, Mr. Osborne?" Kenneth Osborne had been sitting in the conference room with Helen and Mr. Pierce as part of his duties related to being the secretary of the foundation. The governing rules, written by Mr. Pierce, had allowed for decisions to be made between board meetings by any two members of the board, so long as legal counsel was present. This allowed Helen freedom to act essentially on her own.

"That's a good idea. We want to keep him happy, at least until we finish with the first unit. Having him there at night and on weekends makes the construction site more secure. How about we give him a rent reduction?" Mr. Osborne, Helen thought, so often had very practical ideas.

"Yes, then he can spend it however he wants. When you call him, tell him his rent is reduced … what? … 10 percent?"

"That's generous," said Mr. Pierce. "It should give him a good incentive to put up with the inconvenience." That settled, Mr. Osborne excused himself, leaving them to talk about Helen's other business.

"I just don't know about the institute, Mr. Pierce. Have I lost my way or something?"

"Tell me more. Where are the doubts coming from?"

"I started the institute six years ago when I was in Connecticut. At the time, I wanted the institute to be the vehicle for my work. I wanted some scholarly or academic look at the issues of women moving out of bad marriages into some sort of self-sufficiency. I wasn't an academic and didn't want to be. But I thought if people at that level focused on it, things would change. But now, I wonder if I was wrong. Maybe all I created was dead trees. We end up with intellectual papers being written to stick in a file and die a slow death. I think over fifty papers have been produced, all sponsored by the institute, but I don't know that anything else has happened."

"Were you thinking the papers would spur political action?"

"Maybe I did. I was sort of in the 'right actions and right speech' mode at the time. That's probably the nub of the issue right there. My mind wasn't clear enough to make goals that were clear."

"Is it possible that the foundation work eclipsed the institute in your own mind or space or something?"

"It did; I see that. The foundation work is concrete. I can count the people we help. So many housing units. So many kids in a safe place. It's very easy to measure progress."

"Then let's think about how the institute can duplicate that measurable progress you want. You know about the spring meeting where they hope to get universities interested in setting up a graduate program. How about we push for a requirement that every program includes a one-year practicum in a social-service setting or something. That way, we would be creating a new profession of people in the world putting the academic theories into practice. We might even call for an explicit certification as a self-sufficiency specialist or something. Let them come up with the name, the rules and requirements, and all that. Would that move it closer to what you would like to see?"

"You're my resident genius," smiled Helen. "I would really, really like that. For now, I use a network of people to help identify tenants. If there were some trained people who understood exactly what we're doing, beyond the obvious, that would be fantastic."

"So, can we say for now we'll let the institute continue on its path, but we'll direct the path if we can? You know, the institute budget is pretty small, and we could always add fees if we wanted to decrease the financial involvement."

"Let's leave the funding at the current level for a while. Then, if they start off in this new direction, we could sponsor graduate students in some way. We might even consider upping the funding at that point. The important thing is that I have a better vision for the institute as a whole. I'm going to play around with it this year, see where it goes."

Helen felt much better leaving the law office. As she was walking back to her apartment, her cell phone rang. "Hi, Helen, it's Harriet. I would like Alicia's number. I forget to get it when we were together the other day. I'm going to take her with me to see Brendan and show her the apartment house. You can come, too, if you want."

"Thanks anyway, Harriet, but my schedule is pretty tight for the next few days. I'm happy to leave it all in your hands. Let me look up

Alicia's number and call you back. I've never mastered how to look up a number when I'm on the phone." She did that, put the phone back in her pocket, and continued walking. Four steps later, the phone rang again.

"Morning, Harriet, it's Frank Brewer. I think there's a good building, maybe twelve units, on Lower Queen Anne we could pick up on the cheap. How about you and Alicia come see it with me?"

"Today?"

"Yeah, these don't come along often. If I'm right, we need to hop on it."

"OK. I'll do it. Alicia might be a problem, though. Harriet is about to call and get her to go to the Capitol Hill apartment house to meet Brendan."

"Damn, let me get off and call her, see if I can get to her first. I'll call you right back."

Helen hung up with a frown. It was odd behavior for Frank, she thought. He seemed so anxious to get to Alicia in a hurry. It was not as if they would need Alicia to see the place. She let it go and went home. As she stepped out of the elevator, Alicia opened her door.

"Sorry to intercept you like this. Frank said to tell you we'll go at one if that's all right. I'll call him if you need to change it. You know Frank; he's Johnny-on-the-spot when he wants to do something. How is your morning going? Want a cup of tea?"

"No, thanks; I'm good. And one o'clock is fine for me. Who reached you first, Harriet or Frank?" She almost laughed, imagining Frank dialing like crazy to try to beat Harriet.

"Frank talked to me first. I was in the shower when Harriet called. By the time I got out and to the phone, it had stopped ringing. Then it started again before I even got back to the bathroom, and it was Frank." Alicia was laughing when she said it. "Then I called Harriet back, and she sounded a little put out that Frank had beat her. So she and I are going to meet Brendan tomorrow morning. I'll say one thing for the foundation—it has the most active board members I've ever met, and I've met more than my share over the years."

"I hope that's a good thing," said Helen.

"It most definitely is. This is just what I wanted when I moved here. To get involved in a whole new way with new people. It's the best decision I've made in years."

"I really am happy for you. Oh … don't go in just yet. I want to tell you how much I love that drawing. What a perfect gift. Thank you so much."

Alicia smiled. "Fabulous. I wanted you to have it. I'm so glad you like it. And you're welcome. See you at one." They both went into their own apartments.

As Helen was fixing lunch, she received a call from Elsa Dutton. "Helen, I've been working on getting that job announcement to Pam Butler. I think we did it. I went to the professional association list for substance-abuse counselors and got Margaret Suskind's name. I called her, told her where I got her name, and that was that. She knows nothing about you. I said I was calling fifteen counselors and picked them at random. Then I said I was looking for one of their clients for a job sponsored by a foundation. Said the foundation preferred a woman who had one or two small children, an abuse problem that was well under control, and a need for housing plus a wage. I did that yesterday. So, you should know within a week if it worked. If not, let me know, and I'll come up with something else."

"Elsa, you're the greatest. I wouldn't have thought of that. I'll tell Mr. Osborne so he'll be watching for the call."

"Right. Let me know how it turns out. Got to go; client coming any minute."

Helen was always conscious of how busy Elsa was. They never had a chance to say anything off-topic. That had been fine for Helen up until now. But, mulling it over as she went back to her lunch, she thought maybe something was missing.

Helen had to rush to get out of the apartment and down on the sidewalk to meet Alicia. Frank was already driving up the street and pulled over only long enough for them to get in. He drove to the bottom of Queen Anne, then made a very sharp right turn, and went up Olympic Place. He parked in front of a red-brick building. "This is it," he said. "It was built in the early 1930s. Looks great from here, doesn't it?" They both agreed. The building had a classic, balanced look. "She looks like a stately woman," Frank said. "I like it."

They got out, and Frank walked over to a man standing in front of the building. "Gary, good to see you."

"Hi, Frank." They shook hands. Gary looked at the women.

"I want to introduce two of the smartest women you'll meet anywhere. Gary Koontz, this is Helen Smith, and here is Alicia Mayhew. They both sit on the board of the Claudius Foundation with me." The women shook hands with Gary. "Gary's a financial advisor. He deals with high-net-worth clients. He and I have been involved in a lot of deals over the years."

As Frank spoke, Gary led them into the apartment building. There was a wide hallway with a central staircase. On each side of the stairs, the hall led toward the back of the building. "Let me explain the layout," said Gary. "There are four apartments on each floor, two in front, two in back, except for this floor, where one of the back ones was made into a laundry room and some storage lockers about thirty years ago. The ones in back are smaller, but they all have two bedrooms. Going up, they're all identical to the one below them. There are two empty right now, one on this floor at the rear, one on the floor above at the front. So you'll be able to see an example of each type." He led them along the staircase to the back apartment on the right. "There's better natural light in the ones on the right because they're on the street side and facing south. None of them has been remodeled, so they're all the same in that regard." By then, they had reached the door, and he was putting the key in the lock. They went in and started walking around.

"This main bedroom is huge," commented Alicia. "Great windows. Bigger closet than I have in my bedroom. And the tall ceilings are beautiful. Same with all this molding."

"The kitchen is tiny," called out Frank. "Come see what you think of it."

Alicia joined him. "It is small, but with the dining room right next to it like this, you could use the table there if you had to for more work space. But really, I think most women would manage with this. And it's so cute. I love these tall old wood cabinets with the glass in front and the old glass knobs. I don't know about these appliances. No dishwasher, a stove that looks like it dates back to the 1940s, and an oven that doesn't self-clean. Most women still know how to wash dishes, but I'm not so sure about cleaning an oven."

"The second bedroom is small," Helen said as she joined them near the kitchen. "But it's big enough for a double or two twins. You could actually use it for the master, giving the kids the bigger room if you had two or more kids. That way you could use it for a playroom as well as a bedroom, especially if you put in bunk beds. Oh, cute kitchen," she added, as she looked around Frank into the small space. "The cabinets are charming."

"The living room and dining room are really huge," added Frank. "You could put an office in a corner of one of them. And there's plenty of space for something like an art area or train tracks for boys or something."

"There's an amazing amount of storage in here, too," put in Gary. "I don't know if you noticed, but there's that entryway closet, then a walk-in closet as big as the bathroom next to it, plus the linen closet in the bathroom. That's on top of the nice-sized closets in the bedrooms. There's an outbuilding, too. Right now it's used as carport parking. It holds about five cars, I think. It could become large storage lockers, or you could rent it out for RV parking, or even make a studio for artists in there. It has these big skylight things."

They went outside and walked around the apartment building to look at the structure.

"It's in need of a little help," Gary added. "But you can see it makes a significant addition to the property as a whole." They all agreed and then went back to the front of the building to get a general impression of the other buildings on the streets surrounding the apartments.

"What do you think of the location for kids?" asked Frank.

"There's a park down the block, but other than that, this is pretty urban. The good thing is how close it is to a lot of small businesses. Might be pretty easy for someone to get a part-time job. Three small hotels, restaurants all over the place, a convenience store, drive-in food places, dry cleaners, gift shops. Lots of opportunities around. And it's right on the bus line. Plus, a major grocery store two blocks away. This is great for working single people as well as a woman without a car."

"You know," Helen paused, "we don't often think about the parent who gets weekend visitation. Pretend this is not the primary residential parent, but the other one. This really fills the bill for that. Look how close we are to the Seattle Center. A dad with weekends with his kids can take them to the Children's Museum, play in the International Fountain, go the Science Center. Plus all the festivals and things at the center. The kids would have a great time. And the dad could probably care less about how small the kitchen is."

"You're on the money," Frank said. "I should have been the one to think of that."

"Well, you said these women were smart," drawled Gary.

"OK, don't remind me. Let's talk about the deal here."

"Right. Here's the story. The owners inherited from their parents, who inherited from theirs. It's been in the same family since it was built. They all used it as a stream of income. It's been totally depreciated. Right now, they think of it as an albatross. It needs upgraded electrical. The plumbing is old. They just don't want the hassle. But without some rehab, the rents are going down. People don't want the pokey little kitchen with no dishwasher. They want the laundry in the unit. They want a parking space in a nice garage. The owners are getting the typical problems that crop up when you start going downscale for tenants. So, what they can use is a tax deduction by donating it. You give them the money to pay all of their sales-related costs, throw in enough for a trip to Hawaii, they'll probably work with you."

"Oh, my," said Alicia. "Does this happen all of the time?"

Helen started laughing. "No, this is a first."

"We probably want to run some numbers," Frank said. "Drew might be able to give us a rough estimate for plumbing and electrical upgrades. I don't know, but I expect all of the walls need to be taken down to the studs to get at the water lines and what-not. It may be more than we want to tackle."

"Nonsense," said Alicia. "If you get it for almost free, that's just time and some cash to get it fixed up. This is a great place."

"You willing to bird-dog it through to move-in?" asked Helen. "It always seems to take more time than you plan. At least, that's what happens to me."

"Of course I'll do it," responded Alicia. "This is just the kind of thing I need. I spent years planning silent auctions, presentation events, parties for four hundred. This is a walk in the park compared to trying to get fifty women to work together on a fashion show. I can do this."

"Well, in that case, let's talk it over with Edward, see what the legal requirements are. Then we'll ask Drew and maybe Joe McGregor to look at it as well, see what they think. Everybody on board with that?" Frank was reluctant to make any commitments without some further discussion, whereas the women were willing to jump right in. They all agreed to talk to the others and get back to Gary within a week.

As they were in the car driving back to the women's building, Helen said, "This is a big addition for us. That's eleven more units all at once."

"How many do you usually add?" Alicia asked.

"We typically get a place with anywhere from two to seven units," Frank answered. "That's easy to manage without hiring outside companies to do it. Lets more of our assets be targeted directly to the tenants."

"Right," Helen added. "We're trying to get the kids in a good place; that's primary."

"Do we have the right to discriminate by taking only people who have children?" asked Alicia.

"We do. It's a non-profit that owns the building so that gives us a little leeway. I'm not sure exactly how much, but that's something you can ask Mr. Pierce about. He keeps us inside the boundaries."

Frank stopped in front of the building, and Helen got out. Alicia, who was sitting in the front seat with Frank, did not. Helen looked at her, a little confused. "Frank and I are going for a walk around Green Lake. We're meeting George there. Then we'll all have an early dinner at the Bar and Grill. Want to come?" She smiled at Helen.

"No thanks, but it was nice of you to ask. Have a great time and say hello to George for me." Helen turned and walked into the building, smiling. So that's the lay of the land, she thought to herself. Good on Alicia.

❧ ❧ ❧

A full week had passed since the letter from Derrick, and Helen knew she had to face it. She had ignored his other letters over the years, often throwing them in the trash without even opening the envelope, and had felt no guilt in doing so. Now, however, it was not possible. For some reason she had yet to explore, the issue would not dissolve in the sea of a busy life. At the same time, she felt blocked each time she approached the subject of a reply. She did not know whether that was due to her previous failure or something else. What she felt was a growing pressure to respond. She had to relieve the pressure as it was beginning to encroach on her life. After a session of yoga poses to prepare herself, she sat cross-legged on her meditation pillow, did some breathing exercises, and then began her sitting meditation.

An hour later, Helen rose, made a cup of mint tea, and sat at her table. She picked up her favorite pen and a pad of paper and started another draft to her brother.

Dear Derrick,

Forgive, if you can, my delay in responding. It has been difficult to sort through all of the things I could or would wish to say. Even now, I cannot promise to do justice to my thoughts and feelings. I will, however, do my very best. That is a promise I can keep.

My failure to respond was not meant to punish you. My inability to reach out has nothing to do with you. The years at Riggs Erickson deadened my soul. My pain was overwhelming. It required vast time to heal. I can only liken it to being in a coma.

For five years after getting out of Riggs Erickson, I stayed at an ashram in rural New York. The swami led me back to life. It was slow, but he taught me patience. When I was well enough to function outside, I went to Connecticut and worked for a wonderful man in an investigative agency. He hired me even though I was pretty much damaged goods. During all of those years, it took everything in me to get through each day. I became, and still am, a very solitary person. That, in part, is why I did not respond to you. I was too fragile to have any relationship that involved an emotional component. I am getting very good at business and quasi-business relationships, however.

Please, Derrick, be assured that I never blamed you for anything that happened. You were young. You did not have the knowledge or resources to intervene. On my road to healing, I put all memory of you and my love for you in a box and set it high on a shelf in a closet I never opened. I did not believe I could bear to open that box ever again.

Things change, however, and time does indeed both march on and heal. I am ready to step foot on the bridge that will lead us back to one another. This is my first step. I want to hear about you and your family. I want to see pictures of my nephews and my niece. Soon, I don't know just when, I want to see you. Later, I will meet everyone who loves you as much as I always have.

Love,
Helen

Emotionally exhausted, Helen decided she needed a walk. She put on good walking shoes and gathered her coat, keys, and an umbrella, just in case. She walked down the hill, through the Olympic Sculpture Garden, on to Pike Place Market, where she had lunch, and up to Capitol Hill. Since she was already in the area, she decided to walk around the Lenora Apartment Building. She saw Brendan with his son walk down the sidewalk and cross the street to go into the building. She slowed, making sure they were in the door and out of sight before she turned around and went back the way she had come. She did not have the energy right then to engage with anyone. She walked down Capitol Hill toward the downtown area and retraced her steps. Almost three hours had passed before she arrived home.

# Part II

⁂

# JANUARY

New Year's Day dawned sunny, when it finally dawned, just before eight. Helen watched it from her dining room window. She had gotten up in the dark two hours earlier, wondering why she had chosen to live at such a latitude. Going into the kitchen, she poured some more tea before putting a drop of vitamin D on her tongue. Everyone in Seattle, she'd heard, needed extra vitamin D because of the lack of winter sun. She decided to spend half the day on retreat in her own house. Taking a cushion, yoga mat, candle, incense sticks, and holders from her bedroom, she went into the guest bedroom. The room, otherwise, contained nothing. She lit an incense stick and a candle and placed each in its holder. She sat on her cushion and chanted. After twenty minutes, she went into a silent meditation.

After the hour of emptiness, she posed questions to herself. How to live *in* the world but not *of* the world? Was she losing balance, adding too much into her life from outside? Where had she failed in her duty to herself and others? How had she failed in her practices and intentions? These questions filled her mind for her next hour of active exploration.

Helen spent another hour doing yoga poses and then a half-hour in breathing exercises. At this point, Helen had reached a deep level of concentration, her body and mind both quiet, receptive, and open. She started her final hour of silent meditation.

When the last meditation was finished, Helen put her things back into her bedroom and took a shower. Then she had a small lunch of two mandarin oranges, twelve almonds, and a cup of tea. She was ready to start the year.

Checking her files and calendar, Helen saw there were many duties that fell within her "right livelihood" dictum. She felt the most important person to find on New Year's Day would be Pam Butler. It had been over two months since she had last spoken with her.

"Hello, Pam. It's Helen Paige. How are things?"

"So great," said Pam. "I got a job. Can you believe it? My counselor at the rehab clinic told me about it. I get free rent and a thousand dollars a month. The apartment has two bedrooms, so the girls can be here with me. I don't get to keep them here much, but I do see them every day. I'm sure you got a copy of the court order that gave James temporary primary custody when I moved out."

"I did get that. I thought if you wanted to call me, you would have. What are your feelings at this point?"

"They're up and down. Some days, I feel great. Other days, I cry most of the time."

"Tell me more."

"Well, first you have to understand where I am. This is an apartment building on Capitol Hill. I'm the live-in manager, but I don't have to do too much. Be around a lot. When someone has a stopped-up drain or a burner on the stove that goes out or something, I take care of it. I can call repairmen if I have to, but know what? I can do some of it! I'm so surprised. I found this home-repair manual, and I use it all the time. In fact, I even read it at night. Last week, a woman's toilet sort of went out. I took the manual up there and looked in the tank and figured out what was wrong. Went to the hardware store, there's one two blocks away, showed them what I needed, and fixed it myself. Actually, I called my father-in-law for a tool, and he brought it over and sort of helped me. But next time, I can do it myself. And guess what? He *gave* me a toolbox the next day. So, days like that are great."

"And the down days?"

"When I miss the girls. I hate waking up here by myself, knowing Meredith is in the house making them pancakes. That sets me back for hours. I'm so scared I won't get to be their mom again."

"How often do you see them?"

"Oh, every day. I get a bus from here and go see them every afternoon for a while. James is with them then, and Meredith goes home. You know, it's so weird. He and I take them places, like to movies. We even took them ice skating. None of us was any good at it, but we sure had fun. The girls loved it. James brings me home after dinner, usually. His mom and dad spend the night at the house when he goes to work."

"It sounds like things are starting to fall into a pattern for the girls, then?"

"Yeah, they know I'm not living there, but so far, they seem OK with everything."

"It sounds like all of you are on the same page right now."

"Well … we'll see what happens at court, when the judge gets involved. I'm so scared he'll give the girls to James and they'll quit letting me spend so much time with them."

"Pam, don't be anxious about the future. Right now, you're doing really well. Judges don't take children away from either parent without a good reason. And you aren't giving him a reason, are you? No drinking or drugs or anything?"

"No way. I'm so clean I squeak. And I still get random UAs."

"Good. Keep it up. How's James doing?"

"That's different. He's pretty lonely. When this is over, he'll either be living in our house with his parents or living in their basement in their current house. I don't know which is worse for him."

"You aren't so lonely?"

"No … that's the great thing about this job. There are other single moms with kids. My girls have play dates with some of them when they're here. And I've met some cool women. Lots of them are in school or training programs; some of them work part time. They're great. I was so lucky I can't tell you."

"Would James want an apartment there, you think?" The idea came from the air to Helen and almost took her breath away.

"Huh. That's something. Shoot. I need to think about that. It could really work out. Thanks, Helen."

"No problem. Talk to you later."

When Helen got off the phone, she thought about her suggestion to Pam. If James lived in the apartment house, he and Pam could share time with the children just as they had throughout the marriage. Pam would be free to seek outside work for a few hours a day, or a training program. She decided it was worthwhile to pursue the idea further with James. First, however, she would let Pam have a chance to do so. She typed up the results of the phone call for her file and then looked at her list again.

There were a couple of other items she thought she could work on, even though it was a holiday. One was a letter to her brother, something she had been putting off since before Christmas. She breathed in and out slowly, watching each breath rise and fall. Yes, she decided, she could do this.

Dear Derrick,

Seeing you was wonderful. And very hard. Thank you for making the trip during such a busy season. And for bringing all of the pictures. Your family is so special; they sound wonderful. How proud you must be to have such children.

We covered a lot of ground, catching up on some of the years we were apart. We said so much. And left so much unsaid. It is time for me to make a start on filling in some gaps.

I'm sorry you were still so young when I disappeared into marriage. I never thought how devastating it would be for you. Maybe I thought, with a combination of Mom being a little better and you becoming a sturdy and outgoing boy, you'd get by with a little help from your friends, as the song goes. Worse, I probably didn't give it any thought at all. Caught up in the glamour of the Prescott's life and my love for Robert, I checked out of my duty to you. You know, I think, my deep regrets, my sorrow, for doing that to you.

What you don't know, and I had yet to learn, is that Robert suffered from bi-polar disorder. I finally figured it out when I was twenty-eight. I knew something was wrong before then, but didn't know what it was. He went through cycles of being totally manic and then falling into depression. For each new cycle, the highs and the lows were more devastating. When I met him, he was in the manic phase. I thought he was just an exciting, daring, fun-loving character, and that's who I fell in love with. We drank; we smoked pot; we took a few uppers. We partied like crazy. I was a sophomore in college, and I wasn't that different from my peers. After the kind of childhood we had, here I was—free to let go of responsibility and embrace this wild and crazy life. And I did.

His parents, the great Catherine and William Henry Prescott III, were thrilled with me. They knew they couldn't get him married to anyone in their circle, so they were praying he'd find someone "acceptable" on his own. I was suitable in their eyes. I didn't have a name or a fortune, but I was pretty and smart enough to get into college. Best of all, I was malleable because I wanted a life like theirs. Catherine figured she could use those as building blocks to make me presentable to their society friends. So, the marriage happened pretty fast.

Robert had one depressive episode before I married him, but he was on medication for it. It didn't last very long, and I thought he was just in a down mood for some reason. I didn't think much about it. Catherine kept me busy with wedding plans and honeymoon plans. William took Robert off on golfing and fishing weekends. I had no idea what they were hiding from me.

I just read over what I have written. This is something I never thought I'd share, but I believe now that I owe it to you. I don't see how we can have a good relationship going forward if I don't share what made me the person I am now. We did some of that in December when we had dinner. We'll have to do more another time. Share what you want with whomever you feel you need to. Your wife, at the least, should be aware of this. If I am ever going to be part of your life again, she deserves to know my history.

Love and peace,
Helen

There was a great emptiness inside Helen when she finished the letter. She knew the feeling and knew she needed to change it. Grabbing a coat, putting keys in her pocket, she went out of the apartment. Once on the street, she walked toward Elliott Bay. Down the hill on the avenue, all the way to the end, then a left turn, and a right turn, and within a half-hour, she was on the path that followed the bay to the north. She walked as far as she could, turned, and walked back, and then repeated it several more times. As she walked, she watched the ferries on their trips across to Bremerton and Bainbridge Island and the gulls that trailed them. The thick clouds rolled closer and further from her, and glimpses of Mt. Rainier came and went. As she walked, she breathed deeply, counting her breaths and matching the counting to her walking. She felt tension and worry seep away as she walked and walked. Peace returned as the day turned, early, to darkness.

&#128028; &#128028; &#128028;

After breakfast the next day, Helen studied her calendar and her list of tasks. The duplex was finished, so she needed to think about a tenant. And the Lenora Apartments had two vacancies and another probable the following month. She also knew two of the other buildings needed tenants. And the new building on Lower Queen Anne was almost finished with eleven more apartments ready. The easiest way to select the tenants she wanted to attract, she had learned, was to send an e-mail to a group of about twenty social agencies and ask the agency head to pass the information on to the case managers. It usually resulted in ten or twelve applications within a week. Helen and Mr. Osborne could then screen the applicants, check their background, and make the selections.

She called Alicia. "Hi, I would have knocked on your door but thought I might catch you in your nightdress."

"I'm still in it, as a matter of fact. But I do own a robe, Helen. Do you want to come over for something?"

"Only if this is a good time; it's not pressing."

"No, I was just reading the paper. You can come right now. You're always more interesting than the paper."

Helen did not know quite what that could mean but let it pass. Sometimes, with Alicia, it was better not to ask. She collected some files and left her apartment. Alicia had already fixed a pot of tea, and they sat at the dining table as Helen started.

"I thought you should join Mr. Osborne and me on the tenant selection committee for the foundation. We haven't used anybody else before. I think it's time we expand. We only need one of us, technically, but if something should happen, it's always best to have somebody to step in. And," she paused as she lifted her cup to drink and noticed the spicy cinnamon aroma, "did you know Mr. Osborne is a co-owner of that new tea shop?"

"The one by the sewing shop?" asked Alicia. "No, I had no idea. I've been in there twice. You know it just opened in mid-December. Have you been?"

"Two or three times. I haven't figured out the other owner. Have you?" Helen found herself easily distracted from her initial business and into the tea-shop discussion. Something about the woman in the shop had been nagging at her, so it was good to have this chance to try to untangle her feelings.

"I haven't focused on it. Should I?"

"Please do. I just have a funny feeling and can't figure it out."

"Have you talked to her?"

"No, just went in and bought tea and left."

"Maybe you should have started a conversation." Alicia looked straight at Helen when she said it, almost as a challenge to Helen's way of thinking.

"Hmm. Maybe I will. Moving on, let's talk about tenant selection. I brought along some applications so you can see what we're looking at. First, our goal is to find single parents who have such limited means they can't afford decent housing. Other than that, they may have no other issues. It's best, in fact, if they don't. We have a map with the most undesirable and crime-ridden neighborhoods. If they live there, they get moved to the top of the list. That's one group. Then we're looking for parents who are in the process of splitting up. They may have been in good shape in terms of housing, but with the split, they're headed downhill. Those are harder to identify. We make calls to the person who submitted the application, if we know who it is. We call the applicant sometimes to get more data.

"The biggest problem is when the parent has chemical-abuse issues. We don't want our places to end up being the site for a drug deal. We also can't endanger other tenants if we suspect one parent is hostile and will act out. Those belong in shelters for abuse victims or something. Think of us as responsible landlords, not as social workers, although it's hard to separate that out. Sometimes … well a lot of the time, actually, one parent has a restraining order against the other one. You have to check those out with a third party. See if the offending parent is just being set up for a custody issue or something. A restraining order in and of itself shouldn't be a deciding factor, unless you find out the offending party might actually be violent."

"Now, a couple of examples. This applicant, who is one of our tenants, has a history of drug use. So we called the chemical-abuse counselor to find out how likely she is to start using again. You can see from our notes we ended up calling a social worker as well. It's hard to get much information from them. So then, we asked for a meeting and had the tenant join us at a coffee shop near her home. We decided, on the basis of that meeting, she would make a good tenant. So, that's a pretty hard one." Helen put the file down and picked up two others.

"Here are a couple of easy ones. This is a man with one son, aged ten. The main problem was that he and his wife ended up in bankruptcy. He got primary custody because she didn't even want the boy. He's doing well now, so he pays rent. In fact, we've raised the rent a couple of times because he's making good money and has paid off all of the debt required by the court."

"How do we know when the tenant is able to pay?"

"One of the things they have to agree to is for us to have access to the tax returns, current wages, and W-2s. If they're employed, we ask for the wage information each quarter. This man has good earnings and could move out any time but really likes where he is. We'll need to nudge him out soon, I think. We let him stay partly because his son is doing really well in the school near their building and has a lot of friends. We want the dad to find housing that keeps the kid in the same school."

"This second one is more typical. It's a woman with three kids, all under age six. She is a full-time mom, and her child support barely pays for food and clothing. So she gets a free ride on rent. We did encourage her to start an online course in bookkeeping, though. She got a computer from a social agency, and we provide the Internet connection. We want her to do it so she feels that she's trying to move forward in her life. In fact, I heard last month that a local tire-store owner gave her a part-time job handling invoices from her apartment with the computer."

"OK," said Alicia, "I think I know what we're looking for. How do we get the applications in the first place?"

"Here's where I would like you to start. I want the foundation to e-mail this list," and she pulled it out of a file, "of social service agencies. That means you write the e-mail, as a member of the board of directors of the foundation. Then tell them what we want in terms of them passing it on. I have a sample e-mail from last time I sent it out." She handed Alicia another paper.

"How come you use Mr. Osborne's name at the bottom?" asked Alicia.

"Because I like to keep my name off things," replied Helen. "The foundation work overlaps too much with my CASA work. I'm not sure if it's unethical or not. I don't want to ask because it's important to me to do both. So I evade the whole issue. No one knows I'm on the board except the other members."

Alicia looked at Helen. "How can it be unethical to help people? What possible difference could it make if you do both?"

"Well, that's what I haven't fully explored. Someone could make a case that my CASA work enables me to maintain contact with a client by finding them housing and then watching over them. That might be a violation of CASA principles or something."

"Do the CASA clients know you're involved in the housing?"

"No, the closest anyone would have come in the two years I've been doing this is if they saw me go into the Lenora Apartments. I always made sure I went in the back door, and Brendan would sort of sneak me in. Three of those tenants were CASA cases. Now I can't go there anymore since Pam Butler got the manager's job. That's why I asked Harriet to sort of take on the oversight of the building. She knows not to use my name. Plus the CASA clients only know me by the last name of Paige. They could figure out something was strange if they talked to each other and found out two or more had me as the CASA. And that wouldn't seem too odd to them, I don't think, just a coincidence."

"Right. OK. So, I'm going to write the e-mail like this one," she held up a piece of paper, "put my own name on it, and ask for applications. Do those come in as hard copies or as e-mail attachments or what?"

"Most applicants will fill out the form and take it to the social worker or whoever told them about it and have it faxed or scanned and sent via e-mail. They'll go to Mr. Osborne, or they may come straight back to you. If he gets them, he'll e-mail them on to us. We can review them at home or go in and review them with him or whatever."

"Right. I've got it. I'll do it this morning. In my robe, thank you very much."

Helen returned to her own apartment, humming an Indian chant. She felt good. She knew Alicia was as capable as she was herself of handling the applicant recruitment. Alicia, she was learning, was a very accomplished woman in many respects.

Helen was putting various tax-related papers she had collected over the year into file folders, labeling them as she went, when her cell phone rang. "Helen here," she said.

"This is James Butler. Do you have a minute?"

"Yes, I do. What's on your mind?" While she talked, she found her notebook for the Butler case, moved her paperwork aside, and sat at her table.

"I've got a problem. Pam's in this apartment building now; she's the manager. She's talking about me moving into it, in a different apartment I mean, but the same building so we can share time with the girls easier."

"And what's the problem?"

"Well … well …," he stammered as though he didn't know the answer, "the problem is how my parents will feel."

"And how will they feel?" Helen sat forward a little, as though James were across from her. It helped her maintain an open, helpful, but neutral tone.

"They'll be pissed. Sorry. It'll make them mad."

"Who will they be mad at?"

"At me and Pam. For taking the girls away."

"Would you be taking the girls away?"

"Yeah, 'course we would. We'd be on Capitol Hill, and they're in Magnolia."

"How long does it take to get from one to the other?" Helen was disgusted by what James was revealing but fought to keep her voice from showing anything.

"Anywhere from fifteen to thirty minutes, depending on time of day and traffic."

"So …" She hoped he would catch on to the absurdity of his position.

"But my parents are used to being able to get the girls and take them to their house or out to lunch or shopping … They like to drop in to check on them and thing like that."

"They wouldn't drive twenty minutes to see the girls?" Helen tried to sound as if it was an innocent question.

"Of course, they would. They love the girls."

"Maybe I'm a little slow here, James. I'm trying to figure out the problem." She tried to push him to really hear and understand just what it was he was saying.

"They'll feel that we're taking the girls away from them." He finally sounded sure about what he meant.

"So, then, if the girls are in Magnolia now, and Pam is on Capitol Hill, does that mean the girls have been taken away from her?" Helen was direct and cool when she asked.

"No, of course not. And remember, Pam chose to move out. She didn't have to …" He trailed off. Helen wondered if he really believed what he had just said.

"You're how old, James?" Helen knew, but wanted him to say it.

"I'll be thirty-six in May." He paused, and Helen said nothing. A long time passed, long for a telephone call. "I think I get it," James said, with a touch of belligerence.

Helen said nothing.

"OK, thanks for your time."

They hung up, and Helen made notes about the discussion for her file. She wondered idly how much time would pass before someone would call to pursue the subject. And she wondered who might be the one to make that call. When it came, she suspected, either the case would be resolved, or the battle lines firmly drawn. At least everyone would know exactly where each stood, which would be a relief to all of the parties.

❧ ❧ ❧

Helen showered. She stood in the walk-in closet and tried to decide what to wear. At the very back of the closet, she saw a cleaning bag she suspected had been hanging there for as long as she had lived in the apartment. Inside the bag were wool pants, which she put on, and the matching navy jacket, which she also pulled out. Holding up various shirts, blouses, and shells and looking in a mirror, she finally settled on a rose-colored shirt with black stripes. She hunted around the built-in shoe rack and found some low-heeled navy pumps. Then she went back to the bathroom, rooted through a drawer for mascara and lipstick, and made up her face. Finally, she was ready to go.

Helen walked the four blocks to Vanja's Tea Shop and went in. She selected a table close to the back, between the counter and the short hall leading to an office and the restroom, placed her bag and coat on the table, and went to the counter to order. The woman who waited on her looked between forty and forty-five. Tall, perhaps two inches short of six feet, she was not fat or thin but well proportioned in terms of height-to-weight ratio. Helen was taken with her skin, hair, and eyes. The pale skin reflected her Nordic background. Since there was an enclave of Norwegians and Swedes in the area dating back to the fishing-fleet days, this was not surprising in Seattle. The woman's hair was blond, natural, and straight, cut very simply—bangs that almost touched the eyebrows, the rest blunt-cut at the level just below the ears. With very large icy-blue eyes, set well apart, she gave the effect of a frozen maiden.

That coolness was totally offset, however, by her clothing. First was a blazing red turtleneck under what Helen could only think of as a vest with tunic pretensions. The floating sleeves fell to the elbow, leaving the red sleeves of the turtleneck showing from there to the wrists. Composed of a see-through gauze fabric, colored in four shades of purple from deep grape to burgundy and lavender with thin lines of orange, the vest floated to a series of points at the hip. The woman also wore a silver necklace, very chunky, and silver earrings that went with but did not match. The combination of the pale, classic face and vivid clothing was nothing short of stunning.

"My name is Helen Smith. I'm a friend of Mr. Kenneth Osborne. I'd like a small pot of the honeybush tea, please." She hoped that by saying her name as well as bringing in Mr. Osborne's name, she would get a bit of a conversation. Instead, the woman nodded and turned her back to fix the tea. Helen returned to the table and sat. She'd have to do better, she thought.

Five minutes later, when the tea arrived, she tried again. "I've been here a few times. I remember talking about the decor with Mr. Osborne. What you've done is fabulous. Where did you find that wonderful … what is it? A steamer trunk or safari trunk or something?" Helen was referring to a large trunk, set upright on its end, open, with drawers on one side and a hanging section on the other. It was lined with a sprigged paper, yellowed with great age. Small tea towels, embroidered or with lace edging or made of cutwork, hung at various levels on one side. From the drawers spilled lace, scarves in a multitude of colors, ethnic necklaces with wooden beads and shells.

"Yes, it's a steamer trunk. It belonged to my great-grandfather, and he actually used it on the voyage here. We sort of settled on it first, and then built the rest around it." Her voice was very melodious. It sounded as though she had been trained in music with her voice coming from her diaphragm. Helen tried frantically to think of something to keep the conversation going.

"Do you plan to sell the tea mostly in the shop itself or to restaurants?"

"We plan to sell the tea whenever and wherever and to whomever we can."

This caught Helen by surprise, and she laughed out loud. The woman smiled back, and Helen was taken by how beautiful she was.

"Oh, what a great line," Helen said. "Please, have a cup of tea with me. I haven't had nearly enough time to ask Mr. Osborne about the shop."

"One cup, yes, I will. I'll get a cup from the kitchen. By the way, my name is Sonja Lundgren." She pronounced it "sawnya" rather than "sewnya." Walking behind the counter, she returned with a cup.

"Sonja, I'm so glad to meet you. Mr. Osborne, of course, has spoken of you. I know you've been friends for years."

"That's right. I was best friends with his sister from nursery school through college. Kenneth was about nine years older. He used to baby-sit me. He became my other best friend when I was about ten because he was the only person I felt really understood me. Much later, when I was at the University of Washington and he was already working as a paralegal, he introduced me to my husband. They were fraternity brothers at college."

"So your husband is about nine years older than you, right?"

"Yes, he is. We married before I finished college. And now our children are nineteen, seventeen, and sixteen. All boys, unfortunately. I'd have loved a daughter. But they're all at the point where they don't need me so much, except to check in with and make sure they have clean clothes and plenty of food."

"I've seen you in here, of course," Sonja continued. "But you always seemed to have something serious on your mind so I never wanted to bother you with idle conversation. I've been hoping you would have time for a talk at some point. You know Kenneth thinks very highly of you. He hints at some sort of work he shares with you, but you know how discreet he is. I know almost nothing."

"I'll tell you more than you want to know, I'm sure," Helen said with a smile. Inside, she wondered at the comment Sonja made about not wanting to bother her and made a mental note to meditate on it later. She then proceeded to describe the work of the foundation. "And Mr. Osborne is the secretary of the foundation as well as being on the tenant selection committee," she said as a wrap-up to her ten-minute monologue.

"It sounds like a truly worthy organization." They were both almost finished with the tea, and Helen was getting ready to leave. As she was putting on her coat, Sonja said, "You know, I have an idea. What about having a high tea, hats mandatory, at a country club or something, as a fundraiser for the foundation? It would serve two purposes … well, three actually. First and most obvious, it would raise money for you. Second, it would be great publicity for the tea shop. Kenneth and I would be there running the whole thing, and I'd plant the story to the newspaper. Third, it would spread the word about the foundation. What do you think?"

Helen was hesitant. "I don't know. Can I think about it? Could my name or picture be left out? I don't want any personal data getting into the paper."

"We could always have someone else give quotes and things. Kenneth, maybe?"

"We could ask him. But I think Alicia Mayhew might be better."

"Alicia Mayhew, you know her?" asked Sonja. "She's been in here. I recognized her, but I didn't speak to her. She's a pretty well-known woman about town."

"I didn't know that," said Helen. "She's my neighbor. I talked her into being a member of the board of directors."

"Well, you sure went high-profile. Kenneth never said a word about Alicia Mayhew being on the board. She's been the head honcho of about five or six organizations or events that I know of. Hospital auxiliary, a big garden club over on Mercer Island, a capital campaign for the cathedral, a regent at a local college … She's always in the society page for one thing or another. Well, she *was*. Since her husband died, I haven't noticed so much."

"I wouldn't know about any of that. I haven't been in Seattle long, and I don't read the paper. But I know she's really good at helping us in the foundation work. Here's what I'll do. I'll tell her what you're thinking and tell her to get in touch with you if she'd like the foundation to do it. After what you just told me, it sounds as if she's much more qualified than I am to make this sort of decision."

"Fair enough. I hope she calls. And thank you for starting a conversation with me."

When Helen got off the elevator, she knocked on Alicia's door. No answer. She made a mental note to e-mail Alicia about the idea from Sonja Lundgren.

As she approached her door, she realized she didn't really want to go in. Here she was, all dressed up with make-up on. It seemed a waste to sit in the house when she looked good. She decided to go see the progress on the small apartment building at the bottom of Queen Anne.

When Helen parked in front of the building, she saw Frank Brewer's car parked near hers. If it had not been a classic red Corvette, she would never have noticed, but his car tended to stand out. *Good,* she thought to herself, *I hope he's here.* She found the key to the main door in her purse and went into the building. Most of the work had been done, at least all of the work that created a mess. She expected it to be ready for tenants within a week, which is why she had worked on getting applications to start screening.

"Hi, Helen," said Alicia, as Helen entered the building. "We're just looking around. I'm glad we bumped into you." As she was talking, Frank came out of the apartment to stand behind Alicia.

"Hi, Helen," he said. "Come tell us what you think." He stood aside for the women to precede him into the apartment he had just left. Helen was taken aback only for a moment at seeing Alicia and Frank together. She had suspected for several weeks that they had become, at the least, good friends.

"This looks good," Helen said as she walked into the apartment. "I like the new lighting fixtures. They really match the age of the building."

"I found those at antique shops in Snohomish and out on the Olympic Peninsula," said Alicia. "We made three or four trips before I collected enough for the whole building. I needed four that matched or went well together for each apartment so it took a while. Some of them needed rewiring, but some were already fixed. All in all, I paid less for these than I would have for middle-of-road-quality, new ones."

"Wow, Alicia, I would never have thought of doing that. They add such a great touch."

"I sort of get some credit," said Frank. "I did a lot of the driving."

"Fair enough, Frank, so thank you, too."

Helen walked through the entire apartment, looking into all of the closets, opening and closing all of the kitchen cabinets, checking the window locks, and putting her hand on the radiators. She also flushed the toilet, turned on the oven and all of the burners, and ran the water. "Everything that should work seems to work. Did you turn on all of the lights?"

"I did," said Alicia. "But I can see I didn't do what you did, which is smart. I just turned on the lights to see how pretty it looked. I didn't think about functionality."

"We should do this in every apartment," said Frank. "Why don't I start on the top floor, and you two can do this floor and the middle one. Make notes of anything we see wrong." They separated and started the walk-through. When they had all finished and compared notes, they made a comprehensive list. There weren't many items, just a couple of dripping faucets, a non-working oven, and four or five window locks that did not work properly. "Let's check the laundry room, too," Frank said and walked down the hall to the end room. The women followed.

"We should get the keys to all of the doors and make sure they work," commented Alicia. "By the way, who will sweep the stairs and halls and be in charge of the laundry room? Will we have a property management company or something?"

"We need to talk about that," said Helen. "I hope to have tenants moving in before two weeks go by, and they'll need to know whom to call if there's a problem. What do you two think?"

"This building is on the cusp of needing a live-in manager as we have at Lenora," said Frank. "Eleven units is probably too big not to have anybody in charge. But it's a little small to make it much of a job."

"How about we offer one tenant some incentive to take charge?" said Alicia. "We can give the person a binder with names and numbers to call for each problem we think might come up. And he or she will have responsibility for all of the common spaces, picking up trash around the outside, things like that."

"OK, what's the incentive?" said Helen.

"Maybe when we interview the tenants, we could pick someone we think would be good and see what it would take. This close to the Seattle Center, maybe tickets to plays or concerts. Or gift certificates to some of the restaurants. Let them pick three a month and we give a fifty-dollar certificate to each."

"Or maybe tuition for classes down at Seattle Pacific. It's close by," Frank added.

"Those are good ideas. So we'll pick the person and then get creative. Everybody agreed?"

They nodded.

"Done," Alicia said.

"You look nice today. Been out to lunch?" Frank asked. Helen was surprised he had noticed her outfit but pleased that he had.

"I've been waiting for you to say something," said Alicia. "She looks smashing. I love the navy suit, definitely your color."

"Thank you. This was for the benefit of Sonja Lundgren, the co-owner of Vanja's. That reminds me, I want to tell you what she suggested," Helen said. She then related Sonja's idea for a high tea.

"Super," said Alicia. "I can do that, done a hundred of those kinds of things. I'll get together with her tomorrow, if she's free, and we can talk about it. It should be between March and May; that's the best timing. Everybody'll want an excuse to buy a new hat. We need to invite all the Red Hat clubs; they'll have a ball with it."

Helen loved the way Alicia was so enthusiastic about embracing new projects. Inviting her to join the foundation was one of the smartest things Helen had done. Well … not that it was her idea. It was Kenneth Osborne 's idea, and all Helen had done was go along with it.

❧ ❧ ❧

Two days later, Helen printed from her computer over a dozen applications for apartments that had been forwarded to her via Mr. Osborne. Then she sorted through them. One was from a woman with two sons, ages seven and nine. They lived in a section of town known for drug problems, gangs, and even a drive-by shooting that had left an innocent bystander severely wounded. The woman worked as a hotel maid. She was on food stamps and Medicaid. The application included the name of a social worker, Meghan Barnes, for a reference, so Helen immediately called.

"Hello, my name is Helen Smith, and I'm with the Claudius Foundation," she introduced herself. "I'm calling about a client of yours named Carmen Barrios. She applied to lease an apartment from us."

"I'm so glad you called," Meghan said. "I helped Carmen with the application and faxed it in. What would you like to know?"

"We're interested in any alcohol or drug-abuse issues first."

"No problem. I don't think she smokes or drinks, and I know she doesn't do drugs. She's been a client here for two years, so I'm sure I'd have noticed if there were substance-abuse issues."

"Is there a violent spouse or partner who might endanger our other tenants?"

"There was. She's the victim of spousal physical abuse. But it was four years ago, and he was deported as an illegal alien. She hasn't even heard from him for something like three years. She heard a rumor he was in some village near Oaxaca, where they're both from, but I can't confirm that. The reason she comes here is for counseling related to the physical abuse. And she wants to help the children deal with the abuse they saw her suffer. We do some family work as well as individual counseling. The children had some issues at first about their father leaving them, but they're functioning well now."

"Thank you. Is there anything else you feel I should know before I interview her?"

"She's Mexican; I guess you already know that. Here on a permanent visa. The boys were born here. Her English is not great, but she's in ESL and has improved a lot. She wants to speak English well enough to get a desk job at the hotel eventually, instead of cleaning rooms. The kids often act as interpreters for her when she's nervous. So she might bring one of them to an interview. But she'd be a great tenant, and she fits your program requirements."

"Good. Thank you for your time. I'll definitely arrange to interview her."

"Thank you. I'd never heard of the Claudius Foundation before. I'll keep your info on file, if you don't mind. How often do you have housing available?"

"It comes and goes. Right now, we're adding eleven new units in one building and one or two in a duplex. Plus, we have three vacancies coming up in a larger building. Keep us in mind." Helen got off the phone and immediately called the cell phone number for Carmen Barrios.

"Hello, my name is Helen Smith. Is Carmen Barrios available?"

"This Carmen." The voice had a very heavy accent.

Helen spoke slowly and tried to enunciate well and keep it simple. "You want an apartment. I have your application. Can I meet you to talk about the apartment?"

"Si, si, yes, I want apartment. Where is apartment?"

"We have one on Capitol Hill and one on Lower Queen Anne. Where do you want to live?"

"They sound good. I want away. I want apartment away."

"Where do you work?"

"Downtown. Hyatt Hotel on Eight Avenue."

"Either apartment would work well for you," Helen said. "You could even walk to work."

"Can I have apartment?"

"We have to meet you first. When can you meet?"

"I work morning at six. Home two, maybe three. I see you three, maybe four? Where?"

Helen felt they had done well in terms of communicating up to this point. Carmen seemed to understand most of what she heard, though Helen struggled to do likewise. Now she was stuck as she did not want to meet at Carmen's current home and she did not know where else to suggest. "What is best for you?"

"Can see apartment? Where is apartment?"

"Yes, you can see the apartment."

"Si, I want see apartment. Has two bedrooms?"

"Yes, it has two bedrooms."

"Yes, I want apartment. Where is apartment?"

Helen could feel Carmen's frustration and desire both coming through her questions. Helen suddenly realized that, with Brendan gone, she would have to be careful about going to the Lenora Apartments.

"Come first to the office to meet. Then we will drive you to the apartment. The office is at 2011 Queen Anne Avenue. Can you get here?"

"Si, yes, we take bus. Can bring son? He knows read the bus. He say better English."

"Yes, bring your son."

"We come tomorrow? After work?" Helen didn't know whether to be pleased or irritated at being rushed by Carmen.

"Yes, you can come tomorrow after work. Is four o'clock good?"

"Four, yes, we be office four. I say address," and she repeated the office address back to Helen, who assured her it was correct.

When she hung up, Helen immediately called Mr. Osborne and told him to expect Carmen and her son to show up at the office the next day. She told him she did not want to go to the Lenora apartment with Mrs. Barrios if she could avoid it and would try to get Alicia to go instead.

"You could sneak in," Mr. Osborne said. "I could go along and drop you all off in front. If you wear a hat and sunglasses and put on a dress with heels, no one will recognize you. I've never seen you in a dress and heels, so I doubt anybody else has either."

"Mr. Osborne, it's January. Bare legs and sunglasses?"

"Well, wear tights and cute boots. Wear it with a short jacket. And get some big framed reading glasses. That should do it. If everybody's looking at your outfit, no one will actually see who you are."

Helen laughed. "Maybe you're right. I'll check my closet."

"And, Helen, I almost forgot to tell you about a call earlier from Ruth Mellon, who's a nurse in a program called Nurse-Family Partnership. She heard about us from an agency she works with. She helped one of her moms fill out an application and e-mailed it to me. I want to tell you about the program … the Nurse-Family Partnership. They provide early intervention to promote healthy children. A nurse is assigned to first-time pregnant women who qualify for Medicaid. So I guess that means they're lower-income. A lot of them, she said, are teenagers. The nurses become like a counselor and advisor for the mother. They make home visits from before birth until the child is two years old. They're in the home a lot and teach the mothers everything from caring for the baby to looking for work. She sent a flyer about the program to me. I thought you should know about this because it looks like such a good fit for the foundation."

"It does. I'll drop by and pick up the flyer and the application today."

"Good, I'll leave them in an envelope with your name in case you come when I'm out picking up our lunch. I'm going to drop by the tea shop while I'm out, just to see how things are going there. So, either I'll see you or Mr. Pierce will."

Helen went to her computer when she hung up and looked for the program through a Google search. She read about it, including some of the research. So impressed, she went out right then to get the application.

When she returned, she started to add the newest applicant to her pile. Before doing so, however, she felt a shiver, and decided she should read it right away. The applicant was Sahar Dijani, twenty years old, with a baby of seven months. Sahar did not work. There was not much information other than references and the contact number—for Ruth Mellon with the Nurse-Family Partnership, the name Mr. Osborne had mentioned earlier. Helen got on the phone.

"It's Helen Smith. I would like to speak with Nurse Mellon." She paused. "Hello, my name is Helen Smith. I'm from the Claudius Foundation."

"Great, I'm glad you called," said a warm but worried-sounding voice. "I'm really desperate. Well, I'm not desperate, but Sahar is. Her parents are kicking her out, and she needs a place yesterday. It's going to be a homeless shelter unless I help her find something in a hurry."

"Right," said Helen. "Let me ask a few questions. Do you have time?"

"Yes, this is my top priority."

"Tell me about Sahar's situation … some things I should know if we become her landlord."

"Her family came as part of a refugee program from Afghanistan two years ago. They're very traditional. She got pregnant. They've treated her horribly since then. Confined to the house, made to do all the menial work, not talked to … basically shunned and treated as a slave. I met her when she showed up at a pregnancy clinic eight months pregnant.

That was her first contact with an American government program other than the resettlement folks. Her English is good. She has no money or source of money. I'll get her to apply for WIC and food stamps right away. She should be eligible for some kind of welfare grant from the state as well. Her biggest problem will be housing. I'm afraid for her to get a room somewhere or look for a shared housing situation. She's too vulnerable. Anybody could take advantage of her."

"What assets does she bring to the table?"

"Well, she learning to be a great mother. I've been working on that with her. The baby is a girl, but that's a blessing and a problem. If it had been a boy, the family might have been more reasonable. Right now, she needs to concentrate on taking care of the baby. She's under a lot of stress what with the family treating her badly added to the idea she's facing homelessness. She's holding up pretty well so far, but I don't know how strong she is for the long haul. As far as assets, she knows how to clean, cook, get around town on buses, shop, sew and mend clothing. And she's literate, which is better than the norm for her background. She was raised in a rural village."

"Is the father in the picture?"

"No. The most I've got on that is that the father was Afghan, married, a friend of the family in some way. They're close-mouthed about it. Apparently, when the state wanted a DNA sample, he took his family and moved somewhere. No one is saying where."

"OK. I think the best place for her is in the Lenora Apartments. It's on Capitol Hill, right on a bus line. There are grocery stores and other services in walking distance. The building has a lot of mothers with young children so she'll have a chance to get some peer support there, if she knows how to reach out at all. We'll start rent-free until we look at the situation more closely. Does she need furniture?"

"You mean you're offering a place?"

"Well, you said she was desperate, and we have housing, so yes, I'm offering a two-bedroom apartment."

"Wow, this is fantastic. When can she move in?"

"Tomorrow, that gives me a day to let the new manager know. The manager's name is Pam Butler. I'll get someone to e-mail you the address of the building and Pam's number. Call her to coordinate things."

"You don't know what this means. This can make a huge difference for Sahar. Thank you so, so much. This is beyond my wildest dreams."

Helen could hear tears in Ruth Mellon's voice. "You're very welcome, Ruth. You know, it *is* why our foundations exists. We're carrying out our mandate. If you need anything further from us, and Pam can't help out, give us a call."

Helen got off the phone and sent an e-mail immediately to both Mr. Osborne and Alicia, telling them that she had selected Sahar Dijani for an apartment at the Lenora Building. She asked that they coordinate with one another and that one of them call Pam Butler right away to alert her. "I can't do it myself," Helen wrote, "because Pam is a CASA case, and I don't want to have direct contact with her. Please let me know when this is done."

As Helen hit the button to send the message, her cell phone rang. Without checking the caller ID, she said, "Helen here."

"This is Meredith Butler."

Helen smiled to herself.

"It's January, and you said in October that we would have a meeting before Ted and I leave for Arizona. You were supposed to call us in December."

"Oh, I'm so sorry. I got busy with some construction projects, and it just slipped my mind. I apologize. Shall we set a time and date right now?"

"Yes, please. Can we do it tomorrow?"

"I have an appointment tomorrow at four in the afternoon. But I'm good before that. It might take an hour, and I would need to be finished by three. With those parameters, where and when shall I meet you?"

"I'd like you to come to the house. Maybe ten-thirty in the morning? Ted plays golf early. He'll only play nine holes, so he should be back by then. We live in Magnolia."

Helen agreed to the meeting and got the address. Then she got out her files to review the case. She made some notes of what she wanted to accomplish in the interview, which she suspected would not be an easy one. Meredith and Ted would try to convince her that Susie and Janie Butler would be much better off if the grandparents were in charge. She just hoped they would not have a lawyer present. It had happened to her once on an earlier case, and the lawyer was not happy when she simply informed him she could not talk in his presence without Hilary Armistead, the CASA lawyer, present as well. That meeting had ended right there. She did not know why otherwise intelligent people would think such an ambush would work. All the CASAs she knew were too well trained to fall for such an amateur trick.

Shortly after she hung up from the conversation with Meredith Butler, Helen received a call from Mr. Osborne. "Helen, you have this new tenant possibly moving in tomorrow, but you and I will be taking Mrs. Barrios and her son to see an apartment there in the late afternoon. So, I asked Alicia to handle Sahar Dijani and be on hand when she shows up to move in. We'll be stumbling over each other, but it should all work out. Just don't get any more tenant action for tomorrow, or we'll sink."

Helen laughed. "Right. I think I may have overbooked us. But Sahar needs a place right now. She should have come first on my list, in fact, but I didn't know about her soon enough. By then, I'd already committed to Mrs. Barrios. She's such a go-getter I just caved in to her. We should have her see both apartments, by the way, Lenora and Lower Queen Anne. But I warn you, she'll try to get us to give her the first thing she sees. Wouldn't surprise me if she brought a sleeping bag along to claim it."

Mr. Osborne laughed with her. "Got it. Now, this panic made me think about whether it's time to get more help. I wanted to know if I could put it on the agenda for our next board meeting, which is next week. Remember? We canceled December because everybody was busy and agreed to a mid-January meet instead."

"I remember; I have it on my calendar. Send an e-mail to the other members, please, and ask what else they may want to add to the agenda. We've been so busy there's quite a bit to report."

Helen was tired, even though it was only midday. She suspected she had been too involved in too many lives. It was always a draining experience for her, and she knew she had to pace herself. She turned off the computer, unplugged the landline telephone, turned off her cell phone, and went to her bedroom.

Helen sat on her cushion with crossed legs. She started with her breathing exercises, did some yoga, and then moved into meditation. First, she tried to empty her mind but found it was not yet possible. She was still too tied to the emotional content of the new tenants. She went back to breathing exercises, and another half-hour passed. This time, she found, her mind was quiet, and she was able to sit in emptiness. She sat for a long time. It was dark when she reentered her kitchen. She made a simple dinner of an omelet with vegetables and then went out for a short walk before bed.

The next day, Helen arose early so she would have time for some yoga and breathing before her meeting with the Butlers. She felt somewhat overwhelmed, still, by her schedule. She knew that she had yet to deal with several critical issues in her meditation practice. The tea shop was nagging, as well as her on-going involvement with not only Alicia but also Mr. Osborne, Frank Brewer, and now Michelle Lundgren. Far more disturbing, however, was her new relationship with Derrick. The fact that she could not bear even to bring it to the meditation practice told her the contact with him was powerful and disturbing. There was danger, she knew, in ignoring the twinges and subtle warnings she was receiving in her interactions. Her AA meetings could not help her; this was work that she needed to do on her own. She again felt her separation from Swami Rameshrawananda. A trip to India was simply not on, she knew. But she could feel storm clouds brewing.

By ten, Helen was almost ready to go to the Butler's home. She dressed in the same navy pants suit she had worn to the tea shop the previous day. One of her standard tactics was always to dress to meet the expectations or experiences of the client she was to see. Mostly, in Seattle, this meant casual pants, even jeans, with tee shirts, fleece jackets, quilted vests, and sandals (with socks, often), tennis shoes, or walking shoes. Since her clients were of limited means, she dressed down most of the time. That would not do for the Butlers.

She arrived on time and knocked on the door. The home, as she expected, was very grand, complete with large columns and topiary in urns flanking the broad pale-gold granite stairs. Mrs. Meredith Butler opened the door. Helen had actually expected a maid in uniform to do it.

"You must be Helen. Welcome. Please come into the living room." Meredith led the way. Helen noted the entry hall, two stories high, surrounded by balcony rails on the second floor. Meredith Butler was a very well-preserved sixty-five, Helen thought. She had maintained her weight and her youthful figure. Doctors had helped do the same with her face. The living room was big enough for a grand ball and felt cool and formal in the morning's gray light. Meredith led Helen to a large sofa and took a chair next to it for herself.

"Will Mr. Butler be joining us?" asked Helen as she got out her notebook and pen and placed them on the table in front of her.

"He will. He's just now changing. Would you like coffee while we wait?"

"No, thank you, I had a cup of tea just before I left."

"James tells me he called you yesterday."

"Yes, he called to tell me about Pam suggesting that he move into the apartment building where she now lives."

"He says you were pretty hard on him. Accused him of being a mama's boy."

"I accused him of nothing at all," said Helen mildly. "I mostly listened to him talk about the apartment as an option."

"I certainly hope you don't encourage him in that direction. Those children deserve a real home with a yard."

"Yards are nice, if one can both afford one and also maintain one. It can be difficult when one has children to raise and is on one's own."

"Yes, well … that hardly applies in this situation. James has a home with a yard, and we can maintain it very nicely. In fact, my husband Ted enjoys doing yard work."

"I see. Is the topiary his work? It's quite lovely." Helen did not want a confrontation, but neither was she about to roll over for this woman.

Meredith frowned at her but was deflected from further comment by the approach of her husband. Ted Butler, a tall and lean man, entered the room and pulled a chair closer to sit across the coffee table from Helen.

"Hello." He nodded at her. "You must be Helen Paige. I'm Ted. It's good to meet you. I had a friend who was a CASA for a while. He said it got too hard for him; he couldn't detach himself from the children."

"Yes, it's one of the main challenges of the work."

"What is it you would like from us today?" he said.

Helen noticed that Meredith sat back in her chair and left the conversation to her husband. "First, I want to know more about James as a child. It's always good to have some background on the family and social influences."

"James was an easy child, never had any problems, no drugs, and he's hard-working. He's our only child so he was never compared to a sibling or anything like that. He did fine in school but never really liked it."

"What about hobbies or sports or clubs, anything like that?"

"His favorite thing to do was always camping. I did it with him when he was young; then he did it in the Scouts. He was happiest, though, when he was able to go by himself. He started going solo when he was sixteen or so. I remember sometimes he'd be gone four or five days at a time, out in the wilderness. In fact, he pretty much kept up with it until his girls were born. I think he and Pam went camping quite a bit when they first met. I remember he bought a bigger tent about then."

What sort of work did you do, or are you still working?"

"No, I'm retired. I was in the air force for ten years. Then I got out and became an engineering manager at Boeing. Retired seven years ago. Now I golf and play poker." He laughed and shook his head a bit.

"Can you tell me anything about the marriage between James and Pam?"

"Well, that's kind of hard. Pam never really warmed up to us. I think she felt she just couldn't compete or something. Maybe we made her uncomfortable. Then, of course, she started drinking. That's when we finally just gave up on her."

Helen noted that Ted had failed to answer her question, so she rephrased and tried again. "Did James ever tell you how his marriage was going? Whether he was happy with it?"

"James was never much of one to talk a lot. He tends to keep things to himself. So, no, he didn't talk about his marriage. I can't believe he liked the way they lived, but he didn't complain to us."

"Was it a surprise to you when they decided to get a divorce?"

Ted looked confused by the question. He looked over to Meredith. "Were we surprised, or were you, I guess I mean?"

"Not really. With Pam drinking so much, I don't see how the marriage could have been a healthy one. So their decision to split up didn't just come out of the blue."

"Do you know which of them decided it was time to get a divorce?" There was a pause. Helen looked from one to the other, giving each a chance to speak.

"They never said," Meredith finally put in.

"Tell me a bit about the girls," said Helen. The floodgates opened immediately. As they praised the girls and laughed about things the girls said and did, they both relaxed and interacted with one another, almost ignoring Helen. They told stories about times they had shared with the girls at Disneyland and taken the girls on a cruise and to the beach at Seabrook on the Olympic coast. Helen let them talk for about fifteen minutes, taking notes on and off as she looked at them, smiled at the stories, and encouraged their remembrances.

"It's obvious," she interjected at last, "that you and the girls have good times together. They must be a source of great happiness for you."

"They're the best thing that ever happened to us," said Meredith, and Ted nodded in agreement.

Helen took a chance. "Pam said you're good for the girls, and I can see that. She hopes you continue to play a big role in their lives going forward."

Meredith looked skeptical. "*Pam* said that?"

"She did." Helen paused and leafed back through her notebook. "Let me look. I want to get this right." She got to a page she just happened to have marked with a paper clip. "There're no big secrets to what I write; it's going in the report, and you'll see it anyway. Here it is. These notes are a little sketchy, but they're verbatim. 'Meredith is devoted to them.' Then later she said, 'I want the girls to have a relationship with Meredith and Ted.' And later again, 'The girls mean everything to Meredith and Ted.' That's some of what she said."

Ted and Meredith were quiet. They looked at one another. Tears came into Meredith's eyes, and Ted held out his hand to her. She took it and looked down.

"I never knew she felt that way. I was afraid she'd get the divorce and take the kids away and never let us see them." Meredith was subdued.

"Not hardly," said Helen. "Pam is a loving parent, a really good mom. She wants what's best for her girls. And she knows they're best served by having a lot of people who love them. I don't think she'd ever take them away from you or keep you from them." She paused for a minute and then added, "You might want to talk to her about it."

Ted and Meredith both nodded.

Helen got up, saying, "Thank you for taking time to see me. I'll let myself out. You know how to reach me if you need to talk before my report goes in." She walked away, leaving the couple holding hands in their cool, elegant, living room.

❧ ❧ ❧

"This will go fine," said Mr. Osborne as he and Helen prepared for the meeting with Mrs. Barrios. "Alicia and Frank are at the Lenora with Pam and Sahar Dajani. And the nurse, Ruth Mellon, is there too. Alicia called me about two hours ago. They're all busy with the move-in. Frank got one of his friends with a truck and a good back to help out. Alicia said Sahar had almost no furniture, just a chest and one chair of her own, apparently. Oh, and a crib for the baby. So Frank called one of his friends who owns one of those staging companies … you know, where they bring in furniture to put in a house for sale to spruce it up. Anyway, the friend said they have furniture in back that's gotten too worn from all the moving-in-and-out business. She'll let them go through it and pick some stuff out. Plus, Pam is showing Sahar how everything works, like the dishwasher, which Sahar's never had before. Bottom line, they'll be too busy for Pam to even notice you. Then they'll go to Target and get things, like dishes and sheets and what-not. And I have the key to the vacant apartment, which is on the third floor. Pam's giving the one on the main floor to Sahar so she doesn't have the stairs to contend with. So that's all good."

"Great. Make sure you get receipts for what they buy at Target. Those can go to the foundation. They're reimbursable." Helen looked out the window. "I think I see the Barrios."

"What's our plan?"

"We'll show them the Lenora and then take them to the Lower Queen Anne building. I'd really like you to park around the Seattle Center so we can walk through it on the way to the apartment. Especially the skate park for skateboarders, the fountain, the arena, that section. Or maybe let us off there, and I'll walk them through it while you go park closer to the building. Do you have keys for the apartments there?"

"Sure do."

By then, Carmen Barrios and her son were looking for the address. Helen and Mr. Osborne, dressed in his elegant camel overcoat, went down to the sidewalk to meet them.

"Hello, I'm Helen Smith. Are you Carmen Barrios?"

"Si, yes, and my son Rodrigo. Nine years old. He has good English." She had her hand on the shoulder of a boy close to her own height. He was a very handsome child and boldly held out his hand to Helen.

"Good afternoon, Miss Helen," he said.

Mr. Osborne held out his own hand and said, "You can call me Mr. Osborne." He also shook hands with Carmen, saying, "And you can call me Kenneth. My car is right around the corner. Shall we go?" He led them to his car. Helen motioned for Carmen to get in front while she got in the back with Rodrigo.

"I want your mother to see where we are going so she can watch the route and the neighborhood," she said to the boy. "What grade are you in?"

"I'm in fourth grade. My mom is really worried about the apartment. Can she afford it?"

"We can make it happen for her, yes. We are part of a foundation that supplies housing for people who are having trouble making ends meet. So that won't be a problem. We want to find a place you'll all like, so tell me a bit about what you like to do around your neighborhood."

"Our neighborhood isn't safe, so Mom wants us to stay in the house most of the time. We like to climb on stuff, at the playground at school. And we ride bikes when we can borrow them from the other kids. We have one, but it's too small. And we read. We read a lot because we don't have a TV. That's why we're good in school. At least, the teacher says that. Maybe she just doesn't want us to feel bad about not having a TV."

Helen laughed. "Maybe you're right. Have you ever been on a skateboard?"

"Mom says we can't because we don't have helmets." He spoke quietly as he added, "But we've done it. A friend let us borrow his. It's really fun."

Helen nodded. "If I were younger, I think I'd do it. I love to see the kids at the skate park practicing. It looks exciting."

"It is, even when you just go straight down the sidewalk."

Helen was impressed by Rodrigo. He was friendly, respectful, and comfortable talking with an adult he did not know. She wondered if it was his mother's need for an interpreter that gave Rodrigo a grown-up air. She looked up and saw that Mr. Osborne was just turning onto the street in front of Lenora.

"I'm going to let you out here and park. I'll join you." He handed the key to Helen. "It's Apartment 307."

Helen got out with Carmen and Rodrigo, and the three walked straight into the building and went up the stairs, Helen keeping her head down and moving quickly.

"Is mine?" asked Carmen before Helen even had the door unlocked.

"No, I am going to take you to see another one as well. Only after that can you choose."

Carmen and Rodrigo walked into the apartment and started looking around while Helen remained near the door. She heard them speaking rapidly in Spanish, excitement raw in their voices. She did not know what they said, but she could hear they were enthusiastic. Mr. Osborne soon joined her. They heard the toilet flushing, water running in the bathroom, closet doors opening and closing. They joined Carmen and Rodrigo in the kitchen. Carmen was opening drawers and cupboards, checking out the stove, opening the refrigerator. She and Rodrigo talked with one another the entire time, though Helen was at a loss for what they were saying.

"Is good. I want apartment please," Carmen said to Helen.

"We really like it. We don't need to see the other one," Rodrigo added.

Helen laughed. "If you like this one, I think you'll like the other one, too. It's on the way back to Mr. Osborne's office, so it won't take but a minute to stop in and look. Let's go now."

Fifteen minutes later, Mr. Osborne dropped Helen and the future tenants in front of the Children's Theatre at the Seattle Center. As he drove off, Helen started walking through the center. Several boys, ranging from about eight to fifteen, were in the skateboarding park. Rodrigo went straight for them and starting watching.

"He loves skateboard," said Carmen.

"Yes, he needs to get a helmet," added Helen.

"I tell him, I say don't you go board with no helmet. Not safe. Bad for brain, I tell him. Rodrigo smart. He know to keep brain good."

"Yes, Rodrigo is very smart," Helen agreed. They stayed at the skateboard park for a few more minutes before moving on. "The grassy area here is good for kids to run around," Helen pointed out as they walked toward the International Fountain. "This is a safe place if there are two children together and it's not dark. A very nice place for children to play. And have picnics." She noticed that Rodrigo and Carmen were both looking around avidly at the grounds of the center, taking in the Key Arena, the water features and sculptures, the lanes and trees. She hoped it reminded Carmen in some ways of the *zocolos* of Mexico. "Do you like this?" she asked.

"Oh, si, yes," breathed Carmen. "Is beautiful. Apartment close?"

"It is, right over there." Helen pointed out the direction. They walked through the center and out onto Mercer, then over to Queen Anne. "The apartment is four blocks from here." As they walked on, the Barrios talked again together. Helen was struck by their conversation. They sounded more like peers than mother and son, to her ear. There were outbreaks of laughter now and again in their voices.

"Beautiful," said Carmen as they walked up to the door of the apartment building. Mr. Osborne was at the door, holding it for them.

"There are eleven apartments in this building," said Helen. They've just been remodeled and updated. Rodrigo, do you understand what I mean?"

"A little," he confessed, "but maybe not too much."

"Let me explain. They have new pipes for the water and new wires for the electricity. So everything works like new. There is a laundry room on this floor. We only need to look at two apartments here, because the rest are all the same. So, let's go into the one at the top at the front. It will have the best light and be farther away from the street noise. But it means you need to carry everything like groceries and laundry up the stairs. The ones at the back are quieter, probably. So you and your mother need to think about those things."

She led them up the stairs and into the front apartment on the south side. Rodrigo and Carmen started wandering around together as they had at the Lenora—opening and closing doors and drawers, flushing toilets, looking in the oven and refrigerator—all of the time with the constant stream of talking and exclaiming.

"We like this one," Rodrigo said to Helen a few minutes later. "Mom says the stairs are not a problem. She's young and can carry things. And she can have us carry things. She likes the light up here. This is it. She wants to know how much."

"We need to look at her wage statements from the hotel before we will know that. How much does she pay where you live now?"

"The rent is seven hundred. We have only one bedroom so Mom sleeps on the couch in the living room. Then we pay for the trash and electricity. We don't have a phone, except for Mom's cell phone."

"Well, I'm sure she can afford this. It's less than that. And we provide all the utilities, including Internet service and cable television if you ever want it."

"Apartment mine?" Carmen had a huge smile. She grabbed Rodrigo and hugged him. He hugged her back.

"Yes, Carmen, this is yours," Mr. Osborne said and shook hands again with both of them. "We can go back to the office right now and fill out the papers, and I can give you keys. Then you can move in whenever you want." Carmen started crying.

❧ ❧ ❧

Helen was returning from a head-clearing walk. As she got off the elevator, George Pendergast was waiting to go down. "Hello, Helen," he greeted her. "I was just having lunch with Alicia. Her chicken salad is as good as mine, much as I hate to admit it."

"It doesn't surprise me," replied Helen. "I've discovered that whatever Alicia does, she's good at it." They both laughed.

"Alicia gave me more about the foundation and mentioned how busy she is with it. I wonder if there's something I could do to help. I do have free time, though not as much energy as you young people."

"George, that's very generous of you. I suspect we do have something. Why don't I think it over and give you a call?"

"Please do. I'd better not hold this elevator any longer. It's good to see you again. Goodbye." He stepped into the elevator, and Helen continued to her apartment, shaking her head a little. She was baffled that Alicia would choose to maintain a relationship with a man who had been her husband's lover. And even she, who was so curious, could not quite see how to ask Alicia about it.

Thirty minutes later, Helen was writing up the report on the Butler case. By turning it in now, the parties might reach an amicable arrangement without moving toward a trial. Helen felt it was always in the best interests of everyone if decisions could be made by the parents. First, it forced the parents to learn to work together on behalf of the children, even when there were personal issues affecting the parental relationship. Second, the children did not have to see or sense the tension involved in preparing to testify in court. Third, of course, it saved the court time and money.

The phone rang as she was typing. "Hello, Helen here." She was still distracted by what she was writing and hardly noticed she had even answered the phone.

"Helen, it's Michelle Sullivan."

It took a moment for Helen to tune in and recall who Michelle was. "Michelle, hi. I'm just writing up the Butler report. I think we'll get lucky and it will get resolved once they have the report."

"That's especially good news, then, because I'm calling about a new case. How does your schedule look?"

"About like usual … well, maybe busier than usual. This month has gotten a little crazy, I can tell you that for sure. But I don't have any cases I'm active on, now that this one is basically behind me. And I doubt this one will go to trial."

"This case is a boy aged fifteen. It's a divorce case. Looks as if we need to investigate alcohol abuse by mother, and there's a domestic violence accusation against each parent."

"OK. I'll take it on if you want me to. The child is a little older than I'm used to, but I don't see a problem."

"Good, I'll overnight FedEx it today. You have time; trial date is in August. We'd like the report by mid-July."

"That's nice, no pressure there. How are things going?"

"We're running another training session. We need more CASAs, but that's not new. We lost four in the last month. They either burned out or moved or got sick. We hired another lawyer on a part-time basis to take some of the trial work off Hilary. Her name's Virginia Wexler. So you'll be seeing her around, I suspect. We're swamped with cases coming up for trial, so this should help. And thank you for closing the Kirk case and now this one without a trial. It's a huge bonus."

"You're welcome. Good luck. I'll look forward to the case." They disconnected, and Helen returned to her report. She had not wanted to take on another case but knew she needed to do it. Her vow to engage in "right livelihood" compelled her to be in the world working for others. That vow had to supersede her natural tendency to retreat rather than engage.

It was five and already dark when Helen finished the report. She stretched and rolled her neck to relieve the muscles from the time spent in front of the computer. Then she took an energy bar from the kitchen, put it in her pocket, and went to the entry closet for her coat and umbrella. She left the apartment and walked down the hill, eating her bar, and went directly to the small church in South Lake Union. Even though some people had made overtures toward her, she had decided that the meetings there were still the best for her. So far, she had held them at bay successfully without, to her knowledge, offending them.

When the meeting ended, Helen retrieved her coat from the rack at the back of the room. As she was doing so, a man approached her. "I believe your name is Helen," he said. "I'm Gerard. I've noticed that you walk, and I wondered if I might walk part-way with you?"

Helen could not think of any response that would not be a total rebuff. She was stuck. "Of course." She gave in gracefully since she had to give in anyway. They walked out without any further conversation. "How far are you going?" she asked after walking two blocks with Gerard beside her.

"I live on Queen Anne. The twelve-hundred block."

Helen tried not to groan. She'd have to put up with this almost the whole way home. Her other option was to tell him she was going to walk somewhere else, but that opened up another can of worms. What if he said he'd go along? Then she could not go straight home, which is what she wanted to do.

While she pondered this, he spoke. "I've noticed a couple of times that when I'm walking to the meeting you're walking ahead of me going to the same place. Since it's dark out, and we both seem to favor dark clothes, I thought we'd make a more noticeable target for cars to avoid if we were together."

"That's true," Helen said noncommittally.

"I don't talk much," he said "but I listen well. Feel free to talk or not."

"Right," Helen said.

And that was it. Neither of them talked again until they reached Gerard's door. Then each said goodbye. On her own again, Helen breathed deeply. That had not been so bad. He had put no demands on her, which she appreciated. And she had not really minded him beside her.

❧ ❧ ❧

The FedEx package with the new case arrived shortly after ten the next morning. Helen decided to put it at the top of her to-do list. She took a new notebook from her stash on the bookcase. Opening the file, she recorded some basic information on the front page of the notebook and then read through the file.

The father, Norm Easton, had filed for divorce from his wife, Marilyn. Helen's client was Garth Easton, the fifteen-year-old son. The statements from Marilyn and a friend of hers, Sharon Knight, included accusations that Norm had hit Marilyn on several occasions. Marilyn had a restraining order against Norm. He and his friend Rob Jobin both indicated that Marilyn was drunk every night and that she had been abusive on two occasions. One evening, when drunk, she had thrown a skillet full of hot food at Norm. On another occasion, she used a baseball bat to try to break the windows in Norm's car. He had called the police on that occasion, according to his statement. The file included a copy of a restraining order against Marilyn.

Helen called each parent and made appointments for the first interview. The appointments were on a Saturday evening and a Sunday morning, since the father worked during the week and the mother preferred to use her weekdays for other things. Helen made some notes and wrote questions she wanted to be sure to ask at the first meeting.

Then she put the file and notebook away. She was glad she had a couple of days before the first interview. The hostility expressed in the statements made her uneasy. Her own sense of balance and peace was affected by hostile actions and words. She avoided most television shows and movies and was even careful which sections of the newspaper she read. Ashram living, she learned years ago, had made her acutely aware of and sensitive to anger, no matter how it was expressed. She decided a yoga session would probably put her in the right mental space to face the rest of the day.

After the yoga and a lunch of a soft-boiled egg over sautéed spinach on toast, Helen sat at her dining room table, ready to work again. She decided to concentrate on the foundation's board meeting, scheduled for the following evening, and make a list of all of the properties in the portfolio to present to the group. Getting paper, she started the list.

CLAUDIUS FOUNDATION PORTFOLIO

1. Connecticut, Apartment bldg. , 9 units
2. Capitol Hill, Lenora Apts., 22 units
3. Wallingford, single-family house
4. Lower QA, Apartment bldg., 11 units
5. Dibble Ave. duplex, 2 units
6. Green Lake, single-family house, 1 unit not available to rent
7. White Center, apartment bldg., 4 units
8. Shoreline, triplex, 3 units
9. Issaquah, duplex, 2 units
10. Issaquah, apartment bldg., 5 units

As she looked over the list, she was amazed at how the foundation had grown. When she had started it, she had only thought of providing housing for four or five women in a small town in Connecticut. At one point, the foundation had three buildings there, but she had sold two since her decision to move to Seattle. The only building with a live-in, on-site manager full time was the Lenora Apartment Building. The Connecticut building had a property manager. That meant their small board of directors was trying to maintain eight separate buildings with twenty-eight units. She wondered how they would manage as the Lower Queen Anne building filled with tenants. This was definitely something to bring up at the meeting. She then thought about other items she wanted addressed at the meeting and made a few more notes.

The phone rang as Helen was about to leave for a walk. "Helen here."

"This is Ruth Mellon with the Nurse-Family Partnership. First, I want to thank you so much for your fast action on Sahar Dijani. We may have saved her life."

"How is she getting along in the apartment?"

"She's doing really well. She's made friends with Pam, the manager. Pam's girls love the baby. They play with her a lot, which gives Sahar a break. And Pam has sort of taken Sahar under her wing. She walks to the store with her, helps her buy groceries, that sort of thing. The other day, they went to a local Goodwill and bought clothes for the baby. Sahar is coming out of her shell a bit. So it's all good."

"I'm glad to hear it. Your program helping young mothers is a blessing. I wish every city had one."

"Me, too. What I called about is another case. You don't happen to have another apartment up your sleeve, do you?"

"It depends. What's the situation?

"It's a young couple. They're married. They both ran away from home as teens and ended up in Seattle. I suspect you know we have quite a large population of homeless teens. Now they're eighteen and nineteen, been together three years already. I'd like you to interview them. I know they're not your ideal picture because of their age. But when you meet them you may change your mind. How about it? Can I set up an appointment?"

"Yes, the least I can do is meet with them. I'm good tomorrow morning."

"Excellent. I'll bring them wherever you want to meet, maybe ten o'clock? They'll have the baby with them, but it's only eight weeks and shouldn't be too much of a distraction."

"Why don't you bring them to a tea shop on Queen Anne. It's called Vanja's Tea Shop, and it's in the twenty-four-hundred block."

"I know the one you mean. We'll be there."

Helen hung up and called Alicia. "What did you think of Ruth Mellon when you met her at the Lenora?" she asked as soon as Alicia answered.

"And good afternoon to you, too. It is a lovely day for January," Alicia responded.

Helen laughed. "I'm sorry. Hello, Alicia. How's your day going?"

"Fine, so nice of you to ask. And yours?"

"Very well, thank you. Do you have a minute to talk to me?" Helen smiled through the inconsequential chat. Alicia was a tonic to her.

"I certainly do. It's always a pleasure. What can I do for you?"

"I'd like to ask your opinion of Ruth Mellon."

"Yes, Ruth. I liked her. She's competent; that's the first thing that comes through. And she loves her job and her clients; that's the second thing. I guess I'd say she's the perfect nurse."

"Would you trust her judgment if she recommended someone as a tenant for the foundation?"

"I would. She asked quite a few questions the other day while we were getting Sahar settled. And she asked about the other tenants, as well. So she has a good idea of what we're about and who we serve. Why? Does she have another possible?"

"Yes, we're meeting tomorrow at the tea shop so I can decide. Want to come? It's at ten in the morning."

"I'd love to come. If we walk, we'll have a chance to catch up. I have a couple of things I need to talk to you about before the board meeting."

"Excellent, I'll knock on your door about ten. 'Til then. Bye for now."

"Goodbye, Helen. Thank you for calling."

Helen giggled when she hung up. When she realized she was giggling, she abruptly stopped. It was just like the laughing fit she had had the second time she had ever talked with Alicia. There was work to do around the issue. She would need to deal with it in meditation. For now, however, she was desperate for the walk; she needed movement.

As Helen walked along the curve of Highland that overlooked the sound, she felt her body relax. She knew then, as she felt it leave, that she had been holding tension in her body. Stopping to sit on a bench, she enjoyed the perfect view of the sound with the snow-clad Olympic Mountains in the background. Even though it was only ten degrees above freezing, there was a clear sky, and the mountains were visible. As Helen breathed deeply and gazed at the mountains, her mind wandered, and she drifted into a waking meditation state. Into her consciousness floated a picture of Alicia Mayhew. It shimmered, faded, glowed. It was there and not there. Helen watched it, mind empty. Then a wordless knowing invaded her. Alicia was murmuring. Helen felt a message. "It's opening; let it in" was all she could decipher. Gradually Alicia's image faded, and Helen was left with an overall feeling of peace and relaxation.

Helen stood and continued her walk, pondering the meaning of her meditation message. It was not the first time for her; she was a long-time student, after all. She just wished her messages were not so obscure. Other people from the ashram consistently received very clear messages, not like hers at all. She wondered, again not for the first time, if she would ever be blessed with such clarity. Thus musing, she went home, fixed some dinner, practiced her breathing exercises, and went to bed.

స₹ స₹ స₹

Thanks to a heavy rain, Alicia and Helen were walking to Vanja's Tea Shop under a large shared umbrella.

"You know George was visiting me the other day, right?" Alicia asked.

"I do know. I bumped into him at the elevator. He liked your chicken salad."

Alicia laughed. "He did. He asked for an extra helping. He's at loose ends, you know, since Timothy died. He's lonely, which is to be expected. But he still has a lot of energy for a man his age, just as Timothy did. He wants something to do."

"Yes, he mentioned he'd like to be involved in the foundation. What do you have in mind?"

"I'm not sure. He was a teacher and an administrator, you know, so he has skills in managing people and things. He'd be better off with people, I think, since he's somewhat isolated, as far as I can tell. I thought at first he could visit the properties once a month and check on them, but I'm not so sure. First, he'd have to drive. Second, I'm not sure it's enough to do."

"Bring it up at the board meeting tomorrow. We have a big agenda. Let's see if something comes up during that. If it doesn't, we can brainstorm together afterwards. It would also help if you asked him to list three or four things he's good at and another three or four he'd like to try just for fun. Maybe that will give us a little more to work with."

"Good idea. I'll do that today so I can have it in mind for the meeting."

By then, they were at the tea shop. As they stepped inside, Alicia spotted Ruth Mellon sitting at a table with a young couple. "Good morning, Ruth. Hope we didn't keep you waiting too long."

"Not at all. We just got settled; haven't even ordered tea yet."

Helen shook the umbrella out the door, then folded it and put it in a large ceramic urn that already held several others. She joined Alicia and shook hands with Ruth, who had risen to meet her. Ruth was in her mid-thirties, with short curly hair, a round friendly face, and a smile that showed her dimples.

"I'm so glad to put a face to the name," Ruth said. "Alicia's told me all about you … all good of course," she added.

"I'll order tea and scones all around," Alicia said and went to the counter where Sonja was waiting.

Helen smiled and looked at the seated couple. The girl was small with a thin face made interesting by large brown eyes and delicate, arched eyebrows. The boy was thin, looked as if he might be tall, with very straight posture. He looked wary. He had his hand on his young wife's shoulder. Behind him, on the floor, was a baby asleep in a carrying basket.

"Mrs. Smith, I'd like to present Christy and Ben Hudson."

Ben rose slightly and shook hands. "Nice to meet you," he said.

Christy smiled and nodded, not speaking.

Helen sensed the unease in the young couple. "I see your baby. Tell me something about him," she asked, mostly to see if they would relax a bit.

It was Christy who spoke. "His name's Lance. We wanted a short name so people wouldn't change it to a nickname. He's eight weeks old. He sleeps a lot. And he doesn't scream at night, like some babies. He's real good. He wouldn't disturb anybody. I don't let him cry much; as soon as he fusses, I try to get him right away and nurse him or change him or whatever he needs. He's no trouble, really. He wouldn't disturb neighbors or anything." She spoke rapidly once she started.

"He's a good baby, just like Christy says," added Ben. "If she's tired at night, I get up for him, and he's real good. If I just walk around a little and pat his back, he quiets down real fast." Helen could see he was trying to bolster the argument Christy was making.

"I'm sure he's a good baby who won't disturb neighbors. That's no problem at all. We don't rent apartments to people based on a baby crying. Tell me about yourselves. What are your days like?"

Before they could answer, Sonja approached carrying a tray. Putting it on the table next to the group, she passed around five plates, each with a scone accompanied by two containers, one with thick clotted cream and the other with strawberry jam. She then handed out small embroidered napkins and butter knives. The tea, in a large blue pot, was placed in the center of the table. Delicate saucers and cups were handed around. Sonja then discretely picked up her tray and departed.

Alicia poured tea. Helen noticed that Christy and Ben watched the others very closely. They did not touch the scones until they saw Helen use her hands to separate her own in two parts and then put cream and jam on each. They followed suit. Ben had some difficulty with the small handle on the teacup but drank his tea without spilling any.

As soon as they were all settled, Helen said, "I was asking how you spend your time."

"Right," answered Ben. "I work every day, from six in the morning until about four or five in the afternoon. I have two jobs. I work for an electrician in the mornings. He's an older guy and only works half a day. I'm his helper. I drive him to the job and then do whatever he says. He's been teaching me all about the work, but I need to become an apprentice to go further."

"Do you have a car?"

"No, we use a company truck. I go to the company parking lot and get the truck, then go pick him up. At noon, I drive him home and take the truck back to the parking lot. I get a bus to and from there. Then I get another bus and go to the restaurant. It's a breakfast-and-lunch place, closes at three each afternoon. I do dishes and then help with clean-up. I get done about four, sometimes a little later. Then I go home."

"How long have you worked at these jobs?"

"I've been with the electrician for a little over two years. The restaurant job, I've had less than that, maybe eighteen months or so. Do you want my bosses' names? I wrote them down for you and their phone numbers." He stood to reach into his pocket, and Helen noted he was over six feet tall.

"Thank you. Do you have any questions for Ben?" Helen looked at Alicia.

"What do you and Christy do for fun?" she asked.

They looked at each other, and both ended up blushing. "Besides that?" Alicia said with a smile. They blushed worse, and both put their heads down.

"We walk," Christy finally said. "We can't go to movies or things; it costs too much. But we walk, and we play cribbage sometimes. We listen to music a lot; we have a radio. Ben's real handy, so he makes things to sell. He has some tools. He made birdhouses one year when we were near a construction project and we could get scraps. Those sold really well. And he made little signs for people to hang on their beach cottages or someplace. The signs said things like "This Way to the Beach" with a carved finger pointing or "Welcome" or "My Beach House," stuff like that. We got in trouble one place because of the noise of his saw and stuff, but we wouldn't do that. We'd be really quiet."

Ben spoke. "Christy likes to paint. Sometimes, she'll paint while I'm working with wood. And sometimes she'd paint what I made. Like once we made blocks for little kids, and she painted the letters on two sides and then an animal or something on the other side. Those all sold right off, too." The couple seemed to relax a bit more as they talked about their lives.

"Where do you live now?" asked Alicia.

"We rent a room in a house in Burien. The house has four bedrooms. The main guy rents the house and then takes in boarders. We get to use the kitchen and the living room if he isn't at home. We've been there about ten months. He likes us OK, but he's not too happy about Lance being there. The woman in the room next to us is complaining every time Lance cries, so that's why we try so hard not to let him cry."

Alicia looked at Helen. Helen nodded.

Alicia looked at the young couple. "Well, I think we can do a bit better for you than that. Would you like to walk down Queen Anne Avenue? It's quite a ways, but all downhill. Or there's a bus you could get up here and ride down."

"We can walk," said Ben. "Where're we going?"

"We're going to view an apartment. See if you like it," responded Helen.

"How much is it?" Ben asked. "We don't have a lot of money."

"How much rent do you pay for the room you're in?"

"Two hundred a month. But we get everything, water and trash and lights and all that. It's nothing like an apartment would be. We've never lived in an apartment, but I bet they cost a lot." Ben looked worried.

"This one isn't so pricey," said Alicia. "I'm pretty sure you could manage the rent."

Ruth had remained quiet for the entire interview. She smiled broadly when Alicia and Helen exchanged the glance that told her the young couple were going to get an apartment. She nodded her thanks to Helen.

"I think I'll leave you with these ladies, then," she said to Ben." Call me when you can; I'm sure you'll find some pay phones around here. Do you have change?"

Ben nodded. The young couple said goodbye to their visiting nurse and then started picking up their belongings. Ben stood first and handed a large diaper bag to Christy. She put on her coat and put the bag diagonally across her chest. Ben put his coat on and then picked up the carrying basket with Lance. It was obvious they were practiced in being parents who shared the duty of carrying everything a baby required.

"I changed Lance just before we came, and he nursed on the way, so we're good for at least another hour," she told Helen. Alicia went to the counter to pay for their tea and scones, and they left.

❧ ❧ ❧

At six that evening, Alicia joined Helen for the walk to Mr. Pierce's law office. A light rain was falling, and it was cold, though not freezing, and they walked quickly. They were not the first to arrive, as both Joe McGregor and Frank Brewer were already in the small conference room. Harriet Kilcoyne arrived within minutes, and Joe called the meeting to order. After dealing in short order with the old business, he said, "Right. We have a lot on our plate this evening. This is not a formal agenda, by the way. We can take these things up in any order we wish. Who wants to start?"

"I'd like to get some small decisions made off the top so we can get to the more serious things. One item is the new tenants. Let's take the Lenora Apartment Building first. Pam Butler is our new live-in manager, replacing Brendan Riska. We are paying her a thousand a month plus free rent. Next, we have Sahar Dijani, age twenty. She's an Afghani refugee with a two-month-old girl. She is essentially escaping from her family, which became abusive once she got pregnant. She has no income and pays us no rent. We have a possible new tenant who is James Butler, Pam's husband. They're in the middle of a divorce. If he moves in, we'll charge him minimal rent, maybe three or four hundred, depending on what we see from his paycheck stubs.

"Moving on to the new complex on Lower Queen Anne, first we have Carmen Barrios. She's still married, but her husband is in Mexico and has been for three years. He was abusive. She has two sons, ages nine and seven. We'll charge her five hundred; she's used to paying seven hundred. She has no debt, so she'll be in much better shape. I would like to figure out a way to get two helmets and two skateboards or one skateboard and one bike for the boys. Think about that while I finish up. Our final new tenants are Christy and Ben Hudson and their eight-week-old baby boy, Lance. They're eighteen and nineteen, been together three years, married for one year. They're now in a room in a boarding-type house in Burien. Ben works two jobs, total of about forty hours a week, but all at minimum or less wage. They pay two hundred where they are; we'll take them at one fifty. They'll move in on the weekend when they can borrow a car for their things. For them, I'd like to arrange two cell phones and the service. At present, they use pay phones, and he has no way to contact her during the day because she has no phone. We need to change that. And that's it." Helen hoped she had been reasonably succinct. She wanted all of the data in the minutes, as well as all of the board members to hear the names and some details about the tenants, since that was the whole purpose of the organization.

"OK," said Joe. "I'll tackle the skateboard business. I know the owner of the bike shop on Roy, not two blocks from the apartment. I'll go in and set it up with him to give us a good deal and then take the boys in myself, if the mom will let me. Otherwise, I'll take her along." Knowing Joe, Helen suspected the owner would make tax-deductible donations of the items.

"I'll do the cell phone business," spoke up Frank.

Helen gave each of the men a slip with the name and contact information for the tenants and the agency that recommended them.

"Will the young couple need furniture and items for the kitchen and bath?" asked Harriet. "I could make a trip to Target with them, as Alicia did for Sahar Dijani." When Helen looked surprised, Harriet added, "Yes, Helen, Alicia told me about that day," and all three women laughed.

"What are we being left out of here?" asked Joe. Frank then told the story about the day at the Lenora apartments. At the end he added, "Helen was sneaking around with Ken's help, and Alicia was running herself ragged getting Sahar moved in. We probably all slept well that night."

"Sounds like the board is becoming more than a board of directors," said Joe. "That's an item on the agenda I want to address. Anybody else want to go before that?"

"I'd like to bring up one more thing," Helen said, "since I think it will be pertinent to what you want to talk about. I have here a list," and she passed it around, "of the properties the foundation now owns. You'll note the number of units beside each one. The property in Connecticut is the last of three I started with when I formed the foundation there six years ago. Two were sold, and the proceeds went for the Lenora Apartment Building. The last one now has an offer. It's in a good location, and the offer came in at one point eight million, which is two hundred thousand a unit. Probably get turned into condos. I think we should take it so we can reinvest here."

"What about the tenants?" asked Alicia.

"That's not a problem. When I came here, I gradually replaced the tenants as they moved on. The replacements got charged market rate from the beginning. So at this point, they aren't the type of tenants we seek for the foundation. The rents have been coming into the foundation as income on investment."

"Any motion to sell?" asked Joe.

"I have a problem," said Frank. " Before we get to a motion, I think we need to talk about some of the advantages of keeping the place."

Joe was disgruntled. He had another issue he wanted to get to, and had hoped to dispense with the Connecticut property in short order. But he was only the president of the board, and he had obligations to all of the members. "Anybody want to talk about this?" he asked, hoping for no response.

"I do," said Helen. "Frank, can you discuss the advantages in detail?"

"Right," said Frank. "We have a lot of property now, as Helen just showed us. And we have insurance. But a lot of things happen to properties, especially in this area, and a lot of them aren't covered. Think about the mud slides and the rain and wind storms we have. What if one of the properties has serious storm-related damage or the sewer needs to be replaced. Happens all the time. On these properties, that can cost upward of a hundred grand. So having the monthly income from the Connecticut property gives us a cushion. It rents at market, whereas ours don't. So it's a solid source of income for us. Maybe we should keep that property as a sort of reserve fund."

"Anybody else want to add anything before we vote?" Joe was trying to move on to the next item.

"Yes, I want to add something," said Harriet. "I agree, Frank, that a reserve fund would be a good idea. But I'm not sure using the rents from Connecticut are the best way to do it. We could just go ahead and sell, then take a piece of the sale and put it in a separate fund. I could locate a safe investment vehicle with a decent cap rate. That way we have the guaranteed price from the offer on the table, we get rid of having a property we can't use for our housing purposes, and we establish the reserve fund all at the same time."

Frank thought it over. He still wanted to keep the property, but he wasn't quite sure why. Harriet made a good argument; he couldn't deny that. "I just don't know," he finally said. "I don't want to sell, but I'm not able to give you a better reason that I already did."

Joe was irritated. He liked all the votes to be unanimous. That way no one was in a position to say "I told you so" later. Saved arguments.

"Any other discussion before we move on?" He had a slight frown, as though he wanted no answer. So no one answered.

"Can I get a motion to sell?" asked Joe.

"I move we sell the building in Connecticut," Helen said.

"Second," added Harriet.

"Moved and seconded. Any comment or discussion? Seeing none, show of hands in favor. That's five in favor, one opposed. Ken, put it in the record. Shall I go next?"

Seeing no opposition, Joe started. "We're growing. We're getting so big we need help. Plus, look at us squashed up in this room. We need space. So, I've been thinking, and I talked to Edward. He says the business next door, the insurance agency, is cutting down on space. They're letting go of people and downsizing. We can sublease two rooms. One we could use as an office and storage for our files. The other, the big one, would give us a conference room big enough for ten to twelve people. We would enter through the main door to the insurance company straight into a lobby we would share, but only as an entryway, and then go straight to our rooms, which connect. We'd get a name on the door right under theirs and a plaque with a name for the interior door. Cost is four hundred a month. Lease for two years.

"Now, the reason I want the space. We need a full-time employee. The person we hire needs to coordinate our activities, be a central and primary point of contact, send out e-mails on things we all need to know, oversee construction activities, especially since we seem to be adding property left and right, plus handle everything else Kenneth does now. Edward said Kenneth could have the job if he agrees. Over to you, Ken."

"Mr. Pierce did discuss this option with me. I love it. The foundation is my favorite client, anyway. So, yes, please." Kenneth was flushed pink with pleasure. It matched his pink tie, which he wore over a pinstriped shirt in navy, gray, and pale lavender, together with a navy blazer and charcoal slacks.

Helen was totally surprised by this proposal. She had never thought of it. But as soon as Joe brought it up, it seemed so obvious.

"Do we have the income for a salary and the rent?" asked Frank.

"I'll see to that," said Joe. "Figure the rent at five thousand, salary for Ken at one hundred, employee benefits at another fifty, we're talking less than two hundred. We could even throw in a rental car for the foundation and still come in less than two hundred grand a year. I can raise that with a dinner party every quarter. My wife will love it, get it in the society page and all. Helen, you haven't said anything. We won't do anything unless you agree first. This is just an idea."

"Of course, I approve. You've all been so good and taken on so much. Maybe this will help relieve some of the stress. And you know how I feel about Mr. Osborne; he's perfect. His title, I assume, will be executive director of the Claudius Foundation?"

"Whatever title he wants, short of king or emperor." They all laughed. "Now, let's hear a motion on the lease of the room next door and another on the appointment of Kenneth to the position of executive director and another one on his salary."

All the motions, seconds, and voting were accomplished in less than three minutes.

"Moving on, what's next?"

"I have a suggestion." said Alicia. "Mr. George Pendergast, a dear friend of mine, would like a role in our work. He's approaching eighty, but he's spry, alert, and capable. He was a high school teacher and an administrator. He owned the house we bought in Green Lake, and if you recall he has a life interest in it. I've been thinking of what he might add to the foundation. Since we will be buying more property, especially with the sale of the Connecticut building, we need to think about some monitoring of things. Of course, Kenneth can do some of that in his new position. But he might be very busy with the actual buildings as well as applications. I'm thinking about someone who pays attention to the tenants once they're in the housing unit. George is very good with people, both adults and children. He could meet every tenant in person right after each moves in. He could assess any needs, like the skateboards or cell phones, and follow up with that. That would be his primary task, perhaps. Then he could make a telephone contact with each tenant each month. Check on the children, see if anyone is desperate in any way or has a problem the foundation might be able to help with."

"That's good," said Harriet. "Sounds like quite a lot of work. Will we pay him?"

"I doubt he'll want a salary. He has a pension and some investments. But he shouldn't be driving all over the place. So maybe we could offer to pay for taxis for his visits or give him a stipend for it or something."

Joe looked around and assessed everyone's reaction to Alicia's suggestions. "Looks like it's a winner of an idea, Alicia. Let's get to an approval of funding; then you can see if he wants the job. That way we're set to go if he says he'll take it."

"I move we provide a taxi allowance or provide reimbursement of taxi expenses for George Pendergast to visit any and all tenants at any and all times," said Helen.

The motion carried, and Joe looked for the next area of business.

Frank spoke. "I've been approached by some colleagues still active in the business. Now that we're selling the Connecticut property, we can look for more. There are two on the market I'd like some of you to look at with me. The one that I think is the best deal overall is on Seventh West, near Galor, so it's walking distance of where we sit right now. This is a great building for a couple of reasons. Let me explain a bit about it. Think of a big square; then insert two crossed lines to divide it into four smaller squares. That's the building, a big box with four identical units. Each unit has its own entrance with a parking space in front and a small front yard as you approach the door. What you gain with each unit is not just a private entrance and yard, so it feels like a house, but also two sides with a lot of windows on each one. The two sides that connect to the neighbors are where the closets, laundry room, bathroom, one wall of the smaller bedroom, and part of the kitchen are. So you get good noise separation. This place was built in the seventies so it's got fairly modern plumbing and electric. It has gas heat, hot water, and cooking. So it's pretty economical. We can get a good price. It's been listed for over four months, and the owner is anxious. They want to use a 1031 exchange for a place in Southern California that they'll eventually turn into a retirement home."

They all agreed it sounded like a good building. Alicia and Harriet wanted to go the next morning to see it, and Joe said he thought he might like to go along. Helen was somewhat hesitant, feeling she was overstretched, but finally agreed to go when Joe said he'd like her comments when they went.

"Any other business?" Joe asked. He paused, ready to close the meeting.

Then, again, Frank spoke up. "One thing I've noticed is that we have more women than men as tenants. That's to be expected, I know. And in a small building, say four units, I don't see it as a problem. But when you have only women in a place with six or more units, the kids won't be seeing men. I think men around gives a better sense of life.

If boys are raised to think only women raise children, that's the wrong message." Helen was astonished. She and Alicia looked at one another.

"Damn, I should have been the one to say that," said Harriet, voicing the thoughts of the other women.

"It's so obvious when someone actually says it," added Joe.

"Here's what we'll do," said Helen. "Look at the list I gave you. The Lenora has two men now, and James Butler will make it three if he goes in. Darn, now I wish I hadn't put Sahar in there. But let's put men in from now until we have at least seven. Then keep seven at all times."

"How can we do that?" Harriet said. "What if men don't apply?"

"We put the unit on the open market, take any man who looks right, charge market rent. Our charter allows that." This was Kenneth. "It says what our goals are, but our written goals have nothing to do with how we use an entire building. We could own a building as a capital asset with no tenant, as we do the Green Lake house. Even the Connecticut building is an example. It's run as an income-producing property for the foundation."

"Let's set goals for the new building on Lower Queen Anne, then," added Harriet. "I'd say five, just under half. Anybody prefer a different number?"

"Good," said Helen after a short pause. "Let's just put it in the minutes. We don't need a vote on that."

"We still have a raft of applications," said Kenneth. "More have been coming in every day. Do you want me to screen for men to see if we can fill up with qualified fathers first?"

"Yes," said Helen. "I think I prefer men who have visitation rights, even though the children may not have the apartment as a primary residence."

"Do we ever want single men?" asked Joe.

That stumped all of them. The pros and cons ranged from wondering if the women tenants would end up fighting over an eligible man to having a single working male as a role model to having a man around to help move furniture or change a tire. In the end, they decided to just leave the question alone. The meeting was adjourned.

Kenneth approached Helen as she and Alicia were getting ready to walk home. "I want to give you the tenant applications I printed out today. While the meeting was going on, I pulled a couple out and put them on the top of the pile. They're men."

"Thank you, Mr. Osborne," said Helen. "I'll make contact tomorrow. We forgot to put in the minutes when you start your new job. How soon will that be?"

"Maybe three weeks. I need to find a paralegal for Mr. Pierce. I'll be right next door, of course, so I can complete the training and still be around to answer questions, even when I'm not officially employed here."

"You'll still make tea?"

"You know I will. And Mrs. Prescott, Helen, if I may, thank you, thank you, thank you. Oh, and you can call me Kenneth now." They both laughed. He wanted to hug her but knew she was not comfortable with such familiarity. Someday, maybe, he thought.

Helen was exhausted when she returned home. She put the file of possible tenants, unopened, on her dining table and stumbled into her room. She took off her clothes, fell onto the bed, and went promptly to sleep.

❧ ❧ ❧

It was another typical rainy, gray January morning when Helen sat at her small red table to deal with the rental applications Kenneth had given her. She made a mental note always to think of him as Kenneth now. If she ever slipped and called him Mr. Osborne again, he would think he had displeased her, and she did not want to hurt him. Pausing with an application in her hand, she thought about that and looked out the window. She stared at the low clouds pressing down on the street outside and felt the weight of them on her as well. It was difficult to plod through life with such exposure to others. She felt a sudden, deep longing to be back in the ashram with Swami Rameshrawananda. Shaking it off, she faced up to her worldly responsibilities and studied the paper in front of her.

The application Kenneth had placed at the top was from Carl Soyster, father of Rehema, age five, and Darvon, age three. They were currently living south of Sea-Tac. Kenneth had attached a sticky note to the paper, reporting that the particular neighborhood had an increasing problem with gangs and drugs. Carl Soyster was unemployed but collected a monthly check from the government. Helen wondered if he was disabled. The foundation didn't have handicap-accessible units. She made a note in her foundation notebook to put the issue to the board at the next meeting. Then she called Mr. Soyster.

"Hello, my name is Helen Smith.. Is this Mr. Carl Soyster?"

"It is." The voice was a deep baritone. Mr. Soyster sounded like a radio announcer.

"I'm with the Claudius Foundation, and I have your application for a rental apartment. I wonder if I might ask a few questions."

"Fire away."

He was a man of few words, Helen noticed. "Do you know where you wish to live and what size apartment you need? And do you have any special needs we should meet?"

"I want out of this neighborhood because I'm concerned about drug gangs taking over. No special needs."

"I see you have two children, a boy and a girl. How many bedrooms are you looking for?"

"Two would do fine."

"I'll make the reference checks and call you back today. Will you be available at this number?"

"Yes, it's a cell."

She rang off and called the first name given as a reference. "Hello, my name is Helen Smith with the Claudius Foundation, and I'd like to talk with Sergeant Searle."

"Speaking." Another laconic voice.

"I'm seeking information on Carl Soyster, who put in an application for a rental apartment."

"What do you need to know?"

"Basically, what kind of tenant he'll be. We have units that include some vulnerable women, and all of our units include children. We're increasing the number of male tenants. Can you tell me why he would have applied to the foundation?"

"I suggested it when I saw a forwarded e-mail about your org. I'm with a family services unit at Joint Base Lewis McCord. Soyster's wife was killed in Afghanistan last year. She was a reservist with a unit over in Walla Walla, got called up, and the family moved close to the base. After she was killed, he didn't want to live quite so close, so he moved up near the airport. He told me the neighborhood doesn't feel safe anymore. I gave him the application."

Helen liked the clipped military response. It reminded her of Joe Friday, "Just the facts, ma'am." Her mom was a sucker for those old re-runs.

Helen hung up and considered the options. She liked the idea of putting Carl Soyster at the Lenora Apartments. Since she did not want the stress of bumping into Pam Butler if she went herself, she decided she needed someone else to meet him there. She finally called Frank.

"Frank, I have a possible tenant. He's a widower, his wife was a military member, died in Afghanistan. Two children, three and five. I'd like him for the Lenora building, but I don't want the new manager to see me showing him around. There's an apartment there, top floor, that just became vacant. Could you meet this man? Then you could bring him back to the office so I could meet him, too."

"No problem. You want to call and set it up, or do you want me to do it?"

"I will. Give me your availability."

"Today we're at the Seventh Street West place, remember? So I'll be free from there and good to go at three or after. Tomorrow morning is good, but I have an appointment at one o' clock, so I need to be done by noon to give myself time."

"OK. I'll call back."

Helen hung up and called Carl Soyster. "It's Helen Smith again. When would you like to view the apartment? I have a vacancy left on Capitol Hill plus several on Lower Queen Anne. Do you know those neighborhoods?"

"I've a pretty good idea. My GPS can get me to the address. When and where?"

"I've arranged for Frank Brewer to meet you just inside the door at the Lenora Apartments." Helen gave him the address. "Would you prefer four today or eleven tomorrow?"

"Eleven tomorrow is fine. I'll be there."

Helen hung up. She liked the sound of Carl Soyster. Her mental picture of him was a big spreading elm tree. She called Frank back and passed the meeting time and place to him.

The next applicant was Patrick Lowery. Helen called his employer, who was listed as the reference. She went through her familiar opening and then asked, "What can you tell me about Patrick that would make him a good tenant?"

"He'd be a great tenant. He's conscientious. He doesn't drink or smoke. He gets along with everybody, real friendly guy. His wife walked out on him, and they got divorced. She got custody, but he sees his kids every other weekend, Friday to Monday morning. He has two boys and a girl. They're young; the oldest is about eight. He's worked here for over ten years, a stable guy."

Helen was struck by the resemblance in the men she had just talked to. All of them used words sparingly to convey a sharp, informative picture. She thought about it. The question in her mind was, Do they do this because they're *men* or because they're men in *this* location, meaning the Pacific Northwest, or because they're *individually* exceptionally concise people, male or not. The men she had known best in Boston and Connecticut had been much more talkative, especially so. But perhaps those men had been exceptional in a different way. In their case, as for politicians, their way with language *was* their work.

"Thank you for talking to me. I'll get in touch with Patrick." She got off the line and immediately called Patrick Lowery.

"I can show you an apartment in Lower Queen Anne if you like that location," she said after introducing herself.

"That location sounds good. I work on Western Avenue down by Interbay, so it's a short commute. I could even walk it. Being that close to Seattle Center would be great for the kids, too. You know I need two bedrooms, right? I have kids that spend weekends with me."

"Yes, all the apartments in the building have two bedrooms,"

"I'm in. Let's do it."

Helen almost laughed, given her moments-old ruminations on male communication. "I could meet you later today at the apartment, inside the front door. It's on Olympic Place. Let me give you the address."

"I'll be there. I can take an hour off work. I'll skip my lunch hour. What works?"

"How about two-thirty or three?"

"Three it is. See you there."

It was ten o'clock, and Helen had only fifteen minutes before she needed to walk to the Seventh Street building to meet the other board members. No time for yoga, breathing, or meditation. She regretted that but hoped to get to it as soon as she returned.

When Alicia and Helen approached the square pale-yellow building on Seventh Street West, they saw Harriet, Frank, and Joe already walking around the outside.

"Hey, Alicia, Helen," called out Joe. "We're talking about these little yards. Do you think they're big enough to fence off, or will it look funny?"

"I wouldn't fence them," said Alicia. "I'd mark them off with a row of skinny thick evergreen bushes to give privacy. Then we could put in the look of a small English country garden but use green ground cover and plants like oat grass. Put them in thick. Make it low maintenance. Think hosta, lots and lots of it. Add some bulbs for some color. Maybe tulips, daffodils, crocus, day lilies. Then add a wooden bench or a couple of metal chairs that wouldn't rust out. Put in a slate patio for an outdoor grill. Doesn't need to be big, maybe six by four feet. Tell all of the tenants they have to take care of it and give them an instruction sheet. Have George Pendergast check on the yards once a month when he comes for a visit."

"Done," said Joe. "Let's go in. Two of the places are vacant now, and the other two have leases still active, two months on one, four months on the other. They're all alike, as Frank said, so we only need to look at one."

The five board members went into a unit. The front door opened directly into the living room. The unit was carpeted in a gray shag that was spotted and stained. The walls were painted beige, faded and sad looking. "Oh, dear," sighed Alicia. Helen agreed. The atmosphere in the home was depressing. They went into the other rooms.

"The bedroom are a nice size," said Harriett. "The kitchen is great. The eat-in space is good for kids to sit and do homework or make a puzzle or something while Mom's right there fixing lunch and watching them. I like that. And the windows are good as to size, let in a lot of light. But they're single pane. That lets in too much cold air, and it's drafty. I think we should put in really good windows. It's pricey but makes such a difference."

"Good point. Done. What about the flooring?" Joe asked as he made notes in a small spiral notebook he kept tucked into his shirt pocket.

"I'm thinking bamboo flooring throughout," said Frank. "It's easy to keep clean; it's indestructible, looks good, environmentally correct."

"What's not to like?" said Joe. "Any comments, ladies?"

"The color," said Alicia. "It's available in several, from blond to a fairly dark brown, and a chestnut, if I remember correctly. We need to pick a color that goes well with the wall color we select and those kitchen counters and even the bathrooms. Then we can run the flooring in every room."

"This bathroom has blue tub, sink, and toilet," said Harriet. "Do you think all of them are blue? I think ivory for the walls, with chestnut for the floors to warm them up. How would that work for the kitchen?" Harriet was thinking as she talked. "I see this counter is gray, that wouldn't be so bad with ivory. But the counter is pretty bad. Look at the burn marks on it."

Frank picked up on Harriet's comment. "We can replace the counters for not much money. We don't need granite. The new melamine or Formica-like products are really good. We could just go with ivory."

"But then the counters will fade right into the cabinets if we paint them ivory. It sounds dull," Harriet mused. "You know," she opened a cabinet door. "These cabinets are solid wood; they're not the cheap stuff. We could have them sanded down and refinished, bring them back to natural wood. Now that, I think, would be smashing."

"Fine, but let's tell the contractor to do that right off the bat, see if he can restore them well enough." Joe made a note. "Anybody know if

I'll be able to use Patten on this? Or should I go back to the outfit that just did the Lower Queen Anne building?"

"Drew just finished with the duplex, the first side. We could move him to this job next," Helen said. "If our current tenant there is happy, we can just leave him in there, put one of our people in the new side, and wait for the other unit remodel until this building gets done and either duplex person moves out. Then upgrade the older unit."

"We can do that, or we can start looking for another contractor if you don't want the guy who did Lower Queen Anne. Sooner or later, at the rate we're growing, we might need a new guy anyway." Joe looked around for comments.

"I have a couple of people I could call on," said Frank. "But I'd rather hold off if we can. Drew's so good, and he doesn't require much oversight. How about this: Helen talks to the current tenant, sees if he wants to stay where he is without an upgrade. If he's good with it, we'll get Drew started on this one. Or maybe he could hire some more people and take on two jobs at once."

"Good," Joe said. "Let's try to keep Drew if we can. I'll leave that to you and Helen." The group continued to walk around the unit and make suggestions and comments. Joe agreed to be the point man on the project. Frank said he would get together with Drew if Helen would have the talk with the current tenant. It was after noon when they completed the work. The others all agreed to go to lunch together. Helen begged off, citing her meeting with Patrick Lowery and her tenant screening tasks.

She returned to her apartment and thought about taking a break but realized she still needed to work on the tenant list. So far, she had arranged only for two, and the pile contained at least thirty more. She set a timer on her microwave to go off in an hour as she did not want to forget the appointment with Patrick Lowery at two-thirty. With a sandwich in one hand and a pen in the other, Helen rapidly went through applications. She found one more man she thought would work for the Lower Queen Anne building, Jeff Daniels. Mr. Daniels was the father of Katie, age seven. He was employed full time as a building engineer at Swedish Hospital. While the Capitol Hill building would make for a shorter commute, there were no longer any vacancies. Pam's husband

James Butler had finally called to tell Pam he would like the apartment, and Helen had already filled the other units.

"Hello," Helen said, and introduced herself to a stranger for the fifth time that day. She talked to Mr. Daniels and then his boss at Swedish. She decided he would be a good tenant and called him again to arrange a meeting. He was anxious to see the apartment and agreed to meet at four, an hour after her meeting with Patrick Lowery.

"Kenneth, it's Helen," she said a moment later.

"Well, well, I finally made it to a first name basis. You just made my day. What's up?"

"I have two men meeting me at the Lower Queen Anne building, one at three and one at four. I'm pretty sure they're both going to be tenants. Would you be able to see the first one, name's Patrick Lowery, if I send him in for the lease agreement without coming along? Then I'd come with the second man later."

"Will do. I'll have a couple of agreements printed out and ready to go."

"Thank you, *Kenneth*. I'll see you sometime round five, I expect."

"Yes, *Helen*, I'll be here waiting." He could hear her smile, and he smiled, too.

Helen arrived at the Lower Queen Anne building just in time to meet her first of the two potential male tenants. He introduced himself, and they entered the building.

"My wife left me and took the kids. I went to court to get visitation, so I need to think about space for them." Patrick Lowery was confirming what Helen had already heard from his boss. She was opening the door to one of the rear apartments at the Lower Queen Anne building.

"This one is good because it's quieter, but it doesn't get as much light. And the rooms are a bit smaller, overall, than up front." Helen wanted to tell him all of the disadvantages the foundation members had talked about.

"I like this; it has a really good feel to it," said Patrick, walking around the living room. "This room is plenty big. I have a man-sized TV and a recliner. Other than that, I'd just put the couch in here. Let's look at the bedrooms." They did so.

"This bigger one, I'd put in bunk beds. My sons could sleep here; they're five and eight. My girl, she's six, I'd put her in my room, and I'd take the couch. Where I am now, it's one bedroom, and I take the floor. It's just the three nights and only every other week. We'd be fine in here together. Lots of room for their toys too. I could even keep a couple of bikes in the boys' room. Yeah, this is a good fit. How much?"

"It depends on your pay stubs. How much do you pay now?"

"I'm at twelve hundred, but they say it'll go up in two months. Right now, my lease is expired, and I'm on a month-to-month arrangement. I make just over fifty thousand a year."

"Well, we won't charge more than twelve hundred, I can guarantee you that. Mr. Osborne will have to run the numbers for us. We never take more than twenty percent of take-home, and it goes down from there. We'll need to know your child support payments and debt load to come up with the final figures."

"Done deal. I really like this place."

Helen heard the main entrance door open and remembered she had not locked it behind herself when she and Patrick entered the building.

"Hello? Anybody here?"

Helen stepped out of the apartment and saw a very tall, well-muscled man about thirty years old.

"I'm early," he added as he spotted Helen.

"Mr. Daniels?"

"Right. Want me to wait outside?"

"No, come on in here. This is Patrick Lowery. He's just taken this apartment."

The two men shook hands.

"Does this mean I'm too late?"

"No, not at all. We've just renovated this building, and we've only one live-in so far. Do you want to look at this apartment? There're several more like it, all in the rear of the building. Then we have bigger ones at the front. Mr. Lowery, do you mind if we wait a few minutes so Mr. Daniels can look?"

"No problem. And call me Patrick or Pat, either one."

"I'm Jeff. And I can already tell you I'm taking one of these. Love the building, great architecture. And you said on the phone it has all new wiring and plumbing. That's what I like to hear. Plus, my daughter will go ape being this close to the center. The ballet, the festivals, the art classes, she's going to think she went to heaven."

"How old is your girl? Mine's six."

"Katie just turned eight. She lives with me full time. Her mom moved to South Carolina with the jerk she married."

"Ah heer ya," drawled Patrick. The men both looked at the floor and laughed.

It dawned on Helen that they would likely become friends as well as neighbors. "Well, why don't we all go to the office and fill in the lease agreements? Mr. Osborne can give you keys so you can move in whenever you want."

As they walked back up the hill, the men talked. They decided to rent a truck big enough for both men's furnishings and move in at the same time so they could help each other carry the heavy items. By the time they all got to Mr. Pierce's office, the men were practically brothers.

Helen got home in time to change, shower, and have a bowl of soup. Then she grabbed her coat and keys and walked out again. When she was halfway down Queen Anne Hill, she saw Gerard leave his apartment building and turn onto the sidewalk about a block ahead of her. By the time they both reached the bottom, he stopped at a light, and she caught up.

"This is embarrassing," she said. "I feel as if I'm stalking you."

"Well, if you're going where I'm going, how about we walk there together?"

They walked for ten minutes without speaking. Then Gerard said, "My home is in Michigan. The company I work for bought a company here in Seattle. I'm the head of the transition effort to integrate the new into ours. My company rented a corporate apartment for me, where I live while I'm here."

Five minutes later, Helen said, "I moved here two years ago. I lived in Connecticut."

They went to the meeting and walked out together.

"I wonder if you would have lunch with me on Sunday now and again?" Gerard asked. "That gets to be a long day for me."

Helen thought about it. He might be telling her in code that he needed help on Sundays to resist alcohol. If that was it, she had an obligation. "I have an appointment this Sunday at 10:30. It's in Issaquah and will take an hour. That, plus travel time, would get me back here around noon."

"How about brunch at one?"

"OK. Where shall we meet?"

"How about Peso's on Lower Queen Anne? I love the food there."

"Me too. I'll look for you around one o'clock."

They walked the rest of the way home without talking.

❧ ❧ ❧

On Saturday evening, Helen drove to Kirkland to meet Norm Easton. Mr. Easton's home was a 1970s ranch set on a fairly large lot. The driveway sloped down from the street, and the house was built on the hill, sloping down with a walk-out basement in back. Helen noticed the basketball court on the lower yard as she walked up the driveway and then the sidewalk to the front door. The house reminded her very much of the one on the east side of Magnolia that Pam and James Butler had lived in before moving to the Lenora.

Mr. Easton met Helen at the door. He was medium height, medium weight, had medium brown hair and blue eyes. He showed her into the living room, which was tastefully decorated in taupe and navy blue, with a large tan leather couch. It was a masculine room but was softened by pillows on the couch, some lamps with warm copper bases, and draperies of blue and copper stripes. They sat in two navy linen wing chairs that flanked a side table made of teak legs with a round southeast Asian pounded-brass top.

"This is a lovely room," Helen commented.

"Thank you. I had my sister help me. My wife took the furniture that we used to have in here. I like this better, to tell the truth." Norm Easton had a pleasing voice with an open and pleasant face.

"Would you like to start by telling me about when and where you and your wife met?" Helen started the interview in her usual way. She proceeded to ask questions about social background and the marriage and then started on the harder issues.

"In your statement to the court, you wrote about your wife having an issue with alcohol. When did this problem first come to your attention?"

"Good question," he paused. "Let me think. It came on gradually. We often had a drink before dinner and even a glass of wine *with* dinner. I'd say maybe five years ago, something like that, she'd already be having her cocktail when I got home from work. Then she'd have another with me. And we'd go through a bottle of wine at dinner, not just two glasses. But I still had only the one. Even then, it didn't seem out of hand. But we started arguing a lot about then. She'd get mad at me for not picking up my clothes or not filling her car up with gas or something. And she'd fight with Garth. He was about ten or so, and I noticed he started avoiding her. If she came into the room, he'd leave. I put it down to him growing up and wanting to separate a little, which I figured was normal.

"Two years ago, it got bad. She'd be flat-out drunk when I got home. She'd rant and rave and even throw things. Two or three nights a week, she'd skip dinner. I'd pick up take-out for Garth and me. Half the time, she'd just pass out by nine at night."

"What did you do about the situation?"

"What I did was not enough, and not soon enough, obviously. We were in over our heads before I woke up. She'd always spent pretty much whatever I made. She used to blow it at the casinos. I got that stopped. I started putting the maximum in Roth IRAs, and the same with my retirement program at work. I funded Garth's college with the state program. I protected us financially as well as I could. About a year ago, maybe a little more, I found out she'd run up big credit card bills—at one point we owed over ten thousand dollars. She applied for about five credit cards without me knowing and kept the bills from me so I didn't know about the debt for months. I got the cards canceled, and she started just writing checks everywhere. We're talking clothes, jewelry, lots of bars and restaurants. She was going out at lunch and drinking with her friends, and she'd get drunk and pick up the tab. This was three or four times a week. At that point I changed checking accounts and started putting my pay check in a new one.

"She got madder than holy hell at me. By then, we were sleeping in separate rooms and seldom saw each other. I came home one night, and she was in the kitchen. She was cooking pasta sauce for Garth for dinner. When I came into the kitchen, she threw the sauce at me, pan and all. I got burned right here." He pushed up the sleeve of his sweater, and she saw a red scar four inches long, one inch wide, on his forearm.

"Did you seek treatment?"

"Yeah, I went to the walk-up medical clinic in the shopping center; it was about six at night. They cleaned it and put on an antibiotic cream and gave me a shot and a prescription for a pain killer."

"I'll want you to sign a release for me to talk to the clinic. Is that OK with you?"

"Sure, no problem."

"I'll want to talk to Garth. I see from the court papers that he spends one week with your wife in Issaquah and one with you here. How does that work with his schooling?"

"When he's with me, I take him to school in Issaquah in the morning and drop him off. He goes to his mom's apartment after school, and I pick him up and bring him back here."

"That's quite a commute."

"It is, but that's kind of a funny thing. He really talks to me in the car. In fact, we talk more now than we ever have."

"Is this his week with you?"

"It is. He's over at the neighbor's house now."

"How would he feel if you called and asked him to come home so I could talk to him?"

"I don't think he'll mind. I told him he might have to talk to some-one, so he's kind of ready." Norm called his son and asked him to return home. Within minutes, a tall young man with brown hair entered the living room. He strongly resembled his father.

"Hello, Garth. My name is Helen. Could you show me around the house? I need to see your bedroom while I'm here."

Garth looked at his father, who nodded. "Sure, happy to," Garth said.

"I'm going to run to the store if you don't mind," said Norm. "I'm sure you two will be better off without me for a bit." Helen was grateful he had suggested leaving as she would have otherwise had to ask him at least to leave the room while she talked to Garth.

Garth took Helen down the central hall to his bedroom on the right. The room was neat, with the bed made and no clothing on the floor. Helen noted the desk with schoolbooks and a laptop. She saw sports banners on the wall and trophies on a shelf. A skateboard was on the floor of the closet. "Do you keep a lot of your things here?" she asked.

"Yeah, everything. I only have clothes at my mom's."

"Why is that?"

"Because I don't trust her. She might throw my stuff away or ruin it or something."

"Why would she do that?"

"Because she's a drunk." Garth shook his head with disgust when he spit out the answer.

"Do you know that yourself, or did someone tell you that?"

He looked at her with much the same expression. "No one had to tell me. I'm not stupid. She smells, she falls down, she vomits, she passes out, the garbage is full of empties. What does it take to figure it out?"

Helen felt very sorry for Garth. "Why do you spend every other week with her?"

"Because the court says I have to. It's not my idea, for sure."

"If you stayed here, you'd need to change schools."

"That's no problem. I like this one better anyway. I was here before." As they walked back to the living room, Garth said, "Are you going to ask me about my parents and the fights and stuff?"

"No, you don't need to tell me about that. What you can tell me about is yourself. Maybe your favorite classes at school, what activities or sports you're in, who your friends are, favorite teacher, that sort of thing."

Garth looked relieved at not having to talk about his parents and went straight to the other topics. He had a lot to say and was still talking when his father returned.

Helen stood up. "Good timing. We've just finished," she said. Then, shaking his hand as she told Garth goodbye, she walked to the door with Norm. "You've got a great son, there," she said as she walked out.

"I do. And I know it," said Norm.

Helen drove home and immediately typed her notes into the computer. She did some laundry and then sat in a chair in her living room. It was after nine that night when she awoke. After eating an omelet with cheese and tomatoes, she cleaned her kitchen, brushed her teeth, and went to bed.

⁂ ⁂ ⁂

Sunday morning, Helen got up early so she could shower and eat a decent breakfast before driving to Issaquah. When she arrived at Marilyn Easton's modest apartment, it was still raining. Marilyn met her at the door and took her into the dining area, which was separated from the kitchen by a countertop. Helen could see the sink full of dirty dishes. The apartment was permeated with the smell of cigarette smoke and burned toast. Marilyn reeked of alcohol. She looked much older than the thirty-five years Helen knew to be her age.

"What do you need to know?" Marilyn asked. Her voice was raspy.

Helen started the same way she had with Norm, asking how the couple met and what the early years of the marriage were like. Marilyn told the same story Norm had, until Helen asked, "When did the marriage start to go bad?"

"When Norm decided his work was more important than me and Garth. He'd come home late; he'd sit in front of the TV; he'd basically ignore us. Weekends, it was just sports and more sports. He was no fun, never wanted to go out. Then he started getting on my case. One night he hit me, then threatened me with a knife."

"Did you call the police?"

"I thought about it. But he's the breadwinner. I didn't want him in jail or anything."

"Who did you talk to about this?"

"My friend Sharon."

"Where was Garth when this happened?"

"He was in bed; he didn't see nothing."

"Why do you think he hit you and threatened you with a knife?"

"He said it was because I was spending too much money. He took away the credit cards and switched banks on me. I think he was trying to control me by taking away my money."

"In what ways did he control you? Did he make you stay home, keep you from your friends, monitor your phone calls?"

"No, he just took the credit cards away from me. That's how he controlled me."

"Did you think you were spending too much?"

"No. I was just buying things I needed. Clothes, shoes, things like that. And I went out to lunch with my girlfriends once in a while. I had to do that or go crazy since Norm never wanted to go out. I needed to get out of the house sometimes."

"Did you work during the marriage?"

"No, we agreed when we got married that I could stay home. That was our deal. I'd stay home and take care of everything at the house, and he'd work."

"What about now? Are you working?"

"No. I figure if I work, he won't have to pay alimony or child support. So I'll wait 'til that all gets sorted out first."

"I'm sure you know Norm said you drink a lot. What can you tell me about your alcohol use?"

"Yeah, I drink. I'm an adult; it's not against the law to have a drink."

"How much do you drink?"

"Maybe a cocktail and a glass of wine or two."

"Do you ever get drunk?"

"Not much, and I never drive if I've had too much. I'm very responsible that way."

"Have you ever forgotten what you did the day before or had blackouts?"

"Yeah, well, I'm getting older, so I expect to forget some things. I've only had a couple blackouts, nothing serious."

"I have to ask you to have a substance abuse evaluation. That means going to a clinic for an interview and urine test. I'll give you a list of places to do that. It's part of what the judge ordered."

"Yeah, I know. I'll go do that next week."

"And I'll need you to sign some releases for me. I have to talk with the chemical-abuse counselor and get the results from the test. Also, I would like the names and numbers for two or three people you want me to talk to. They should be people who have known you for some time, and they should be able to talk about the relationship between you and Garth."

"You know Garth's not so happy with me right now. He's being a snotty teenager. It's normal for him to go through a stage of rebelling against me so you shouldn't put much stock in that."

"Yes, I understand about teenagers and how they sometimes behave."

Helen concluded the interview and got the signatures and collateral information she needed. She left the apartment and took deep breaths, enjoying the clean air after the musty, smoky air in the apartment. Even standing in the rain by the car was a relief.

She returned to her building two hours later, left the car in the underground parking garage, and walked down the hill to Peso's. She arrived only ten minutes late. When she entered the restaurant through the crowd gathered around the entry, she saw Gerard waving to her from a table. She joined him.

"Hello, I'm glad you made it," he said.

"Thank you. Sorry I was late. I could have run down the hill, I suppose, but I'd probably have fallen."

"I wouldn't want to have brunch with a fallen woman."

Helen laughed.

They ordered and talked about the news. Both knew something about the possibility of a major-league basketball team coming to Seattle, so they talked about that for a minute, then broadened to the pros and cons of major league sports in general. When brunch arrived, they ate and turned to another safe topic, the gridlock in Washington, DC. Then they talked about the presidential campaign and the victory of Barak Obama to a second term. After several tentative probes, being careful to say nothing too controversial, they discovered their political positions were similar. Then brunch was over, and they started the walk up the hill.

"Can I entice you to have dinner with me one night this week? I promise it's only a dinner. No obligations. No agenda. Just a dinner."

"In that case and with those provisos, I accept."

"Thursday?"

"Thursday. Yes."

"If I may, I'll walk you to your apartment building. I'll be there at six o'clock on Thursday evening. I'll get a reservation at Moorage, if you don't mind."

"I love Moorage; it's my favorite restaurant on the hill."

"Excellent; mine, too."

They walked up the hill, not talking again until they were at the door to the lobby of Helen's apartment.

"Nice building. I'll see you right here, Thursday, six o'clock."

"Yes, I'll be here. Goodbye until then." Helen turned and went into her building.

❧ ❧ ❧

It was five o'clock Wednesday evening. Dark had descended. Helen was sipping tea, standing at the window, watching the rain. The landline phone rang. "Helen here," she said.

"Helen, I'm not sure you remember me, but we met several times. I'm Stewart Prescott, your cousin by marriage. Uncle William asked me to call you. He doesn't want Aunt Catherine to know about this. He's in the hospital. He's dying of pancreatic cancer. It's vital to him that you come and talk to him. It's his last wish. He told me to tell you why he asked *me* to call. He said he knew if he had his attorney call, you would think it was about something it isn't. He needs desperately to talk with you. He told me to do whatever it takes to get you to come to him. I'm at a loss. I have no idea what it would take. Please, I'm begging you. Not on his behalf, on my own. He's desperate to see you. I know he can't die with any kind of peace unless he does. What can I say?"

Helen was quiet, frozen almost. She started to talk, but nothing came out. She breathed in and out. Four times, five times. She cleared her throat. "I don't know if I can do that."

"Please, whatever it takes. Anything. Do you need money? I can get the tickets; I can do it right now."

"No, I don't need money."

"What? An escort? I can come and get you. If you can't fly because of health, I'll get a private plane for you. What? Tell me. Anything."

"It's nothing like that. I need time to think about it."

"That's what I can't give you. He's fading. He's eighty-five, Helen. He's in the hospital to die, not to get treated. He's on a morphine drip for the pain. We're talking any day here. We don't have time."

"I just don't know."

"Helen, he's dying. If it were you, and you had one chance to talk to one person, wouldn't you want the person you choose to make an effort?"

"Yes, I would."

"Whatever is between you and Uncle William, I don't know or care what it is. It can't keep you from reaching out to him. Please. Let me call the airline and get tickets. Please let me do it. There's a red-eye straight here tonight. Please, Helen."

"Yes, I'll go."

She heard a huge sigh. "Thank you," he said softly. "Thank you. I'll call and get you a seat on the flight tonight if that's OK with you."

"Yes, I'll go tonight."

"I'll have a driver meet your plane. I'll get you a room at Parker House. I'll meet you there to take you to the hospital. Will that work for you?"

"Yes."

"Wonderful. Now, could you give me a cell number? We'll need to be able to reach each other while you're here. I'll give you my numbers if you have a pen." He waited for her to get pen and paper and write down the information. "And I'll call you back in a half-hour with the flight info. Helen, I can't tell you what this means to me. My father died twenty years ago, and Uncle William has been so good to me. This is something I can do for him. Thank you for helping me." He hung up.

Helen stood there, phone still in her hand, staring out the window. Soon the phone started beeping, telling her it was off the hook. She put the handset back down, and the beeping stopped. She stood, looking out the window. Half an hour later, when the phone rang, she was still staring out the window. This time when she answered, Stewart Prescott gave her the flight number and boarding time. "I'm sending a car to get you at nine o'clock. I need your address." Helen gave it to him. "I'll tell the driver to call you as he approaches so you can meet him on the street."

Helen hung up and moved to her bedroom. Everything she did was in slow motion. Her body felt so heavy she could hardly get it to move. She got a suitcase from her closet and started packing.

Much later, in the executive suite at Parker House, she could hardly recall the actual flight. It was morning in Boston, a very cold but very sunny January morning. The knock on the door was soft. She opened the door. Stewart Prescott was about fifty-five years old with gray hair. He was tall and distinguished, wearing a camel overcoat and a cashmere navy scarf and holding a pair of beautiful leather gloves, soft and supple. His face would have been handsome, and was, but a somber sadness hung on it, pulling it down.

"Hello, Helen, I'm Stewart," he said.

Stewart escorted Helen to the private room at Mass General. "I'll be around. Call me on my cell when you're ready to leave." He left her at the door to the room. She breathed deeply, then pushed the door open.

She walked to the side of the bed. William Henry Prescott III looked at her. He was alert, and if he had not been in the bed with an IV hooked to his arm, he would have looked like the powerful business and political figure that he was.

"Helen," his voice still had power and resonance, "thank you for coming. Please pull up a chair. Sit where I can see you." Still giving orders. Helen did as he asked.

"I've been thinking about this for years. In my head, I've been over and over what I could say to you. I owe you an explanation. Much more than that, of course. It's taken me thirty years to get to this place. By that, I mean a place where I can see clearly what I did. The damage I caused. How my pride and arrogance destroyed everything and everyone." He saw her face. "Helen, I need to say this. You need to hear this. Don't turn away. Truth is too hard to come by." He was interrupted by a nurse entering the room.

"I'm fine. I don't want to be disturbed. I've had the drug. I don't need anything. I need time alone with my daughter-in-law." The nurse withdrew without speaking. William turned back to Helen.

"I need to tell it from the beginning. Just listen, Helen. You don't need to say anything."

Since she had said nothing as yet and had no desire to say anything, this was an unnecessary comment.

"I think, when I look back on it all, it started when I was about forty. Robert's brother, William Jr., was starting college. Robert was only about seven years old then. The Vietnam War was going full blast; it was 1968. That was a pivotal year. Riots in the street. Burning flags and draft cards, protests on every college campus. Martin Luther King was assassinated that year. So was Bobby Kennedy. Somehow everything in life was huge, just sort of touched with this amazing weightiness. I was just making money. Lots of it, of course, as I was expected to do. The holy grail in our family for generations was to amass more and greater wealth. We lived for it. But now, with the country falling into chaos, it seemed crass. I thought about Joseph Kennedy and how he raised his sons to be president. He took a sordid beginning and created this whole myth. I wanted that." He stopped talking and sipped water from his cup.

Helen could see that he was reminiscing. It was as though he had forgotten her as he told his story.

"I forced William Jr. to join ROTC. He was a peaceful kid at heart. Never got into fights with other kids. Didn't like sports. He liked playing the piano and going to the theatre. But I forced him into ROTC. What a goddamned tyrant I was. Then, when he graduated, he went into the air force. I wanted him to be a fighter pilot. I was determined he should see combat. Needed it for a war record later, you see. PT 109 and all that shit. I planned for him to be this war hero, come back and run for political office. Never asked him what he wanted. He never fought me on any of it, just did what I told him." William closed his eyes. He breathed deeply, rested.

Helen rolled her shoulders and neck. She waited.

He opened his eyes. "William Jr. couldn't pass the physical for flight school. Some damn thing, I can't remember. Not serious. Like flat feet or color blindness. We talked it over, and I told him to go into intelligence. I knew, you see, that he could get to Vietnam if he got into the

544th ARTW. That's air recon. He could be in a B-52 on bombing runs. I knew all that. So that's what he did.

"The war was closing down. Nixon was going to get us out of there no matter what. Kissinger was running back and forth to Paris then. Peace talks. So this was going to work for me. William was trained and in the field, making flights, right on schedule. Then he got killed. Wasn't even in the air, a freak bomb or grenade or something lobbed into the air base. Just like that; it was all over." He gulped and sobbed, his shoulders heaving. He reached for the water and drank, closed his eyes. "Sorry," he murmured. "Still hurts." He rested.

Helen waited.

"It took a while for me to get over that. All of my dreams and plans, buried with my son. He never wanted any of it … Did I tell you that? He did it all to please me. To make me proud. What a prick of a father I was. But I wasn't done. Remember, Robert was only eleven when William Jr. got killed. So, you see, I still had a chance. Still had skin in the game. I could still be the father of the president.

"So, I started over. I paid attention to Robert. I'd never done that before. It was going along pretty well. Robert wasn't as smart as William. But he had more charm. That was just as good. Remember, it's politics we're talking about. Nobody gives a shit about smart; they want charisma. We were still in good shape. But when Robert was sixteen, something happened. It was like a switch got turned off or something. He started getting moody. Then he'd be higher than a kite. He'd steal liquor, and he and his friends would party all night. It went on and on. We thought he was just a teenager, acting stupid. Then one night he overdosed on his mom's Valium. We thought he'd just made a mistake. But the doctor in emergency said he'd been talking about suicide. We had him taken to a small private hospital. Very discrete. No records kept, that sort of thing. I figured if we kept a lid on it, got it all fixed, you see, the plan could still work." He stopped again. His hands trembled. His face was gray.

Helen stood.

"I think this is enough for now. You need to rest and eat."

"Don't go. I'm not done. I need to do this." He was trying to reach for her, hold her in place.

She put her hand on his. "I'll be back. I promise you. I'll go back to the hotel and rest. I'll be back."

"When?"

"In four hours. Give me four hours to rest. Then I'll come back. I promise. I swear it to you."

"OK then. Four hours. No more."

"No more," Helen said.

She left the room and called Stewart. He came to take her back to the hotel. He said he'd pick her up in time to get back to the hospital in four hours. Helen went into her hotel room, arranged for a wake-up call, and fell onto the bed, still in the clothes she'd worn on the airplane.

Four hours later, Helen was sitting in the chair next to William's bed. He had revived. He was back in command. He took up where he had left off.

"So, Robert got treatment. We got the diagnosis. They called it manic-depressive disorder, back then. Now it's called bi-polar disorder. Don't know why they change the name. They're no better at treating it today than they were back then. Anyway, there was the medication. We watched Robert like a hawk, made sure he never skipped his meds. They didn't make the problem go away or anything. Just made the dips and rises more moderate. Think about taking the Rocky Mountains and turning them into the rolling hills of Virginia. That's about what it's like. We got him into college. He started getting a little worse, but he was still fairly stable.

"By then I was having doubts. I could see problems ahead. I knew Robert could never get any higher than maybe municipal council or something. Not even mayor of a city. That hurt. Bad. It took months for me to accept it. Then Robert met you. He was what, twenty-one years old? When Catherine and I first saw you, we were ecstatic. You were this young, beautiful, totally innocent thing … like an angel. And you seemed to really like Robert. Well, my hopes suddenly revived. If I couldn't be the father of a president, maybe I could be the grandfather of a president. God, I was an asshole. All about me. Me, me, me. Unbelievable. Just saying it makes me sick." He stopped, rested, sipped water.

Helen waited. She was very good at waiting.

"We had to keep you from learning about Robert's illness. We coached him. We reminded him every day not to say anything. We told him to stay on his meds. I took him away for weekends so you wouldn't have long stretches with him. And it worked. He asked you to marry him. We rushed the wedding, and there we were. Catherine had worked as hard as I had on the whole damned, demented project. I can't believe we did it. Then we started waiting for the pregnancy. I'm surprised we didn't have you secretly tested for fertility before the marriage. We were sick enough to do it if we'd thought of it." He closed his eyes again.

"So, you finally got pregnant. Twins, yet. Gave me two chances again. I was back where I had started. And I still had time to make it happen. Then the boys were born." He started sobbing. Tears rolled down his cheeks.

Helen, tears in her eyes as well, stood up. She got tissues and dabbed at his face and at hers. She held his hand. He squeezed hers. They didn't talk. Seconds passed and turned to minutes. William finally breathed very deeply. Helen did so as well. She resumed her seat. William opened his reddened eyes.

"Oh my God. I know what I did Helen. Wish to God I'd been a different man. I ruined so many lives. My own is the least of it. Forgive me, Helen. Please forgive me."

"I do. I forgive you."

He closed his eyes.

Helen left the room.

Stewart came when summoned and took her back to the hotel. "I want to leave tonight, Stewart. William and I are done. Get me on the evening flight to Seattle. Please."

He agreed, and they drove the rest of the way to the hotel without speaking. She took a hot shower and then climbed into bed. She knew she needed to meditate and breathe and do yoga. But she couldn't. She gave in to temptation and escaped into sleep.

Two hours later, the telephone woke her up. "Helen, it's Derrick. Stewart told me you were in town. He said you were leaving at eight tonight. I want to see you. Will you let me take you to an early dinner?"

"No, Derrick, I'm exhausted. Stewart must have told you why I'm in town."

"He did. But I really want to see you. Please. Maybe just tea downstairs in the hotel? Just an hour? Please?"

"OK, Derrick. Just an hour. Meet me in the lounge in thirty minutes." She got up, brushed her hair and teeth, and put on some clothes. It was early evening when she went down to the lounge.

Derrick was above average in height, with thick dark brown hair. Helen thought he was a very attractive man. His smile was infectious, and she smiled back at him when he stood to hug her. Everything about him was warm, from his hug to his burgundy shirt to his deep brown suit.

"I wanted to bring Danica; she wants so much to meet you. But I could tell you were exhausted so I told her maybe next time. You're tired; I see that. But I just had to see your face. Danica said next time you come she really wants you to stay at the house."

"We'll see. I don't know that I'll come back. Boston holds nothing good for me."

"I know. I know that. I understand. It's hard, Helen, to want you in my life and know you don't want to live near me. But I understand why you feel this way. We thought, Danica and I, that we could take a summer vacation to Washington State. She and the kids are planning it. That's part of why I wanted to see you. They have maps and brochures like you wouldn't believe. They want to go to the San Juan Islands, rent a place there for a week. And we want you to be with us. Darren asked if you knew how to kayak. I'd told the kids how athletic you were when we were young. I remember you took me in a canoe, at least once. How old was I?"

"You were maybe seven or so. I was about sixteen, then, as I recall. And I took you in a rowboat, too. Remember that? You fell out."

He laughed. "I do remember. I was reaching for something I'd dropped."

"It was that baseball cap that was too big for you."

"That's right! I still have that hat! It's a Red Sox hat." They both smiled at the shared memory.

"We were thinking after the islands we'd go to Mt. Rainier for a few days. Danica wants to get us rooms at Paradise. You know where that is?"

"Sure. I love it up there. I've gone there the last two summers and stayed at Paradise to hike. It's so wonderful. And so impossible to describe."

"So, will you join us for the San Juans and for Paradise? Renee said she wants a room right next to you, unless you want one off on your own."

"I want one in the annex. They're the only ones with private baths. The lodge ones are great, but the bath is shared. Sometimes it's way down the hall, depending on your room. The food, by the way, is excellent."

"So … this means you'll join us?"

"Derrick, you're a sneak! You did this when you were little. You'd talk to me about something, all innocent like, and then somehow I'd end up agreeing to do something I'd never intended to do."

"Yeah, it still works. My big sister, still falling for the same routine."

They both laughed, and Helen shook her head slowly. "I'd forgotten how much fun you were."

"I never forgot how much fun you were. You were my mom, my sister, and my best friend. All in one."

Helen's eyes watered. Derrick reached for her hand and held it. They were silent for several minutes.

"Say you'll come." Derrick spoke very quietly. Helen nodded, and squeezed his hand.

❧ ❧ ❧

Three hours later, Helen boarded the airplane and took her seat in the first-class section, as she had on the earlier flight. She had the window seat with no one next to her. She suspected Stewart had paid for both seats to ensure her privacy. She closed her eyes and tried to relax. It was hopeless as she had known it would be. Her mind was no longer in her control. The talks with William and Derrick were so heavy, so full of emotion. They were overwhelming her defenses. She wanted to hide in the ashram and chant with the fellow devotees. She wanted to escape into the nothingness.

The flight attendant came by with a tray full of champagne flutes, offering the tray with an inviting smile. Helen took a flute.

"Mrs. Prescott … Mrs. Prescott … wake up." She heard the voice and felt a tug on her blouse. She heard, as though from a distance, several voices.

*we need to get her off the plane everybody else has gone call for a wheelchair is she ill has she had a heart attack call the pilot what's the problem she's not sick she's drunk we can't leave her here grab her arm and pull her get her carry-on and her purse we don't want any liability get the guy with the wheelchair to help where will we take her we don't want liability the airline doesn't want responsibility why did you give her so much I don't think I did she must have taken it when my back was turned my God how many bottles did she drink I see at least four and I gave her two drinks myself and she had champagne at the beginning let's get her in the chair damn drunks where will I take her we can't leave her sitting in a wheelchair stupid cow get her out of the airport we don't need this drunk slut get her away from the airport check her purse does she have money get a taxi just the way I wanted to spend my night what if she gets robbed or murdered I hate nights like this we need to avoid liability a private car use the service we use we could give her our car yes good idea give the driver extra check her purse see what she's got did she have a checked bag why on my date night get her in the car give him the address off her license tell him to just leave her at the door or something here's keys give him a big tip there're hundreds give him two hundred tell him to get her inside a door she has keys tell him to figure it out that's what we're giving him money for let's hurry up and get rid of her*

Helen felt cold air on her face and someone trying to stand her up. She was so tired. Then movement. Then sleep. Then cold air again. Then being pulled and falling and getting picked up. Outside, inside. Bing bing. She was leaning against a wall, then a lighted hall. She was left standing by a door. She had a key. She tried to put it in the lock. It wouldn't fit. She was so tired. She went to sleep.

"Helen, Helen, get up." She opened her eyes and saw the door next to her head open. She felt pulling. Alicia's face floated above her. "Come on, Helen, help me out." Alicia pulled, and Helen tried to stand. She got to her knees, and Alicia pulled her up. She was standing. Alicia got her arm all the way around Helen's waist and started pulling her down the hall. The walls slid around, up and down and around and around.

"I'm sick. Going to be sick."

"In here." Alicia pulled her into the guest bathroom and led her to the toilet. Helen went to her knees and started vomiting into the toilet. Over and over. She groaned. She started crying. Alicia got a towel from the other bathroom and put it in the sink. She turned on the cold water, saturated the towel, rung it out, and starting wiping Helen's face and neck.

"I want to die. Let me die."

"Not until you sleep. Come on." Alicia tugged Helen, got her into a standing position, and guided her into the bedroom. She dropped her on the bed. Then she took the cushions from the floor and rolled up a small blanket and propped Helen on her side. She covered her with a blanket and left her in the room alone.

Two days later, midmorning, Alicia was leaving the building when a man standing near the entrance stopped her. "Do you know Helen?" he asked. She looked him up and down. Nice coat, good leather shoes, well shined. Hair trimmed. Shaved. Good looking.

"I do know Helen." Noncommittal.

"Thank God. I've been out here for three hours. I'm so worried about Helen. I don't have any way to reach her. Is she all right? We were supposed to meet Thursday for dinner. Is she sick?"

"In a way," Alicia said slowly.

"Oh no. Is she hung over? Is she on a binge?"

Alicia was shocked. "Why would you say that?"

"Just tell me. I have to know. I can help her."

"She came home from the airport two nights ago, late. Drunk. Now she's sober," Helen said. "She isn't talking or eating. She stays in her room. I hear her chanting, and I smell something, incense, I think. Sometimes I hear her moving around."

"Does she respond when you call out to her?"

"Only twice. Just said she was fine. What's going on? I'm worried sick."

"She'll be fine. She needs time. Do you have any food for her?"

"I was just on my way to the store. I'm trying to think what might appeal to her."

"I'll come with you. I know what she needs. I'll make it." He was very decisive, and Alicia felt he knew exactly what he was talking about.

"OK. Let's go. I have a grocery bag to carry it home in."

An hour later, Gerard was in Helen's kitchen, chopping vegetables, when Alicia's phone rang. "Yes? Good. Bring it up in the freight elevator. The code is 4713." She went to the door and propped it open. "That's the Macy's truck. I got tired of trying to sleep on the floor so I called yesterday and told them I needed a couch in a hurry. It's here."

Three men came down the hall with a large couch, and Alicia showed them where she wanted it placed in the room. They put it there and left. Alicia looked at it from several angles. Then she went to her own apartment and returned with pillows, which she placed on the couch. She went back to her room and returned with two blankets folded up in a large basket. She placed it on the floor across from the couch. Satisfied, she joined Gerard in the kitchen. "What's cookin'?" she asked.

Gerard laughed. "I'm making a chicken broth with that stewing hen I bought. I put it in the pot and added the organic broth so it'll be extra strong. Then I added onions, carrots, celery, and garlic that I sautéed with some herbs."

"It smells fantastic."

"That's the idea. We want the aroma to be seductive enough to pierce Helen's shield. So far, she's barely conscious we exist. We need her to eat and drink. Then she'll gradually come around."

"How do you know this?"

"It's a 'been there, done that' sort of thing." He looked through the cabinets and drawers. "Help me look for a tray. I found a tea pot and a mug. I need a small bowl, too." They looked but could not find a tray.

"I'll go get one," said Alicia. She went to her apartment and returned with a bright red metal tray. Gerard put a small pot of tea on the tray with the mug next to it. Then he put two small mandarin oranges in a bright blue bowl. A piece of toast, buttered, was on a matching blue plate. The toast was cut into four triangles. Alicia put a folded cloth napkin on the tray.

"OK, let me see if this works." He went down the hall. "Helen." He said it quietly while knocking softly on the door. "It's Gerard. I'm going to put a tray inside the room for you." He opened the door, knelt, and pushed the tray far enough into the room so that he could then pull the door closed. He went back into the kitchen.

"Now what?" asked Alicia.

"We wait," said Gerard. He started working with the vegetables again.

"What's Helen doing?"

"I can't say exactly, but it's bound to be some version of what I call contemplative prayer."

"How long?"

"As long as it takes."

"I haven't told anybody. I've been staying in the apartment. When the phone rings I take messages or give people a story. I've been frantic, not knowing what to do." Alicia was relieved to have someone share her worry.

"That's good. We don't want to make it harder for her to face people when she comes back."

"So, what next?"

"Same thing. One of us needs to be here all of the time. What's your schedule?"

"I don't have anything I need to do that I can't fob off onto someone else. That's what I've been doing so far."

"Good. You can go home whenever you need to change or shower or take care of your own business. I'm good for at least two days, with a short trip home for clothes and supplies. I can call in and cancel my work."

"You'll do that? How well do you know Helen?"

"I barely know her. We went out for brunch once. But that's not important. Everybody I work with knows I need time now and again. They're good with it."

Gerard checked his pot. "I think this broth is finished. I'm going to strain it so I can give her a cup. Then I'll make vegetable soup with the rest of it. Do you know if she has any cheesecloth?"

"I'll just go down the hall and get some from my place. It'll be faster than going through the kitchen again." She left and then returned with the cheesecloth. Gerard located a ladle. He spooned some broth from the large pot into the cloth he had spread over a measuring bowl with a spout. After straining the broth, he poured it from the measuring bowl into a small sauce pan. He set it on the back burner, turned to a low simmer.

"That will concentrate it, which will be even better for her."

He went down the hall to Helen's room. The tray was outside the door. The oranges and toast were gone, leaving peels and an empty plate. The tea pot was empty. The mug was gone. Gerard picked up the tray and took it back to the kitchen.

"This is good. I'll wait a half-hour and then take her a cup of broth."

He went to the living room and sat on the couch. "Any books or magazines around here?"

"No, but you can go look around my place. There's lots of reading material there. It's right across from the elevator." Alicia handed him a key. He soon returned with several books and magazines. He sat in the living room on the couch, put his feet on Helen's ottoman, and opened a book. Alicia sat in Helen's chair for a while.

After ten minutes of silence, Alicia said, "I'm going home to change and shower and take a nap. See you in a couple of hours. Is that all right?"

"Sure. I'll be here."

Alicia left.

When she returned three hours later, she said, "I'm sorry. I fell asleep and just got up."

"No problem."

"How's Helen?"

"She's fine. She had her broth. I gave her some vegetable soup a while ago."

"Has she said anything?"

"Not yet."

"What can I do to help?"

"Maybe you could stay while I walk down to my place. I'll bring an overnight kit and change of clothes. Are there any towels and soap? That guest bath is empty."

"I know. I've been going back to mine. While you're gone I'll stock hers from my place. I'll bring towels and a bathmat while I'm at it. How about shampoo and soap; want your own or shall I provide?"

"I'll do that. See you in a bit. Do you have a key to the main door so I don't need to buzz or anything?"

"Yes, take Helen's keys. They're in that basket on the entry-hall table." Gerard picked up the keys and left. He was back in an hour, carrying a gym bag. He went into the bathroom. "I'm going to shower now," he announced, and closed the door.

Alicia sat in the living room watching the rain dribble against the window. She heard the shower and then an electric toothbrush or shaver or something. When Gerard returned, he was wearing a beautiful thick silk robe, Asian, with a wide belt. He had pajamas and slippers on. "Sorry to be so informal, but I plan to sleep on the couch, and I hate sleeping in my clothes."

"Fine with me. Don't blame you. Do you think Helen would mind if I went home and slept in my own bed?"

"Helen doesn't care. She barely knows we're here. Think of her as being in hell fighting with the devil. When she wins, she'll come out. She'll be worn out. She won't care what we're wearing or what we've been doing. 'Course, she may notice her empty living room has a big beautiful couch, but that's your problem, not mine." He smiled at her.

Alicia laughed and then left.

❧ ❧ ❧

It was Monday morning. Gerard made an omelet with vegetables for Helen's breakfast, added toast with jam and a glass of tomato juice, made spicy with hot sauce and Worcestershire, and fixed a pot of black tea. He went to Helen's bedroom door, knocked, knelt, and pushed the tray into the room. Then he closed the door. It had become routine by now. He had gradually increased the amount of food he placed on the tray over the weekend. This was the first complete meal of average portion size.

Two hours later, Helen emerged, carrying the tray. She took it to the kitchen. "Good morning," she said.

Gerard was reading the paper in the living room. "Good morning," he responded. He noticed the dark circles around the eyes and the gaunt appearance of Helen's face. She looked thinner, too. It was all to be expected, as he knew only too well.

"Thank you," she said.

"You're welcome," he responded.

Helen fixed a cup of tea and went into the living room. She looked at the couch. "Nice. Is that yours?"

"No, I think it's yours. Alicia had it delivered. We prefer this to the floor."

"It's beautiful. Alicia has good taste."

"She does."

Helen sat in her chair and sipped her tea. Gerard continued reading the paper.

"It was a one-off," Helen said after a silence of some minutes. Gerard put the paper aside and looked at Helen. "The last time was 1992. I know what caused it. I know what I have to do to prevent it."

Gerard nodded. "Enough said." He waited.

"What day is it?"

"Monday. You came home from the airport Thursday night."

"Thank you."

He nodded.

Alicia entered the apartment. She came into the living room. Seeing Helen, she smiled. "Welcome home," she said.

"Thank you. It's nice to be back. That's a beautiful couch."

"I thought it looked good in here; matches the chair."

The two women smiled at each other. "You ready for some news?" Alicia asked. When Helen nodded, she continued. "Let me tell you what's been going on at Lower Queen Anne. The Hudson kids, Ben and Christy, moved in last week, the day after we took them there, I think. It sounded as if it took them a whole hour to move in; they have so little. Later Harriet picked up Christy and the baby while Ben was working. They went to Target, bought the store out, carried some of it home, had the rest delivered. So now they have a bed and some furniture. Carmen Barrios and her two sons are in. That may have happened before you left; I'm not sure. Joe McGregor went over and took the boys to the skateboard shop. The boys haven't come out of the clouds since. Then, this weekend while you were taking a break, the two men moved in. Patrick Lowery and Jeff Daniels. Ben Hudson saw them carrying things in and went to help. They all started talking.

"I was there yesterday, and they approached me about the outbuilding. It turns out that Jeff—he's the building engineer at the hospital—and Patrick used to have shops in their homes when they were married. Patrick, by the way, is a plumber. They both still have tools and all those man-things the hardware store carries. And you remember Ben and Christy talking about the things Ben made and sold, the house signs and blocks for kids and that sort of thing. Anyway, the three of them are talking about turning the outbuilding into a workshop and studio. Christy said the skylights would be great for her painting, and they could separate out a space for her under one of those and build around it so the dust from the men working with wood wouldn't be a problem. They're making up drawings and floor plans. I thought I'd warn you about this little cabal in the making so you'd be prepared when they want to talk about it for real."

"Do you remember that whole conversation about having men around as role models for children?" Helen asked. "This sounds like just what's happening. Those two boys of Carmen's will be seeing and hearing these men working around that shop. That's got to be a good thing."

Alicia laughed. "It sounds as if you've already made up your mind!"

"I guess I have," Helen agreed. "They'll have to run it past Drew Patten if they want to do the work on their own time. We could provide materials. Drew could pull permits from the city, make sure they do it to code and make it safe. And they'll need some security precautions. If it's full of tools, it could be a target for thieves. Plus, it might become an 'attractive nuisance,' as the law and insurance companies put it. The little boys could get in there and get hurt around the electric saws or whatever. So that needs to be addressed."

Gerard interrupted the women. "Hold it. I know this is none of my business, but I've been a patient bystander here. Could someone please tell me what's going on? What's this about all these people moving around and building a workshop? Are you two women construction foremen or something?" Gerard looked confused and frustrated. The women both laughed at him. He took it well.

"Fair enough. I'll tell you, if Helen agrees, of course." Helen nodded her permission to Alicia, who continued. "We're both board members of a foundation that provides housing for low-income families with children. We're talking about an apartment building near here that the foundation purchased and upgraded. The first four tenants moved in during the past week, and we're talking about them."

"Well, thank you. Makes perfect sense. And now, dear ladies, it's time I went home. Helen, I left my business card on your kitchen counter. Please call me within the next two days." He went into the bathroom to collect his things.

Alicia looked at Helen with curiosity. Helen said nothing. Gerard came out of the bathroom with the gym bag he had arrived with. He said goodbye and left the apartment.

"What's next?" Alicia said, after a moment.

"Next is that I go back to my life. I'm going to start with the CASA case I was working on before I went to Boston."

"Then I best leave you to it. I'm going to go home and collapse."

Both women laughed.

"Alicia, I'm so sorry for everything I've put you through. I don't even know how to begin to make up for it. But never believe I don't know how difficult this has been."

"Helen, it's never too difficult to help a friend," Alicia said. "When you're ready for pay-back time, you can invite me over for a cup of tea. That's thanks enough." She started to hug Helen, but turned it into a pat on the arm. Then she left.

Helen went to the kitchen and located the card from Gerard. It had "Mirador Industries" at the top, followed by "Gerard Lodge, Ph.D." on a line halfway down. Under his name was "V.P., Operations." Below and to the right were two telephone numbers, one of which was labeled mobile. Helen took that to mean it was a cell phone. She taped the card securely inside her cupboard door.

Then she went into the dining room and located the file on the Eastons. Within minutes, she was back to her routine. "Hello, my name is Helen Paige. This number was provided by Norm Easton. Is this Rob Jobin?"

"Yes, Norm told me to expect a call from you."

"Good. Then you probably know I'm assigned to represent Garth, his son. Is this a good time for you to talk?

"Yes, I'm alone. I can give you maybe fifteen minutes."

"That should be enough. Perhaps you could start by telling me how long you've known Norm and Marilyn and how often you were around the family as a whole." The call lasted less than the fifteen minutes Helen had been given, but she learned a lot in that time. Rob had known Norm since childhood and was the best man at the wedding. He and Rob had remained close since that time and saw each other on a weekly basis. Rob reported that he had watched Marilyn become increasingly unhappy in the marriage and then had started noticing the drinking. He was present on the occasion when Marilyn had attacked Norm's car with a baseball bat. It occurred on a Sunday in front of Rob's house, where Norm and Garth had gone to watch a football game. It was Rob who insisted they call the police. He gave Helen the name of the police officer and the police case file number. He said Marilyn had been seriously drunk. It was also Rob who insisted on Norm getting the restraining order. Norm was trying to protect Garth from learning about Marilyn's problems, according to Rob. Helen thanked him and hung up.

Then she called the police department and asked to speak to Patrolman Agate, the officer involved in the car-bashing incident. She left her name and number and asked to have the officer call her. She was still typing up the notes from her interview with Rob Jobin when the phone rang.

"Helen, here," she said.

"This is Patrolman Agate. You called?"

Helen related the incident, giving the case file, location of the incident, and names. "Oh, yeah, I remember that," the officer said. "The woman was drunk. I took her keys and waited around while she called a friend to pick her up. There wasn't too much damage as she wasn't very strong and was too drunk to even aim that well. In fact, as I drove up she took a big swing and missed and fell down." Helen thanked the officer, hung up, and started typing again. When she had written up notes from both calls, she made her third contact of the morning.

"Hello, my name is Helen Paige, Is this Sharon Knight? I'm working on a custody case involving Garth Easton. Is this a good time to talk for about ten minutes?"

"Sure, it's a good time. What do you need from me?" asked Sharon.

"I'd like to start with how long you've known Marilyn Easton and how often you've been around the family."

"Well, I've known Marilyn maybe a year, year and a half. I've never seen her husband or the kid."

"Has Marilyn talked about her son to you?"

"Not too much, just the usual bitchin' moms do. Like I complain about my kids to her, and she does the same. She said Garth's just like his dad. They're disrespectful toward her, and Garth never does what she tells him to. She said she'd be glad when he got old enough to move out."

"Does she talk about what's going on in her marriage?"

"Yeah, she's not happy with it. But she don't know what else to do. She's never worked and doesn't want to. So she's pretty much stuck, she said. And she's really pissed he filed for divorce."

"Did she ever mention any abusive or violent behavior?"

"Yeah, she told me he hit her a couple of times."

"Did she show you bruises, maybe a black eye or cuts, anything like that?"

"No, I never saw anything, just heard about it."

"What do you and Marilyn do when you get together?"

"We go out for lunch, sometimes out for a cocktail. Her husband's loaded, you know, so she treats. Sometimes there're four or five of us. And I've been shopping with her. She loves to shop. Good taste, too. We have a blast. Marilyn is a kick, lots of fun to be with."

"Well, thanks so much for your time, Sharon." She hung up and wrote up her notes. It wasn't often that the collateral for parent A presented a case for parent B. She would eventually need the intake interview from the substance abuse counselor and the results of the urine tests. Since Marilyn had yet to complete those actions, Helen might not receive results for weeks. She made a note to call Marilyn every week to follow up on whether she intended to comply with the court order related to the chemical abuse assessment. Then she made a note to call the medical clinic to verify the burn on Norm's arm. She also decided to interview at least one teacher and either one or two of Garth's friends. She made a note to call Garth after school and get names and numbers.

Helen stopped for lunch. She found soup left over from Gerard's cooking. She smiled to herself as she reheated it in a small pan. After lunch, she returned to her room. She spent the next two hours in yoga and breathing exercises. Then she sat on her cushion and, for the seventh time, studied her recent use of alcohol. Her failure to pay attention to her needs, she knew full well, had been responsible for the relapse. She had no intention of repeating it. Blaming the relapse on the emotional toll of the trip to Boston was inappropriate. It would place the blame on others for creating the pressure. That would be a failure to take responsibility for her own actions. She could and should have created boundaries and fences around herself. Satisfied, she rose and went into the dining room.

Helen started on the rental applications. She was especially in need of a tenant for the duplex. Then she recalled the earlier conversation about pulling Drew Patten off the second duplex unit remodel to put him to work on the Seventh Street West property. She called Kenneth Osborne.

"Hi, Kenneth. Helen here."

"Helen, I'm glad you're better. Alicia answered your phone the other day and told me you were under the weather. Sorry I haven't called in to see you. My bad."

"No problem, I wasn't in any shape for visitors. Do you have a minute?"

"Sure, fire away. I have a new paralegal, so there's a lot more time for me to handle the foundation work already. What's on your mind?"

"I recall that I was supposed to call the tenant in the duplex and see if he wanted to stay or wait to move to the other unit while his is remodeled, and then decide whether Drew would work on the duplex or the new place. Catch me up on where all that stands as of now."

"OK. This happened while you were sick. Drew said he'd love to run a second crew and do both jobs. So you're supposed to get the current tenant either to move to the remodeled unit or to move out so Drew can start the other side. He's already ordered everything for it and wants to start as soon as we give him the word."

"Got it. Do you have the current tenant's contact information?"

"I do. Let me pull it. Ready? It's Rick Cleveland. I have the cell." He gave it to her. "And don't forget, we gave him a 10-percent reduction in rent for staying in the unit till now. His old rent was nine hundred, so now he pays eight hundred ten a month."

"Thank you for that, Kenneth. I'd forgotten all about that incentive. I'll e-mail you after I talk to him."

"One more thing, Helen. Do you remember the last board meeting when Frank said he had two properties to look at, then we only did the one on Seventh Street West? Well, he said since we're now selling the Connecticut property we should go look at the one we forgot about. He and I are going there tomorrow, and we'd like you to go along. That's what I called you for when you were sick. Frank said he saw it already, and the nice part is that it's already in good-enough shape to move tenants into. No need to renovate. Since we have so many tenant applications, I thought it might not hurt to see what we think."

"You're right. What time are you going?"

"Frank's picking me up at ten in the morning. We could drop by for you at the same time."

"Count me in. I'll be on the sidewalk at ten."

Helen disconnected, then dialed again. "Is this Rick Cleveland? I'm Helen Smith from the Claudius Foundation."

"I'm Rick. I wondered if I would get a call, been expecting it. You going to kick me out?"

"Not necessarily. I know you've seen the renovation next door. It's complete, and now we want to renovate the unit you're in. What we can do is offer to move you into the finished unit. After it's done, you can then choose which one you want, if you decide to stay on."

"And the catch?"

"What catch?"

"How much will my rent go up?"

"Nothing, no extra charge. And we'll keep the current incentive in place so you'll pay eight hundred ten now. Then, when we've finished the work, you'll go back up to the nine hundred."

"I get to stay at nine hundred, in a new place. Gas fireplace, upstairs laundry, new shower. And no more bubble-gum pink bathroom. And the open kitchen with the bar. Is that what you're saying?"

Helen laughed. "Sounds as if you've been touring the unit as we've been doing the work. But yes, that's what I'm saying. The units will be identical, right down to shelves beside the fireplace and the arches."

"I'd be a damn fool to turn that down. And my mama didn't raise no fools."

"It's settled, then. Goodbye." She hung up and sent an e-mail to Kenneth to notify him of Mr. Cleveland's decision.

At ten the next morning, Helen was standing on the sidewalk, and Frank and Kenneth drove up. Kenneth got out and insisted that Helen take the front seat while he moved to the back. Helen was grateful. Sitting in the back of the little red Corvette wasn't her idea of a good time.

"I want you to see where we're going, look at the neighborhood," Frank said. "I'll swing past the building, then go around a few blocks so you can get a feel for what's there."

The building was in Ballard, an older neighborhood just north and east of the ship canal. The building, named Fleetwood Arms, was located on Fifty-third Street Northwest, right off Eleventh Avenue Northwest. It was less than a block from Gilman Playground, a large grassy area with ball fields. Frank drove around the smaller streets and then took a short tour of the main business area. Market Street, the commercial hub of the area, was full of small restaurants, shops, nail-and-hair salons, and other businesses. "I checked the crime stats; this is a good neighborhood," Kenneth said from the back seat. Frank drove back to the building and parked right in front. The building itself was two stories. It had two separate entrances.

Frank got a set of keys from his glove compartment. "The Realtor gave me the keys this morning. He's got them all marked. We can go look at several of the apartments. Looks as if there are about four different designs. Let me explain the basic plan while we're looking at it from the front. The building is basically divided into two identical halves; they don't connect. Each has an entrance hall. From the entrance you go to any of the first-floor apartments. Or you can go up the stairway to the second floor, where you can enter any of those apartments. The ones on the top are larger. There are five units up there. Three of them have two bedrooms; two of them have three bedrooms. On the main floor, there are six apartments. Five of them have two bedrooms; one is a single bedroom. So, we have a total of twenty-two apartments, eleven accessible from each main entrance."

By now Frank had led them to the entrance on the right. He consulted a paper. "Now, in this section, we have four vacant units, two on each floor. There's a three-bedroom on the top, so why don't we see that and then a two-bedroom up there. On this floor, we'll look at the one-bedroom. We can go next door to see a two-bedroom in a different location, with a different floor plan."

They went up the stairs and in the three-bedroom unit that faced the street. The unit had new paint, and it smelled fresh. As they started looking around, they commented to each other.

"Well, it's pretty plain," said Helen. "Nothing special about it, really. But the rooms are a good size. The bathroom is clean and looks as if they just caulked everything. Nice linen closet. No laundry. Is there a laundry somewhere in the building?"

"I don't think so," Frank said. "Tell the truth, I don't know. We'll look when we go back down. I agree it's plain vanilla. We've had some charm with that Olympic Place gem and that duplex. Maybe we're getting spoiled."

"I think the kitchen is good, and I like the way it overlooks the dining and living room," Kenneth said. "The parents would like the open concept here. I don't know the age of this building, but that may have been a modern and radical thing when it was first built."

"You're probably right. I think it was built in the 1960s; I'll have to check."

"The smallest bedroom is pretty small," Helen said. "But it's functional. If there were four kids, you could give them the bigger rooms and have the parent in here. It's not spacious, but it could handle a double bed. That would give the kids a little more space."

"Let's look at the two-bedroom," Kenneth said.

"This is darker than the other one—it's on the back with a building right behind it. But still, I think it's suitable for our tenants," Helen said. "And again, the open-concept kitchen to dining room area. So that's good."

They moved downstairs. The one-bedroom unit was at the very back, near a back entrance to the building. They went into the unit and stood in the living room.

"Well, it's not too roomy," said Frank. "I don't think I see a parent with a kid in here. How about you, Helen?"

"I agree. I suppose we could just charge market rent and get a single person in here."

"I have an idea," said Kenneth. "If there's no other laundry, how about we make this a laundry room? It would be great for that, plenty of room. You could even put a lounge area in the bedroom where people could sit and read while they wait for the laundry. Or do puzzles with the kids. Or nurse a baby. Make it sort of a hang-out area. It would give the single moms a place to sort of meet up and get to know one another."

Helen smiled as she said, "Kenneth, you're a gem. That's perfect. And we could stock the kitchen with a teakettle and coffee pot, some mugs, small plates. Put up some curtains. This could be a real asset to the tenants."

"Let's check what's out back," said Frank, and they moved out of the apartment and through the back entrance. It was two steps down to a small paved area. Trash cans took up one section off to the right. There was a storage shed near the back. Frank checked the key ring, found a small key, and used it to open the shed. It was about ten feet wide and six feet deep. It was empty, with a cement floor. "Well, what would we do with this?"

"Use it for bikes, scooters, strollers, and outdoor play things," said Helen. "We could provide locks and chains of some kind for each person, maybe wire off some locker-type thing. Then keep the main door locked and give everybody a key."

"That works," said Kenneth.

"So, are you thinking another laundry area in the other section?" asked Frank.

"Yes," said Kenneth. "If the layout is the same, I think we should. That would be ten apartments sharing one laundry. Maybe three washers and three dryers. Plus a couple of tables for folding things. Maybe a hanging rack for things that go on hangers. That's about right, given the size of the space, if we use the bedroom for a lounge."

"Let's go look at the other two-bedroom," said Frank.

They left the first section, walked to the other entrance, and went inside. The vacant two-bedroom was on the first floor, at the front.

"This is good," said Helen. The two bedrooms were both large. The kitchen was very large, with the eating area taking up one-half the space. It had a built-in bench going from the corner outwards against each side wall. A built-in table was in front of the bench arrangement. "Looks as if you could seat four adults or six kids here without even needing a chair."

"I think I like this unit better than the three-bedroom upstairs," said Kenneth. "The living room seems bigger, even though it's not the open concept we saw upstairs."

"So," said Frank. "What's our overall opinion? Yes or no?"

"I'd vote yes, depending on the price," Helen said. "It *is* in good shape, as you said, and we aren't going to do renovation work, except for the laundry rooms, which we'll need to price out. But we have a lot of good tenants waiting, and this is a great location in terms of the park for the kids, the nearby shopping, and bus stops."

"The asking price on this is two point two million," said Frank. "That's pretty steep for this location, I think, especially since we'll be taking it down from twenty-two units to only twenty."

"That's a lot of money," said Helen.

"Could we get a mortgage? Could we even pay off a mortgage?" Kenneth was frowning as he considered what he was saying.

"Well, I can make a phone call," Helen said. "See if I can shake something loose. We'll have the 1.8 million from the sale in Connecticut."

"We need a chunk of that for renovations at both Lower Queen Anne and the Seventh Street West buildings. Those are huge. Plus we may need operating funds for those. We aren't asking much rent for Lower Queen Anne, and Seventh Street West will be under construction for maybe six months, so no rent from there. Plus we've lost the income from Connecticut we'd been using."

"Darn, I forgot about all that," said Helen. She paused. "Frank, here's the deal. You see if you can get it for two million. Don't make it firm, no written offer. Just tell the Realtor that's the absolute best we can do and see what he says. Then, if he says it might be accepted, I'll make a call and try to get the two million. If we can do it, we'll have to leave the laundry rooms out for now. When the rents can cover it, we'll put them in. Maybe we can get the plumbing roughed in, though. Then, if we can get a donation of one or two machines for each side, that would help. We could look for grant money for that." Helen was speaking in a musing tone, thinking as she went along. "Kenneth, talk to Alicia. I suspect she knows about organizations that donate money or give grants or something. If she doesn't know, she'll know who *does* know."

"I'll talk to the Realtor about a deal, Helen," Frank said. "But I have another idea, as well. I'll tell him the seller could go for a tax deduction on this to make it work out for them better. I'll suggest we write it up as a sale for 2.2 million with cash up front of two million and a note for two hundred grand, simple interest of 3 percent, pay-off in ten years. Then they can turn the note into a donation to offset the capital gain they'll have. I'll also suggest they donate six washers and dryers, three for each side. Front loading. Can't hurt to ask."

"Run that past Mr. Pierce and ask if he can draw up an offering letter along those lines. Great idea, Frank. I keep wondering why I didn't think of having a board of directors before I moved here. Each one of you makes such a contribution. I just can't thank you enough."

"Helen, don't be daft," Frank said. "Working on the foundation is the best thing any of us do. You need to understand that once people get to a certain age and have enough money, they get a little jaded. Or bored. Or something. Plus, if they've been in a winner-take-all type of profession, as real estate is, they've probably done a few things they regret. Maybe they had to elbow somebody out. Throw their weight around. Do a little pushing and shoving when the umpire wasn't looking. Maybe a lot worse. Then you come along and ask them to put themselves aside for a while and lend a hand to someone who needs it. You talk about the children and making a difference. You tell a few tenant stories. Hell, it's like a chance to atone for a lot of stuff. That's a huge incentive, let me tell you. This is a big opportunity to make up for a lot. So, don't thank us. We're getting plenty reward just helping out."

Helen bowed her head. She swallowed, which was hard to do.

Frank looked at Kenneth, surprised. Kenneth shrugged, then went over, and put his hand on Helen's back and patted her. "Helen, you're not going to embarrass us men, are you?"

Helen started laughing as she looked up at him. "Absolutely not. Wouldn't think of it."

They all laughed, tension released.

Two days later, in the afternoon, Helen was in Mr. Pierce's office. The tentative agreement on the Fleetwood Arms building had been accepted, subject to the foundation paying two million, in cash, at closing. They even got the laundry facilities, thanks to Frank's persuasive powers. Helen instructed Mr. Pierce to call the Prescott family lawyer.

"Mr. Hancock, please. It's Mr. Pierce from Seattle." Edward found the telephone encounters with the esteemed opposition counsel much less daunting and much more enjoyable each time he called. He still, however, stood and turned his back to the door when he made them.

"Yes, Mr. Hancock. I hope your January isn't too harsh." He paused, listened, and laughed. "True, if we want the snow, we drive a half-hour, enjoy it, and come back to the rain." He paused and listened again. "I heard … Yes … Yes, the reason for this call is to request a donation of two million dollars so the foundation can acquire a building with twenty apartments. Yes, it's a very good price. The seller is making a donation of significant equity … Yes, our negotiator is extremely talented. Thank you, Mr. Hancock. Goodbye."

He joined Helen and Kenneth in the conference room. "All set, they'll transfer the money today. We can close next week if we like the results of the inspections . Are those scheduled yet, Kenneth?"

"They are. One today, one tomorrow. I'll be on site for both."

"I'm going call possible tenants," Helen said. "Tell them they can move in fifteen days from today. Can we get keys, Kenneth, so we can show them the apartments? How many are vacant or coming vacant within the month?"

"We have seven vacancies right now. Three more will be vacant by the end of the month, but one of those is the other one-bedroom, so that doesn't count. Then you need to know size. Three of them are the three-bedroom ones, the other six are two-bedrooms. We didn't talk about a manager. What do you want to do about that?"

"I think we should try to get a tenant as a live-in, just like at Lenora," Helen responded. "That's worked out really well. Of course, both Brendan and Pam are naturals for the job. I don't know if we've just been lucky or whether we can expect to find another one just as good."

"I agree that's the best idea. Otherwise, I might have to take on the duties myself. Which would be fine with me, of course. But having a person right on the spot is a real advantage to the other tenants, I think."

"OK. As I screen the applications, I'll be on the lookout for a potential manager. Meanwhile, if you'll excuse me, it looks as if I've got some work to do."

Back in her apartment, Helen hung her coat and went directly to her bedroom. She removed her shoes and sat on the cushion. Then she lit an incense stick. Closing her eyes gently, softly, she started chanting.

Two hours later, Helen was on the telephone. "Hi, my name is Helen Smith, and I'm with the Claudius Foundation. Is this Gloria Parinelli?" The potential applicant was a woman aged thirty-two, with four children. The older girls were ten and eight. The twins, one boy, one girl, were seven.

"I'm so glad to get this call. The hospital social worker told me about your foundation and gave me the application. We could certainly use a break."

"Tell me a bit about your situation, Mrs. Parinelli."

"Right. My husband died last month. He was sick for two years, since the twins were five years old. He had lung cancer, so it was a really bad time, and he wasn't unhappy to have it over with, God rest his soul. I had to quit work to take care of him the last year. So, with no one working and hospital bills so high, we ran into financial trouble. The medical insurance where he worked wasn't that good, and mine was nothing to brag about either. So we had to take out a mortgage on the house. Now we have to sell the house. We can't afford the payments on the mortgage any more. So, we've got it on the market, and we need to move. This is so hard. The kids just lost their dad, I lost my husband, and now we lose the house. But, that's the hand we're dealt, so we'll have to play it out."

"What sort of work did you do?"

"I was the office manager for a small contractor. He did re-models, mostly. I took care of the books, answered the phone, typed up the bids, did the payroll, ordered supplies, paid the bills, sent out invoices. Anything that came up, I did. He was always at the sites; he was a hands-on worker, not just a manager of the crew. He hired people for each job, like framers or roofers or electricians. Whatever he couldn't do, he hired to get done."

"And you can't go back to the job? "

"Not now. Maybe in a couple of years or so. Right now, the kids need a full-time parent. Bobbie and Brenda barely remember one parent the way I was tied up with my husband the past year. Ariel, the ten-year-old, has had to fill in. Leah tries to help, but she's only eight. They all need a mother right now. They deserve it, and I'm going to do it, no matter what."

"What's your financial situation? I don't need details, just the overall picture."

"Well, the kids will get support checks from Social Security, and I think I do too, but I'm not sure. We'll have a little left over from the house sale, I hope. Our savings is mostly gone, but there's enough to help a little. I probably qualify for food stamps, but I'm not even sure about that. This past year has just been a blur. I haven't felt up to checking into anything, what with spending most of my time at the hospital."

"How much room are you looking for in an apartment?"

"I doubt that's up to me. We'll have to make do with what we can afford."

"Well, would three bedrooms do, even if one of them was pretty small?"

"Sure, I could put all three girls in one room. They share now so that's no problem. Give the smallest room to Bobbie; he doesn't use much space. I'd have a room of my own. Yeah, three bedrooms would be a luxury."

"Would you like to meet me at a place tomorrow? Would the children be in school?"

"They would be. I could come midday, after they leave, be home before they get back. Say ten or eleven, depending on where I'm going."

Helen gave her the address and told her about where the Fleetwood Arms was located. They agreed to meet at ten.

Helen made notes from the call and then called two more possible tenants. She arranged for one of them, Ricardo Torres, to meet her at the apartments at ten-thirty. She called Alicia to see if she wanted to go along, but Alicia was not home. Then she ate dinner and started down the hill to the church in South Lake Union.

Two hours later, Helen and Gerard were walking back up the hill after the meeting. "So, tell me more about this foundation," Gerard said.

Helen talked about it for some time.

"And," he said at the end of her talk, "you're going tomorrow to show two tenants some apartments?"

"Yes, I have one at ten and one at ten thirty."

"Mind if I tag along?"

"What? Why?"

"I just want to. I'd like to see what these tenants are like and how you handle it and how it works. I'm interested."

"Of course, you can come along. I'll drive by your place and pick you up, or do you prefer to meet me there?"

"I'll let you pick me up. What time?"

"I'll need to get you at nine fifteen. It'll take about forty-five minutes to get there from here."

"Right."

They approached Gerard's building, and he said, "See you tomorrow, then." And he was gone.

Helen walked on, up the hill. She didn't know what to think about Gerard's desire to accompany her the next day. Of course, she knew almost nothing of his background. In general, however, it was odd, she thought, that a vice president of a company would want to watch lower-income people look at apartments. But then again, Gerard was probably not typical. After all, how many men cooked chicken soup for a drunk and slept on the couch?

The next day, Helen went for an early-morning walk. When she entered the building on the way back, she noticed that the mail had arrived and collected hers. Shuffling through it absently while she was in the elevator, she stopped when she saw a letter from Boston. Her stomach tightened. Her first impulse was to throw it away. Her second was to tear it open and read it. Her third, and the one she heeded, was to put it on the dining room table and resolve to look at it later.

Helen changed clothes, ate a piece of toast, and retrieved her car from the garage. Gerard was on the sidewalk outside his building when she pulled up.

"Morning," he said as he got into her car.

"Good morning," she responded. She paid him little attention as she concentrated on the drive, other than to say, "Frank is going to pick Alicia up, and they'll join us there."

"Frank?"

"Sorry. Frank Brewer is on the board of the foundation. He was a Realtor. He finds a lot of the properties for us and advises us what to offer. He's a huge help." They drove the rest of the way in silence.

Alicia and Frank were on the sidewalk in front of the Fleetwood Arms. Helen parked and then introduced them to Gerard, having forgotten that Alicia had already met him.

An old sedan pulled up in front. The tall woman who approached them was wearing a rubberized car coat, tennis shoes, and jeans. Her face was lined and plain, but she had a good smile with laugh lines. "I'm Gloria Parinelli," she said. She shook hands with Helen as she introduced herself and then shook with each of the others.

"This is quite a committee," she said. "Is it an interview process?"

Alicia laughed and took over the conversation. "We never thought about what this would look like from your point of view. This building is a new acquisition, so we're looking at it for the first time along with you. And another potential tenant is on the way, so we need to separate and show both of you around."

"Let's do this," said Frank. "Helen said she thought you'd prefer a three-bedroom, right?"

"I would. If I end up in two, I'll share with my son, Bobby; he's seven. We have two twin beds; I'd use those. I have three girls. Bobby's twin is Brenda. She'd share with her older sisters, Ariel and Leah; they're ten and eight. The girls are used to sharing, and I'm not sure any of them would want to be away from the others. These past two years have been rough, and I think they've bonded a lot."

The group was moving to the door of the right-hand unit as they talked.

"The three-bedrooms are all on the upper floor," said Frank. "There are two styles, and we have one of each available, one in each section. We'll show you both. It means carrying laundry and groceries up a flight."

"I don't think that should be a problem. With four of us to carry, we can manage."

They went up the stairs to the first of the three-bedrooms. All went in, but Frank and Helen hung back as the others looked around since they had already seen this unit. The two talked quietly.

"What's your impression of her?" said Helen. They were near the entry, a good distance from the others, and could not be seen or heard.

"She's straightforward. Honest, good handshake. I'd say she's competent at what she does and knows herself."

Helen looked at Frank. He was always a source of surprise to her. His exterior looked like the successful businessman, but his ability to handle people and to size them up seemed more like the skill of a psychologist than of a salesman, which is what she thought Realtors mostly were.

"This is a nice apartment," Gloria Parinelli said. "We could live in it."

"Let's go look at the other one," said Frank. "I haven't seen it myself."

They all walked to the second entrance to the building. Upstairs, they entered the three-bedroom none of them had seen. It was on the southeast corner of the building, and as they entered, they were all aware of how much lighter and brighter this unit was than the one they had just left.

"Wow," said Frank. "That's good light."

The floor plan was unique. Two bedrooms were to the left of the common living core, which was composed of an open-concept kitchen and dining and living room. The master bedroom was on the right of the core. It had an attached bathroom. The two bedrooms on the left shared a bath.

"This is fabulous," said Gloria. "The girls and I would fight over the master bedroom, of course."

"And you'd lose the fight?" Gerard asked. It was the first time he'd said anything. Helen had almost forgotten he was there.

"I would," Gloria agreed. "But I'd make a deal. If they get the master bedroom, they have to clean the master bath on their own. So I'd win by losing." She and Gerard shared a laugh.

Alicia had stayed at the entry with Helen this time. "Do you think she's manager material?" asked Alicia. "I think she is."

"I do," agreed Helen. "And Frank's on the same page."

"Well, time for the hard part," said Gloria after inspecting the kitchen and looking out the windows. "What's the rent on this?"

"What rent have you budgeted for?"

"I can pay maybe fifteen hundred, depending on which utilities are included. I have enough to do that for a little over a year. Then I have to go to work, and what I can pay when that happens, I'm not sure about yet."

"Well, here's the deal we can offer," said Frank, after getting the nod from Alicia and Helen. "We could give you this for the fifteen, and throw in all utilities. But we have another deal as well. We could give you this apartment, rent free, throw in the utilities and a new television we'll hang up on the wall, and ask you to be the live-in manager. It's twenty apartments, so there might be quite a bit of work. You take that on, we pay a salary as well as the rent. Salary would be two thousand a month."

Gloria stared at him, mouth half open. She looked up and down. Tears came into her eyes. "I'll take it," she said. "Excuse me." She went into the master bathroom and closed the door.

The rest all looked at each other and then walked around the apartment. Helen was looking out the window onto the street and saw the other applicant arriving. She said, "Frank would you run down and meet him, please? His name is Ricardo Torres."

The others watched from the window as Frank met Mr. Torres and went into the other side of the building. Gloria came out of the bathroom and saw Alicia, Helen, and Gerard all looking out the window. She joined them. "Looks as if your first tenant is here, Gloria. You ready to meet him?"

"I am. I'm ready for anything. I am strong, I am invincible, I am *woman*."

They all laughed together, all familiar with the song.

Later, after instructing both Ricardo and Gloria to meet with Kenneth at the office to fill out the rental agreements and, in Gloria's case, provide employee information, Helen drove Gerard back to Queen Anne. "Do you want me to drop you at work somewhere or back at your building?"

"The building is fine. I can work from there today. I remind you, Helen, that we were scheduled for dinner at Moorage. Are you ready to make good on that?"

"Same provisos?"

"Same provisos."

"Tonight?"

"Tonight."

"Six thirty, meet at six fifteen?"

"Six thirty, meet at six fifteen."

"Yes."

"Good." Helen dropped Gerard off at his building and returned her car to the parking garage.

Upstairs, she went into the kitchen and fixed tea. Then she stood at the dining table, tea in hand, and looked at the envelope from Boston. The upper left corner said "William Henry Prescott III." She stared at the letter for some time. She breathed quietly, gradually extending both the inhales and exhales. Then she went into her bedroom. She spent the rest of the afternoon there in meditation and yoga postures. Then she showered, dressed, and went downstairs. Without opening the envelope.

Gerard arrived on time, and they walked to Moorage. They had a slow and leisurely dinner, sitting at the small table in the window on the left side of the door.

When they were eating the appetizers, Gerard suddenly started talking. "My father was a priest," he said. "A Catholic priest."

Helen looked at him with curiosity but kept silent.

"He left the priesthood when my mother was pregnant. She died of breast cancer when I was seven. When I started college, my father became a Cistercian monk. He's in the Holy Cross Abby in Berryville, Virginia."

Helen thought this was the strangest story she'd heard in a long time. And she heard more than her share of strange stories. She wondered what response she should make. Then she knew.

"My father died when I was twelve. My brother Derrick was almost three. My mother went so far into her grief, and for so long, I became the *de facto* mother. When I went away to college, she was better so I became a pre-teen, where I'd been at my father's death. And I did all the stupid things I hadn't done, only worse."

They were both quiet after that, except for the comments on the food. It was excellent, they both agreed. They shared an entrée so they would have room for tea and dessert. When they finished, they walked companionably back to Helen's building and parted.

Helen took off her coat. She went into the dining room and looked at the envelope on the table. She thought about opening it. Instead, she went into her room, undressed, put on her nightgown, and sat on her cushion. She chanted for an hour, sat for an hour in the silence, and went to bed.

The next morning, Helen contacted Garth Easton's high school. She asked the secretary if the signed release giving the school permission to talk to her had been received. The secretary looked around and found the release. "What I would like," Helen then said, "is the name of the teacher who knows Derrick the best. Who do you suppose that might be?"

"Well, let me think," the secretary said. "I could find that out. Why don't I ask around and call you back?"

"Excellent, thank you," said Helen. "Please just leave the name and contact number on my answering system if I'm not available when you call. Thank you so much."

"My pleasure," responded the secretary.

Helen recorded the call in her notebook, sat back, and thought about what she should do next. Her eyes wandered into her living room, and she focused on the couch. She rose, walked into the living room, and looked slowly around. It was starting to look like a real room in a real home. The couch, the bright pillows, the big basket in the corner, all added a warm and lived-in look to her room. The books and magazines Gerard had brought in gave it a personal feel. But, she thought, the walls looked suddenly naked. She put on her coat, added her wallet to the keys in the pocket, and went out.

There were a number of art galleries on Queen Anne. She wandered into two of them located on the main avenue but saw nothing that pulled at her. There were nice pictures, and several would have been a good decoration in her room, but they did not *involve* her. Then she remembered the gallery on McGraw, up past the hardware store. It always had wonderful local artists on display, and she had often stopped to look in the windows when she was walking. The gallery was several blocks away, and the walk there and back would take over a half-hour. But it was a nice day for a walk, cool for Seattle, a bit less than forty degrees, but sunny. And she was trying to take care of herself. So … she did it. She breathed deeply and enjoyed the walk.

Inside the gallery, Helen wandered slowly, taking in each picture of the six or so featured artists on display. Then, from across the room, she saw a picture at the far back wall near the restroom door.

She walked toward the painting, drawn to it by something she could feel but not understand. This was her painting. She knew that without any thought at all. The painting was very like Monet's "Poppies Blooming," without the female figures. It was a landscape, with the light coming from the left down a rolling hillside. The lower part of the hill was covered with poppies, but not brilliant red ones. These looked softer, more faded. The sky had huge white clouds, not perfect white clouds in clumps, but sketchier, rolling across the sky. In the far distance, on a hill to the right of center, stood a pale gold stucco building with a red roof, probably a red tile roof that one might see in Tuscany or even Mexico. It was a large building, perhaps an old monastery or castle, but without all of the turrets. The light on the meadow was soft. On the left, on the slope above the poppies, were two dark figures, dimly seen. They may have been walking, or working in the field, perhaps. The overall scene was one of great peace. It was contemplative. Yes, she thought, this was her picture. The price was twenty-seven hundred dollars.

She looked about for the gallery owner, who had been watching from a desk in a far corner opposite the restroom entrance. She nodded, and the woman approached her.

"I'll take like this one," she said. "I'd like it delivered and hung."

The tall, distinguished older woman nodded. "An excellent choice. Alister Weatherby, the artist, is up and coming. He's already attracted quite a following, and his work will certainly appreciate over time. It's an excellent choice."

Helen largely ignored what the woman said. It mattered not to her if the artist was up and coming or down and going. And it mattered not whether the painting appreciated or depreciated. She simply held out her credit card. The woman gave a small bow and took Helen back to her desk. She ran the credit card, had Helen sign the slip, and made arrangements for delivery of the painting. Helen left the gallery.

On her way back to Queen Anne Avenue, Helen decided to stop in at Vanja's Tea Shop. When she entered, Sonja was waiting on a customer. She had about ten canisters of tea leaves in front of her and was using a scale to measure tea and put it in small brown bags. She and the customer were talking to one another. Helen went to a corner table, took off her coat, and sat facing the window. She felt that by doing so she could watch the street and be less disruptive to the business going on behind her. There were books on shelves right next to her. If she were reading a book, she guessed, she would definitely not be disturbing the sale going on at the counter. She picked up a book at random and opened it near the back. She glanced down and read.

*It is very quiet.*

*The morning sun is shining on the gate-house which is bright with new paint this summer ... the wheat is already beginning to ripen on St. Joseph's knoll. The monks ... are digging in the Guest House garden.*

*It is very quiet. I think about this monastery. I think about the monks, my brothers, my fathers.*

Helen felt a shiver down her spine. What book had she happened upon? She checked the front. *The Seven Storey Mountain* by Thomas Merton. How utterly strange to find a book, and then a passage, that so matched her feeling when she selected her painting. She wondered, not for the first time, if her meditation work was somehow skewed or off-kilter. Her messages, if this was one, were always so difficult to decipher. Did this passage refer to her picture? And why bother with that? Was she supposed to go into a monastery? No way, already did that, if you count the ashram. That left only the story Gerard told last night about his own father. Oh, Lord, what the hell should she read into that?

Helen closed the book very firmly and put it back. Then she selected another book, this time with more care. *Ten Keys to Modern Japanese Flower Arrangement.* Just try to make something out of *this*, you spirits of whomever. She was quite absorbed in the pictures and instructions in the book when Sonja pulled up a chair next to her.

"All done with the customer. Thank you for waiting so patiently."

"No problem. Looked like a good sale."

"The best. That's the owner of a restaurant downtown. She took samples of twelve different teas. She's going to have a taste test with some friends and customers. She wants a unique and sophisticated offering of tea for her restaurant. So ... I see good sales ahead." Sonja was obviously very pleased.

"Great news. How's business in general? Think the shop can make it to the first year? I hear that's the hardest goal."

"I think you're right. We did some business projections before we decided to move forward. We're actually way ahead of schedule. So *that's* all to the good."

The way Sonja said it caused Helen to look sharply at her face. She saw something but didn't know what. She decided to just ask. "And what's to the bad?"

Sonja sighed. "If I bring a pot of tea, do you really want to hear it?"

"I want to hear it whether you bring the pot or not."

Sonja went behind the counter and returned quickly with a pot of tea and two cups on a tray. "Don't tell anyone. Especially don't tell Kenneth, promise?"

"I promise."

"It's my husband. Oskar. He's been acting strange ever since I started this. He's supportive; it's not that. And he did put up the money. At first, I thought he might worry that I'd skip fixing his meals or something, but it's not that. I can't put my finger on it."

"What about his actual behavior has changed?"

"Tough question. I think part of it is in his look. He seems more *noticing* about me. He looks longer at my clothes and at my face and hair. As if he's studying me or something. But he's never said anything."

"You're a very attractive woman, Sonja. And striking. Unusual even. I'm sure I don't have to tell you that. But, did you go out much before this? On your own, I mean."

"Interesting. No, I didn't. I went to things at the children's school, of course, lots of things. I met Kenneth for lunch about once a month for years now. Other than that, I just play bridge one day a week with three friends. And I've done that from just after we married."

"So it's been fifteen years that he's always had you in the house or where he pretty much knew who you were with?"

"That's true." She looked straight into Helen's eyes. "Are you suggesting he's jealous?"

"Do *you* think he's jealous?"

"It never occurred to me."

"Well, I don't know. I've never met your husband. I just ask questions. I don't have answers, you know."

"Thank you, Helen. You've at least given me a place to start. I think I can take it from here."

They finished the pot of tea, and Helen went back to her apartment.

The letter was still sitting on the dining table. Maybe some secret part of her hoped it would go up in a puff of smoke. She did not want to deal with it. She sat down at the table and stared at it. When she did not feel anything in particular, she decided to chance it. Slowly, she opened it.

Dearest Helen,

First, thank you for coming to see me. I'm grateful. Eternally grateful.

There is much I said to you. There is much I did not say. Now to continue. I am writing this myself. No eyes but yours and mine shall see this. I tire easily. It will be in short parts. Forgive me if it is hard to follow.

I believe you started Claudius for revenge. You don't agree, I'm sure. You know my love of Hamlet. The choice of Claudius is thus clear to me. Search your own heart.

Revenge you have had. But God has used you, Helen. For his own ends. You were the means for God to reach me. Egotistical, I know. But look at it. You have taken upwards of ten million from me. That's nothing. Nothing at all. What you *left behind* when you took, that's the thing. You made me very curious. I like to satisfy my curiosities.

I had an investigator. Land records alone tell a story. The buildings in Connecticut. The tenants. The children. I see your trail, Helen. You leave footprints. I don't know why you moved to Seattle. I know Doyle Judd died. I know it hurt. Maybe that's why. I still follow your trail. I have photographs of your buildings. I love the new apartment building on Olympic Place. You have good taste. Today, two million more I sent. Another twenty apartments. Good work, good price. I am proud of you. Of what you have done.

Now, Helen, do you know yourself what you do? You seek atonement. Your whole life, since the accident, has been one of atonement. You know that, I know that. But what happened, Helen, is that you have been transformed. Your revenge against me has been turned, *transformed*, Helen, by God, into your redemption. But you redeemed me, too, Helen. You made me a part of the Grand Plan. You didn't mean to. I know that. But watching you use my money has transformed me. My money became the instrument for my atonement. God is playing with us, Helen. He's playing a game. The pay-off for him winning is our souls.

That's all I can write today. Exhausted. But not dead yet, Helen. Not dead yet.

William Prescott

Helen marveled at her father-in-law's stamina, if nothing else. Old and dying he might be, but he always wanted the last word. And he always got it. She railed against him in her mind. She wanted to hate him but could not. She wanted to hurt him but could not. He frustrated and challenged her. Even now, he reduced her, in his letter, to the role of a pawn in his life. She had been his pawn; she knew that. He was telling her she still was. She hated the very thought.

She went into her bedroom for another session of yoga, chanting, and meditation. She needed to build stronger fences. She needed to control her mind and her emotions. She needed her disciplines. Thank God for the training from Swami Rameshrawananda. She was finally beginning to believe that, as he had said, she could learn to no longer lean on him.

࿔ ࿔ ࿔

Three days later, Helen was still working her way through the applicants for the apartments. One of her constant fears was that she would miss a child that needed her help. It was so hard to tell which were the more critical cases from the applications alone. Each applicant she talked to seemed perfect. She was frustrated that her number of apartments never seemed sufficient. It was one of the many things that made her feel inadequate, one of the many things that she dealt with through her meditations.

The phone rang. "Helen, here," she said absently.

"Helen, it's Kenneth. We need to call an interim board meeting. How about tonight?"

"Sure, tonight's fine for me. What's it about?"

"Money, the sudden appearance of. Plus anything else you want to bring up."

"Sounds intriguing, I'll be there. Seven?"

"Yes, I'm calling everybody right now. Will let you know if we can't get a quorum and need to reschedule. Otherwise, just show up."

Helen hung up and went back to her applicants. The one on top was a woman of thirty-three named Liz Talcott. She had two children. The first she had listed as Asian son, five, and the other as Russian daughter, three. She listed her occupation as "full-time mother/editor." All those things together were quite unusual. She had never had an application that announced ethnicity or cultural heritage of children. Helen decided to call the mother.

She noted the number, called, and introduced herself. "Tell me what you are looking for in an apartment," Helen said.

"Mostly a decent place, safe neighborhood, and where we'll be accepted for who and what we are. I guess I'd say I need a *tolerant* place. We've seen some real dives. A couple of times, the look on the person showing us the apartment made it clear we weren't wanted."

"Is it that your children are adopted that creates the problem?"

"Partly. Dato looks Asian, which he is. And Tanya looks like a non-specific American, but she still speaks more Russian than English. We got her only six months ago."

"You say 'we.' Are you with someone who will be living with you?"

"No, that's the whole reason I'm out looking. My partner and I broke up a month ago. We're selling our house and both moving into apartments. She's a physician and works full time, so she's in good-enough shape. And she'll pay child support. But I'm the full-time parent. I can get some editing gigs, but it'll be hit-or-miss with no guarantees. So, based on that, the social worker I talked to at DSHS suggested I see if I can get a subsidized apartment until the kids are settled in school and the US. Then I could go back to full-time work. DSHS can't help because I'll have the proceeds of the house sale. But I want to use that to set up college funds for the kids. Half for that, the other half so I can pay for dance classes and vacations and the things that make life worth living. I don't want them to grow up poor or to think of themselves as poor."

"OK. I think I understand your situation. We have a building that I believe would fit you well. It's just a couple of blocks from the Seattle Center. It's small; there're only eleven apartments. I have a two-bedroom unit available there. It has good-sized rooms and great storage, and we just finished a total renovation. If you want bigger, I have a three-bedroom in Ballard. Would you like to see both of them?"

"I would. You know now I'm gay, plus the kids are foreign. Is that going to be a problem? I can't risk letting the kids see people look at us funny over and over."

"It's no problem. And most of the people we put in the units seem pretty broad-minded to me. I know the ones near the Seattle Center better, since I've personally shown four of them the places they live in. One is a single Hispanic woman with two boys, one is a really young couple with a new baby, and two are divorced men with children either full or part time. They're all very friendly. The other building is the Fleetwood Arms in Ballard. It's bigger, twenty units, and has a live-in manager. She's a widow with four children. She seems totally down to earth, been through a lot. We all liked her right off, the four of us who were with her when she came to look at the apartment. I'd have her meet you when we go there so you can make up your own mind."

"Sounds good. Tomorrow's good for me if it fits your schedule."

"Yes, I can make it in the morning. How about I give you the address for the Lower Queen Anne place and meet you there at ten? After we see that, you can follow me to the Fleetwood Arms in Ballard." They made arrangements and Helen got off the phone.

She was running out of apartments. They had already selected five for the Fleetwood. And now she might be down to only three left in the Lower Queen Anne building. The newest building at Seventh Street West was still two or three months away and, even then, would offer only four more units. She counted the number of applications in front of her. Twenty-six. She could not take them all, and there were several more on the way, according to Kenneth. Making decisions like this was so hard.

She made a cup of tea and took it to the living room. Then she went back for the applications, sat on the couch, which was as comfortable, she had found, as her chair, and sipped her tea. Her eyes wandered up to the painting, which had been delivered and hung the day before. She found it even more wonderful in her living room than it had been in the gallery. She felt very peaceful and quiet inside looking at the picture and sipping her tea.

Then she started looking through the applications again. She stopped at one from a man. He was fifty-two, quite a bit older than her tenants. But on the application, he noted two children, ages six and ten. The older child was Sage; the younger was Payton. Sexless. Interesting, especially living with a man over fifty named Mike Calvert. She had to get this story.

Helen called and introduced herself. "Mr. Calvert, can you tell me what sort of apartment you have in mind?"

"Sure, one I can afford." He laughed, and she did as well.

"That aside, what about size?"

"Well, I'd really like more than one bedroom, which is what we have now. I sleep on the couch and put the two kids in one room. Which they don't like."

"Why not?"

"Because Sage is ten, and she wants *space,* she tells me. Payton's a boy, a pretty typical boy, and a typical six-year-old boy doesn't have as much respect for a big sister as the big sister thinks she's entitled to. Plus, he leaves his stuff around and gets into her stuff, she says."

"Tell me about yourself and the children." Helen didn't want to come right out and say, "Are you the father?" but she really did want to know.

"I'm on disability from the city. I was a fireman for over twenty years and got injured on the job. I'm divorced, years ago. I have a daughter who got into drugs and is totally messed up. She lost the kids to the state, and the kids got put in foster homes. As soon as I found out, I got them out and got custody. That was two years ago. So now I have two kids. It's not so bad. In fact, we get along fine. We just need a bigger place."

"Well, it sounds like three bedrooms would be better than whatever you have now. So I can offer the last three-bedroom unit in a place called the Fleetwood Arms in Ballard. Would you like to tour it with the children? See what you all think?"

"Depends. I don't want them to see something they want and then not be able to give it to them. How much is it?"

"What do you pay now?"

"Eight hundred plus utilities. Another seventy-five for parking."

"I think we can do better. We'll have to run the numbers, but I suspect we can get you in for under eight hundred and give you the utilities for free. And there's plenty of parking in the neighborhood."

"Sounds good. That neighborhood is safe, isn't it? We're in Marysville now, and I don't know that neighborhood."

"The neighborhood is very safe. We only buy in neighborhoods after we've checked out the schools and the crime rate stats. And this building is in good shape physically, not run down, no mold; clean and freshly painted."

"I'm all over that. When can we see it?"

"I'm meeting with someone there tomorrow. I could call you and let you know when I'm more sure of the exact time, which I think will be just before noon. Would that work?"

"It can work. I want the kids to see it, so I'll tell the school I'm giving them a day off. They're both great students; they can afford to miss a day. And I don't want to make any decisions without them right on the spot. They need to feel they have a say in whatever goes on in their lives, given the rough start they had."

"I understand. I look forward to meeting all of you tomorrow."

❧ ❧ ❧

Helen arrived at the board meeting a little late. "This is the last time we have to squeeze into this room," said Kenneth. "We're moving into the larger quarters next week. With Mr. Pierce joining us tonight, it's really past time."

Helen joined Joe McGregor, Frank Brewer, Harriet Kilcoyne, and Alicia Mayhew. Kenneth took a seat at the head of the table. Mr. Pierce joined them as Helen was getting settled.

"Call this special meeting of the board to order," said Joe McGregor. "We can dispense with the reading of the minutes of the last meeting and the treasurer's report. Combine the minutes of this one with the last one, Kenneth, as an addendum. Now, Mr. Pierce, I believe you have information for us."

"I do," replied Mr. Pierce. "I was approached as your legal counsel by an attorney for a foundation, which I agreed to leave unnamed. We will refer to it as the benefactor foundation for our purposes. The attorney informed me that we have been awarded the sum of five million dollars." He stopped, waiting for the rustling in chairs and sharp intakes of breath to subside. "There are only two conditions. The first is that the gift shall remain anonymous. I agreed that even the board and all of its employees," he looked significantly at Kenneth Osborne, "must remain uninformed. The second condition refers to the uses to which the money may be applied.

"First, one million dollars must be prudently invested. Both the capital and the earnings that flow from it must be kept separate from all other funds. They are to be earmarked for two purposes. The first is to effect repairs and maintenance on existing and future properties. The donor requires us to undertake professional reserve studies and create a budget and timeline for required repairs and replacements for each property, both those currently in the portfolio and any new ones. This is to include, but not be limited to, such items as roof repair and replacement, parking structure or parking lot upkeep, repaving, and associated needs; updates and upgrades to existing electrical, mechanical, heating, and plumbing and sewer systems; redesigned and updated landscaping. The second use is to pay for the reserve studies themselves. There must be one conducted when each property is acquired and each five years thereafter. Current properties are to have reserve studies spaced out, one each six months, until all are complete, and then once each five years thereafter."

"And the remainder, the other four million?" asked Joe.

"The remainder is to be used to add more properties to the total portfolio. The condition here is that the properties cannot be purchased if they cannot be used for the intended residents within four months of purchase. There are minor provisos attached. For example, we can renovate and update on a schedule. Example, if we get a property with six units, and have the first one ready to move into within four months, and then one each four months after the last one, you actually have twenty-four months to complete the renovation, one apartment at a time, and that meets the criterion."

"Is that example part of the agreement or contract or whatever it is you made?"

"It is. We went back and forth on that issue. I know how much you all like to upgrade and remodel everything so I tried to make it so that you could do it. The other side was holding out for immediate tenancy. This was our compromise."

"Can we spend the funds on the upgrades or only on the basic purchase price?"

"That came up as well. We put in a clause that funds can be used for updates and remodeling only if the work does not exceed 20 percent of the purchase price of the building. If it exceeds that, excess can and must come from other sources."

"Are we supposed to vote on whether we want this money," asked Alicia, "since a no vote is an admission of terminal stupidity?"

They all laughed.

"I think we can just say the board graciously accepts the money and the conditions as agreed upon," said Joe.

"I don't know what to think about this," Helen said. "Why would someone give us this much money and not want to tell us who he or she is? Who's behind the benefactor foundation?"

"I have an answer for that," said Joe. "I do the same thing myself, not that I ever give five million to anybody," he hastily added. "They don't want us to come at them every month with a new and bigger request. People with money to donate get bombarded with requests. This is a way to protect themselves."

"All of the conditions on use of funds, is that normal?" asked Helen.

"This is actually pretty specific and detailed, in my book," said Alicia. Frank, who also sat on many boards, agreed with her.

"So, does that mean the benefactor foundation knows a lot about us?" asked Helen.

"That's a fair bet," said Joe. "But we do have to file pubic documents with the government to insure we're operating within the laws governing our non-profit status, so it's not a big secret."

Helen suspected the money was from William Prescott, but she was not going to tell the board that. She never used his name or acknowledged her past relationship to him to anyone who did not already know about it or did not have to know about it. And she was not about to start.

"The benefactor did us a big favor," Joe went on. "Beyond money, of course. They're suggesting we do something we should have been doing anyway. We haven't been preparing for the long haul on our buildings. The roofs will need replacing someday, and heating systems will wear out. We haven't put money aside for those eventualities. So what the benefactor foundation has done is *demand* we create the structure and means to do it. There's a good business head in there somewhere; this isn't just a do-gooder organization."

"We need to do that with everything," Kenneth said. "That's what I'm trying to do now that I'm full time. We need a better system, with written instructions, on everything from selecting tenants to setting rents to handling the rental income. That's going to be my job for the next six months."

"I should mention," Helen said, "that my current source of money is probably going to run out very soon. The benefactor is gravely ill. However, I can also report that we received two million from him to pay for the new building, the Fleetwood Arms, so we can be grateful for that."

"I need to go see that building," said Joe. "I think I'm the only one who hasn't. And since we're now adding more buildings with the money Edward just mentioned, I think we should try to name the buildings if they don't have names. Calling them the duplex or the Lower Queen Anne gets a little more confusing in my mind than saying the Lenora or the Fleetwood."

Several of the others nodded their agreement with his comment.

"So, I'm in the business of looking for property again, right?" said Frank. "My question is, do we want to go big or small? We could spend the entire five million on one, or break it up. What's your preference?"

They talked it over for some time. Frank was saying, "The biggest advantage I see to the small buildings, say four to twelve units, is that the tenants have a chance to build a tight community. Especially if we have—"

A knock on the outer office door stopped the discussion.

"Who's that?" said Frank.

"Oh, oh, I forgot to mention," said Alicia as Mr. Pierce headed for the door. "I invited George Pendergast to sit in on the meeting. I wanted him to meet everyone and tell you about his work with our tenants."

"Hello, everyone," George said as he appeared with Mr. Pierce. "I do hope I'm not intruding. I could remain in the outer office until such time as I'm properly invited in."

He said it with such a warm smile and such charm that there was no way anyone would suggest he do other than join them. They all shuffled their seats around as Mr. Pierce went to his private office and returned with a client chair, which he put at the table for George. While he was gone, Alicia introduced George to Joe and Harriet, the only members who did not already know him. George sat in the chair provided, a small smile on his face.

"George, you're always welcome to our meetings. In fact, why don't I move right now that George be an honorary member of the board and always be informed of meetings, to which he is always welcome," Frank said.

It was immediately seconded and passed.

George was grateful and bowed his head once to acknowledge their kindness. "So, where were you when I interrupted?"

"We're talking about the ideal size of the next buildings we should acquire. We've come into an inheritance, so to speak, and we have to spend four million dollars on new housing. We're discussing pros and cons of bigger versus littler."

"George, you've been to all of the places, now," said Helen. "What do you think?"

"Well, I can contrast the Lenora with Lower Queen Anne, and then address the two-unit house in Issaquah and the triplex in Shoreline," responded George. "I'm not willing to comment yet on Fleetwood Arms. Starting with the first two. The size of Lenora, with twenty-two units, makes it more difficult for a group feeling to arise. There are some excellent relations involving maybe two or three of the tenants, but there remains a lack of major common ground that brings all of the tenants together, or even large groups of them. The new project involving sharing of strollers is an example. It has brought together those women with children in strollers. But many of the tenants are beyond stroller needs. And even the ones who are using them will quit in a few months or years. Thus, they will tend to have the same grouping, which will be built around children's ages. You tend to get that anyway, given how children interact with age peers, so the stroller doesn't necessarily promote something that wouldn't happen otherwise.

"Turn now to Lower Queen Anne. The annex project, which by the way is what they call it, has brought every single current tenant into contact with the others. Now, there are several things that have contributed to this outcome, and I don't believe you could duplicate the project. But let's look at it not as a template to be copied exactly but rather as an exemplar, to serve more along the lines of an inspiration or broad example to follow. It has brought the youngest tenants, the Hudsons, into close contact with both Mr. Daniels and Mr. Lowery. The latter two men, of course, were bonded within minutes of meeting one another. One must wonder if they were related in a previous life. It's quite remarkable. Both of them are about Carmen's age, and they enjoy teasing her. And she enjoys the teasing. Her sons are fascinated with the tools and the workshop and spend hours with the men, who treat them as sons. And Carmen treats Christy Hudson as a daughter she never had. Carmen takes care of Christy's baby while Christy paints. Those are the first four tenants in the Lower Queen Anne building, and they've created a very close community. Whether new tenants will join in that community has yet to be determined.

"Now, here's the issue. Is the annex project responsible for that? Or does it come from the people who were chosen to be tenants? Or from the size of the building? I suspect it's all three. You have two of the three possibilities that you could attempt to duplicate: the project and the size of the building. But you can't do much about the personalities.

"Now let's turn to the Issaquah house and triplex in Shoreline. The two residents in Issaquah became best friends. They are two stay-at-home mothers. They have most dinners together; they go to the movies and for walks; they both go to the school programs together. They're essentially a family, and I doubt they ever move out of that house. The triplex is just the opposite. The three tenants barely know one another. Their friends and activities are totally separate. So, in those cases, I think the idea of trying to control or create something is far less likely. The personalities will dictate what happens. Now, you know I'm not a sociologist so this is just small-sample observational data."

His audience, especially Joe McGregor, was impressed by George Pendergast's knowledge and ability. First, he had shown intimate knowledge of some of the tenants, at least in the Lower Queen Anne building. Second, he had quickly understood the question and was able to grasp its essentials. Third, he had organized his thoughts and created a logical, coherent presentation off the cuff. *Remarkable,* thought Joe to himself.

"Given your analysis, then, what do you think an ideal size of building would work best for our tenants?" Frank asked.

"My guess is somewhere between eight and twelve units. Big enough for some variety, small enough so that everyone could be involved. Again, though, that's just a guess, a WAG as my old friend used to say."

Alicia laughed. She knew just whom he was referring to.

"I give. What's a WAG?" said Kenneth.

"A wild-ass guess."

They all laughed, Joe hardest of all.

"Anybody else have anything to add?" Joe asked.

"I do," said Alicia. "I was over at Fleetwood Arms to take fabric. Mrs. Parinelli is going to make curtains for the lounge. It was after school. Her two girls were in the lounge doing homework. And another girl was there as well. They were all talking about teachers and boys, things girls do. And I was struck by how great it was that they had this space away from their moms where they could hang out together. Yet their moms knew they were safe. So I think some kind of common room is a good idea. Also, Mrs. Parinelli was going to show a new tenant how to sew curtains because the other tenant wanted to make them for her apartment. So we have gotten a couple of benefits from that room already."

"Well, I'd say we're working toward a consensus here," Frank said. "And I even have a few ideas. Down on Nickerson, about the six-hundred block, there are quite a few small apartment buildings. Some of them look like those old two-story motels from the sixties and seventies where you park in front of your own door or near the stairs. I don't like those because the rooms in front, with the windows, are exposed to everybody who walks by. So that's not what I'm talking about. It's the others, sort of big box-type buildings, that I'd like to check out. They look like the right size. The location is good. How about I start there?"

"Good, Frank," Joe said. "Go for it. Now, I have another issue to bring up. We need at least one more board member. If we're taking on more properties with this new cash, we're going to need more help. Anybody with an idea about whom we should recruit?"

"I have a name," said Kenneth. "It's Oskar Lundgren. Anybody ever heard of him?"

"Sure, I know Oskar," replied Joe. "His family's been around for several generations. They came from Norway as fishermen, three or four brothers, as I heard it. They started with one boat they moored in that place where Chinook's is. They own half of those fishing vessels down there now, I think. Plus the chandlery shop, a warehouse or two, and who knows what else. They made their real money in canneries and have a couple of them in Alaska. Old family around Ballard. What made you think of him?"

"I'm good friends with his wife. She mentioned to me that he's thinking of stepping down as the head of the family business and letting a nephew run it. She said he never had time for a hobby, and she's worried what he'll do with himself. So it might be a good fit. He's a really good guy."

"He is that. I've always respected him. He and I worked a project together for a boys' club. Yeah, he's a good guy. You want to approach him or shall I?"

"Why don't you? I'm sure he'd rather think he was approached because of his achievements than for being Sonja's husband. Otherwise, he might think it was her idea."

"No problem, I'll call him tomorrow. Thanks for suggesting him, Ken."

"That reminds me about something I want to bring up before I forget," said Alicia. "Oskar's wife Sonja started a tea shop on Queen Anne. Kenneth is a partner," she nodded toward him, "and Sonja and I are having a high tea at the country club as a fundraiser for Claudius and some publicity for the shop. We're charging a hundred dollars a head. We're planning for one hundred fifty guests. No costs to deduct because everything's donated. So we'll have fifteen thousand for the foundation. I was thinking we should start a separate fund and then use the money for tenant improvement or entertainment or something. We think we can do this every six months, make it a spring and fall event."

"Nice. Can anyone come, or is it only by invite?" Kenneth asked.

"Anyone who shells out a hundred can go, right, Alicia?" said Frank.

"Precisely," said Alicia.

"Oh good, put me on the list. I don't care when it is; I'll drop everything else to be there. I want a table for four," said Kenneth. "And I know just what I'll wear."

"We're about done here," Joe said. "Anybody have anything else?"

"Just a quick report on Fleetwood. Our manager is Gloria Parinelli, and she's great so far. We have three of our tenants in now, and two more will look tomorrow. Most of the tenants who were there when we bought it are looking for places to move to, so more units will be available soon."

"On that note," said Joe, looking around, "this meeting is adjourned."

❧ ❧ ❧

The next day, Helen drove to the Lower Queen Anne apartments and parked behind the building near the storage/carport structure the men were turning into a workshop. She walked to the front of the building to meet Liz Talcott, the woman with the adopted children. Liz was walking down the sidewalk with the two children, having parked some distance away.

Helen introduced herself. "I'm really sorry the rest of the tenants aren't here. They all are working. I should have suggested we actually come in the evening around dinner time so you could see them."

"Well, we'll look now and maybe meet them later. I drove around a bit and saw how close this is to the Seattle Center. Great location," said Liz.

Helen thought Liz looked a lot like a busy mom with two little children. Hair pulled back in a ponytail, she was wearing jeans and a loose sweatshirt that had a few stains. No coat. Dato, the boy, had straight black hair and dark slanted eyes. His sister, Tanya, with pale skin, black eyes, and high cheekbones resembled her adopted brother in many ways. Both were solemn.

They all entered the building, and Helen took them to one of the larger two-bedroom units on the front, on the main floor. "This unit has two bedrooms. At the Fleetwood Arms, I have a three-bedroom. But this building, I think, meets a lot of your needs in other ways."

"I love this architecture," said Liz. "The picture rails, the fabulous moldings … Look at those baseboards; they must be six inches high, at least." She wandered about, the children following closely. "Oh my God, this kitchen is so fabulous. Look, it even has the original built-in fan with the chain. And look, it works!" She had unlatched the chain and the fan was running. "Who has that anymore?"

She walked around the living/dining room section. "This is huge. I could put my office in the living room, right by this great window. The kids could play in here when I'm working, plenty of space."

She went into the bedrooms. "OK, I grant you three bedrooms would be nice. But this one is possible. The kids are little enough for now to share. So I'd put them in the bigger room, and I'd take the little one. There's a ton of storage space. I could get by with what's here."

"Are you ready to see the other one with three bedrooms?"

"Sure, I'm parked down the street."

They arranged for Liz to follow Helen and arrived at the Fleetwood Arms about forty minutes later. Gloria Parinelli had been watching for them and was waiting at the entrance when they arrived. She shook hands with Liz and introduced herself.

"Would she be in the one next to me?" Gloria asked Helen. "The other tenants moved out three days ago, and I just got it painted."

Helen nodded. Liz carried Tanya and held Dato's hand as they ascended the staircase. Liz walked through the apartment. "I want to show you the laundry room," Gloria said. They all went to the ground floor and back to the old apartment that had been remade. The laundry room, which had been a living room, now contained three washers and three dryers. There were two folding cafeteria-type tables. Shelves over the appliances held various types of detergents, spot removers, dryer sheets, and bleach. Each was labeled with a tenant's name.

The kitchen area was tidy. There was a red kettle on the stove, a coffee maker, and baskets with red-checked napkin liners, filled with creamer, several types of sugar or sugar substitutes, stirring sticks, and small napkins. Four large pitchers were lined up nearby with large plastic glasses on a tray near them.

What had been the bedroom was transformed into a sitting area with a small couch and two comfortable chairs, all on a large rug that created a conversation nook. A card table in one corner had two chairs pushed under it and a half-completed puzzle on it. A floor lamp was nearby. The closet doors had been taken off, and shelving installed. There were books, puzzles, children's games, and toys neatly arranged, some in baskets, on the shelves. Two side tables and a coffee table completed the furnishings. The overall effect was of a well-organized, clean, and welcoming family room.

Oh, my," Helen said. "You've really fixed this up great. And I love those curtains."

"Yeah, me and the kids had a lot of fun doing this. Alicia Mayhew brought the fabric over. The furniture is from our family room. I had space in the apartment for the living room stuff, but I thought I'd have to send this to Goodwill. It fits great in here. The girls like it because it reminds them of the house. They spend time here every day. It's a great space for them to hang out together and get to know the other kids in the building."

"Thank you for showing me the apartment and this lounge area," Liz said to Gloria. "I think," she said, turning back to Helen, "that this apartment would be good for us, but my heart tells me to take the one on Lower Queen Anne. I think it's the children's theatre and the whole Seattle Center vibe that these two will need."

"I understand," said Helen. She gave Liz instructions for meeting with Kenneth to complete the lease agreement. Liz left, and Helen returned with Gloria to the entrance of the building. "I expect a man here in a few minutes. I'll bring him up when he arrives and introduce you." Gloria returned to her own apartment.

Less than fifteen minutes later, Mike Calvert arrived. Helen introduced Mike to Gloria and let her take over. Gloria introduced herself to the two quiet children and talked to them while she led the group to the open apartment. She walked around with them, pointing out the advantages of the apartment, from the generous rooms to the well-appointed kitchen. Then they all went downstairs. Gloria mentioned her own children and talked about how much her girls, Ariel and Leah, loved the lounge. Sage asked their ages and sounded enthusiastic for the first time. They talked about what movies the girls had seen and what kind of music they listened to.

Mike stood back with Helen and listened. He nodded and smiled at her. "I think you made a sale," he said quietly. "And it would be nice to have a woman like Gloria around when Sage has questions she doesn't want to ask me. Gloria is a real homespun-lookin' woman."

Helen agreed, though she did not say so. Helen let Gloria give instructions on the lease agreement, shook hands with Mike, and left. She felt it had been a very productive day. Two excellent tenants in two apartments that filled their needs. Four children well placed in safe environments. Mission accomplished.

❧ ❧ ❧

At five, Helen took a shower. She stood in her walk-in closet and stared at her clothes. She finally selected a pair of teal pants with a matching teal cardigan and a striped blouse of teal, pink, and white. A pair of pearl earrings completed the outfit, and she added make-up as a special touch. She stood in front of a full-length mirror and decided she looked pretty good.

At six fifteen, Gerard arrived, and they walked to Moorage for dinner. It was cloudy, and they had umbrellas, just in case.

When Helen took off her raincoat, Gerard looked at her. Slowly. "My," he said. "Very nice."

She smiled, feeling her effort was well worth it.

They declined drinks and gave the wine list back when it was presented. Then they ordered. "Does the chef have any foie gras this evening?" Gerard asked. The waitress excused herself and went in the back. "I suspect they do, given the other things on the menu," he said to Helen. "Do you like it?"

"Very much," she answered.

Then the chef came out. He introduced himself as the owner. "My wife says you wish foie gras. Is this correct?"

"It is correct."

"May I ask your preferences for cooking? Sautéed, in a mousse, as a pâté?"

"Sautéed please, with toast points, perhaps."

"Excellent. Thank you," he said, and returned to his kitchen.

When it came, it was perfect. They shared it, rolling eyes at one another with delight. Gerard had ordered cassoulet while Helen had asked for a rabbit dish. When the entrées arrived, they each gave the other a taste.

"I was married," Gerard said. "It didn't take. It was over in three years. That was twenty years ago."

"I was married. I'm a widow. Technically. Legally. The marriage was over eight years after it started. I was twenty when I married."

They both declined dessert but had tea.

"I had a good day," said Gerard. "We had a tough engineering problem. Been at it for over a month. Finally had one of those ah-ha moments, and the problem is solved."

"I had a good day. Placed two tenants in places they will love. Four children in safe housing."

They finished their tea and walked home in silence. A very nice silence, Helen thought. They parted at her door, and she went up to meditate for an hour before going to bed.

Next day, mid-morning, Helen was sitting on her couch admiring her painting, sipping tea, resting. The phone rang. *Darn*, she thought, and almost did not answer. But it might be someone who needed her. "Helen here." Briskly.

"Helen, this is Catherine Prescott."

Helen's heart started pounding, and her hands, she noticed, were wet. The handset of the phone was slippery. She said nothing.

"I'm in town. I would like to see you. We need to talk."

*No we don't*, Helen thought, but she did not say it and remained silent.

"Would you prefer I go to you? Or would you like to come to my suite at the Four Seasons?"

"I'll go there." She definitely did *not* want her mother-in-law in her home. Not now. Not ever. No way.

"In an hour? About eleven? I'll have lunch sent up."

*Oh, not lunch. She expects me to be there over an hour?* Helen hesitated. She tried to think of a way to back out altogether. Short of being unbearably rude, something she considered quite seriously, she could not think of anything. "Fine, give me your room number, please."

An hour later, Catherine Prescott opened the door of the penthouse suite. *Always the best*, thought Helen. *She can't bear not to have the best.* Helen was carefully dressed in a deep blue St. John knit suit with navy nylons and pumps. She wore simple white gold earrings and a white gold brooch with diamonds surrounding a pale pink/orange tourmaline. Catherine looked Helen over and voiced no disapproval.

"Thank you for coming, Helen. You may put your coat over the chair here," pointing, "and have a seat," pointing toward the couch in the living room of the suite. Helen did as she was instructed. She sat, knees together, legs to one side of her midline. Hands gently touching one another in her lap. Back straight, not leaning on the couch. Exactly as instructed by Catherine all of those years ago.

"I know this is a shock to you," started Catherine. "William does not know I'm here. He's in the hospital. I went to him this morning, then had our pilot bring me straight here. I'll go back in the morning and see him tomorrow afternoon in Boston. So he'll never know I came here."

Helen said nothing. She wondered at the Prescotts. Each of them was getting in touch with her after an absence of almost twenty years, each intent on the one not knowing what the other had done. During her married life, they had worked together as a unit, of one mind and one goal.

"Now Helen," Catherine finally continued. "I'm seventy-nine this year. William is dying. I mentioned he's in the hospital. He's in and out mentally. He's on morphine, so sometimes I can't really talk to him. I'm not sure where he stands with God, Helen, and it's a source of great pain to me." She paused. She had a small lace handkerchief and held it briefly to each eye, being careful not to smudge the mascara. "What I want, Helen, is to find a way of reconciling him with you. I know he feels you and he have treated one another very badly. He needs to forgive and be forgiven before he can face God. I'm sure of it. I want to help bring this about for him."

Helen was thunderstruck. She did not know how to approach this conversation. It was like a Band-Aid on a wound that had been left on too long, and now it was so stuck there was no loose corner to grip to rip it off. A knitted scarf with no thread to pull to unravel it. It was a ball with nowhere to start. Catherine looked at her, obviously awaiting a response.

"I've wanted this for a long time, Helen. I've tried, over the years, to get William to let me talk to you. He always forbade it. I prayed to the Virgin Mary. I did novenas. I talked to the priests over and over. I want you two to come to terms with what happened."

"And you, Catherine, have you come to grips with your part in it?" Helen was moved to speak, finally.

"What do you mean? What did I do? This was between you and William."

"Catherine, you were the one who told me to go to Riggs Erickson. You drove me there, remember?"

"But that was for your own good. You were killing yourself with booze and pills. That was to save you. I tried to save you."

"Save me? I was going to divorce Robert. You knew that. You put me in Riggs Erickson so I wouldn't leave him. What about before I married him? You knew his ups and downs. You knew he might be suicidal at times. You never told me. I was a young kid, Catherine, and you kept this huge secret from me so I would marry him."

"You wanted the marriage, Helen. You wanted the money, the name, the prestige. The illness was just something that came along with it. I think you don't remember what was going on, Helen. You were out of it most of the time."

"I remember. Robert and I did drugs every weekend. He started me on uppers and downers before I was even twenty years old. When he was high, he wanted me high. He introduced me to alcohol. Poured me some whenever he poured something for himself. But I thought this would just last a year or two. I never knew it wouldn't stop. You could have told me that, but you didn't.

"Even years after we married, we were still the life of every party for blocks around. For miles around. You knew that. You never intervened. You never tried to stop either one of us. Where were you? You were the adult."

"Helen, you and Robert did that. I had no control over either of you. You must take responsibility for that yourself. You must learn to forgive yourself."

"Yes, I know what I did. I'm learning to live with that. But what about you, Catherine? When I was going through it, not knowing why we were so 'out there,' you knew the truth. You knew Robert was ill. You should have told me, warned me. When I finally found out, for God's sake, I was twenty-eight. Twenty-eight, Catherine. Eight years after I was married. You let me marry him without knowing. Then you stood by for eight years while I tried to follow him up and down. Always higher up, always lower down. I was confused. I didn't know what to do. But you weren't. You knew all along."

"I stepped in. I saved you." Catherine was calm and reasonable.

Both of them were calm. And reasonable. Each telling the truth only the one could see.

"You *saved* me? No, you *imprisoned* me, Catherine. You took me to Riggs Erickson. Your nice, private, exclusive hospital. You must have given them one beautiful donation to get them to keep me there. I was just as drugged at Riggs as I was before I got there. Did you know about that, Catherine? That they kept me on tranquilizers and sleeping pills? I just floated across the days. And months. And years. Almost five years. You wanted me there, and you kept me there."

"Helen, it was the treatment you needed. You were very ill by then. The drugs and alcohol almost killed you. You've forgotten that."

Helen was suddenly very tired. There was no way. She could see it. Catherine and she could *never* agree on what the past had been like. They each had a story, a truth, and could not accept any other truth.

"What, exactly, do you hope to accomplish by coming here, Catherine?"

"That's what I've been trying to tell you. I want you to forgive William so he can forgive himself and you and be reconciled to God."

"William has a lot of things to be forgiven for, Catherine. What about when he forced William Jr. to go into the air force? He was ultimately responsible for that death. Then Robert's dea—"

"Stop, Helen! You're not being fair. Not another word. William was not responsible for our sons. I refuse to hear it." For the first time, Catherine had raised her voice, not to the shouting level, but close.

"OK, Catherine. What, exactly, is it that you want or expect from me?"

"I want you to go to William. Fly back with me tonight. I want you to ask his forgiveness for your part in the accident. When he hears it straight from you, I know he'll forgive you. Then you forgive him, and he can find his way back to God."

Helen was too shocked to respond for some time. Catherine dabbed at her eyes and stared at Helen. Finally Helen cleared her throat and spoke quietly. So quietly that Catherine leaned forward and cocked her head so her ear was pointed at Helen's face.

"Catherine, I cannot do it. I cannot do it because I had nothing to do with the accident. I'd been in Riggs Erickson for over a year when the accident happened. I was in rural upstate New York, for heaven's sake. How can I tell William I had a role in that? He won't buy that, Catherine. He may be ill, but he'll never buy that."

Catherine started sobbing. "Helen, I came all this way. I've prayed. I've done everything I can think of. I love him; he's my life. This is the one thing I want to bring him. He must have peace with God. He *must*."

"Yes, he must. And I want that for him. But he has to make that peace himself, Catherine. You and I cannot make it for him."

Helen was drained. She could not recall feeling this empty in years. And she wanted a drink. She really, really wanted a drink. She got up, got her coat, and left. She took the elevator to the lobby, and sat down. She looked at the lounge. It would be so wonderful to go have a drink. She got out her cell phone and punched in numbers. "Gerard? I'm in trouble. I'm at the Four Seasons." She listened, closed her phone, and walked out the door. She stood on the sidewalk and waited.

❧ ❧ ❧

Gerard turned off I-5 and followed his printed directions to Cloud Mountain Retreat Center, about two hours south of Seattle. He stopped the car, helped Helen load her things into a small cart, got back in the car, and left. He had not talked to her the entire trip.

Helen went into the main building, checked in at the front desk, and went to her assigned room where she remained most of the time for the next ten days. She went to the main building for meals and sometimes joined both the sitting and walking meditation periods. Several times, she walked the fifteen acres of trails by herself. Mostly, she sat and breathed. When guests for the scheduled retreats came and went, she joined them. At the beginning of each retreat, she helped people carry things to their rooms. At the end of each retreat, she helped clean the center and prepare for the next group. Each day, she spent an hour chopping vegetables. She felt herself grow stronger and stronger.

Finally, on the eleventh day, she called Gerard. "It's Helen. I'm ready to rejoin the world," she said. She was very calm, very peaceful. It occurred to her to wonder at Gerard's availability. It seemed that whenever she called, he had nothing to do but meet her needs. Odd, she thought.

❧ ❧ ❧

On the second day of her return Helen, tackled the work on her table. She had a very busy schedule. *This is good*, she felt, then wondered at the feeling. For many years now, she had considered her work as that, *work*. Now, she found, she could move toward it, not just willingly but also eagerly. The first thing on Helen's schedule was the Easton case. She had two messages from Mr. Leston, Garth's math teacher. She called his direct number. "This is Helen Paige, Garth Easton's CASA. Is this a good time to talk?"

"It is. I have this period free before my AP calculus class, so we have a good twenty minutes. I've had other calls from CASAs over the years so I know the kind of thing you're looking for." He had a very masculine voice, but its overall tone was friendly and helpful.

"Then perhaps you could just tell me a bit about Garth."

"Right. Garth is a great kid, first of all. He's very mature for his age. He takes his work seriously; he's always prepared for class. He's an excellent student. But, beyond that, Garth is good for his fellow students. He's sensitive, very sensitive for a boy this age especially. When he sees another kid with problems, he walks over to help. I saw him one day, maybe a month ago, approach a girl in the hall at her locker. She had her head in her locker, probably crying. Garth went over, put his hand on her back, and just stood there by her. He whispered something to her after a few minutes. She laughed. Then they went off down the hall. I know for a fact it was not his girlfriend, just a girl he knew. That probably tells you everything you need to know about Garth."

"Yes, it tells me a lot. So you think Garth should have a major say in who he lives with, I take it."

"I do. The decision should be all his."

"OK. That's all I need from you. Thank you for your time." She hung up, wrote up the notes, and looked over her file on Norm and Marilyn Easton and their son Garth. Then she checked in with the substance abuse clinic that Marilyn had said she would use for her evaluation. They confirmed what she suspected, that Marilyn had not made an appointment. Helen decided to write the report and send it in. She could always conduct an update investigation if Marilyn complied. Meanwhile, everyone would be on notice of her recommendations to the judge, which might break other things loose.

She stopped two hours later, report completed and "send" button pushed. Michelle, her supervisor, would now review it and then send it up to Hilary for further comment and editing. They would decide whether further investigation was necessary to make the report more complete. Helen knew, however, that very little would need to be done. It was a straightforward case with no complications or nuances. A drunk is a drunk is a drunk. She certainly knew that.

Helen turned to the foundation work. She called Kenneth Osborne on the new dedicated phone line.

"Claudius Foundation, Mr. Osborne speaking," he answered.

"So, you've moved in?"

"I have. You must come see me, Helen. I get lonely in here."

"Well, you can always go see the properties, get out a bit."

"Yes, I plan to. But for now, I'm still working on things in the office. I'm setting up those reserve studies, creating files for each building, organizing the financial details. I'm starting a separate account, probably a savings account, for the money from fundraisers, like the high tea Sonja and Alicia came up with. And Joe's dinner parties to pay my salary. Somebody might come up with more of those. The rent proceeds are really growing now, and those we'll use as operating funds. I'm a little confused, since the rents are growing enough to take care of routine maintenance on all of the buildings, and then some. What do we do with the 'and then some'? The new reserve account will be growing too. I'm interviewing some investment counselors to help us decide where to put that money. I'll have them present to the board after I meet them and do a first screening. I'm not about to make those decisions on my own. I'm probably overdoing all this, but you never know. If we get another huge donation, we'll be big enough to get super serious, and I want all of the systems in place."

"I knew you'd be perfect for the job. You're always thinking ahead and right on top of everything."

"Well, thank you, ma'am, always pleased to serve."

They laughed. Helen felt good. Kenneth always made her feel good.

"Now, what can I do for you today?"

"I need an update. I've been out of town."

"Yes, so I heard. Alicia told me you'd suddenly gone on vacation. We have to get used to it, I know. So here's the scoop. Frank's all excited about two new properties. They're both owned by the same company, a small investment group. He is trying to get a better price by buying both, and he's negotiating hard. Meanwhile, Alicia took the applications you left on your table when you went on vacation, and she and I have been going through them. We've placed three more tenants in the Lower Queen Anne and another four in the Fleetwood Arms."

"My word, seven tenants in about ten days. Fabulous."

"We were rather proud of ourselves. In fact, we went out for lunch to celebrate how great we are. We took Frank along, of course."

"I'm glad," said Helen, "Alicia works hard for us. She doesn't have to, you know. So I'm really glad she's enjoying it."

"She's lovin' it," Kenneth said, with exactly the same voice as the McDonald's commercial.

"Signing off," Helen said, and hung up. Next, she called Frank. "Any chance I can look at those two new buildings you're talking about?"

"Helen, welcome home. Am I glad to hear your voice. And yes, how about today, this afternoon? Like in an hour. That work for you?"

"It does. Give me the address, and I'll meet you there." Helen hung up and decided to walk. It would take almost an hour, she thought to walk to the six-hundred block of Nickerson from her apartment. She changed into good walking shoes. Then she grabbed an umbrella, insurance in case the current sunshine turned to dark clouds and rain, which could happen in any given five-minute span in Seattle, and left.

Helen met Frank at a two-story, red-brick building built into a slope that came down to Nickerson at a shallow angle. Beside the building, about twenty-feet wide, on each side, was space for parking. The slope in that section had been leveled, and a concrete retaining wall about twelve feet tall supported and held at bay the hill at the back. On the sides, the walls descended toward the street at the same angle as the hill. The building itself was solid looking with large windows on all exposed sides.

As Helen was talking to Frank in front of the right-hand parking area, a black sedan pulled up, and George Pendergast exited. "Good afternoon," he said as he approached them. He shook Frank's hand and gave Helen a quick hug. She hugged him in response without even thinking about it and then was shocked. She tried not to show it. This was the first time she had hugged someone in over twenty years.

"Frank, thanks so much for inviting me to the look-see with you and Helen. I love buildings, just love them. What do we have here?"

"Here we have nine units. This is a lot like the Lower Queen Anne. In fact, I suspect they were built at the same time, maybe even the same builder. The brick and the windows look identical. The floor plans are a lot alike. Here we have only two stories, not three. Four units on the first floor and five on the second, all with two bedrooms. Two units on each side and a smaller one in the middle of the back on the second floor. Each apartment on the side is identical to the one above it. Now, here's the critical part. You can see how they put in a tall foundation so the sides of the building on the ground floor would clear the parking wall by about four feet. That leaves room for those windows you see. At the back, there are no windows. That's why there's no apartment at the middle of the back on the ground floor. The two ground-floor units at the back, one on each side, have no windows on three sides. None on the back wall, none on the wall that adjoins the apartment to the front, and none on the wall that abuts the stairwell in the middle of the building. Plus, the back units on the ground floor look out on the parking lot. We need to pay a lot of attention to that when we see the units. This building is empty. The owners thought it would sell better with no tenants."

"Why would that be?" Helen asked. "It's supposed to be an income-producing property, isn't it?"

"I believe they thought it would be worth more as a tear-down. Somebody could buy it and put up a three-story building. Put in all first-floor parking so you get more space to work with on the sides. Then elevate the top floors. You could probably get the city to re-zone for about four, maybe up to six, townhouses, depending on the size. Their only mistake was the housing bust of 2008. This place has been empty since then, sitting on the market. No one can get funding for a townhouse project. The banks aren't lending. So, they're sitting on this, waiting out the recession in building, hoping to make a killing when things turn around. Meanwhile, of course, the place is costing them money."

"What's the asking price?" asked Helen.

"Two point two million. But I don't think we should pay that. So … we're talking."

"Let's go inside," said George. The entrance space was small, just large enough for the door to swing inward with a couple of feet to spare. Directly ahead was the stairwell leading to the second floor. To the left and right of the stairs were two hallways, each with two doors leading to two apartments. A third door was placed at the rear of the hall on the left.

"That's the mechanical room," said Frank, pointing to the back door. "It has a boiler. This place has radiant heat; you'll see the radiators in each room. The water in the boiler is heated with natural gas so it's pretty cheap to heat the place." He opened the door on the left-side, front apartment. It was much like the Lower Queen Anne apartments, just as he had said. The same beautiful millwork, wide baseboards, cute but small kitchens, huge closets, lots of storage.

"This is a great apartment, and tenants who like the Craftsman look will love it," said Frank. "But now let's look at the back unit." When they entered the apartment behind the one they had just left, they immediately noticed the difference in the light. This unit, with light on only one side, did not have the same feel as the other unit. "It's only the two units that have this issue since the ones above these have the full back wall with windows. What do you think?"

"I think I wouldn't want this unit, even with the fabulous millwork and great closets," Helen said. "How about you, George?"

"I feel the same. But I know for a fact, Helen, that most guys aren't as light-crazy as you and I are. Half of them never open their curtains or blinds. It's why we have the term 'man cave.' A man probably wouldn't mind this so much. But this is on the east side. Let's go look at the west side unit."

They did.

"Oh, no, this really is a cave," Helen moaned. The living room, with weak west light on the gray winter day, was depressing to Helen. "It might be good in the summer, but this would give anybody a depression in the winter."

"Now, here's what I'm thinking," said Frank. "If this were the common space, how would that work? We could use the large living-dining section for something like a party room or community lounge. Maybe a

big-screen television for sports days like the Super Bowl. Then the bedrooms could be designated craft rooms. One for the kids, one for teens
and adults. The women could bring in their sewing machines, scrap-
booking items, whatever. Add a couple of folding tables for projects;
you'd be all set. Put in good recessed lighting in all of the rooms with
dimmer switches. It cuts us down to just eight units for the building,
so we need to think about that."

George spoke. "Well, it still makes the lower edge of what we agreed
on at the special meeting, in terms of number of units, so that piece still
works. Yes, I like the idea, Frank. What about you, Helen?"

"I sure like it better than putting a tenant in here. And a common
room, the natural light doesn't matter so much. They're only in here
when they want to be. Or with a project or people they want to be with,
so that's a different story. Like a dim restaurant."

"OK, we done here? Ready for the other one?"

Helen and George nodded to Frank, and they locked the apartment
doors and left the building.

"We can walk to the other one, named Canal Place."

They crossed Nickerson and walked about two blocks further west.
They were in front of a narrow gray stucco building that extended backwards for a long way. It was on level ground, but at the back there was
a fence, and beyond the fence, a drop-off to the Ship Canal.

"This one has five units on the first floor, six on the second. There's
a one-bedroom on the upper right side, on top of the mechanical room.
We turn the one-bedroom into a common space, leaves us with ten units,
still in our goal range. As to types, we have four with three bedrooms
and six with two bedrooms.

"That's a good mix," said Helen. By now they were in the two-story
building. The stairs were to their left. There were six stairs, then a landing and a turn to the middle of the building, and the stairs continued
to the second floor. "How many units are empty?"

"Three right now. Four more tenants are on month-to-month so
we can give them notice right away if we need to. The other three have
seven or eight months left on the current lease. Let's go see the one on
this floor first. The other two are upstairs."

They entered the unit into a small entry space. A coat closet was on the left, and the kitchen on the right. The dining area and living area extended ahead, and a hall to the left led to the bedrooms. The guest bath was in the hall, while the larger bedroom had an attached bath.

"This building was probably built twenty years ago. You see the difference, more modern layout, carpet rather than wood floors. This is more like Fleetwood Arms," Frank said as he stood in the living room while Helen and George poked about in all of the rooms.

"The advantage here," Frank added, "is, of course, that it's newer. You get some great views from the units at the back, out over the canal. The rooms are smaller than in the other building, and there's less storage. But it works well for us."

"What's the asking price?"

"They want two million, which is a little high."

"So, what are you thinking of offering?"

"Well, if it's good with you, I'd like to go for a package deal, and offer three million five hundred for both. It'll be more than that by the time we go back and forth, but I won't go as high as four million."

Helen and George looked at each other. "Sounds good to us," George said, and Helen nodded her agreement.

"If we get both, can we name the other one Sabrina?" George asked.

Helen and Frank looked at each other. "I don't care; I have nothing in mind. Sounds good to me," Helen said. Frank agreed.

George looked very pleased.

"Is that your mom's name?" asked Helen.

"No, my first cat." They all laughed.

❧ ❧ ❧

It was nearing the end of January, and Helen was again facing a large pile of applications. She called Alicia. "Hi, Alicia, Helen here. What's your schedule today? I'd like some help with an initial screening of these applications … Good. Yes, I'll fix lunch for you. No problem."

After she hung up, she decided she had best check the kitchen. Promising lunch was easy; delivering on it might be harder. Then she remembered her trip to Trader Joe's four days ago. She had brought home a new product, flatbreads from the freezer section. She opened her freezer and checked. Yes! There it was, a French flatbread with mushroom and Emmental and Parmesan cheeses. Perfect. She'd make a salad to go with the flatbread. She checked the cooler section. She had baby spinach, some arugula, a Persian cucumber. On the counter, she had organic cherry tomatoes. She could make a vinaigrette. This would be great, a lunch the envy even of Alicia—she of the chicken salad stuffed in tomato! Helen was actually humming when Alicia knocked.

"Hi, Helen, I'm ready to go."

"Good 'cause I've got a lot of applications. You know Kenneth put out an e-mail to the social agencies last week, and we've been flooded ever since."

"Did we close yet on Sabrina and Canal Place?"

"No, but Mr. Pierce has it set up for tomorrow, and the owners already gave Frank the keys so he could start showing tenants."

"What price did he finally pay?"

"Three million eight, so we still came out two hundred thousand to the good. We have to put that aside until we can add enough to it to buy something else. Either that or come up with some fancy upgrades in a hurry. All we really have is two common rooms, one in each building, and that's just furnishings, no real remodel work."

"Yeah, Frank's really good at making deals. We're lucky to have him."

Helen looked at Alicia. "Are some of us luckier to have him than others?"

Alicia looked back but did not blush or laugh. "That's something I need to think about, Helen. He's left me some openings, but he's leaving me a lot of space so I don't need to walk through. And I'm reluctant to give any green lights."

"Do you know why you're so hesitant?"

"I do know. It's my marriage. You know I never had a serious relationship before I married Timothy. So I don't even know what a serious relationship looks or feels like. Hell, I'm not sure I even know what sex is supposed to be like after learning I only ever had it with a gay guy."

Alicia started to laugh when she said it, and Helen started laughing as well. They both ended up in a fit of laughter that brought tears to their eyes. Each time they looked at each other, they broke into giggles ending in breathless laughter. It was just like the time in Alicia's apartment in the fall. That, too, was precipitated by Alicia's startling comments.

When they were once more composed, they started on the applicant files. "How many are we looking for?" Alicia asked, sorting the papers into three stacks on the table in front of her.

"Good question. Let me count them up while you take notes." Helen looked through the files on the units. "We have eight units in Sabrina, all two-bedrooms, but one is a much smaller unit than the other seven. Then we have ten in Canal Place. Four of those have three bedrooms, the other six have two bedrooms. And we now have more free in the Fleetwood Arms. Let me see ... we have eight there, and two of them have three bedrooms. Plus there are two left in Lower Queen Anne, all two bedrooms. How many is that?"

Alicia started adding. "We have twenty-eight total. Of those, six have three bedrooms. And one is small. That seems like a lot of apartments to fill."

"It *is* a lot of apartments to fill," responded Helen. "Do you think we should get Oskar involved in this part? Have you even met him? I haven't."

"Yes, I have. Frank and I took Oskar and Sonja to dinner while you were gone. He's really nice. And he's so devoted to Sonja; you should have seen it. I think he'd be happy to help out. He's real down to earth for a guy with his kind of money. He's sort of blue-collar, but in a good way, if you know what I mean."

"Yes, I think I do know what you mean. So, think he'd be willing to meet a couple of tenants and show them around? After one of us went with him the first time and showed him how we do it?"

"Sure, I think he'd get a kick out of it, really."

"OK. You can call him and ask how he'd feel about it. If he's really into it and wants to help with the selection, he could meet us here. If he prefers just to meet the potential tenants and show them the apartments, he can do that after we get some selections made. I'll start now. What are these three piles?"

"This pile," Alicia said, "is the 'probably not' batch. They're single people or married without children. The second batch is the 'absolutely first' batch. They're recommended by social workers or filled out with the help of a social-agency employee, and they're desperate. The person who recommended them made a note in the application about them. The third batch are people with kids at least part time for visitation, but not particularly desperate right this minute."

"Got it," said Helen, and she took the second batch.

"If Oskar wants to help with this part, shall I tell him to bring his own chair?" asked Alicia, teasingly.

Helen smiled back at her. "I hear you. I'll buy a couple of chairs next time I have a chance. Did you see my painting?" She pointed to the living room.

"I did. I was afraid if I said anything you'd take it down. It's perfect. If I'd seen it first, I'd have bought it for you." She went to her purse and extracted her phone. Helen started on the files she had selected.

The first file grabbed her attention immediately. It had come through Elsa Dutton, the social worker Helen had contacted to arrange for Pam Butler to apply for the job as live-in manager at the Lenora Apartment Building. Elsa had written "GET HER A PLACE NOW" on the bottom of the application and signed her name to the directive. The applicant was Lorie Davenport. She had a son, Bradley, age ten. Her daughter, Ashley, was seven. There was no indication, other than "divorce pending," written in the space for marital status, that a problem existed. Helen rifled through her Rolodex, picked up her cell, and walked into the living room to call Elsa Dutton.

"It's Helen Smith from the Claudius Foundation."

"Thank God. I was hoping you'd call. I tried your number several times last week and couldn't get you. I couldn't find a number for the foundation, either. I was hoping you'd see my note on Lorie's application."

"So what's the deal here?"

"It's an ugly divorce. The husband has threatened both Lorie and the kids. There's a restraining order so he's not to go near them, but you know how those things are. Right now, Lorie and the kids are with an aunt of hers in Aberdeen. He won't look there. But she wants to get back to Seattle. She thinks he'll cool down really soon, but for now, I'm uncomfortable. So, I want her where other people are around during the day and we can keep her under the radar. She'll use a mail drop for mail and home-school the kids for the rest of the year."

"Well, I'm not sure. I'm thinking about the other tenants in the building. I can't be putting anybody in danger."

"We talked about that. The father is a high school teacher. He's mostly just mad as hell about the divorce. He was never abusive, and there's nothing in his past that suggests he'll go off the deep end physically or mentally. We think the threats were not credible. I was the one who insisted on the restraining order. Lorie didn't think it was necessary. He's in counseling now for anger management. Ordered by the court. His counselor reports that so far he's gone to every meeting and shows remorse for the threats he made. He's never owned guns and is against gun ownership. So, I'm probably overreacting. But I just don't want to take any chances."

Helen thought about it. She could understand how a man might make loud threats when told by his wife that she was leaving. It was an issue she had often faced on the CASA cases; and it was as often the wife who made threats as it was the husband. Mr. Davenport's later actions, such as getting into an anger-management counseling program and showing remorse for the threats, provided some reassurance that those threats had been impulsive and perhaps hollow.

"Well," Helen finally said, "we'll meet her for sure. When can she come to town?"

"Any time. She only needs three hours' notice."

"Tell her to be here tomorrow at eleven. I think the best place is the Fleetwood Arms. Tell her to meet me there. I'll give you the address."

"I'll be there, too, if you don't mind."

"No problem; that's fine." Helen got off the phone and called Gloria Parinelli. She asked Gloria to be home for the tenant showing and asked if perhaps Mike Calvert could be around as well.

"I'm sure he could," said Gloria. "He's around most of the time. I'll just tell him today when I see him to stay home in the morning."

With that arranged, Helen was ready to move on to the next application. Alicia stopped her by saying, "I talked to Oskar. He'd like to help on the selection process, but he's tied up today. He'll go tomorrow, though, to be around when you show a couple of apartments. And he'll work on the applications next time we do them."

"Good. I guess I'll meet him tomorrow, then."

"Yes, you will. I overheard you making arrangements to be at the Fleetwood Arms at eleven tomorrow and told him to show up there and introduce himself."

"You're not coming?"

"Helen, you have Elsa Dutton coming. I heard you talking to her. And Gloria and Mike, plus you and Oskar. Don't you think that's enough people to scare the pants off the poor tenant?"

Helen laughed. "Yes, I suspect it is. Point taken." They went back to the applications.

Helen looked at one from a man. Daniel Fortnuss was thirty-one years old and had an eight-year-old son named Nicholas. His son was with him every weekend and one night during the week. The person who had recommended him was Donald Jackson, a social worker who wrote, "This man deserves it more than anyone I know," in the section for comments. Helen was intrigued. She called the social worker's number. "I'm Helen Smith from the Claudius Foundation."

"Is this about Daniel Fortnuss and Nicholas?"

"Yes, it is. What can you tell me?"

"Daniel was convicted of car theft five years ago when Nicholas was three. He was an unwitting accomplice but took a plea so he wouldn't face a longer prison sentence. His attorney talked him into it. As it was, he served two years. He got out early but has trouble getting jobs because of the conviction on his record. He was an accountant, so you know he won't be able to get any jobs that require him to be bonded or handle money. I have letters from the arresting officer, the prosecutor, his parole officer, the warden at the prison, two of the guards, his in-laws, his ex-boss at the accounting firm. Every one of them is genuine; I checked them all out. This is a great guy with a real bad string of luck. I've managed to get him part-time work here and there, and everybody's been glad to have him, but no one has a full-time job. No big company will take him because of the criminal record. This guy needs a break. He and his wife were divorced while he was in prison. She's a nurse, works weekends, so that's why he has Nicolas every weekend. She'll vouch for him, too, by the way. So, as it is now, all he can afford is a crappy room in a crappy house in a crappy neighborhood. He hates that his boy has to see him like this."

"Got it. Can he meet me tomorrow at noon at an address I'm about to give you on Nickerson, near the Ballard Bridge?"

"Sure he can. You mean you'll help him?"

"I may be able to. First I want to meet him."

"Great, I'll call him right now and pass it along. How will he recognize you?"

Helen smiled. This person thought just as she did. "Tell him I'll wear a wild red hat with a feather on it. That should work."

Helen got off the phone and went to the kitchen to fix lunch. Alicia picked up an application and talked to her about it while she chopped the salad vegetables.

"Listen to this, Helen. This came through the visiting-nurse person. What's her name again? I can't read the signature."

"Ruth Mellon."

"Right. She wrote a little note. It says, 'Please consider, a definite fit.' The applicant is a single dad with a child, age fourteen months. His name is Jacob Abramowitz, and his daughter is Sarah. Hmm, think they're Jewish? Anyway, he's employed. Looks like at a freight company. They live in south Seattle; don't know where the address is. I'll have Kenneth check the crime map and the stats. But isn't it odd that Ruth Mellon would be working with a single dad? I thought her program concentrated on pregnant women."

"Give her a call; she's in my Rolodex."

Helen overhead the conversation while she put the flatbread in the heated oven and finished the salad.

"Hello, is this Ruth? I'm Alicia Mayhew with the Claudius Foundation. Yes, fine, thank you. How are you? We think so much of your organization, you know. I tell everyone about it." Pause. "Yes, you saw that, did you? We're so excited about it. We're still planning some of the door prizes. We decided to sell raffle tickets ... That's what we thought. So one of prizes is a week at a condo in Miami Beach, one is two tickets to the Seahawks-San Francisco game in a private box, another is airfare to Hawaii." Pause. "Oh good, bring friends."

Helen found herself smiling. Her conversations were so business-like compared to Alicia's rambling friendliness. People must think their organization had a split personality. But, she had learned, both styles were equally effective.

"Now," said Alicia, "what can you tell me about Mr. Jacob Abramowitz and his daughter, Sarah?" She listened for some time and then said. "That does fit us. I'll give him a call. And thank you for thinking of us ... Yes, I look forward to it as well." She hung up.

"Here's the story. Jacob was away in Israel reading Torah, and Ruth was working here with his wife throughout the pregnancy. They didn't have any money, and the wife was staying with her parents. Just before Sarah was born, the mother contracted eclampsia and died shortly after giving birth. Jacob returned. He and the in-laws didn't get along, so he found a job as a bookkeeper at the freight company, got a place of his own, and took the baby. Ruth said he's doing well with her. She started walking last month and is on or ahead of schedule in every regard. Most of Jacob's money goes to the day-care place so they live in a single room."

"Oh no." Helen's voice was subdued as she heard the story. "That's a heartbreaker."

Helen placed a piece of flatbread on a plate beside a large serving of salad and handed it over the bar to Alicia. Then she passed over silverware and napkins. After she fixed her own, she carried it around to sit at the table with Alicia, and they settled in for their business lunch.

"Helen, this is fantastic! The flatbread is out of this world, and the salad is heavenly as well. Thank you."

"You're welcome. You want to call Jacob or shall I?"

"I will. When can we see him? Tomorrow you're already booked with the Davenport and Fortnuss cases. Plus Oskar will be there, so you'll probably spend time with him ... I could see him, maybe take Frank along."

"Good, then you make the contact with him. What places will you show him?"

"I'll start with the Lenora; I think there's still room there. I like it for him for two reasons. First, the whole stroller thing, I bet he still uses those. More important, there's a synagogue and a Jewish school on Capitol Hill. I know there's a great day-care in that school as well. How about if I offer to pick up the day-care tab?"

"Fine by me. Sounds as if you've got it worked out."

The next day, Helen arrived at Fleetwood Arms fifteen minutes early and waited at one of the entrances. Elsa Dutton arrived with Lorie Davenport immediately thereafter. Elsa was introducing Lorie to Helen when a man approached them. He was tall, broad in the shoulders, and looked very strong. He was about fifty years old, perhaps older. It was hard to tell because his face was bronzed and his hair was blond with subtle streaks of gray. He looked like someone accustomed to hard labor under the sun or at sea. He was dressed, however, as a businessman. He wore a charcoal overcoat, open, with a navy suit under it, and highly shined dress shoes. He looked more as if he should be strolling on the streets in New York or Boston rather than Seattle. *A very striking man*, thought Helen.

She turned to him and asked, "Are you Oskar?" He nodded. They shook hands, and Helen turned back to the two women. "This is Elsa Dutton and Lorie Davenport. Ladies, may I introduce Oskar Lundgren. He's new to our foundation, and I wanted him to see the building and get a feel for our work." They shook hands all around, murmuring their hellos quietly. Helen described the basic layout of the building as they stood in front of it. Mike Calvert came out of the building and joined them. "Here's a tenant, Mike Calvert," said Helen, and introduced him.

"Gloria said to bring Lorie on up; she'd like to show her the apartments," Mike said. They all walked inside and up the stairs to Gloria's apartment. Gloria came out to join them, and Helen introduced everyone.

"So, what are your children's names and ages?" Gloria asked Lorie, leading her down the hall.

"Bradley is ten and Ashley is seven."

"Wonderful!" exclaimed Gloria. "I have seven-year-old twins, Brenda and Bobbie. And my daughter Leah is eight. Both girls have been hoping for someone their ages. My other daughter is ten. Mike's grandkids are ten and eight, but the ten-year-old is Sage, a girl. So Bradley is a bit outnumbered. We're going to have to tell Helen back there," indicating the group following them down the hall, "to order up another couple of boys age ten for him." Everyone laughed. At this point, Gloria was unlocking the door to an apartment. "This is three bedrooms. Your kids probably don't want to share."

They all entered the apartment. Lorie and Oskar started looking around. Oskar pointed out the open floor plan to Lorie, and they talked about how furniture could be arranged to make the most of the space. Mike, Gloria, Elsa, and Helen remained closer to the entry. Elsa talked in a low voice. "I want her looked after a bit. I think everything will be fine, but there's a husband involved who may create an issue."

"I'm right down the hall," said Mike. "I could leave my door ajar. Better yet, I might even be able to rig up an alarm of some kind. We used them all of the time in the fire department. Maybe something like what we gave handicapped people so we'd know where to look for them in a large building. I think I can work something up that would make you and her both feel safe if that's what we're talking about."

Elsa looked relieved. "That's exactly what I'm talking about. Just a precaution, but an important one for me."

Oskar and Lorie returned from looking at the bedrooms. "This looks perfect, and I love the location," said Lorie.

"Wait 'til you see our lounge and laundry space," enthused Gloria. "We all love it, especially the kids. They hang out and play music and games and stuff. It's fabulous. And you can always do a load of laundry or fold clothes or set up a sewing machine in the laundry section so you can keep an eye on things if you're concerned. The laundry section is huge, so we've even put in a couple of comfy chairs. Actually, we have two women who're teaching each other sewing down there in the evenings, using one of the folding tables. Neither of them is much good at it yet, but they seem to be havin' a good time."

"It sounds wonderful, but I'm concerned about finances," said Lorie. "How much is this apartment? It's awfully big."

"What does your budget look like?" asked Helen, taking Lorie into the kitchen area. The others moved out into the hall to allow the women to talk privately.

"I've budgeted a thousand a month, not counting utilities. I think I can manage that."

"Well, then you're in good shape. We can get you in here for eight hundred, and the utilities come for free."

"Really? Eight hundred total?"

"Really. Eight hundred total."

Lorie looked relieved. Her shoulders dropped, releasing tension that had been stored there without her awareness. "The kids will be so happy to be back in the city. This apartment will be heaven for them. And I really like Gloria; she's made me feel at home already."

"Yes, Gloria's a wonderful manager. And wait 'til you get to know Mike and his grandchildren. I think you'll like them just as much."

They exited the apartment and went downstairs to the lounge and laundry spaces. Gloria and Mike both showed Lorie the gathering spaces and games, and then he took her outside to show her the storage shed for bikes. Helen asked Gloria to give Lorie instructions for filling out the lease agreement.

Helen and Oskar left the building and stood outside on the sidewalk so she could answer his questions about the process.

"Well, that's pretty much how it goes," Helen said. "Some buildings don't have live-in managers, like Gloria, so we show them everything ourselves. It's best if you've seen each building so you know where to park and how to find keys and what the layout is so you don't waste a lot of time. Any questions?"

"I do have a question. When Lorie asked about the rent, you took her aside and talked. Do you have a list of rents, or how do you handle that?"

"We don't have a sheet with suggested rents because we don't base our rent on market prices. Our budget is such that we don't really need the rent to be very high at all, only enough for repairs, taxes, and insurance. The procedures are all being formalized right now, since Kenneth came on board as a full-time employee. We weren't so big as to need written instructions until the past four months, during which we've added dramatically to our inventory of apartments. So this will all be easier from here on in, as soon as Kenneth gets some standard procedures written up. And he'll also keep a list of all the apartments that are available or due to become available soon, and he'll pass that on each time someone goes to meet a potential tenant.

"Meanwhile, going back to your question about settling on a specific rent for a tenant right in front of you, always answer questions about how much the rent will be with a question of your own. 'What's your budget?' or 'How much do you pay now?' or something similar. Then make sure you go lower by a decent percent. If they say eight hundred, go to six. If they say four, go to two. Keep in mind that we're not in the business of making money on these places. We're in the business of getting kids into safe places and reducing stress on the parents or guardians. On the other hand, we don't give free rent unless we have a good reason. It takes their pride away. They want and need to pay something, and it's better if they think it's fair. When we give free rent, we trade it for something, like being the manager or maintaining the grounds or cleaning common spaces. If it's a bigger place, like this, we throw in a salary, depending on the person's need. There's always something you can think up that gives them some pride. That's critical.

"After we see them and settle on a place, they fill out the rental agreement with Kenneth Osborne. That gives us access to financial data. It tells us if we did a decent job with the rent. Then, as they get themselves squared away, maybe get a job or promotion, we gradually increase the rent until it gets to market. When they're totally independent, we suggest they move on so we can rent the space to someone who needs it more. If they're just making it, like two tenants in a duplex in Issaquah, they just stay on and on."

"I see. Wish I'd known about your foundation a long time ago. We often had fisherman and marina workers who could have used a hand."

"The foundation came to Seattle only a few years ago. But you're right; we haven't been very high profile. We have only a few places, and they fill up fast with the network of social services we use. If we had a huge budget, things might be different. On the other hand, we've grown a lot in the past six months, which is why we need more help, like you." Helen smiled at him. "And thank you, Oskar, for coming on board."

"My pleasure. This looks like my kind of thing. I really like the tenants, Mike and Gloria, now Lorie … all good folks. Great organization you've got."

"Thank you. Are you ready to meet another tenant? I'll tell you about him. He's a new type for us." Helen told Oskar everything she had learned about Daniel Fortnuss and his eight-year-old son, Nicholas. "They won't need a big apartment. Nicholas will only be there weekends plus one night a week. He lives primarily with his mother. In this new building we're closing on today, Sabrina, there's a smaller unit. That's the one I want him to take. So ... do you want to ride with me or follow me? It's on Nickerson."

"That's close to where I'll be going after, so I'll follow you."

"OK, don't be shocked when you see me in a red Viking hat when we get there." He looked a little surprised, but she didn't elaborate.

Helen put on the red hat with the feather as she got out of her car in the parking area of the Sabrina. Oskar parked next to her and laughed at her hat. "You really meant it," he said, smiling.

"I did." She laughed as well.

"You must be Helen. I'm Daniel Fortnuss." The man speaking to her was approaching from the other parking area. He was of medium height with very thick brown hair. At first glance, the hair reminded Helen of pictures she had seen of Bobby Kennedy. As he got closer she noticed he had a very pleasant face and wore dark-framed glasses. Helen revised her thinking: he looked like Buddy Holly. She smiled at her own stereotypes and shook his hand.

"I am. I'd like to introduce Oskar Lundgren. He's on the foundation board as well. He hasn't seen this building, which we're calling Sabrina. Shall we go in?"

Both men exclaimed over the interior. "Look at this millwork, amazing," said Oskar, and Daniel agreed.

"They don't do this anymore. What a shame. And look at these wide-plank floors. Beautiful." Daniel was obviously taken by the building. Helen had taken them first to the dark apartment that would become the common space.

"We feel this apartment is too dark," she said. "So it will become common space." She described the activities and furnishings the board had talked about. "And we're going to put up a huge television on the wall for sports events," she added. The men grinned at each other.

"Must have been a man in on those decisions," said Oskar. Daniel nodded agreement.

"You're right. It was George Pendergast, as I recall. If you move in, you're bound to meet him. He tries to visit each property every month, and he knows most of the tenants."

"If he's the big-television guy, he just became my best friend," laughed Daniel. Helen was charmed. She could see why Donald Jackson provided such a strong recommendation—and why the people who wrote letters in support of Mr. Fortnuss all spoke highly of him as well.

They climbed the stairs. "I'm going to show you an apartment that has two bedrooms. One of them is quite small. There's a lot of storage space and closets, however. The kitchen is small. All the kitchens are; it was how they were designed back then, and we're not going to tear out walls in this building." They had reached the apartment in the middle back of the building.

The two men went in and started looking around. Helen listened to the comments. Both were very impressed. They rejoined her. "What's the rent on this? It looks like it's going to be way out of my range, unfortunately. It's an amazing apartment."

Helen nodded to Oskar to take over. "Well, what's your budget?"

"Not much. I work whenever I can, but it's hard. I can't be an accountant anymore, you probably know why. While I was inside, I studied construction. I do taping, drywall, some masonry, pretty much anything that doesn't require a license. I can do electrical and plumbing, but not legally as a contractor or anything. So far, I've met six or seven contractors who give me work when they need the help. To answer your question, I can budget maybe seven or eight hundred; that's about it."

"Well, I think we can put you in this apartment for five hundred a month, and we'll pick up the utilities, including cable television." Oskar turned to Helen and said, "It's wired for cable, right?" When she nodded, he added, "We can throw in the Internet connection as well, and we have a new laptop in case you need one."

Daniel's face turned solemn. He turned and walked away. He took deep breaths. He came back and held out his hand, which was shaking slightly. Oskar shook his hand and put a hand on his shoulder. "Welcome home, Daniel." Daniel nodded.

After Helen parked her car at her apartment building, she walked straight to Vanja's Tea Shop and ordered a small pot of tea from Sonja, who had two other customers. She sat down at the table near the back of the shop and made notes to herself in the small leather-covered notebook she'd purchased from Sonja earlier. When Sonja brought the tea, Helen said softly. "I met Oskar. I think I'm in love."

Sonja laughed with delight. "I know. He's wonderful, isn't he?"

Helen nodded in agreement. "All is well?" she asked.

"Well and getting better. You pegged it. Thank you."

Helen nodded, and Sonja returned to her counter and her customers.

❧ ❧ ❧

When Gerard and Helen entered the Moorage that evening, the owner greeted them and then seated them at the same table in the window. He did not offer them drinks or the wine list. They were quiet at first, looking out the window at the people walking past in the drizzle, not really a rain, just a little moisture to make things sparkle. The soup came, and they both started eating.

Then Gerard spoke. "I hated my father when he entered the monastery. Blamed myself, of course. Standard story. He wouldn't have left me if I'd been better behaved. Smarter. A better son. I went to college. He provided for it. Then graduate school. After a PhD in physics, I decided I'd rather be an engineer than a professor. Back to school. I was shy but good at designing and creating things. Very good. Got some patents. A girl heard about me. A cheerleader-looking girl. You know the type. Blond Barbie doll."

He ate his soup, and they waited for the entrées. Helen was learning about the way Gerard worked.

"I went to college on a scholarship," Helen said after a long pause. "I met Robert Prescott there, and I thought I fell in love. His parents wanted us to get married. They wanted some grandkids, and I was the ticket. I was the cheerleader."

The soup bowls were taken away.

"Our marriage was a disaster," Gerard said, taking his turn in the conversation. "She wanted money. She got money. She still gets money. She got pregnant once but didn't want the baby. I did. She got an abortion. I divorced her."

Entrées arrived. They ate, giving one another a bite, savoring the food.

Helen spoke. "Robert had bi-polar personality disorder. He was up and down. He used drugs and drink. I did too. I followed him up and down. I went way down. Then I got put in an institution to dry out. My parents-in-law sent me there because they were afraid I'd leave Robert. They didn't want that. Then I lost more years of my life to prescribed drugs in the institution. Finally, I woke up and left. Then I found a swami. He had an ashram. Upstate New York. Isolated. I lived there for five years. I recovered. He taught me how to live."

They had tea. Helen talked about the new buildings the foundation had purchased. She mentioned the donation to the foundation. "I think it's from my father-in-law," she said.

"Are the buildings nice? Tell me about them." Helen described the Sabrina and Canal Place. Gerard laughed out loud when she told him about Sabrina being named for Kenneth's first cat. They were walking home at this point.

"That's the first time I've heard you laugh," said Helen.

"Stick around. I'm on a six-month schedule. Maybe you'll hear it again."

Helen laughed. "Goodnight, Gerard, and thank you for dinner."

"Goodnight, Helen."

Helen entered her building.

As she sat on her cushion, breathing, Helen's thoughts drifted to Gerard. She wasn't sure where her friendship with him was going, or if it was going anywhere at all. She knew, however, that she was increasingly comfortable with him. He made her a better person, she thought. That was enough. It was more than enough. Then she entered her silent meditation.

❧ ❧ ❧

Helen had barely awakened the next morning when her phone rang. She left her bedroom where there was no extension and went into the dining room, getting there on the fourth ring.

"Helen, it's Stewart Prescott. Uncle William died last night. Aunt Catherine asked me to call and tell you about the funeral arrangements. If you wish to come, we'll send the plane for you."

"No, Stewart, but thank you for the call. And I appreciate the offer of the airplane very much. But this is something I don't think I can or should do."

"Aunt Catherine said you'd probably feel that way. I'm so sorry it didn't work out differently. I think you and I could have been friends. And the family is small, you know. We could each use someone going forward."

Helen was surprised by Stewart's comments. She had no reason to believe they would have become friends under different circumstances. But there was no reason to dispute him.

"Tell Catherine my thoughts and prayers are with William as he meets his God. Tell her that as precisely as you can, please. And tell her William and I reached an understanding. That might be helpful to her. She doesn't know I went to see him, I think."

"I never told her. I promised William I wouldn't. I don't know if he ever did or not."

"Was his end comfortable? With the morphine taking the pain away?"

"It was very peaceful. Aunt Catherine and I were there. We knew it was close. He was ready; he told us so. Then he went to sleep. That was it."

"It sounds like the way he might have wanted then, given the illness."

"Yes, I think it was."

"Goodbye, then, Stewart."

"Goodbye, Helen."

She went into her bedroom, sat on her pillow, and concentrated on William. She tried to reach into his soul. All of her anger and bitterness were long gone, she discovered. An honest compassion was present. She meditated for two hours without moving. A faint message, she felt, was hovering. As always, it was opaque. But it was just enough to act upon.

Helen got up and went into the dining room. She called Kenneth Osborne and told him she would be gone for a few days. Then she slipped a key and note into an envelope and put it under Alicia's door. The note asked Alicia to see if Oskar would help go through the applications remaining on Helen's table and make sure there were none that required action in the next couple of days. After that, she packed an overnight case and drove the three hours to Portland. She parked and walked the streets in the rain, had lunch at a small vegetarian restaurant, got back in the car, and drove another hour west to Cannon Beach on the Oregon coast. It was cold. She walked on the beach in the wind. Then she spent the night in a small hotel, almost deserted.

The next morning, she drove north to Westport, a small old fishing town on the Olympic Peninsula in Washington. Chateau Westport, an old hotel, had rooms overlooking the beach, which Helen found especially restful. She liked leaving the window open all night so the sounds of the sea flooded over her as she slept. There was a maritime museum, which she toured, and then she ate wonderful razor clams, a unique local delicacy. The Grays Harbor lighthouse was just down the beach on a historic trail, and it was a walk she found both beautiful and meditative. The next day, she drove to Grayland, a nearby village, and learned about the local cranberry bogs and the October Cranberry Festival and then poked around the many small antique shops. Back at her hotel room, she had time and space for quiet meditation. She spent hours both days looking at the ocean from her room. Sunset was a beautiful time. The clouds over the sea parted each evening, and the sky was streaked and glowing with gold and pink tones. She talked to no one, except for the wait staff at the establishments.

She kept William close to the front of her mind. When not thinking about him, she thought of Catherine. Catherine would be lost without William; he was the center and purpose of her life, once her sons and grandsons had gone. All of their dreams, their hopes, had died one by one, until both of them were shells. Very rich and busy shells, but shells none the less. *She still has Stewart*, thought Helen. *At least Catherine has him.* Given how well Stewart had treated Helen, she felt he would be at least as attentive to Catherine.

Three nights after she left, Helen returned to Seattle. She felt cleansed. She was saddened by William's death. In the end, he had been as good to her as he could be, given where he was. She was at peace with him.

Alicia knocked on Helen's door the next day. "Hi, got a minute?" she asked when Helen responded.

"Sure, I've got lots of minutes. Come in and let me get the tea ready." Alicia sat in the living room on the couch and waited. Soon Helen brought the tray and put it on the coffee table before sitting in her chair. "What's on your mind?" she asked.

"First, let me bring you up to speed. I've been dying to tell you about Jacob Abramowitz. Remember him? The single father with the little girl?" Helen nodded. "He's a super nice guy. Very quiet, but very nice. Turns out his parents wanted him to be a rabbi. He never wanted it. He applied to law school at the University of Washington and he's been accepted to start this fall. His congregation agreed to foot the tuition. I offered the day-care, as I told you I would. His parents finally relented and will give him a stipend for the three years of law school, just enough for food and baby clothes. So, with our free-rent option, he's all set."

"Nice outcome. Sounds like a good tenant, and we wanted another man in the Lenora."

"And then we placed two more tenants in Lower Queen Anne so that leaves just one place vacant there. Then we put another two in Fleetwood so that's up to eleven tenants; no more are vacant right now, but we have some who'll be moving out within four months. Then we put two more in Sabrina, leaving five more available. We haven't put anybody in Canal Place yet, so it still has ten units."

"You put six tenants in while I was gone? On top of Jacob? That's amazing! Who did it all?"

"We all did. Harriet did a couple. Oskar did two with Frank along on one. Joe even did one. I did the other one."

"I'm beginning to think I'm not necessary. The organization runs like clockwork."

❧ ❧ ❧

Two days later, Mr. Pierce called. "Helen, it's Edward Pierce. I've received a call from Mr. Hancock, the Prescott family attorney. He wants you and me to fly to Boston, and he's sending the private airplane to pick us up tomorrow. I told him I'd call him back after I spoke with you."

"I don't know why he wants me there, or you. Did he say? I don't have any reason to go to Boston."

"He told me he plans to read the will of William Henry Prescott III. He says it's imperative that you're there. He can only read it, in fact, if you are. That's one of the provisions. He also said he thought I should be there to give you any advice you might want. He added that he feels you may want some support. Does any of this make sense to you?"

"No, what should I do?"

"Given the demand in the will that you be present, I think you should be, to protect yourself if nothing else."

"Protect myself from what? What can William Prescott possibly do to me now? He's dead."

"I don't know, Helen. Did he support you? Were you dependent on him in some way? Or did he have information that could hurt you?"

"No, nothing like that. I had an inheritance from my husband. That's my personal financial support. William has nothing to do with it. It must be something connected to the foundation. That's the only thing we have in common."

"Well, whatever it might be, I think it would be wise to go. Is there someone you'd like to come along with us. Would that help you?"

She thought of Gerard. That was the only person she could think of whom she would want next to her if something awful came up. But she felt it was too much to ask. He had already come to her rescue twice.

"No, just you and me. That's enough. We're both strong."

"You're right," Edward said. "We're both strong. I'll make the arrangement and get back to you."

❧ ❧ ❧

Helen and Edward Pierce sat together on one side of a conference room table in the law office in Boston. Mr. Hancock sat at the head of the table. Catherine Prescott sat with her nephew, Stewart, on the other side.

"I shan't take too long. I wish to present the basic outline of the will. It divides William's estate into three parts. One part goes to Catherine, one to Stewart, and one to the Claudius Foundation. I shall present the particulars of each part to each of you in private in a moment. First, however, I must read a letter to all of you. This was written a week before William died. He wrote it in my presence and gave it to me with instructions to keep it until today, then read it aloud, and then give it to Helen." He took the letter from a folder. Helen could see it was on the same paper, with the same ink, as William's previous letter to her. Mr. Hancock began reading:

My dear Helen,

Soon Hancock will reveal to you my plans and dispositions. Now I want to tell you why. Most people like me leave a legacy. Big time. Think the Carnegie libraries. The Guggenheim. Hell, think of Harvard. It's supported by legacies. They call it the endowment fund. I was going to add to Harvard's endowment, you know. And maybe have a wing of a hospital built and my name put on it. Oh yes, I was going to have my name stamped on this and carved in stone on that.

But you've changed me, Helen. Watching you and your work has inspired me. I saw you take all of that pain, all of that suffering, and turn it, transform it, into the Claudius Foundation.

*You* are my legacy, Helen. A truly living legacy. Your work will live after you, I believe, because of who and what you are. I trust you totally. I know you will do wonderful things. Things that would make me so proud.

At first, I thought about setting up a separate foundation. The Franklin and Stephen Prescott Foundation, I was going to call it. Put you in charge. But that would be about me again, Helen. And I'm a little sick of me. Ego is a tough thing. It's hard to kill it.

But I came around, in the end. This is not about me. It's not about my name. It's about the work. Living life as it should be lived. The ideal life. That means it's about you. So, it's yours. Do as you will. I know it will be right. And good.

God bless you, Helen.

# Part III

❧

# APRIL

Joe McGregor called the board of directors' meeting to order at six sharp. "We missed the regular February meeting altogether, then got busy last month, so let the record show the March meeting is being called to order on April 1, and add it's April Fool's Day while you're at it." He looked around. "List everybody who's present. I ask for the minutes of the last meeting to be accepted as provided to each member, and I ask for the treasurer's report to be dispensed with. Can I have a motion and second on each of those items, please?" It was done. "We'll vote by show of hands, all in agreement on accepting the last minutes as provided … Unanimous … All in favor of dispensing with the reading of the treasurer's report … Show of hands … Unanimous." He looked over at Kenneth Osborne to make sure he was ready to proceed.

"Next, any old business?"

"Yes, I'd like to report on the high tea," said Alicia. "It was held as planned on February 24 at the Sandpoint Country Club. All available tickets were sold. A raffle was held for donated prizes. The total for the day was thirty-four thousand dollars. Some attendees simply wrote a check as a donation. We asked two of our tenants to tell their stories. It was those, I believe, that opened checkbooks. At this point, I would like a discussion on the use of the money. I should add that this will be a regular event. It was very popular with the attendees and will be repeated twice a year."

"If that much comes in twice a year, we do need to think about where it should go," said Frank. "I move we set up a separate account and designate the money for specific uses."

"I have an idea," said Oskar. "We could use it directly for the tenants. Maybe even let them decide how to spend it. That way we contribute to the community development and cohesion idea."

"So, maybe the bigger buildings would have a general meeting to decide, something like that?" Joe asked. "How do we allocate the money? Maybe so much per tenant and make it equal? So a little place gets less money than a bigger place?"

"It makes sense," said Harriet. "Let's say we give five hundred per tenant. The little place may decide each tenant gets the five hundred direct. A bigger place … let's say, ten units … might decide to spend the five thousand on an upgraded common room with computers and printers."

"Why don't I run it past some tenants on my regular visits?" suggested George. "We could find out where they stand. Maybe they just want to blow it on Mariners' tickets or a day at a ski resort. That's the sort of thing these folks don't get much of."

"Right, good thinking. So for now how about we ask Ken to set up a separate account with the money and have George come back to the next meeting with ideas." Joe looked around for a consensus, then asked for a motion and a vote.

"Moving on, any other old business?"

"Yes, if I may, given I'm not a board member?" asked George.

"Shoot," said Joe.

"There's just a feeling I have. It's that little duplex on Dibble. Mr. Cleveland is the stable tenant there. You finished the remodel of the second unit last month, and we moved in a tenant two weeks ago. So I went to visit. The tenant is a man with two children. The boy is Gavin; he's ten, and his sister, Ava, is eight. I just didn't like something. The children were too quiet. And the girl sort of clung to the little boy's hand. The dad pretended to be funny, but I don't know. I smelled beer, but he had been working, he said, and was thirsty. It was early afternoon, so I didn't think too much about it. I don't know why I'm bringing this up, but it's been bothering me."

"I remember him," said Harriet. "I showed him the place. The children weren't with him; they were in school. It was in the morning, as I recall. And you know, George, I didn't like him. I can't tell you why. It's nothing I can put my finger on. But I didn't feel I had a right to deny housing for him and the children without a good reason, so I let him have it."

"George, thank you and you too, Harriet," said Helen. She felt a shiver run through her while George was talking. This was something she had to pursue. "I would like you to give me the name and number of the tenant when this meeting is over. I'll follow up. This, by the way, is exactly the kind of thing I want to you report. And you don't have to wait for a meeting. Call Kenneth or me at any point."

She turned to look at all of the board members and met every one of them eye to eye. "This goes for everybody from here on out. If you show someone around, and you have any negative vibes, anything at all, don't commit to renting. Say you'll get back to them. If you just don't like them, as Harriet did with this man, then don't commit. We can always take a little more time to be totally sure. The bigger we get, the more important this is. Never ignore your instincts. Please."

"Enough said?" Joe asked. When Helen nodded, he opened the floor again.

"I should report on the reserve study issue raised in our last meeting, which was the special meeting in January, if you all recall that," said Kenneth. "Seems like forever ago. So … I set up files and started getting the reserve studies conducted. I've got a good company, and they gave us a discount because we're a non-profit. I told them we really are non-profit and invited them to make a donation; that's how I got the discount. Anyway, they've completed the studies on everything except the Issaquah house, the duplex on Dibble, and the Seventh Street West project. So far we're in good shape. There's nothing pressing at any of the places that needs to be done in the next six months. So that's all to the good. It's mostly a matter of making a schedule for each building and then a master schedule for everything we own. I just have to do that, then get the work done as it comes due per the schedule."

"Any other old business? How about a report on how we spent the five million we got in January?"

"I'll make a report on that," said Frank. "We put aside the one million for the reserves and the studies. We have a professional to invest it, Washington Wealth Management Group. Then we spent most of the rest on Sabrina and Canal Place. We had maybe two hundred thousand left, some of which went to the common rooms in those two buildings."

"Good enough," Joe continued. "And on the addition of Oskar Lundgren to the board, let the record show that he accepted and is now a working member—make that a hard-working member—of the board. Not for the minutes ... I want to say, thank you, Oskar; you've been a real asset. I speak for all of us when I say that."

"Now, on to the new business," Joe continued. "Helen, how do you want to go about this?"

"I've asked Mr. Pierce to present this part on my behalf," Helen replied and nodded to Edward to take over.

"The foundation has received a considerable donation. I'm the only one who knows exactly how much it is. Helen wanted it that way. She knew it would be a hefty amount so she left the room while I learned what the legacy consisted of. What I will say is that we need the foundation to think bigger, a lot bigger. Helen is concerned that if you know the actual number it may make it too difficult for you to proceed in an orderly fashion to absorb the funds. So the funds are invested and earning a good profit as we speak. What you as a board must do is think about how you would like to grow. If you get a system in place, one you're all happy with, it will make the whole foundation work better."

"Could you give us some kind of parameters here?" asked Oskar. "Like, are we talking owning enough buildings to house every tenant who might be eligible in the entire Puget Sound region, something like that?"

"That's not a bad way to think about it," Edward answered. "You could start with the idea that your goal would be to house every person you wanted to who met your basic purpose, only broaden it to think about the entire state of Washington. In other words, would you want to start in Spokane, as well, or Vancouver, if that were your ultimate goal? If you think that way, it could lead you to consider a broader evaluation of how you now operate. Broader than a member of this board finding each building."

"That's a lot to get our heads around," said Harriet. "For example, who would we trust to do our work in a different city? How would we find people? How would we watch over them? That's a lot to think about."

"Worse," said Oskar, "we like what we do in part because we're so close to the end product. We meet and get to know these people. We care about them. We know their stories. We see the look on their faces when we give them housing. If our job starts to be managing a group of people in Spokane, we won't have that."

"This is exactly the discussion I want you to have," said Edward. "These are just the issues that determine how wisely you use the money. You don't need to start at the end point. You just need to figure out each step and plan for the future as it becomes more clear."

"You know," Harriet said pensively, "this is like having our fabulous little foundation, which we all love, suddenly become like the Gates Foundation at the bottom of the hill. It does great work, but it's huge, and the ones in charge are so far removed from the people they help. I don't think any of us would be as happy there as we are here."

"Is it because we're power hungry?" mused Kenneth. "Here, we're like gods, deciding the fate of people. We really do change lives sometimes." There were a lot of heads nodding in agreement.

"I like to think of it as giving people the opportunity to transform the lives of their children," said Helen.

"I think of our work as opening doors," said Frank. "People opened doors for me in my life. But I had to make the choices. I had to look at the door and see what was beyond it and then do the work to walk through it."

"I didn't know I was joining a group of philosophers," Joe said, and they all laughed.

"We didn't either," said Oskar.

"The work itself made us into philosophers," said Harriet.

"How about this? How about we all keep thinking about it? At our next board meeting we'll talk more. Meantime, if you get an opportunity to move in a good direction and want to go with it, then e-mail

Kenneth with the proposal. He'll e-mail it to everybody else, see how it floats, and we can go ahead. I know you all like to run with the ball the minute you get it in your hands, so I don't want you having to wait a month to take advantage of something."

"Mr. Pierce, as usual, you've proven yourself our perfect counsel," Helen said. "While we've been talking, my mind has been roaming over the possibilities. I'd like to start stretching out from where we are—like having a mini-branch in Bellingham or Marysville—but have just one person in charge up there, and have that person find one building, get it ready, and fill it. Then one more building. That way we could train someone and still have the person close enough to make in our image, so to speak. If we did that, then eventually, that person could move to Spokane, Escondido, or Kansas City and repeat it. Or if one of us moved, we could start another one."

"Would this person be a volunteer, a board member, an employee?" asked Kenneth.

"I think an employee. How much bother is that?"

"Not much," Kenneth replied, "if it's one more employee. If we get a bunch, then we'll need a bookkeeping person to do payroll. That's not my strength. For now, I just let the accountant do it. But we'd need to change that if we take on more. It's a waste of money for an accountant to be doing a simple task, like weekly payroll." Kenneth was making notes as he talked.

"But here's what we could do. I could hire a part-timer, say four hours one day a week. Let the person start by setting up a system. Do the payroll once a week. Then up to two days a week, same four hours. Have him or her take over the rent checks. Deposit the checks and enter them into a system I created for each building. Provide me a monthly report. Then, as we grow, bring the person on four half-days a week and eventually full time."

"Good thinking, Kenneth. Now let's stretch that," said Joe. "When we get to six or eight buildings in the Bellingham area, the rent job will get bigger. So the person you hire might want to split the job up. Let a new person come in a half day a week to do payroll, and the first person becomes the rent expert. We start out in Spokane, get another couple of employees, and then both of them become full time. If you think that way, you'll pick the kind of people who can grow into bigger jobs, and they'll be people you can work with well."

Edward Pierce sat back, satisfied. The board was beginning to grasp and deal with the possibilities of the new infusion of money. *They have no idea*, he thought, *of just how big they're going to grow. They'd all quit now if they knew.*

"So, am I in the market for more buildings?" asked Frank.

"You are," said Helen. "And I'm going to send out an e-mail for more tenants. We have the building on Seventh Street West. How close to occupancy is that?"

"I checked on that last week," Harriet put in. "It's almost there. I'd say another week, maybe. You could show people now if you wanted."

"So, I have those four units; plus Canal Place has some. Frank, get a place that's ready now. Then you can look for some that need rehab. I don't see any reason for us to change the way we do things. Meanwhile, if I get someone for the northern area, maybe you can help with the first building selection."

"Right. And I'll make some contacts up there, see if I can find a Realtor I like who can help the new person."

"Well, I'm ready to go home and have a drink and think about all this," said Joe. "Can I hear a motion to adjourn this meeting?"

After receiving a motion and a second, Joe took the vote and the meeting was adjourned. Harriet put her hand on Helen's forearm as everyone else rose to leave. She leaned over and said, quietly, "Helen, may I speak with you?"

Helen nodded, then said, "First, Harriet, can I have just a moment to get this information from Kenneth on the duplex tenant?"

"Of course, take your time," Harriet said, and rose from her chair. She added: "I'll be in with Edward. I have some business with him anyway."

Helen and Kenneth went to Kenneth's desk and pulled the file on Martin Larch. He was thirty-nine with two children, as mentioned by George. His application had come from someone who worked for Goodwill Industries. Helen copied off the name and number for follow-up the next day. Then she and Kenneth talked about how the meeting had gone while Helen waited for Harriet to finish her business with Edward. It was only a few minutes.

Harriet said, "I wonder if I might have perhaps a half-hour to talk with you."

"Of course," responded Helen. "Where and when?"

"How about at the little wine bar just down the street … Don't worry," she added hastily, "I know you'll only have water or tea." Helen was embarrassed by that since she did not realize others on the board were aware of her alcohol issue. "How about now?"

"This works for me," Helen said. "And I do like the place. It's such a relaxing atmosphere. And the young couple that owns it is so dedicated. I actually go there quite a bit, mostly for the goat cheese and caramelized onion flatbread."

"Good, we can share small plates," Harriet said. Harriet was a midsized woman of perhaps sixty-five. She was always superbly dressed, especially for Seattle, in professional yet stylish suits and pumps. Helen had never seen Harriet in slacks or jeans of any type.

They put on coats and walked a block to the wine bar. It was not busy, but not empty. About half the small tables for two were occupied. Harriet led Helen to a table, somewhat removed, on the side wall with no one at either table next to it. They removed their coats and sat. Helen said nothing, waiting for Harriet to take the lead. Harriet busied herself with the menu for a moment, then looked up, nodded to the waitress, who was also an owner, and gave the order. "We'll have goat cheese with caramelized onion flatbread, a plate of olives and cheese, and the duck confit," she said. "I'd like a glass of the New Zealand Sauvignon Blanc and my friend will have …?" she looked at Helen.

"Club soda with lime," Helen responded. Harriet made sure the server noted it and then turned back to Helen.

"I want to ask a favor regarding an apartment," started Harriet. "But you need some background first. Not many people know my personal history, but I feel you should, first, because I'm on the board with you and, next, because I feel we're becoming friends, and this is something so pivotal you need to be aware of it."

The final comment made Helen uncomfortable. She had believed she could keep friendship out of the equation, even when she and Edward created the board. Now she realized how foolish that was. People could not work closely on something so emotionally laden as the Claudius Foundation without having it spill into their private lives. It was not like a meeting of the Lions Club or a committee for a community center. A meeting once a month was not in the cards. This was a major commitment of time and effort and had become more so. The projected growth, with the new legacy, made that even more apparent.

"Of course, whatever you wish to tell me," Helen said.

The drinks and small plates arrived.

"I was married in my late twenties to an Iranian; he called himself a Persian, as did many of them. A very handsome and personable man. I was head over heels. We met at business school at Harvard. He came from a wealthy family. They weren't related to the Pahlavi family, the royal family, that would be. But they were heavily involved in the monarchy's financial dealings. He was Muslim, but it didn't mean much to me at the time. I was a liberal; everybody could be whatever religion he or she wanted to be. When we finished our MBAs, we went to Iran. I went to work for an American financial institution and handled personal investments for wealthy people. Very wealthy people. My husband had a similar position but different clients. Mine were more international; his were more Persian."

As she talked, they ate, Harriet sipping her wine very slowly, interspersed with eating olives and crackers with cheese.

"I had a son after just a couple of years. A wonderful little boy. My husband became more religious after our son's birth, which I don't think is terribly unusual. Pretty soon, he was keeping to the five-prayers-a-day ritual. Then he started being a bit bossy toward me. The lectures at the mosque on the role of the female were apparently causing him to view his American liberated wife a little more closely. He was becoming critical of everything I did.

"We lived in a sort of compound, the family compound with all of the generations. I thought at the time it was wonderful. All of those built-in babysitters who really loved our son as much as we did. And lots of servants, of course. Everyone had lots of servants.

"You probably don't recall any of this, but demonstrations against the monarchy started in 1977. The Shah fell, went into exile, in 1979. Our son was four in seventy-seven. The marriage had deteriorated badly by then. My husband was increasingly radicalized by the imams at the mosque. By seventy-eight, he said I had to quit work and stay inside unless accompanied by a male relative. I refused. He quit our bedroom and told his family to ignore me until I became a good wife. Well … if you read the book *Not Without My Daughter*, you have a good idea of what I was enduring. He basically kicked me out of the country in late 1978. Took me to the airport with one bag. Said if I didn't get on the plane and leave, I'd be out in the street. I had money, of course, and a good job. A company that stood behind me. But I couldn't have a life in Iran. Things were ugly and getting uglier. In the end, I left." Harriet was completely dry-eyed as she related leaving her son in Iran.

Helen nodded in sympathy, not sure what she should or could say. "You never saw your son again?" she finally asked softly.

"No, not to this day. I've been totally cut off from him and his life since he was four years old. He is almost forty years old. I don't know if he's alive or dead."

Both women were quiet for some time.

"I'm telling you this so you'll understand why I'd be drawn to the foundation. The kid angle. I don't have any, but I want to work to make their lives better. It makes up for a lot. Maybe I should have fought harder. Found a way to smuggle him out. I just don't know. It didn't seem possible when I was there. I had no voice, no power, inside the family compound. Looking back, I'm not sure I ever had any time alone with my son, except for maybe the first weeks. I didn't even realize what a communal son he was, like all of the children. My brothers-in-law had wives and children in the compound, and it was the same for those women. Worse, really. They couldn't work. They were Persians. Our mother-in-law was the boss where the wives and children were concerned."

"Harriet, I'm so sorry," said Helen, and meant it totally.

"Thank you, Helen. I needed to tell you that story. It will help you understand where I'm coming from. Everyone sees me as this strong woman who's made it in a man's world. That's not so unusual today, of course, but it was a pretty big deal back when I made it. You need to know some of what's behind that public façade of mine. So … the other thing that brings me to this point on this day is … I want to commandeer an apartment."

"Commandeer?"

"Well, not by force of arms, of course. But I want to take one over for my own purposes. They're not purposes antithetical to the foundation, however, or I'd never suggest it. I want you to give an apartment to a young Iranian woman with a child."

"We do that all the time. What's different in this case?"

"She's not indigent. She has some money."

"Then why do you want her in our place? Why not just rent something on the market?"

"I want her around the kind of people we help. I want her to see them and understand them. Share the common room. Have them in her place for dinner."

"Why?" Helen was confused.

"Because she's the daughter of a very wealthy family. She's done what I couldn't do. She brought her child with her. A daughter. She's been in the country for two years now. No one's after her. They were at first but legally, through the courts. She's in the clear now. I think the family washed their hands of her. She got the money because when she came they put some in an account for her, thinking she was just going to be here a while, maybe a year, visiting an older sister in Los Angeles. She was going to keep her sister company while her sister's husband traveled a lot in his work. Then they'd all go back together. She transferred the money out as soon as she got here. It's enough to live on for about two years if she's frugal, which she is. By then, we hope she'll be able to get a job. She already is picking up work as a translator; she knows three languages besides English and Farsi. She works from home via computer translating all sorts of documents."

"So, you want her in one of our apartments? Any idea which one?"

"Yes, I want her in the Lenora, where Sahar Dijani is. They can give each other some support, and she can help Sahar. It's a win-win for both of them."

"Fine by me, then. Sounds as if she'd qualify on her own. Did you check with Pam, see if something is available that's suitable?"

"I did. She has one coming open in two weeks, and I asked her to hold it for me. Said I wanted to check in with you, and then I'd let her know."

"Fine by me. It's all yours."

"Thank you, Helen. You know I won't make a habit of it."

The women smiled at each other and finished their small meal.

As Helen walked back to her apartment, she thought about Harriet. The cool, professional woman, competent and respected. Helen had already grown fond of Harriet and, now, seeing her in a more three-dimensional view, admired her even more.

❧ ❧ ❧

At eight in the morning, Helen was up and ready to work. She had been bothered by the duplex tenant and still felt uneasy. She called Goodwill Industries. "My name is Helen Smith, with the Claudius Foundation. Someone in this office recommended a Mr. Martin Larch for housing. Can I speak to the person who may have done that?"

"Mr. Larch works here on a part-time basis. It could have been anyone. Or maybe he filled out the paperwork himself. He'll be back around noon today. Want me to have him call?"

"No, thank you. It isn't that important. Thank you for your time." She hung up the phone. The feeling she'd had about this intensified. She looked up the cell phone for Rick Cleveland, the tenant in the other side of the duplex.

"Rick Cleveland? This is Helen Smith from the Claudius Foundation."

"Yeah, hi. Hope you aren't calling because you came to your senses on the deal you offered me."

They laughed as both remembered their previous conversation.

"No, nothing like that. This is about the tenant that moved into the other unit."

"Oh, him." Rick's voice was flat.

Helen's stomach started hurting. "Him. I'm getting bad vibes. Tell me what's going on."

"Well, I'm not sure I'm in a position to do that. What kind of tenants does the Claudius Foundation usually have?"

"We exist for one purpose, which is to find safe housing for children. Our goal is to get them from a bad situation to a good one. Tell me anything I need to know."

"Well, those kids aren't in a good situation, I know that. I never had kids, but there's a problem. They're scared and nervous, I think. Especially little Ava. She's afraid to be without her brother right next to her. They spend time with me. Met me when I was puttering around the yard. They're really nice little kids. Their dad lets them come over to my place whenever they want. And that's happening more and more. I bought a couple of games and some movies so we have something to do when they're here. I feed them dinner and started keeping snacks around. That should tell you something."

"Right. You won't hesitate to call the cops if anything happens, right?"

"I'll call. But what can I do?"

"I don't know just yet. I'm going to make a few calls, see what can be done. Do you know anything about the mother?"

"He cusses a lot about her, calls her a bitch, a whore. In front of the kids. Apparently she deserted them all."

"Right. Thank you, Rick. Let me give you my cell. Call me any time. Any time at all, please. Especially if you're worried about the children. I'll be working on it."

Helen hung up and called Elsa Dutton. She told her the situation. "What can I do?" she asked.

"We could report it to the Child Protective Services, but that's about it. We need some kind of reason. How about the school? Often that's where these investigations are initiated. The teachers usually know the best."

"I'll find the school and call. Good lead, Elsa. Thanks." She hung up again and looked on the Internet for the elementary school closest to the duplex on Dibble. She called and asked to speak to the principal. After holding for ten minutes, Helen was connected with someone.

"Hello, how can I help you?"

"I'm calling on behalf of two of your students. Their names are Gavin and Ava Larch. I'm concerned about them, and I wonder if their teacher has noticed or reported anything. An investigation by CPS might be in order."

"And who are you?"

Helen was stuck. It wasn't going to sound good. But she didn't know what else to do. "My name is Helen Smith. I'm with the Claudius Foundation. We provide housing for the Larch family. We've had reports from the neighbor and a visitor to the home that the children may not be safe."

"I'll take it under advisement," said the principal, who never bothered to introduce herself. "I'll also make a note to talk to the teachers. I'll ask them to talk to the children. I'll also tell them to be aware that there might be an issue and ask them to keep an eye out for anything. We'll take it from here. If there's anything suspicious, we'll take action."

Helen felt the words were correct, almost as though the principal was reading them from a prepared sheet of paper. She was not sure this was sufficient, and it certainly was not the response she had hoped for.

She called the CASA office next and asked to speak with Hilary Armistead, the director.

"She's at court today. She has back-to-back trials and settlement hearings. Can she call you tomorrow?"

Helen agreed to wait until the next day to talk to Hilary. She did not like it, but she was out of ideas. The few phone calls and the frustration of being unable to find someone who was as worried as she was got to her.

She went back into her bedroom. She lit an incense stick, lit a candle, and sat on her prayer rug, legs crossed. She breathed and chanted, trying to calm herself and find balance. Analyzing her actions, examining her behavior and feelings, she tried to discern what was appropriate and what was a response to her own background and issues. It was a deeply difficult task. Finally, she cleared her mind and tried silent meditation. After a half-hour, she admitted she was still too unsettled for the meditation to be productive. She blew out the candle, rose, and went back to work. First, however, a peanut butter/banana sandwich followed by a cup of tea.

An hour later, Helen was sitting at her computer with her CASA files in front of her. It was finally time to review the Butler case. She had a report from the counselor at the substance abuse clinic and the results of five random urine tests. All that was needed at this point was the final contact with the involved parties. First she called James after making sure it was noon so she would not disturb his sleep.

"James, it's Helen Paige, your CASA. Can you tell me how things are going for your girls?"

"Sure. It's going real good. I'm in an apartment upstairs from Pam. It's small, but since we have hers as well, it all works. Right now, I'm making sandwiches, and we're all going to walk to a park for a picnic in a half-hour."

"Do you feel the current situation is one you can both live with?"

"Yeah, we're both happy with it, and the girls seem good. They've made some friends here, so in a way it's better than when we were in the house. They're learning how to get along in a big group. I think they're better off, really, than when we were together."

"How about Pam's drinking? Is that a problem for you?"

"Pam doesn't drink. I haven't even seen her with a beer since I've lived here. She's no drunk, that's for sure. I'm in and out of her apartment often enough that I'd notice. And she's too busy, anyway. She knows every tenant in this place, and half the time, she's running around with one or more. There's an Afghan woman she sees every day. And a Jewish guy is here now, too. She watches his little girl some evenings when he studies."

"OK. I wanted you to know I'll be completing the report on your case and sending it in. You and your lawyer will get it before the week's out, probably."

"Right. Thanks, Helen." James paused, and Helen sensed he wanted to add something. "You remember our last call? In January? You asked me how old I was."

"I remember."

"It got to me. At first, I was pissed. I kept thinking about it. I even talked to a buddy at work on break about it. He laughed at me. Said I deserved it … Anyway, I thought about it again. And you were right, you know. I can't believe I was that stupid. My parents and I ended up in a fight, but it didn't last too long. We have a better relationship now, actually, than before all this happened. So anyway, thanks."

"You're welcome, James." She was gratified to hear he was finally becoming his own man, which would also make him a better father.

Next she called Meredith Butler. "Hi, it's Helen Paige, the CASA for the girls."

"Hello, Helen. Are you working on the report?"

"I am. I'll be sending it in today. Is there anything you want to add or want me to know before I write up my recommendations?"

"I don't think so. I suspect you know the situation very well indeed. You know we see the girls several times a week. And we took them to San Diego last month. Spent some time at the zoo, played in the surf. Had a great time."

"I didn't know that. I'm sure they enjoyed it, and Pam was probably happy for the break."

"She was. Have you seen her and James lately?"

"I have not. Been busy with other cases."

"Well, I think they're having a contest to see who can lose the most weight. They're both doing well with it. Pam having a job makes a big difference. She's a lot more self-confident. The girls are happy, I'll say that. She is a good mother, you know."

"Yes, I know she is. Those girls are lucky to have you and your husband, plus a mom and dad, all who love them to death. Very lucky girls."

"They are. And we are. I know the job of a CASA is tough. One of my best friends did it for a few years. She burned out."

"Yes, that's easy to do."

"I don't think I have anything to add to your case. I think I know how it'll turn out. And we're good with it."

"Thank you, Meredith. Enjoy your little girls. Goodbye." Helen closed her cell phone, ending the call. She wrote her update, finished the report, and sent it onward.

An hour later, she was having tea and looking over her notes from the most recent board meeting. The phone rang. "Helen here," she said, distracted.

"Good afternoon, Helen. It's Michelle. I just got your draft on the Butler case. Looks good. Everyone's on board? They'll settle?"

"They'll settle. This is a closed case as soon as we send this out and tell the lawyers to help them make up their parenting plan. There's another issue I want to talk to you about. I have a call in to Hilary, and she's supposed to call me tomorrow, but as long as I have you, I want to run it past you as well." She told Michelle about the Martin Larch situation.

"I can understand how upsetting this is, Helen. I can't think of anything we can do until we have some kind of evidence. The teachers are usually the first line of defense, just as you were told. If it were a CASA case, that would be different. We could send you in and have you nose around. But other than that, I think your hands are tied."

"I'm so frustrated," said Helen.

"I know. I'm frustrated every day in this job. Taking care of children is just the toughest thing you can do. I hear you."

"Yes, I know. So let's move on. What else is on your plate?"

"Glad you asked because I have another case I could sure use you on. It just came in, and I think we should get on it quick. Want to hear about it?"

"Sure, fire away." Helen felt the foundation was looming in front of her, like a child desperate to be born. But she still had the CASA work and could not let it drop. It was an anchor and a pair of wings. Both.

"This is a strange case. Three kids, all elementary age, oldest is ten. The father is in the navy. He's been re-assigned to the Pentagon. He's there already, on orders. He tried to get the kids before he left, but the court dragged its feet. He hired a private lawyer to try to get the kids, but the court doesn't seem happy. The mom has the kids here and wants to keep them here. There's some evidence that she has an older child by a different father. That child, who's fifteen, may or may not be abusing the kids. The mother may or may not be abusing prescription drugs. The dad sounds frantic."

"Got it. Send it on over." She got off the phone and returned to her reading of the foundation meeting notes. Then she made a decision. She looked up a number and dialed.

"Hi, is this Ruth?" she asked.

"It is," came a voice with a decided giggle in it. Helen was reminded of Ruth Mellon's welcoming and friendly round face. She could not help but smile at the voice.

"It's Helen Smith from the Claudius Foundation. "Do you have a minute? It's not about our mutual work."

"Sure, what's up?"

"I have a proposition for you, and it's something I shouldn't talk to you about while you're at work. You can give me a number to call you after work, or we can set up an appointment."

"I can meet you over my lunch hour tomorrow. Will that work for you?"

"It will. Where in the city are you?"

"All over, that's what the 'visiting' in visiting nurse is all about." They both laughed. "Tomorrow, I'm in Wallingford around my lunch hour. Is that close enough?"

"It is, and I know the perfect place," Helen said. They made an appointment for the following day.

The next afternoon, Helen and Ruth were sitting in a coffee shop. "I asked for this meeting for a couple of reasons. First, we have more apartments available. But I also want to know more about you and your career plans."

"Career plans? I don't think I know what those are." She laughed. "I was so lucky to get to nursing school. I have student loans that won't quit, but I did it. Then I got even luckier to find this job when I got fed up with straight nursing. I come from a long line of folks who work hard and don't get very far, so this is huge for me. I'm like the star of the family. So, as far as plans, I haven't thought beyond where I am right now."

"Do you love what you do? Would you ever be willing to think about something different?"

"Well, I do like it, parts of it anyway. I help people, and that's what I want to do. I didn't like hands-on nursing, I did it only two years before this came along. I've been doing this for five years now. I'm good at it."

"Here's what I have in mind. You've seen a bit about what the foundation does. We find buildings, and then we fix them up if they need it. Then we find people to move in. The people may or may not have an income. But they have children. Our real goal is to make sure children at risk have a safe and secure housing situation. I'm sure that's all pretty clear to you, right?"

"Sure, you helped Sahar Dijani and the Hudsons. I'm still active on both cases. They're doing great, by the way. Sahar has picked up work at the local dry cleaners. They give her alteration jobs. She takes the things home and does the job and returns them. She loves it. The Hudsons, well, what can I say? That new apartment, the annex out back, it's great for them. And the neighbors are so friendly and supportive. This is a life they could only have dreamed of before the foundation helped them."

"That's wonderful to hear," said Helen. "We have someone who checks in on our tenants, but he hasn't mentioned Sahar, so that's especially good news. And I've heard about that group of tenants where the Hudsons live. They sound like a huge family at this point. And that leads me to what I want to talk to you about. The foundation wants to expand, probably in the Bellingham or Marysville area. We need someone to start up an office and do what we do. We'd help until they're ready to go it alone. I'm asking if you're interested."

"It means giving up my job. As I said, I have student loans. I'd love to do it, but I can't really take on a volunteer job."

"I'm sorry, I didn't explain that part. We'd pay a salary."

"Oh, well … but I'm not qualified."

"Do you know how to contact people, talk to strangers, set up a filing system, organize your day, make appointments, drive around to meet people, fill out applications?"

"Sure, I do that all the time."

"Then you're qualified."

"Well … that's good. But I make a good salary now. And I have benefits."

"How much do you make? Just a range … I'm not being nosy."

"I make just over forty thousand a year. Plus I get paid vacation time. And health insurance."

"So, let's see what I could offer to entice you away." Helen paused. "I could offer a salary of seventy-five thousand. Health insurance. Company car. Paid vacation. We pay for your move. And the deposit and first month's rent on a new place to live. And set up an IRA for you of ten thousand a year. And pay off 20 percent of your current outstanding student loan balance every year for five years until it's paid off."

Ruth looked at her. "You're serious?"

"I'm serious. But here's something you need to think about. You'd have to move up there. It's too far to try to commute. That means leaving the city and your friends. It would change your life."

"It sure would. I'm from Stanwood. Halfway between Bellingham and Marysville. Bellingham is as big a city as I ever wanted to live in. My friends and family are from around there. You're asking me to go home, a huge success story. Where's the paper for me to sign before you change your mind? I'm in." She was smiling broadly, dimples showing, short curly hair dancing.

"You may want to start by talking to your boss and giving your organization enough notice to find a replacement. Then introduce the replacement to your cases if they want you to. That way you aren't burning any bridges. Always smart. Then find a place to live, and we'll look for office space near there. You can take the lead on that. When you find something suitable, we'll send someone up to sign the lease on behalf of the foundation. Then you need to spend time in our office talking to Kenneth. He can give you the scoop on files and organizational systems. Frank Brewer will want to spend time with you. He finds most of our buildings for us. Your salary begins the day you give your notice. If you need an advance, let me know."

They talked for another half-hour and then parted. Helen felt confident in her choice of Ruth. She decided to e-mail everyone on the board as soon as she got home so they would all feel included in the first baby step of their growth.

Later that day, Helen went for a long walk, first heading to the Seattle Center and strolling around. Then she went to the Olympic Sculpture Garden. The sun was shining, and Elliott Bay was smooth, the ferries plying back and forth. Helen alternately watched the ferries and studied the outdoor artwork. Some of it she loved. Some of it confused her. After several hours, she returned home and fixed two fish tacos for dinner. About eight o'clock, when she was dressed in pajamas and robe, reading, her phone rang.

"Helen? It's Rick Cleveland. You should come here. There's a lot of noise next door, like someone's hammering. I went out and yelled to see if everything was all right. Martin opened the door and cussed at me. The kids went out the back way while he was doing it. They hid out in the bushes. A little while ago they knocked on my door, and I let them in. They're downstairs now. What shall I do?"

"Is the hammering going on now?"

"Yes, worse."

"Call the police, report a disturbance. I'll be there as soon as I can."

Helen hung up and called for a cab. Then she hurried into her bedroom and put on jeans and a shirt. She threw some fruit from a basket on her kitchen counter into a shopping bag. Grabbing a fleece jacket and her purse, she went out to the sidewalk. A taxi arrived shortly thereafter, and she directed it to the duplex. A police car was in front. She paid off the taxi and went to Rick Cleveland's door.

"I'm sure glad to see you," he said, opening the door wide for her. She could see two children huddled on the couch, the girl holding onto the little boy. Both had brown hair and very large brown eyes. They had been crying.

"Hey, you two, my name is Helen. I think I know your names. Are you Gavin and Ava?" They both nodded.

"Oh, I'm so glad. I was told you would be here. I was told you were scared and needed some grown-ups to help you. Is that right?" They both nodded.

"I thought so. I have good angels. They tell me everything I should know. They told me to bring you some grapes and oranges and an apple and even a pineapple. I don't know why. What are we supposed to do with those things?"

"Eat them," said Gavin. Ava nodded her agreement.

"Are we supposed to eat them with popcorn?" asked Rick, joining in the session.

"Yes!" said Gavin with enthusiasm.

"OK. I know how to make that," said Rick. "Do you want to watch *Shrek* while I make popcorn?" They both nodded. Rick turned on the DVD player and put in the movie. He and Helen moved into the kitchen.

"What's going on?" Helen said softly.

"The cop is still over there. I met him when he drove up and told him I have the kids."

Helen cut the pineapple into chunks and the apple into slices and placed them with the grapes on a platter while Rick put the popcorn into a large bowl. They joined the children on the couch. Rick sat on one end next to Gavin. Helen sat on the other end next to Ava. Ava soon rested her head against Helen, eating grapes and watching the movie. Less than an hour later, there was a knock on the door, and the policeman beckoned Rick outside.

Rick soon returned and told Helen quietly that the cop would like to talk to her. She went out and stood with the cop on the covered porch.

"Could you identify yourself please?" asked the cop. He had a notebook open and a pen in one hand. Helen felt what she thought her CASA clients must feel when someone was writing down everything they said.

"I'm Helen Smith. I'm on the board of directors for the foundation that owns this building. Mr. Larch is a tenant of ours."

"I'm going to call CPS to come for the kids. That a problem?"

"Yes, it's a very big problem. The children are traumatized. They can't be separated. The girl would be in serious trouble. Can we locate a relative? Mr. Cleveland and I could stay with the children until a relative could arrive."

"You're not an approved foster-care parent, are you? Mr. Cleveland isn't. I already asked."

"No, but you can check me out with a lawyer named Mr. Pierce. And two other members of the board. Mr. Joe McGregor or ..." Helen hesitated. She had been going to give Frank Brewer, but her instinct suggested another name. "Or Mr. Oskar Lundgren."

"Oskar? He knows you?" the cop was suddenly interested.

"Yes, he's also on the board. Our foundation's primary concern is the safety of children. He can tell you that. Meantime, while you make calls, perhaps I could get the older child to tell me the name of a relative if you haven't already gotten that from Mr. Larch."

The cop was suddenly very serious. "He's in no condition to give us much. I've already sent him to Harbor View for a mental evaluation. So, yeah, see if you can get a name of a relative. I'll make a few calls."

Helen returned to the living room. Ava, she noticed, had fallen asleep. Gavin, eyes heavy, was staring at the movie. "Gavin? Do you have a relative? Like a grandma or an aunt?"

He nodded slowly. "Grandma McHale lives in Ocean Shores. She calls every day. And we see them, sometimes every week, sometimes not. And when we get to go there, Grandpa takes me fishing."

"Do you know Grandpa's name?"

"Yes, it's Ethan."

Helen quietly left and met the police officer on the porch. She gave him the name and location of Mr. and Mrs. Ethan McHale. He called it in to his supervisor and asked if the McHales could be contacted.

Within a half-hour, things were sorted out. It was decided to leave the children in the care of Rick and Helen until the grandparents could arrive and take them to Ocean Shores. Helen went back to the children. Rick went upstairs for a while and then returned. He picked up the sleeping Ava and took her upstairs. He returned and walked the half-asleep Gavin up with Helen following. He had folded out a sleeper sofa in the second bedroom upstairs and made it up for the children. Gavin crawled in beside Ava and was asleep in an instant. The adults went back downstairs.

"I'll go next door and survey the damage," said Rick. "The cop gave me the keys."

He left and was gone about thirty minutes. Helen ate all of the remaining fruit on the platter and the few kernels of popcorn at the bottom of the bowl.

"It's not so bad," Rick said when he returned. "Most of the damage was to the furnishings. Looks like he used a baseball bat. The television's shot to hell. The table and chairs in the dining area are totally destroyed. Looks like you'll need a new refrigerator; he bent the door. A few holes in the wall, but that's just drywall repair. Doesn't look like it affected any of the wiring or anything."

"That could have been a real disaster," said Helen. "Thank God the children were able to escape. Think for a minute if they had been little, four and two, for example."

They were both horrified at Helen's words.

"Don't go there. It's over. The kids are fine. This is now. Stay here."

Rick was determined not to dwell on what had not happened. Helen thought that was a pretty sane response. She decided to follow suit.

"You go on up to bed," Helen said. It was after midnight. "I'll sleep here on the couch so I'll hear if the cops come or the McHales arrive."

"Good enough. I'll spell you in four hours. There's a blanket in the trunk over there." He pointed, then yawned, and went upstairs. This was the first time Helen had actually looked at the duplex apartment. It looked fantastic, she thought. Then she tried to pretend to herself she had not also thought, *especially for a man.*

Rick Cleveland had a navy couch with navy-and-white striped side chairs. The couch faced the fireplace. He had made a cabinet of beautiful wood for the television that hung on the wall above the fireplace. It had sliding doors that retracted around the edges when the television was being used. Closed, they sported a painting of the sun setting over the ocean. He had white linen panel draperies on the windows, hung from thick rods painted navy. Over the gleaming oak floors, a large navy and white rug with a wavy pattern anchored the furniture grouping. A white coffee table completed the look. Very nautical. Masculine, but sophisticated. Across the room was a mirror with an ornate frame that mimicked scrimshaw. Under it was a parson's table, black. Under the table was the trunk Rick had pointed out to her. It looked like an old seaman's locker. She went to it and withdrew a Pendleton wool blanket. Under it was a pillow, so she took that as well. She lay down on the couch and went promptly to sleep.

It was still dark when Helen awoke to a soft knocking. She staggered up and unlocked the door. On the porch was a couple who looked to be in their late fifties, early sixties. They looked fit. And solemn. She asked, "Are you the McHales?"

"Yes, Ethan and Lorraine. How're the kids?"

"They're fine. Still asleep upstairs. Come on in." As they entered Rick descended the stairs. He greeted them quietly.

"So, what's the plan?" he asked.

"We talked it out on the way here," started Ethan. "We really need to step in and take the kids. Our daughter basically ran off with another guy. He didn't want any kids around. She lives somewhere in Oregon, doesn't keep in touch. Shows you what kind of mother she is. Martin insisted on keeping Gavin and Ava. God knows why. He suffers from mental illness. We tried to get custody once about two years ago. But when he's on his meds, he seems normal, so we lost. We can't move here, can't afford it. So we've been trying to keep close contact. We call Gavin every day after school. And we come over once a week. Sometimes Martin lets us have the kids for the night, sometimes not. We stay in motels. It's expensive."

"Do you have room for the children?" asked Helen.

"Not so much, but we can sleep in the living room and give them the bed. We lost our house two years ago in the bust. We have a one-bedroom apartment now. The job market is lousy. I worked for over forty years at a cedar-shake mill, but that disappeared some years ago. The spotted owl put paid to the lumber industry in Grays Harbor County. So we're all just trying to get by ever since. I'm still ten years out from Medicare. It's rough."

"But we can make do. We can still take care of the children," Lorraine was quick to add.

"That's right. The kids come first," Ethan hastened to support Lorraine.

"Maybe we should go see what we can do about the children's clothes and things," Rick put in. "The house is a mess, but I don't think Martin went upstairs. The kids shouldn't see it, though. We could get some boxes from the storage shed out back and pack their things, at least enough for the next week or so. Then I'll use my truck to bring out anything else you'll want." They all agreed to Rick's plan. Helen stayed in the apartment with the children while the others went next door and started packing things. She got her notebook from her purse and started making some notes.

When the McHales returned to Rick's home, she asked them to join her at the dining table. "Does either of you work?" she asked.

"I work at the school cafeteria in town. It's not much, four hours a day, five days week. No work during the breaks and the summer, of course. I'm paid by the hour. Ethan gets pick-up work here and there. Some carpentry, boat repair, installing new windows, painting, deck-building. He's real handy."

"I've been thinking," started Helen. "I'm with a foundation that buys and fixes up housing units for people with children. Are there many vacant multi-family properties for sale in Ocean Shores?"

Ethan and Lorraine looked at each other, frowned, and gave it some thought.

"There are," Ethan said. "There's always a ton of for-sale signs around there. People who bought beach property and never built on it. Or bought a beach house and don't go to it. You know, Ocean Shores was sort of founded by a group fronted by Pat Boone back in the … I don't know … maybe the 1950s when he was a big deal. It never took off. Too rainy for people, I think. Anyway, a bunch of money got spent, lots of things were built, and it's been limping along ever since." Ethan seemed to know the area well.

"Would it be possible for you to find a four- or six-unit place, maybe?"

"Probably, like I said, there's always lots of stuff for sale. What do you have in mind?"

"I'm thinking the foundation could buy a property and have you fix it up, one unit at a time. You could move into the first unit with the children while you fix up the rest. Give you a little more room."

"I can't afford to fix it up; materials cost too much."

"Oh, that would all be picked up by the foundation. And you would get a salary as the general contractor. Hire out all the work you wouldn't want to do yourself. It would be a cost plus your salary contract."

"Well, that sounds good, but I doubt we could afford the rent once we got it fixed up."

"That can be worked out. We don't need to worry about it. The important thing is for you to locate a couple of properties right away. I'll come out and look them over with one of the other foundation members.

Then we can get started. The sooner we have Gavin and Ava in decent housing with enough room for everybody, the better."

"Amen to that," said Lorraine.

"I'm going to run out to the store and get some food for the kids' breakfast. Know if they eat bacon and eggs?" Rick asked Lorraine.

"They eat everything," she responded. "If you look under those baggy clothes they wear, you'll see their ribs. No one's ever paid enough attention to their meals. We always bring food when we visit."

"Got it. I'll run out now. They might wake up any time." Rick got his coat and keys and left.

"I can start looking for property the minute I get back," said Ethan. "How soon could you get there to look over what I find?"

"Hopefully within two days. There are several of us, and most of us have flexible schedules. It sounds like an all-day trip, right?"

"A long day. Plan three hours each way on the road, just to be safe. Traffic is bad at the Lewis/McCord section of I-5, and sometimes it's backed up here in Seattle. Then add in a meal or two, and a couple of hours at least to look at property."

"I'll make sure everyone knows the time commitment. I don't think it'll be a huge problem."

They heard the children, and Lorraine went up to them. Helen heard excited little voices, then giggling. She heard the water in the bathroom running and the toilet being flushed. Soon the two children tumbled down the stairs in a race and ran to their grandfather. He grinned as he settled them round him on the couch. "You hear you're goin' home with me?" he asked. They nodded.

Rick appeared in the kitchen, coming in through the back door. "Good to see you guys up," he said to the children. "Should I fix pancakes or bacon and eggs?"

"Bacon and eggs and pancakes," yelled Gavin.

"And syrup," added Ava.

"Will do. I'll get right on it."

Helen decided her job was done, so she called a taxi. While she waited for it, she exchanged phone numbers with Ethan. He asked about the price range for the property he was to seek. Helen told him to worry first about the property and let the foundation worry about the price. The taxi arrived, and she left. It had been an exhausting night, and she had not slept well. When she got home, she went to bed. It was not yet eight in the morning.

Later that afternoon, Helen contacted Dr. Anna Schofield, one of the directors of the New Life Institute. She asked for an opportunity to discuss the results of the meeting in March, during which the issue of a new graduate program had been discussed. Dr. Schofield suggested a date two days hence when she and Dr. Harold Collins would both be available. They agreed to meet at noon, over lunch, in the foundation's new office. Helen notified Kenneth. He was delighted to act as host for the meeting and insisted on making all of the lunch arrangements. He had a caterer in mind, he said, that he had been anxious to use.

The institute, started about the same time as the foundation, was supported entirely by funding from the latter organization. She suspected Mr. Pierce had informed the group about the talk she and he had had in October. As a rule, she left the institute to the academics, but the decision to make it more relevant to her work had caused her to rethink the level of commitment she was willing to make going forward.

After the call to Anna Schofield, Helen felt she had done enough for one day. She knew she still needed to monitor herself and her involvement in the world and retired to her bedroom. First, she practiced yoga for an hour. Then, she did her breathing exercises. Finally, she felt ready for her silent meditation. Incense was burning in a holder, and the smell took her back to her ashram. A great peace descended. Deep into her meditation, she was dimly aware of a presence. She relaxed and let it flow, feeling surrounded as love poured through her. Her body tingled and then hummed, a pleasant, constant, humming. She floated on a lake of humming.

When she came out of her meditation, three hours had passed. She glanced at the clock on a crate near her bed. Six. She had to hurry.

She stood on the sidewalk, dreamily watching the lights and the people. She hardly noticed when Gerard approached her, and she fell into step with him without speaking. They went to Moorage and sat at their usual table. Gerard watched her but did not break her silence. He ordered for both of them.

Halfway through the beet terrine, she shook her head. "Hi," she said.

"Good evening to you, Helen," he replied.

"I know. No one told me. I just know," she said.

"I believe you."

"January. The five million. It was from you. Why?"

"Because I want to be part of it."

"You want a more active role?"

"Not right now. Maybe sometime. Now I have my own work."

They ate in relative silence and then walked home.

"How long since you've been to a meeting?" asked Helen.

"Can't remember."

"That's not so good."

"Maybe you're right. Maybe tomorrow. You?"

"Maybe tomorrow."

They reached her apartment.

"Goodnight, Helen."

"Goodnight, Gerard."

And they parted.

In the morning, Helen received a FedEx delivery with the file she and Michelle had discussed. Helen fixed a cup of tea and sat down to read it. Commander Kirk Becker was the father of daughters, Mia and Claire, nine and eight years old, respectively, and son Zach, seven. He had divorced Diana two years earlier. Diana was given primary custody because Commander Becker was on sea duty and often away, sometimes for as long as six months. He had requested shore duty so he could become the primary custodial parent. However, his shore duty assignment was the Pentagon. He had moved to nearby Alexandria, Virginia, six months earlier. Now he was trying, from that distance, to gain his objective of having the children live with him. In support of his request, he had attached various letters, including one from a housekeeper and another from the agency who had placed the housekeeper in his employ. He stated the children had confided to him their older step-brother was abusive toward them, both physically and sexually. He believed the mother knew this but was unable to change the situation.

Diana stated that she was an excellent mother. She said the three younger children were not being harmed in any way by their older brother. She maintained these were lies told so that Commander Becker could obtain custody and thereby be relieved of the obligation to provide her with the child support ordered by the court. She submitted statements from a minister and a friend who supported her statements.

As Helen read the case file, she made notes and decided on her strategy. She got a new notebook and recorded the necessary information in the front of it. Then she looked at the clock and started her calls. She figured she had three hours before she needed to get ready for the institute meeting.

"Commander Becker, please. Tell him it's Helen Paige from Seattle, acting on his request." She waited less than a minute.

"Commander Becker." The voice was very businesslike and very male.

"Hello. I'm Helen Paige, the CASA appointed to your case. You may want to give me other numbers so that I can reach you, other than at work, if you prefer."

"I will but feel free to catch me here as well. Everybody in this office, and it's a small one, knows about my situation and will find me whenever you call. No matter what. This is a top priority."

"I understand. The first extensive phone call may last as long as an hour, so I would prefer to have you at home for that one so we won't be interrupted. Meanwhile, I have a few questions we can probably take care of now."

"Shoot."

"Who in the Seattle area knows you and the situation with the children well enough to comment? They also need to be willing to talk to me."

"That would be the neighbor, for one. Her name's Roxie Stowe, with an *e* on the end. Hold on, I'll look it up." He paused and then read out her number. "A second person would be a teenager named Marie Louise Rainey. Marie Louise babysat for my kids quite a bit." He rattled some pages and then read another number. "I don't know if the school there has a counselor or not. I didn't think to follow up on that angle when I was there, but I'd like you to do it."

"Good, you've been helpful. I'll start with this. Can I call you when you're off duty?"

"Right. In about four hours. Let me give you the home phone." He read it off. "And thank you, Ms. Paige. We really could use some help on this."

"Good-bye, Commander. I'll talk with you later." Helen hung up. She did not want to accept thanks from someone when she was uncertain of the direction her investigation would take. It often happened that, as the case proceeded, the facts she thought she knew turned out not to be facts at all but, rather, subterfuges or misleading interpretations. Truth with a large *T* often turned out not to be true, even with a small *t*. She made notes of her call and entered the names and phone numbers given to her in the front of the notebook.

Then she placed her next call. "Diana Becker? This is Helen Paige, assigned by the court to represent your children. Is this a good time to talk?"

"Yeah, sure. What's this about? Is my husband causing trouble again?"

"The court has ordered me to do an investigation—"

"What the hell for! I've already been investigated!" She was agitated.

"Basically, I just do what the court orders me to do. I'm a volunteer. I'm not given a lot of extra information." Helen maintained an even voice, not reacting to the anger Diana Becker expressed.

"It's just my husband causing trouble. Just ask the questions an' I'll answer them. But that's all it is. There's nothing to *investigate*."

"Good, then it shouldn't take too terribly long. But I do need to come to your home and see where the children live. That's a basic requirement for everything else. And I'll need to talk to the children. Maybe watch you fix their dinner or something. That should do it, that plus talk with you. When is a convenient time?" She had tried to sound reasonable and accommodating.

"No time is convenient. But if it has to be done, maybe this weekend?"

"Sounds good. Is Saturday early afternoon a good time? Would everyone be around then?"

"Sure, that works. You can come when we eat lunch or dinner, either one."

"I think I'll take lunch. How about I arrive about ten thirty, talk to the children for a bit, observe lunch, talk to you a bit, and be on my way. Would that work?"

"Sounds fine. You know where we live?"

"I have the address, let me repeat it to be sure it's correct." She did, and it was. "See you Saturday at ten thirty," she repeated. Then she closed her cell phone and noted the appointment on her calendar.

She immediately called Roxie Stowe. "Hello, my name is Helen Paige, and I'm assigned by the court to advocate on behalf of Kirk Becker's children. Is this a good time to talk?"

"Yes, it is. I'm happy to tell you what I know."

"Thank you. First, what can you tell me about the situation with the children?"

"I can tell you they're in a bad place. The problem is that Diana can't decide which children to protect. On the one hand, there's her son by her first marriage. His name is Andrew, and he's fifteen. On the other hand, there're the little ones. They're Mia, Claire, and Zach. Andrew's always had trouble accepting the commander's children. He's jealous that they have a father. He picks on them unmercifully when he's left alone with them. I've heard them from my place, right next door. He mistreats them, even hits them. And I saw him one day forcing the girls to undress and dance. I put a stop to that. Another day, he tied Zack to a tree, with duct tape of all things. I had to use a pair of scissors to get him loose. That's just what I see and hear, mind you. I can't help but wonder what goes on inside the house where I can't see it."

"What did Diana do when she learned of these events?"

"That's just it. She says she *talks* to Andrew. She told me after the duct tape incident that it was just boys playing. But Zack was scream-ing and scared to death by the time I got there. Andrew had walked off and left him there. When I mentioned the girls being forced to undress, she said Andrew was just curious, and that it was natural for a boy his age to be curious. That's the whole problem. She just dismisses it. She stands up for Andrew."

Next Helen called the babysitter, Marie Louise Rainey. This turned out to be a seventeen-year-old who took classes at the local junior college, having already completed her requirements to graduate from high school. She was home studying when Helen reached her.

"Andrew's a tyrant," Marie Louise said. "No two ways about it; he's a tyrant. Mrs. Becker is blind not to see how he treats those little kids. Mia hates him. She told me he threatened her once. Said if she told on him he'd kill Zach. He tried some of that stuff on me. I think he figured that since he's a lot bigger than me I'd just take it. I told him if he ever laid a hand on me I'd have him arrested. He believed me. He knew I meant it. I must've told Mrs. Becker twenty times that he hit the kids or made them do stuff, but she just won't hear it."

Helen asked a few more questions, then said goodbye, and closed her cell phone. She'd heard enough to be convinced. She called Commander Becker and told him she would be interviewing him in a few hours, after she returned from a meeting. She also asked for a fax number so she could send him a release, which she wanted him to sign and send to the fax number she would provide. This would give the children's school personnel permission to talk to her about the children. After preparing the top part of the release she called the school for the fax number, then sent both items to Commander Becker.

Just before noon, Helen walked to the new foundation office to meet with Drs. Schofield and Collins of the New Life Institute. She had made up her mind. If she did not hear anything to convince her otherwise, she would start winding down the institute. She knew now what she wanted it to produce. If she could not get what she wanted, she would simply try again with a different structure. The work was too important to continue to leave entirely to others.

Helen, Dr. Anna Schofield, and Dr. Harold Collins were eating a wonderful lump crab appetizer in the conference room when Helen started her conversation. "Tell me about the spring meeting, please."

"It was very productive," Anna began. "We moved it to Boise, which Mr. Pierce suggested. Good turnout, over twenty schools were represented. The most important outcome, I think, was that we came to a consensus around the idea of two tracks for the graduate program. One would be a Master of Science instead of a Master of Arts. So instead of a thesis there would be a practicum, or internship. There would be one year of theoretical classroom work followed by one year of guided internship in the field. We would select or approve of the venues and the level of supervision for the internship and ask for a complete report at the end to qualify for the degree."

Then Harold took over. "The other degree would be the PhD, the academic degree. The requirements, however, would turn on the issue of the dissertation. We would demand that it be based on data collected from the field, actual working programs involved with women's independence and self-sufficiency in some way. It would then be possible for someone to complete an internship, just like the MS students, and later use that experience within the dissertation."

"There were some student representatives at the meeting," went on Anna. "They were determined to 'keep it relevant,' in their words. My question to you is: is this something you feel is in keeping with the institute's goals and where it should be going?"

"It definitely is," said Helen. "It's gratifying to me, actually, to hear these plans. I think the institute could support the effort in a couple of ways. We could provide locations for the internships if we find suitable supervisors with the experience and credentials you need. We could also provide stipends to the students."

The three of them finished their lunch, made a point of thanking Kenneth profusely for arranging it, and went their separate ways. Helen felt much better about the institute. She decided she would continue to support it a few years longer to see if the students were able to contribute productively toward the goals she had in mind.

When she returned home, it was almost time for her phone interview with Commander Kirk Becker. She reviewed her notes from the previous conversations and created a list of questions and issues for the coming phone call. After a change of clothes and a brief yoga session, she felt clean, balanced, and ready for the interview.

"Commander Becker, are you ready for this interview?"

"I am. Let's go."

"Why don't you start by telling me about your children. I'd like to get a feel for their personalities, what they like and don't like, that sort of thing." Helen really wanted to know if he had spent enough time with, or cared enough, to understand his children.

"Right. We'll start with Mia. As the oldest, even though not by much, she's always acted as a little mother to the other two. She's old for her age, which is a pity. She's a stoic. She takes whatever's handed out and tries to shield the other two. She's also very smart. Good in school. She understands people, knows whom to trust and whom not to. I'll give an example. She told me her principal at school acts interested but isn't, but her teacher, Ms. Ross, is interested but tries not to act like it. I thought that was perceptive, especially after I'd met the women.

"Moving on to Claire, she's very sensitive. Her feelings are easily hurt. She cries over things, whether it's a bird killed by a cat or seeing someone hurt. When she told me about Andrew hitting Zach, I think she cried more than Zach did. She relies on Claire more than she should. And she's hurt more by not having a decent mother. She's also very loving. She'll put her arms around Zach and give him a hug any time she thinks he's being mistreated. Other little girls tend to like her a lot, and she has a ton of friends at school.

"Zach is a tough little guy. He sometimes goads Andrew, I suspect. That's why Andrew takes after him so much. He puts up with Claire's hugs because he doesn't want to hurt her feelings. So he's pretty aware of what's what. In fact, I think Mia and Zach sort of team up to protect Claire. And they all put up a united front against their mom. She's let them down so much they've sort of formed their own protection society, and it works well for them. But let's face it, they're way too young to be expected to fend for themselves. Also, Zach attracts other boys like a magnet. He's got some real leadership qualities."

Helen had never heard an assessment like this from a father. It sounded as if he had made a study of his children. "Do you know anything about a duct-tape incident?"

"Sure do, Roxie told me about it. Later, I got the story from Zach as well. The girls had gone shopping with Diana, so it was just Zach and Andrew at home. They got in a fight about cleaning up the kitchen, I think it was. Andrew's a pretty big kid; I think he's about five eight. He twisted Zach's arm around his back and dragged him outside, held him against a tree, and then wrapped him up around the shoulders and ankles with the duct tape. Zach kicked him a couple of times before his feet got taped. Made Andrew even angrier. Then Andrew said he was going inside to get a hammer and beat him to death. Zach started screaming, and Roxie heard it and rescued him. That scared me when I finally got it out of Zach. I don't know if Andrew was bluffing, and Zach wasn't sure either. He knew enough to scream like hell though."

"Tell me your plans if you were to get custody."

"I've hired the housekeeper. I rented a house with a basement apartment, and she's already moved in. The house has four bedrooms. I can send a lease and a description from the rental listing, if you need it. We're close to schools; the house is in a nice neighborhood. There's a club with a swimming pool two blocks away for the summers. I work pretty long hours; that's why I'll need a live-in housekeeper. I'm sure it'll take the kids some time to adjust, but it's not any different for most military kids. And as I said, Zach and Mia are strong, and Claire makes friends pretty easy, so I think they'll do fine. It beats putting up with Andrew."

"OK, I think that's probably enough for now. I'll meet the children this Saturday. You can ask them how that went. I'll be working on the report as I go along, so it should go reasonably fast. I've already talked with both of your collaterals, and I'll talk to someone at the school this week."

"Good, I'd like to have them here ASAP. I'm just not comfortable with them so far away where I have no ability to protect them. I really want this to come off."

"Right. I understand your concerns. I'll call back if I need anything."

She got off the phone and typed her notes into her computer. All she had to do was the observation of the children and the interview with the mother and the mother's collaterals. This case, she thought, would not drag out as some did. The lines were finely drawn, and the options were straightforward. The children either stayed in Washington State or moved to Virginia.

❧ ❧ ❧

Helen got a call the following morning from Ethan McHale. "I found three places that fit. I went to look at them yesterday. Actually, I looked at seven, but these three are the best. When can you come to see them?"

"You've already looked at seven? You *are* a dynamo. You never told me that about yourself." They both laughed. "Let me call around, see who I can talk into coming with me. I'll get back to you in a couple of hours." First she called Alicia.

"Yes, I'd love to go. And I think we should plan to stay overnight. That way we're not driving out early and back late, tired as a hostess after a long dinner with twelve guests who don't get along. But, now I think about it, we shouldn't have all the fun. Why don't I send an e-mail to the whole board, even George, and see if anybody else wants to go. This might be fun. Ocean Shores is someplace we all know about, but I'm not sure we've all been there. I know I haven't. Leave it to me. Now, when?"

"Well, I need to be back by Friday because I have a Saturday CASA case visit, so I should go tomorrow or Thursday."

"OK. I'll get back to you later today. Bye, Helen."

Helen was ready to call the Becker children's school. It was early, but she suspected teachers and administrators arrived early. She asked for the principal. "This is Helen Paige, and I'm a CASA for three of your students," she said. "You received a release of information from Commander Kirk Becker so that I could talk to the school staff. I wonder if you have it and can now talk to me."

"Just a moment, let me go check," said Margaret Applegate, the principal. She soon returned to the telephone. "Yes, I have the release. Who will you wish to interview?"

"I could start with you. Do you know the children? Their names are Mia, Claire, and Zach Becker."

"I know the children." Ms. Applegate was non-committal.

"Can you tell me anything about any type of abuse. I'm talking about physical, sexual, emotional, verbal, or any other type."

"I can tell you that I saw bruises on their arms and legs. That's on all three of them. There were bruises on Zach's back as well, but I did not see that on the girls. Zach said they were from a brother named Andrew. The girls refused to name anyone. I have notes on this, and I reported it to CPS, as required. I also talked to their mother. She said she'd take care of it. That's the extent of my personal knowledge."

Helen could tell that Ms. Applegate was well briefed in how to respond to official or unofficial inquiries. Everything she said exonerated the school board and the school personnel of responsibility for whatever happened. She followed the letter of the law in all respects. No lawsuits need be filed.

*ঽৢ ঽৢ ঽৢ*

Alicia called back before five. "The whole board wants to go, but Sonja has a dinner party planned so she and Oskar can't," she said. "It's as if the rest of us are having a convention. We'll go tomorrow. We want to see at least one place tomorrow, maybe two, depending on when everybody gets there. Then spend the night, see the third place on Friday morning, and head back here by noon. Does that work for you?"

Helen couldn't believe that so many would travel to Ocean Shores. On the other hand, it could be sort of nice. She had mixed feelings. Then she realized that if she drove by herself and allowed some time to be alone in her room, she would probably do fine. At least she knew and was comfortable with everyone on the board. And she liked them all, very much. This might work out.

"Sounds good. I'll drive myself so I have some flexibility. Is there someplace to stay out there?"

"Yes, I've already made reservations at a hotel/condo thing. I booked eight rooms, told them I'd give a final count tomorrow morning when we left town. Some people may want to spend two nights. I asked for rooms with an ocean view. We'll just take our chances on what we get, but TripAdvisor ratings were pretty good."

"Well done, Alicia. I'm looking forward to it. We can stay in touch via cell as we drive out so we can tell Mr. McHale when to expect us."

Helen decided attendance at an AA meeting would be a good idea before the trip, and she walked down the hill later that evening. When she got to the meeting, late, she saw Gerard. He nodded and smiled at her, and she smiled back. Afterward, they walked home together.

"Dinner tomorrow?" he asked after a silence of fifteen minutes.

"I'm going to Ocean Shores to look at property for the foundation. In fact, most of the board, it seems, is going as well."

"Mind if I end up there? I'd like to look at the property."

"I'd like that. I'm driving early tomorrow, and I was going alone, but you can come with me."

"What time?"

"Leaving at eight."

"I'll be on the sidewalk."

"Done."

They walked in silence and parted at Gerard's door.

Helen practiced yoga for an hour. As she lay in bed waiting for sleep to engulf her, she wondered why she had invited Gerard to go along. Now the board members would see and know he traveled with her. They might think she and Gerard were a couple. She thought about that. She had not been part of a couple for over twenty years. *What a strange concept.* She drifted off.

❧ ❧ ❧

Ocean Shores was an untidy, ill-formed, half-baked sort of resort town, Helen thought. They drove around several streets. There were the typical businesses—a scooter-rental shop, beach-souvenir shops, miniature golf, a go-cart race track, and too many fast-food places for such a small town. Then there was the strip near the beach, which was lined with several hotels.

"The town has fewer than six thousand residents," Gerard reported. He was reading from his iPad. "Wikipedia doesn't say anything about the economy. It reports on a murder, race-related, in 2000. Some white guys harassed some Asians all weekend during the Fourth of July; then the Asians fought back. A white guy got stabbed. Hung jury."

"That's the big news? That's the Wikipedia information for the town?"

"That's it. Other than the attempt by Hollywood celebrities to make it into a big-deal resort and that falling through."

"Poor little town."

"There's a jetty and a state park. We might want to check those out."

"Maybe there'll be time. We're in the lead, I suspect. Shall we go to the jetty or a tea shop first?"

"They only have coffee shops, but we can go there and order tea. Let's do that."

"Right."

The trip had been a largely silent affair, which seemed to suit both of them. They stopped once in Aberdeen for lunch. It was a popular place, very noisy and crowded. Helen and Gerard had eaten in silence, listening to the chatter and watching the people around them. Helen was now ready for a bit of conversation and did not mind having tea, though she also would have liked to walk the beach. Maybe later.

The coffee shop was deserted, except for the barista. She seemed very happy to see them but disappointed that she would not be making fancy lattes. She had probably had training and was proud of her skills, and here she was, putting hot water in a throwaway cup and handing out tea bags. Life in the big city.

"So, Helen, why are we looking at property in Ocean Shores?"

"It's because I met a couple, the McHales, who've agreed to have their two grandchildren live with them full time. They only have a small apartment. So …"

"I see. Why not turn them into a part of the foundation work, right? What size building are we going to see?"

"I don't know. Now that I'm out here, I don't see much. Mostly single houses or those hotels along that strip we saw when we drove around. We'll see what's what when we meet Ethan McHale. He's the one who located the properties here."

Helen called Ethan from the coffee shop and got the address for the first property. She then called the other board members and gave them the address. From those calls, she was able to estimate that everyone would be in Ocean Shores by two and suggested they all meet at that time.

She and Gerard had almost an hour to wait, and decided to go see the jetty and walk on the beach. They parked in a lot near the jetty and got some beach shoes from the trunk of the car. The sun was out off and on. Clouds scurried and raced around the sky, blowing in from the sea. At times they looked threatening, as though a cloudburst was imminent;

then the clouds would dissipate, and bright sun would appear. They watched waves break on the jetty and then walked along the flat shore, watching seagulls. An eagle soared, then dipped close to the water, and soared away again. The wind and waves made enough noise that talking would have been difficult, even had they been the talking types. It was very peaceful and relaxing, and they smiled at one another now and again in delight at the setting. At a quarter to two, they returned to the car, cleaned their feet of sand, and put their shoes back on. Then they drove to Duck Lake and located the address of the property.

"Hi, Mr. McHale," Helen said as she approach the man standing in the driveway of a large house.

"Call me Ethan. Makes me feel like myself," he responded. He shook hands with Helen and then with Gerard when they were introduced. "You can see there's a lot of for-sale signs around here. It's typical. Sometimes I think the whole town is for sale. Duck Lake here is a beautiful place so things on the lake are more expensive, but still nothing like where you live, I'm sure."

While Ethan was talking, two more cars drove up. Alicia and Frank got out of the red Corvette while Joe McGregor and a woman got out of an SUV. Joe introduced everyone to his wife, Gabrielle. No one had ever met her, which Helen thought was odd, since Joe often talked about her involvement in parties for fundraising activities. Gabrielle was a short woman with short gray hair and a slightly round body. She was very friendly and introduced herself.

"I've heard so much about you, all of you, that I feel I've been friends for years. And I can't thank you enough, Helen," she said, turning to Helen, "for giving my husband such a wonderful job. He likes this much more than his so-called real work. I think it relaxes him, too."

A blue sedan appeared and was followed by a Jaguar. Kenneth got out of the passenger side of the sedan, followed by Edward, who was the driver. The Jaguar was driven by Harriet. George Pendergast got out of the passenger side, surprising Helen. They all came over to be introduced to Gabrielle and Ethan. Helen took this opportunity to introduce Gerard to everyone. She said his name, and added simply that he was a friend of hers.

"What do we have here?" asked Edward, turning to the matter at hand.

"This looks like a sprawling two-story," said Ethan, "but it was turned into a four-unit place about ten years ago. I don't think it's what you have in mind, but I thought it would be good for an overall picture. The advantages of this place are that it's on the lake with all of the units having a balcony overlooking it. The building's about twenty years old. The place hasn't been beat up like some of the properties along Ocean Shores Boulevard. Those need painting every other year, and anything metal left out for a single season rusts out. That would be railings on stairs, bicycles, grills, everything. Rust is a huge problem out here. And the wind blows sand around a lot, so there's a sort of scouring action from that, and the paint really suffers. This will be important when we talk about maintenance costs later. I'd like to show you one of the units. They're all pretty much the same."

Ethan had a key to an upper unit. They entered the main door. To both the left and right were doors, each with a number to indicate a unit. The stairs ended in a small landing with two more doors, each with a number. They went into the unit on the right and then spread out and starting looking around.

"Well, at least it has two bedrooms, which is usually one of our requirements," said Frank.

"This kitchen is pretty hopeless," said Harriet. "It's fine if you're renting the place for a week, but it would never do for a family living here. No storage. Two pans, a skillet, a set of dishes, that's about all there's room for. You need more than that to fix meals for children. At least a big pot and a colander for pasta."

"No oven, that's a problem," added Alicia.

"Is this typical of the other units in the place?" asked Joe.

"It is. This place has these little galley kitchens probably because the owner thought he'd make a killing renting the units out to vacationers. But it's too far to the beach, I think, to make that proposition work. And, as you've pointed out, it's too cramped for a family to use it as a home. Maybe a single person, that's about it."

"What's the asking price?" asked Frank.

"He's asking six hundred, which works out to one and a half per unit. That's really high for here. Explains, maybe, why it's been on the market for over a year. Ready to see the next one?"

They all agreed and followed Ethan to their cars. He led them to the small downtown area and parked in front of a bank.

As they stood on the sidewalk, Ethan pointed to the building. "Note that this is an older building, two stories, takes up most of the block. The whole building is for sale. On the first level, you got the bank, a real estate office, a mortgage broker, a laundry, and a small cafe. Those are all income-producing rentals. It's the top floor that's the housing. We have six units up there, all with two bedrooms. They have parking around the back and an enclosed staircase to the upper floor. Five of the units upstairs are rented, but there's one vacant. We'll go there now." He led them around to an alley and a parking area; then they went up the staircase, which was enclosed behind a locked door.

The unit they entered was recently redone. It had hardwood floors and triple-pane windows. The kitchen was modern, with granite counters and stainless steel appliances. There was a small dishwasher. A bar separated the kitchen from the dining area, which led directly to the living space. A hallway led to the back area, which contained two bedrooms, each with its own bath.

"This is nice," said Alicia. "I could see a woman and one or two kids living here. I think they'd feel safe, between the downtown location and being on the second floor. And this place is clean, good closet space in the bedrooms. Love the windows. What do you think, Frank?"

"I could see it. What do the numbers look like?" he asked Ethan.

"Numbers aren't my strong suit, but I did try to work it out," said Ethan. "This building is one million, asking. I don't know if that's firm or not. There're two units upstairs that haven't been redone yet. They will get fixed up next, according to the Realtor, so they'll look like the one we just saw. The rents for the commercial part are in the thirty-four-hundred-a-month range, all together. Those spaces all have separate meters and pay their own electric. Water's provided for everybody but the laundry. They somehow put that on a separate meter. The apartments, the updated ones, rent for four hundred. You'd have to figure out if that fits the budget. I was mostly looking at a place for multiple families."

"Well, this is a potential. But how does Lorraine feel about this? Could she live here with Gavin and Ava?"

"I asked her that. Brought her by early this morning to see it. And she says there's a lot to like. We could sort of divide the bigger bedroom so the kids would have their own space. I'd make a built-in unit like a ship's cabin. You ever seen that? A bed built over drawers, maybe shelves or drawers on each side. A curtain or blind can close off the bed, or you can put a wall divider in high enough to give privacy, then put shallow shelves or hooks or something on each side of the wall. You can also put the beds on the common wall divider unit, then use the part from there to the opposite wall for a fold-down table/desk combo with shelves over it. We could make do."

As Ethan talked about how he would provide private space for the children, Helen was noticing how confident and capable he appeared. She whispered to Gerard, "That sounds fabulous," and he nodded in agreement.

It was getting dark as they finished viewing the second property. Harriet recommended that everyone go to the hotel and check in. She suggested they meet at six thirty in the bar of a restaurant called Alec's by the Sea. "It's about the only place here that offers sit-down dinners and isn't a pub, so I think we should give it a try."

Ethan declined to join them when they enthusiastically invited him. He gave them the address for the following morning's property, suggested they meet there at ten. He then confided he had promised to take his grandchildren to a fish-and-chips place they loved for dinner. "I have to take them. It's like a huge treat, and they need it." Everyone agreed his first duty was to the children, particularly after the traumatic experience leading up to the move to Ocean Shores.

Helen and Gerard registered at the front desk and went to their rooms. They met up in the lobby within minutes so they could have another walk on the beach. With flashlights in hand, they found a wooden walkway that led to the water through a break in the high dunes that hid the beach from view. It was quiet except for the shushing sound of the gentle waves. The moon appeared and disappeared behind fast-moving flat clouds, and the breeze off the ocean was chilly. Helen and Gerard, warm in their Windbreakers, walked for over half an hour in silence, Helen breathing deeply and floating into a very calm space inside herself. As they walked back to the hotel, she said, "I love this; I love walking the beach. It makes me meet myself."

"That's a lot of astounding and amazing alliteration," Gerard said.

Helen laughed. "Does anyone but me really appreciate you?" she asked, not expecting an answer.

"Not really. No one I can think of." He sounded perfectly fine with that. But the comment made Helen think hard about a few things as they meandered back to the hotel.

The group of ten was not unusual at the restaurant, where vacationing family groups were the norm. It was a quiet place. Between being a weeknight and being in the off-season, there were only a few small groups or couples scattered in a fairly large space. No loud music drowned out their conversations or caused them to shout over one another to be heard. Helen, who typically shunned group dinners, felt relaxed and comfortable. She and Gerard sat at one end of the table, across from Harriet and George. Gabrielle McGregor was next to George, and Joe McGregor was beside Helen. They all talked about the places they had just visited.

"I think we're all in agreement that the first place is hopeless, right?" Joe asked, looking up and down the entire table. Everyone nodded agreement.

"I liked the place here in town, though," said Alicia, sitting at the far end of the table away from Helen. "But are there enough people who need housing in this town who fit our profile to make it a sensible option?"

"I looked into that; Harriet and I did together, actually," said Kenneth. "We made a few phone calls. There's a large community services place in Aberdeen, plus Harriet called the local Catholic Church, and we checked in with the police, just to get a feel for the social-service kinds of needs out here. It turns out this entire area, which used to be very prosperous, is on its heels. The employment situation is horrendous because of the loss of timber-related jobs. They're trying hard to attract industry, but it's slow. Sort of one step forward, one step backward. If you remember those big pontoons they're building for the new floating bridge, they are coming from this county, so that helps a little. And some wine things are starting up. You may have noticed the Westport signs about a winery there. This place could be good for specialty agriculture, given it's essentially a rain forest. They've got the cranberry thing going, but mushrooms should be big out here, and aren't. And you could grow greens year round, like organic spinach, bok choy, kale, chard, things like that. Use greenhouses. Lots of water here. Plus, of course, they have the razor clams, which are fabulous, if you haven't tried them."

"And they're missing the boat on advertising this part of the coast," Harriet added. "Look at Quinault. That place is gorgeous. George and I are going up there tomorrow when we leave here. I booked us into the lodge up there. And a new beach town called Seabrook is just up the road twenty minutes. We drove through that on the way here. Lots of cute houses, maybe two hundred, in this little New England lookalike village. Hopefully, that'll draw some action. I've read about it in *Sunset* magazine as well as in the *Times*. There's even an artist out here who's also a film director, and he made a small independent film last fall. I'm going to talk to him tomorrow, too. All in all, there *are* a few bright spots to offset the faded, tired little town we're in."

"Bottom line, I think," said Kenneth, "is that there's this sort of countywide resignation or depression. The priests, who run about four churches out here, said some of the parishioners have got themselves involved with alcohol and drugs. The divorce rate soared after the timber industry fell apart and, again, with the new recession. Lots of financial stress. So we have a fairly large needy population."

By now the food had arrived. Only three people had ordered cocktails when they first arrived, so Helen and Gerard were inconspicuous in their non-drinking. Another two, Joe and Gabrielle, ordered wine with dinner. Conversation lagged as they all devoted themselves to the food and then picked up again a bit later.

"Helen," Kenneth asked, "did you see the write-up in the *Seattle Times* on the high-tea benefit?"

Helen could tell that Kenneth wanted to share. "No, I don't read much of the paper. Tell me all."

"It was fabulous. I even got my picture in there. And Sonja. Wow, you should have seen her outfit. It was a bright geometric in red, orange, yellow, with dashes of navy. But the style! It was like a tunic, over a longer tunic, over a longer tunic. Three layers, all the same print, one sort of floating and swishing over the next. And her boots! I don't know where you would find something like that. They were soft leather, with buttons, like from the Victorian era. Bright red, yet. Stunning. No one but Sonja could pull that off." Kenneth was almost swooning just describing it.

Helen started laughing, and Edward joined in. "I think you liked her outfit better than she did," said Helen.

"I probably did," he said, with such wistfulness that this time even Gerard started laughing. Kenneth, ever good-natured, joined the laughter.

They all ordered coffee or tea, and some asked for dessert. Most of the other customers had gone, and the group was very relaxed. Helen was struck by how comfortable this group, ten people very different one from the other, was.

"We're so lucky," she said. "I don't know how it happened, but this is a wonderful group."

"How did you all get together?" Gabrielle asked.

"We connected one at a time," said Edward. "Helen came to me for legal advice. Then, when she told me about the foundation, I thought of Joe. He and I had worked together before on a benefit, and I thought he was so good at keeping everybody on track."

Joe picked it up from there. "That's right. Then I said we needed another person. Harriet and I were both in Rotary for a while, and I liked the way she tackled some tricky assignments, so I suggested her."

"I'm the one who brought in Frank," Harriet continued. "Since we were into property, I thought his expertise would be useful. I'd had business dealings with him." Helen recalled that Harriet had been a financial advisor to very wealthy clients, as well as possessing an MBA from Harvard.

"Helen brought me in," added Alicia. Neither Helen nor Kenneth corrected her or acknowledged that it was Kenneth who originally put her name forward.

"Helen was the one who was responsible for it in the beginning," added Kenneth. "And Helen is pure gold."

"No," Gerard countered, "Helen is forged steel. Gold is merely ornamental and soft. Forged steel is made under tremendous pressure, sometimes at extremely high temperatures. That makes it incredibly strong. It's far more valuable than gold." Gerard, who had been silent up until then, had spoken very matter-of-factly.

Everyone at the table was thunderstruck. At first, no one said anything. Then Kenneth said, "Oh, my," breathlessly.

"That's the most amazing compliment I've ever heard," said Joe.

Helen blushed furiously. Everyone else started laughing. Gerard looked almost smug.

Later, in the car going back to the hotel, Helen hesitantly began a conversation she had been wanting to have. "Gerard," she started, "are we good friends?"

"We are. Not as good as we will be someday, but good nevertheless."

"What will it take to be better friends?"

"Trust."

"You're talking about me, not you, right?"

"Mostly."

"What do I do to get there?"

"You don't *do things* to get there. You just *arrive*."

"How do you know when you *just arrive*?"

"You'll know," he said.

Later, in her room, she practiced yoga. Then she sat on the floor and breathed. After fifteen minutes of breathing, she started a silent meditation. She felt vibrations beginning low in her stomach, gradually engulfing her entire being. A low humming accompanied the vibrations. She felt very alive, almost electric. It was unworldly and peaceful. She sat and basked in the feeling. And hummed. When she arose, it was after two in the morning. She slept.

※ ※ ※

The address of the property they went to view the next morning was at the south end of Ocean Shores Boulevard. From the road, the building looked like a small compound of patio homes, such as were popular on the East Coast in semi-retirement golfing communities. These, however, were two stories, and it looked as if the second story topped the ever-present dunes.

"This is a strange deal," said Ethan as he gathered the group around himself. "These were built in 2007, just before the housing bust. The builder went broke. The financing was from some investor group. I think it's called a TIC, which stands for tenants in common. They had a mortgage held by some strange combination of banks or insurance companies or something. The whole thing was a mess, everybody suing everybody else. Bottom line, it finally got clear of all that. Now a small outfit in Olympia has clear title. These were originally designed for individual owners. There're two buildings. If you notice that glassed-in rectangle in-between, that sort of ties them together. Each building has four units, each unit has two stories. These buildings were angled weird on the lot, sort of like half a pie each, sitting side by side. So every unit has a private balcony that overlooks the ocean but not the other balconies. Plus they all have a private raised patio that sits on short concrete pilings. The patios are protected from the wind by the dunes. One good thing is the choice of construction materials. The patios and balcony floors are that new composition stuff that looks like wood but isn't. It's mold and rot proof. The siding is similar to metal, but some other product. Again, mold proof, rot proof. That saves on maintenance and repair costs."

He walked them closer to the buildings, which were set back about forty feet from the road. "These are all empty, by the way. I understand the owners prefer to sell to a single buyer. Ready to look inside? I've been in this home once, but I've never see the other units." He led them to a small door beside one of the garages. "If you parked in the garage, you'd just enter the house from there. Otherwise, if you've been on the beach, you get in through this door."

They walked through the empty garage, which was built for one car but was wider than a typical one-car garage. It had built-in storage cabinets and shelves, and a work table was at the front end with pegboard above.

"I think they figured some people would want to use this as a workshop," Ethan continued. "There's plenty of room to park two cars in tandem in the drive, so you don't need the garage if you don't want to put your car inside. Some people out here cover their cars with large custom tarp-like things. Some tenants may not even have cars."

They entered from the garage into a large mud room. There was a closet, a built-in bench with drawers below, a row of hooks for hanging coats, and a clothes washer and dryer, separated by a laundry sink. At the far end was a door. "That's a shower and toilet," said Ethan. "Notice the wood floor. No high polish to get scratched. It's a working floor. This space would be for people to clean up after coming up from the beach. Shower the sand off their body. Leave the sandy towels here, and the boots and beach toys, stuff like that. The sink you could use to clean razor clams and sea shells. You leave all the sand right here instead of dragging it into the house. Or if you're coming in from the workshop, you leave all of the grease or sawdust or whatever in here. It's well thought out. Actually, you'll see that the whole place is like this. Somebody who designed it knew how beach people live."

They all went into the main living space and started looking around. The main floor had an open kitchen. The sink was built into the two-level counter and bar that separated the kitchen from the dining and living areas. "You could stand at the sink peeling vegetables and still look out at everybody and even all the way to the dunes," said Harriet. She and Gabrielle were in the kitchen. The large patio with composite decking had French doors leading out to it from both the dining and the living area. The patio itself had raised planting boxes around three sides.

"This kitchen is great," said Gabrielle. "Two or even three people could be in here at the same time, working and not interfering with each other. Love the gas range. Do you have natural gas out here?"

"No, everybody has a propane tank," said Ethan.

"There's a bedroom back here," called out Frank. "With its own bath."

Ethan said, "I think this place was built thinking about two families sharing it, or maybe grandparents and parents with three or four kids, all coming out for a week at the beach. So the grandparents would have the main-floor bedroom, in case the stairs are too difficult. There's a master suite upstairs, plus two smaller rooms. You could put bunk beds in each of them. They're too small for a set of twins, I think."

They all went upstairs. The balcony Ethan had talked about earlier was accessible from the master suite. It overlooked the ocean, as they had suspected. "This is fabulous," said Kenneth. "The closets are good sized, and there's a sweet bath between the two little bedrooms. But this balcony, that's the real draw. If I had a chair, I'd sit out there all day."

"Let's think about our tenants," said Joe. "How would they use this?"

They were all quiet as they thought about it.

"OK," said Harriet. "You've got a woman with maybe two kids. She puts one in each room; she takes the master. There's enough room in here for a little office-type space for her private papers and things. Put a lock on the door. Then, she can rent the bedroom downstairs if she wants to. Maybe a friend who's lost her job, something like that."

"Or a retired person or a parent," added Ethan. "We have a lot of older people out here. They've been here all their lives, and the timber loss hurt them bad. They've burned through a lot of their savings, and they're on social security. It don't stretch too far. They live in a trailer in a crappy trailer park. Then they move in here with their nephew or niece or a younger friend who waits on them in the coffee shop in town. So here they are, with a nice bedroom in a modern little house. Sit on the patio, putter in the workshop, watch the kids when they get home from school, walk the beach, dig a few razor clams now and then. Maybe put some flowers in pots on the patio. It's a good life." Ethan talked as though he had several people in mind. The others looked at him and one another.

"Let's look at the other building, just because we're here," said Alicia. "By the way, how come you have free rein of all of these places, Ethan?"

"Because I have a Realtor friend. He knows me from way back. He gave me the code to the lockboxes."

Ethan led them back through the garage, and they walked the length of the first building. A large glass structure jutted out about twenty feet toward the road. They entered it through a door on the side nearest the building they had just left. Another door, directly opposite, led out to the next building. "Now this is a strange deal," said Ethan. "My wife and I were wondering what it's for. You see the slate floors. We thought maybe a party room or something. Pretend a wedding was out here, and the guests rented all the units. This might be where they'd have a reception or a brunch or something. My wife said a quilting club would come out, and this is where they'd all put their sewing machines. So I guess that must be what the designer had in mind. There're convection heaters, six of them, so you'd only heat the place when you wanted to use it."

"There's your common room, Helen," said Harriet.

They all went out the other door and into a unit on the other side of the common space and looked around. "This is the same," said Harriet. "I guess we knew that, though."

"The views are slightly different, given the way the buildings sit one to the other, at an angle. Other than that, I guess they're all identical," said Edward.

"That can't be," said Gabrielle. "The two end units in each building have windows on two sides; the middle units don't. We haven't been in a middle unit. Bet it's a different floor plan."

They all looked at Ethan, and he started going through keys.

"We can get in one, soon as I figure out how," he said. He was trying to read the writing on tiny tags attached to keys. "Here it is, I think."

They all left the unit they were in and followed Ethan. He located a key to the door near the next garage. Soon they were inside, and they scattered.

"This is a lot different," yelled out Frank. "There's no window in what was the main-floor bedroom." He came out into the living area. "There's no door to it. See, they can't call it a bedroom without a window so they leave it open and call it an office. But people would put a bed or a sofa bed in there and use it like a bedroom anyway."

"There's no difference in the rest of this section, the living section," said Gabrielle. "But there's got to be changes upstairs."

They all went up.

"Same deal," said Frank. "The back bedroom isn't a bedroom any-more. They took some of the space and added it to the front bedroom and made this into a little nook-type space. I suppose you could use it for a computer or television room. I see they've put cable connections on three walls. So, with this house, you could put the kids in the master up here, or one or two in the master, another in the smaller front room. Mom would take the area downstairs, I guess."

"A mom or dad with one kid would fit this. It would be pretty roomy for just two, though," mused Edward.

"If the parent worked at home," Harriet said, "like a writer or seam-stress or accountant, maybe, that would make sense. Maybe someone who used the Internet for work."

They all thought about the possibilities and then wandered out, following Ethan back to the parking area.

"What's the asking price for this?" asked Frank.

"I think it's 1.3 million," replied Ethan.

Frank continued, " So, what's that … about 160 a unit? Say roughly 180 for the better ones and 140 for the ones without windows. That's a bit steep for out here, given the market. I'd say tops would be 170 for the best, 130 for the others … Well, we could always make an offer, see what happens."

They all looked at one another. "I still like the one in town. I like it just as well," said Alicia.

"There's no reason you can't have both," said Edward, who knew the money situation. "The question is, can you manage them, and are they needed out here."

"We can definitely fill them with the kind of tenants we want," said Harriet, and Kenneth nodded vigorously in agreement.

"Ethan," said Helen, "do you think you could take on the job of maintaining both places, maybe fixing up the other one the way you were talking about when there're two kids involved?"

"Oh, yeah, that's not much work," said Ethan.

"We could train you in what kind of tenants we like. Give you appli-cation forms and lease agreement forms. We could screen the first set of tenants for you, if necessary."

"Yeah, I could learn to handle that. And Lorraine's real good with people; she could do that, too."

"Where would you and she want to live?"

"I'd say out here. Lorraine would fill that patio with bright ceramic pots and flowers and things. She loves container gardening, as she calls it. Even has books about it. And I work with wood, so that workshop would be great. Plus, this is a good place for Gavin and Ava. I think they could use the beach for walking off their stress. Life hasn't been easy for them, you know."

"How are they doing?" asked Helen.

"Better. Ava's quit holding onto Gavin all the time. She and Gabrielle sort of hang out, so Gavin can be with me. He has a friend at school, met him the first day. They've been back and forth to the two homes. In fact, if we were here, I think this friend would come out to visit a lot more. The apartment's a bit small. Two ten-year-old boys need space."

"Good. Well, give us a minute alone to talk," said Joe.

The board members stood together in a rough circle, with the others a short distance away. They talked softly.

When they joined together again, Joe said, "Well, Ethan, here's the deal. Frank's going to make offers on both places. If we get both, you'll be the overall manager at a salary of fifty thousand a year, plus free rent at one of these end units out here, health insurance, a retirement plan, and a car leased by us. Is that a deal you can live with?"

Ethan's eyebrows shot up. "Damn straight," he said. He and Joe shook hands; then the others followed suit.

"He's a good man," Gerard said as he and Helen went back to her car. "Your board did a good job picking him and making that offer. I doubt he'll ever let you down."

"I think you're right," said Helen, and she fished her car key out of her jacket.

❧ ❧ ❧

Saturday morning, Helen drove to Bothell for her meeting with Commander Kirk Becker's family. The house was in a quiet residential neighborhood, a fairly typical middle-class area north of Seattle. The houses were built on rolling hills, not nearly as steep as Helen's Queen Anne neighborhood. Diana Becker's house was on a slight slope going up from the street. The driveway led to a two-car garage. The garage door was up, and the garage itself was filled to a height of about four feet with boxes, bikes, old chests, bins overflowing with what looked like discarded clothing, gardening tools, and the like. Two paths existed to provide access to the various boxes and chests. No cars would fit in the garage, that was for sure.

Helen parked on the street and walked up two short flights of stairs connected by a landing halfway up. The yard was full of bushes and spring flowers, all interspersed around large boulders. There were so many tulips it reminded Helen of the tulip festival in La Conner, a major bulb-producing area not far from where she was making this visit. Hosta was pushing up, leaves not yet unfurled. Primroses left from the winter were peeping out, still blooming. It looked like a yard that was well loved, or at least had been at some point in the past.

When Helen knocked, the door was answered by a woman pushing forty and holding her own. She looked good in her jeans and wore a rather tight-fitting turtleneck that showed off her body well. She was athletic, perhaps a competitor of some type, and obviously worked out regularly.

"Come on in. I'm Diana," she said. "We're still organizing ourselves. Saturdays are hectic around here with the kids going in different directions. Zach's at a soccer game; he'll be home soon. The girls and I are heading to the city for a shopping trip after lunch, so they're busy figuring out what they want. They're upstairs, so we can talk in the dining room if you want some privacy."

By now, Helen had entered the home, and they were both walking down a hall to the back area of the home. The dining room was right off the kitchen. They sat at a table, and Helen took her notebook and pen from her bag on the chair next to hers.

"Do you have any questions for me before we start?" she asked Diana.

"Mostly just why we need to do all this again. I thought it was all settled. Once he left, there shouldn't be any more issues, as they say."

"Well, I don't think I know much about that," said Helen neutrally. "All I'm told is that there's been a request for a change in residential time, and the judge ordered a CASA to make a report. That's me."

"Then let's get started and get it done," said Diana without rancor. "I'm sure there's nothing that needs changing, but if that's what Kirk wants, guess we'll go through it again. Long as I don't have to pay."

"Why don't we start by you telling me when and how you met him?" Helen proceeded as normal through the first part of the interview. Once Diana was comfortably into the life-sharing groove, Helen started the more sensitive part of the conversation.

"Let's turn to the children. Can you give me a sense of what they're like?"

"Sure. Mia's the smart one. She gets good grades, teachers love her. Claire, she's sort of a cry-baby. She goes emotional on me all the time. I keep hoping she'll toughen up. I try not to react to her, hoping it'll help. Zach, he's a fireball. Always running around and gettin' into trouble. He runs with a little pack from the neighborhood. He falls out of trees and climbs on the garage roof, stuff like that. All boy."

"Do they get along well?"

"They do. They stick together a lot. Sometimes a little too much. Like Mia won't let me take just her out for a girl's time. She insists Claire always come along. Claire's like a wet tissue, so sometimes I think we'd have more fun if it was just Mia and me."

"Has she ever said why she wants Claire with her?"

"Not really. She talked about not wanting to leave Claire around Andrew, but that's just silly."

"Who's Andrew?"

"He's my older son. By my first marriage."

"And how does he get on with the other children?"

"Well, he's so much older; he's fifteen, so he doesn't have much to do with them. He and Zach fool around a bit, but that's all. I think he likes the girls good enough."

"Has he ever been harsh with them?"

"Harsh?"

"Ever mistreated them? In any way?"

"Is that it? Is that what this is about?"

"This is about the children and how they get along. Sure, that's always what I ask about. That's my job. I'm the advocate for the children."

Diana was suddenly less friendly. "Well, you can take what people say and stuff it. It's just not true."

"What's not true?"

"Anything. Whatever you've been told. Everybody is always picking on Andrew. I get fed up with it."

"Tell me about Andrew. Why would people pick on him?"

"Well, he's big for his age. He's physical. Strong. So I think that intimidates people a little. When people are scared, they overreact to things. That's what I think's wrong."

"Can you give me an example?"

"Sure. One time, the school called and talked about bruises on the kids. They suggested maybe Andrew was beating on them or something. But it turns out they were all just playing around, wrestling. 'Course little kids get bruises. They bang around and push each other, and they'll get bruises. It's nothing."

"The children said they'd just been wrestling?"

"Andrew told me. The little ones didn't say much of anything."

"I heard about a duct-tape incident. What can you tell me about that?"

"That's just the same kind of deal. Andrew and Zach were playing. Andrew tied Zach to a tree. It was just all part of a game."

"So you're not worried about the safety of the smaller children?"

"No, I just told you. There's nothing to it. Just people picking on Andrew 'cause he's big for his age. It's not fair, really."

"What isn't fair?"

"That Andrew gets blamed for things. He's a good kid. And it's hard for him to see other kids with dads who care. Kirk never really took to Andrew, and I think that's the problem. So Andrew has a little anger in him, and sometimes he might act out a bit. But it's nothing, not really. He's a good kid, like I said."

It was approaching noon, and the door opened. "Hi, Mom, I'm home," said a small boy's voice. It was quickly accompanied by the boy.

He was a well-built, sturdy-looking child, wearing shorts and a soccer shirt. "What's to eat?"

"Go get your sisters. Tell them it's time for lunch. This is Ms. Paige. Say hello, please."

He gave Helen a smile and a short handshake, said hello to her, and took off for the stairs, yelling at his sisters on the way.

"That's the fireball," said Diana. "Now, you want to watch us have lunch, right?"

"Right, I'll sit over there in a corner." Helen gathered her things and retreated to a corner of the room.

The girls entered the dining room and went into the kitchen, nodding a quick greeting to Helen on the way. The older girl was just getting tall and rangy. The younger one was as short as her brother but very thin. A bit too thin, Helen thought. They all had sandy-colored hair and fair skin.

The three children all helped with lunch. They got the makings for sandwiches from the refrigerator and spread it out on the dining table and chattered away. Zach was describing plays from his game. The girls were listening and teasing him a little. One of them told a silly joke. The children did most of the work with the mother taking care of drinks. She poured lemonade from a large jug into three glasses and heated coffee in the microwave for herself. As the children were getting out paper plates and napkins, a tall man-child entered the dining room. He startled Helen, who had not heard him coming.

This, Helen knew, was Andrew. He was, as reported, large for a fifteen-year-old. He looked like a football player. He roughly shoved Claire away from where she had been taking the tops off the mayonnaise and mustard. She cowed and then went around the table to where Mia was standing. Mia glared at Andrew. Andrew started making himself a sandwich. Diana entered the room, smiled at Andrew, and went to him. She kissed his cheek and put her hand in his hair, ruffling it. "How's my big protector?" she said. He continued making his sandwich.

"The girls and I are going shopping after lunch. Anything you want?" Diana looked at Andrew when she asked.

"Yeah," he said, not looking back. "I could use a couple shirts. Pullover. Not that damn green color. And no purple, neither. Red or navy. Or black." He elbowed Zach away from the Fritos. Zach stood his ground. Andrew backhanded Zach across the face. Zach stumbled back. Diana said nothing.

"Can I go to Danny's house while you're gone?" Zack asked his mother.

"I don't care. See if Danny's mom will have you," said Diana with disinterest. "Honey," she asked Andrew, "what're your plans for the afternoon?"

"I'm going to hang out here, watch sports maybe." He talked around his food, standing while he ate. The three younger children made their sandwiches, stepping around Andrew and trying not to get too close to him. They sat on the opposite side of the table, eating. It was very quiet. No one talked. The children kept their eyes on their paper plates. Zach and Mia ate their sandwiches. Claire, who had fixed only a half sandwich, tore it into small pieces and ate only a few of them.

"I'd like to talk with the children," Helen said. "Mia, it looks as if you're finished. Can you show me your room?"

"Sure, can Claire come?"

"Just us at first; then she can," said Helen. She and Mia left the room and went upstairs. The room the girls shared was neat, especially for two girls their ages. A skirt was lying on the floor, and some art supplies were scattered on a small table under the window. But the twin beds were made, and the wood floors were clean. Dresser drawers were closed.

"Tell me about you and your brothers and sister," started Helen.

"Andrew's not my brother. Zach's my brother, and he's great. He tells jokes and makes us laugh. And he stands up for Claire. Claire's nice to everybody. Too nice, sometimes. It's like if Susie gets hurt, Claire's the one who feels it. More than Susie does."

"What's your father like?"

Claire's face was a combination of a smile and the beginning of tears. "He's great. We wish he was still here, so bad. Mom's good, but she just doesn't see it. We miss Dad a lot. Especially Zach."

"What do you want to happen?"

"I want to go live with Dad. I know he's trying to get us. Mom can come see us there. I feel safer with Dad around."

"Can I come up?" It was Claire.

Helen nodded to Mia, and Mia told Claire to come on upstairs. When Claire entered the room, Helen asked Mia to leave them alone.

"I'll be in the bathroom getting ready to go," Mia said to Claire.

"Tell me something about yourself," Helen said to Claire.

Claire looked around the room. "I like art," she started. She moved to the closet and took out a plastic bin. "Let me show you." She withdrew some things. "This is my favorite friendship bracelet. It's from Susie, my friend, but I made one just like it for her. And I painted this." She held up a painting. It was splashed with bright colors, abstract, like a well-controlled Jackson Pollack. It was striking.

"I like that. It has a lot of life and movement," said Helen. Claire looked gratified.

"I think so too," she said. "I did it when I was really happy."

"You're not so happy now?" Tears rolled out of Claire's eyes, and she shook her head softly back and forth.

"I'm so scared all the time. Since Dad left. My tummy hurts."

"What scares you?"

"Andrew. He hits us. He tried to take off my pajamas once, but Zack made him stop."

"Did you tell your mom?"

"I tried. But she shushed me. She said I was telling tales to make Andrew look bad. But I wasn't telling tales. I was telling the truth."

"OK. Thank you for talking to me Claire." Helen rose and went downstairs.

"Come on girls," Diana yelled up the stairs. "Get a move on. Time's draggin' on." She turned to Helen. "You done here?"

"I'd like to talk to Zach. Is he going somewhere?"

"Yeah, he's goin' to a friend's house. It's just down the block; maybe you could walk with him. ZACK!" she yelled. Zack appeared from somewhere, carrying a baseball glove and a bat. "Ms. Paige here would like to walk with you to Danny's. That OK with you?"

"Sure. I'm going now," he said to Helen. She retrieved her things from the dining room, and the two of them walked out the door.

"What's Danny like?" asked Helen.

"He's funny," said Zach. "And he likes baseball, so we're going to play in his back yard. It's flat, not like mine."

"Did you know your father and mother are trying to decide the best place for you to live?" Helen knew her time with Zach was short and decided to go straight to the end point of their conversation.

"Mia told me. Does Mom know Dad's trying to get us?"

"She does. Well, I *think* she does. She should know."

"She might not. She's not real smart."

"Why would you say that?"

"'Cause she thinks Andrew's a good guy. He's not. He's a bad guy."

"In what way?"

"He's mean. He's always hittin' us. He keeps trying to get Claire alone. I think he'll take off her clothes and hurt her. Mia and me try not to let him alone with her."

"If you leave to go to your father's house, what about your friends and your soccer team?"

"I'll make new friends. Find a new soccer team. Dad says navy kids do it all the time. We can do it, too. It'd be better than having to watch out for Andrew all the time. This is Danny's. Are we done?" They had arrived at a well-maintained house, set on a level lot, as Zach had said.

"Yes, we're done," said Helen, and waved goodbye as he left her and walked up the driveway. She returned to her car and went back to the city.

❧ ❧ ❧

Helen was at her computer, typing up the extensive notes from her trip to Bothell to see the Becker family. When she finished her transcription tasks, it was early evening. She still had two calls to make. Diana Becker had provided the names and numbers for both a sister and a friend. Helen decided to keep working. Talking to the sister was the next item on her list. She got her notebook and punched in the number for Deborah Sikes. "Ms. Sikes? I'm Helen Paige, the CASA assigned to Diana's children. Is this a good time?"

"It is. Diana said she'd given my number. How can I help?"

"I just have a few questions. Perhaps you could start by telling me how often you see Diana and the children."

"Oh, quite a bit. Diana and I have always been close, I'm two years older. But I look younger," she said with a laugh. "We're probably together once or twice a month. They come over here for dinner once a month, and we'll go to a movie or on a picnic or skiing or something once a month. That's about it."

"What is your impression of the children?"

"Well, Andrew's pretty much the same all the time. The smaller ones have been gloomy lately, probably because their dad's gone. I think it hit them hard. Claire especially. I notice how she tends to cling to Mia a bit. And she sort of lost her sparkle. But basically I think they'll come out of it."

"How does Andrew treat the smaller ones?"

"Well, that's a problem. He either ignores them or bugs them. He'll just sort of push them aside or even pinch or hit them when he thinks no one is watching."

"What's behind that? Any ideas?"

"I'd say he's jealous. They have each other, for one thing. Plus, of course, he never really had a dad of his own. When Diana and Kirk married, Andrew was living with my mom. So Kirk wasn't around him much. Plus, of course, Kirk was at sea a lot. Then the little kids came along, and Kirk was busy with them. Andrew never felt part of the family. He and Diana are close, but there just wasn't space, so to speak, for him in the larger family."

"Did he ever live with his father?"

"No, never." For some reason Helen could not deduce, no one ever talked about Andrew's father. Since it wasn't part of her case, so far as she could see, Helen had no right to delve into the mystery she sensed around the issue.

"So, if something happened—if the court said the smaller children could live with Diana only if Andrew lived elsewhere—what would happen, do you think?"

"You mean the court could say that?"

"I don't know what the court might do. I just wondered."

"Well, he can't go back with my mom. She's getting too old for that. I guess he could come here, but I'm not sure my husband would allow that. He's not real fond of Andrew, when it comes down to it."

"Do you think Diana plays favorites at all where the children are concerned?"

"No, I don't think so. She's a good mom, and she loves all of them. She tries to protect Andrew a little, I think, but that's because he's had a tough break. But she works at treating them all the same."

"What can you tell me about the relationship between Commander Becker and his children?"

"Oh, he's a good father, no doubt about that. But let's face it, he's career navy. That's no life for children. He's gone too much."

"Right now he has shore duty. He told me it's a three-year tour."

"Yeah, three years maybe. Maybe not. Then what? There's no security there."

"Right. Well, is there anything else you think I should know?"

"That's about it. If I think of something, I'll call you back. Your number's in my cell log."

Helen then called Suzanne Cowper, Diana's friend. She introduced herself and then asked, "What can you tell me about the Becker children?"

"Those kids are so nice," said Suzanne. "They're well behaved. Smart as can be, especially Mia. And Zach is all boy, a great little kid. Claire is sweet and friendly. I like all of them."

"How often are you around them?"

"About once a week. A lot of Wednesdays, we'll go over there for dinner or have them over here. My husband works late that night, so we have dinner on our own. Two of my kids are six and seven, so all the kids have a great time together."

"And Andrew?"

There was a long silence. "What about him?" Caution in the voice.

"Does he get along well with your children?"

"My children are all younger."

"Does he join in playing with them?"

"Like I said, he's a lot older. They don't have much in common." Helen's antennae were up. She decided to play hardball.

"Mrs. Cowper, I'm an advocate, a volunteer, assigned by the court to represent the Becker children. I'm trying to find what's best for them. Please pretend for a moment I'm assigned to your children, trying to find out what's best for *them*. With that in mind, would you leave your children alone with Andrew for the afternoon if you went shopping?"

A long hesitation, then, "No, I wouldn't."

"Thank you, I know that was hard to say."

"Diana's a good friend. She's a good mom ..." More hesitation.

"But ...?"

"Well ... she doesn't seem *aware* of everything."

"I see. I understand. Thank you for your time. I appreciate it, and I promise you've done the right thing for the children."

Helen now felt ready to write her report. She had all of the information she really needed to say what had to be said. By the time she was finished with the conclusions, she knew the report would hurt Diana. As so often, the conclusions would first be denied, then cried over, and perhaps, eventually, accepted. The report might also provoke angry phone calls to Helen, something she was accustomed to. She was also aware that Diana might call the CASA office and demand Helen be removed from the case. The anger some parents felt when they received the report was one of the reasons Helen never used a landline attached to an address for her CASA work. It was why there were extra locks on her door. It was why she used a different name. Being a CASA was not something anyone did for fun, as far as Helen knew.

It was full dark. Helen thought about walking down the hill to a meeting. But then she decided she was not in great need of a meeting, other than with herself. She went to her room and sat on her rug.

☙ ☙ ☙

The phone rang Monday morning while Helen was having her second cup of tea and looking out her living room window.

"Good morning, Helen. It's Stewart Prescott. I hate to be calling again, but I have to."

"It's fine, Stewart. What is it?"

"It's Aunt Catherine."

"Anything I should do?"

"Yes. You should come and see her."

"Is that her idea or yours?"

"It's hers. She's in the hospital with pneumonia. William's death, you know, it just took everything out of her."

"Yes. I understand. It doesn't surprise me."

"So … you'll come? Want me to send the plane?"

"Let me get back to you. I need to think about it. I have things here that I have to take care of before I rush off as I did last time."

"Certainly, call as soon as you can, please."

Helen sat at her small table and wondered who she should talk to. Her first instinct was to tell Gerard. Her second was to call Alicia. They were the people who had been privy to the disaster following her last trip to Boston. She did not want a repeat of that experience. That was the most important thing, she finally decided. She had to do whatever it took to avoid a repeat. She called Gerard.

"I hate doing this," she said when he answered. "Please, feel that you can say no."

"I know how to say no. What do you want me to say yes to?"

"Going to Boston on a private jet. Maybe two days, I'm not sure."

"Yes."

"Yes?"

"Yes."

"Right, I'll get back with details."

"Fine."

Helen called Stewart. "I can come. Please send the plane. Will it be tomorrow?"

"No, I took a chance. It's on its way. It's scheduled to land at Boeing Field in four hours. There are two pilots so they'll just refuel and turn around. I'll send a car. Same hotel suite?"

"Yes, and one for my friend. Last time I needed a friend and didn't have one. Big mistake. And please don't tell Derrick I'm coming. It's too hard if Catherine is as difficult as William was."

"I understand. Thank you, Helen, I know how difficult it is for you."

"Thank you, Stewart. See you when I see you."

Helen called Gerard. "A car will get me in about four hours. Then we'll pick you up."

"Dress code?"

"I'm going to see a sick person in a hospital. I won't be partying."

"Got it. Just a jacket and tie for dinner, then."

"If that."

"Yes, Helen, that. Bring your teal pants and sweater, please."

"That's Seattle, Gerard. I'll take something Boston. You'll like it."

"Good enough, I trust you."

She hung up. He had used the word. Now what did that mean? She had no time to think about it. But she would remember it. For now, she needed to make arrangements. She called Michelle, her CASA supervisor.

"Michelle? I have to go out of town, family emergency. I just wrote up the Becker case; I'll send it right now. It isn't quite finished, but it's far enough for you to put on the top and bottom and process it if you want. I think it should be done sooner rather than later. And you might want to call the father and send him a copy directly when you send it to his lawyer. I know he'll want to see it right away."

Then she called Kenneth. "Hi, Kenneth? I have to go out of town, family emergency. I just want to make sure we're moving on the two Ocean Shores properties."

"We are. Frank made a deal on that group of condos. A really good deal. He made it Saturday, and it was accepted within the hour. Edward believes he'll have it closed in ten days. Shall I call Mr. McHale?"

"Please do. Tell him to be ready to move whenever we close. How about the other one, the one in town?"

"Frank's still working that. He's fighting for a better deal."

"Tell Mr. Pierce to tell Frank we want it, even if we have to pay too much."

"Will do, but you know Frank. He's a natural miser when it comes to our money."

"He is that, and he's a godsend. I just don't want to lose the chance to pick up those units. I think that area could really use some decent housing."

"I agree. And such a beautiful beach. I can't believe it's never been really discovered. I can see how people who think *Hawaii* when they think *beach* don't like it, but give me a break. It's fabulous for people who understand the Pacific Northwest. Did you walk along the beach?"

"I did. I loved it. And the sunsets were so wonderful. If the economy ever comes back, and Seattle keeps growing, I think it will eventually come into its own. There are a lot of people who can appreciate a quiet natural setting like that. Meanwhile, we need to get the children out there into some decent housing."

"I hear you," said Kenneth. "Oh, I have something else. Should we try to find a tenant for the duplex on Dibble?"

"I have pretty strong feelings on that. We put a lot on Rick Cleveland when we rented that apartment to Martin Larch. Rick came through big time for those kids, Gavin and Ava. So let's give him a key and send any tenants through him. He can show them around and decide if he wants them. I think he'll do a good job on selection; then we can make the terms. You want to handle that?"

"Sure. I'll make an appointment to see him. Take a duplicate key. We still need to get the repairs done, and we have to move out the stuff Mr. McHale didn't want. I'll coordinate that with Mr. Cleveland as well. I'm thinking we'll get Goodwill or Salvation Army to come out and just pack it up and take it away. You have any problems with that?"

"I don't, but check in with Lorraine in Ocean Shores. Make sure there's nothing there the kids want."

"Got it. Will do. Oh, I forgot something else. Ruth Mellon found a place in Bellingham this past weekend. She called me this morning. I called Frank. He's going to meet her after she gets off her job tonight. He and Alicia will meet her there for dinner and to see the place. Frank lined it up with a Realtor there."

"That's exciting. Our Ruth is a go-getter, isn't she?"

"Yes, and I like her. I haven't met her, except on the phone, but she sounds like an Energizer Bunny, and I can't wait to see her."

"Good. I know everything's in good hands. I'll check in when I get back."

"Bye, Helen."

"Bye, Kenneth." She hung up and went to her closet. She took her suitcase off the top shelf. Then she reviewed her conversation with Gerard. Sounded as if he wanted a nice dinner. She thought about it and then packed the navy St. John knit and good jewelry. She threw in a younger-looking, swishy sort of dress as well, and some sandals that went with it. Since her legs were her best attribute, she thought she might as well take advantage of it. Then she packed medium-weight slacks with two coordinated tops. Underwear, sleepwear, hose, socks, sandals, and shoes. Makeup and personal items. Done. Then she looked around and rethought. Private plane, no security, plenty of help to carry things. She got a small hold-all and put in her yoga mat, meditation cushion, rug, and some incense sticks. Plus a loose-fitting top and pants for yoga. Done. Again.

The driver arrived and loaded Helen's two bags. He stopped for Gerard, who had one bag and a briefcase. Gerard kept his briefcase with him. They said little in the car. The driver took them directly to the operations room, where a man met them and took charge of their bags. A pilot escorted them directly to the airplane. On board, they sat across from one another, a table between them.

Helen debated how much to tell Gerard. Finally, she started. "My mother-in-law is in the hospital with pneumonia. She's asked that I come to talk with her. Well … listen to her might be a better way of putting it. She's much better at talking; I do the listening."

"Sounds fun. You have my cell; it'll always be charged and in service. How about yours?"

"The same."

"Which parts do you want me available for?"

"The parts after she talks to me."

"Right."

They were quiet for some time, Helen reading from her iPad while Gerard worked on a laptop. Helen was relaxed, which surprised her. She should be extremely nervous, she thought. She leaned her head against the seatback and fell asleep.

"Helen."

She heard the sound of her name, soft, low. She opened her eyes.

"Would you like an omelet?" Gerard asked.

"I would. I think I'm hungry."

The steward was preparing a tea tray. He put it on the table between them, Gerard moving his laptop aside.

"Yes, we would like omelets," he said to the steward. "Both the lady and I will have avocado with Gruyère and prawns. Wheat toast." He looked at Helen for confirmation, and she nodded agreement.

"How did you know what I'd like?"

"The other choice was ham and cheese, and that didn't sound so good."

"You're right. Good choice."

The food came, and they ate. Gerard went back to his laptop. Helen looked out the window.

After some, time she spoke. "Gerard."

He looked at her.

"Would it be nosy of me to ask what you're doing?"

"Of course not. I'm not sure you'll find it interesting. I have a knotty engineering problem. We're designing a device that will be inserted in a person. I'm trying to make it do everything it needs to do. Then make it very small. Then make it easily accessible to a syringe. And then get the best shape and design for the space."

"Good heavens. What will it do?"

"Replace the current insulin pumps, which have problems. It'll take over the market. Change the lives of diabetics. Then we'll come up with similar devices that feed off this one, do different things."

"Is this what you do for a living?"

"This is my work, yes."

"That was a careful answer."

"It was."

"Will you work on this while I'm at the hospital with my mother-in-law?"

"Maybe a little. But I'll be seeing some people, too."

"You know people in Boston?"

"A whole lot of people."

"Why is that?"

"I taught at MIT for a long time."

Helen thought about that for a while. A professor at MIT. If it was for a long time, as he said, then he was tenured. It took a lot to lose a tenured position. In fact, she wasn't sure it was possible.

"Is that where you were when you had problems?"

"I had the problem before and during. I kept it together, though. I did my work. A little teaching, a lot of research. Drinking was confined to Thursday afternoon through Sunday evening. That was my schedule. Free time only."

Helen said nothing more. She had pried enough. Her CASA work, on top of the investigative work in Connecticut, was turning her into an interrogator, and she knew how irritating that could be.

When they landed, Helen called Stewart. It was too late to see Catherine so she arranged it for nine in the morning and told Gerard. He had been on his phone as well. "Can you be ready for dinner ninety minutes from now?"

"I can."

"Good."

They checked into their rooms at Parker House, and Gerard told her he would knock on her door to escort her to dinner. Helen hurriedly took a shower. She dressed with care. The swishy dress in shades of teal, aqua, and greens. Hose with a greenish tint. Sandals with medium-high heels. Discrete diamond studs. She checked herself in the mirror. This was the classic elegant look she intended, and she was comfortable with it.

Gerard arrived at her door. He paused and just looked. "Is this for me?" He tried to sound casual, but she caught the admiration.

"Of course. I don't know who else would see me."

"Everyone within range," he grinned.

"Well, I wouldn't wear it in Seattle."

"Does this mean we have to travel a lot?"

"No, I got my money's worth years ago. That's the nice thing about really good clothes; they last forever."

As the taxi was driving them to the restaurant, Gerard started talking. "I lived in Jamaica Plain for a long time. It was close enough in, easy to commute from, and has a lot of old houses chopped up into apartments. Either that or they were originally built that way. I don't know. But they're cheap. I had one for years and years. The restaurant we're going to, Ten Tables, opened in 2002. I was one of their first ten customers, I think. Used to go every week, at least once. I was new to sobriety. I told them upfront I couldn't have alcohol. They remembered. Never offered me the option. Plus, the food is fantastic. The owner farmed in Connecticut. Has a passion for food from the ground to the table."

"Is it named that because it only has ten tables?"

"That was true then. Small and cozy. I don't know if it's changed."

They had a wonderful meal. Helen found she was able to relax and enjoy herself even though she knew the next day would be a trial. "This is wonderful," she told Gerard. "I would have been spending the evening on a meditation cushion, but this is even better. More relaxing."

"Ah, I'm moving up. But I don't want you to be so relaxed with me that you fall asleep all of the time. You already did that once today."

"I'm not going there," Helen said with a smile.

He smiled back.

They were quiet for a time, and then Helen said, "My mother-in-law dominated me. I was afraid of her, but I modeled myself on her. I wanted so much to fit into her world. I tried and tried. But I had my husband as well, so it was like two worlds. One was all parties and drugs. The other was theatre and ballet." She shook her head. "I don't know how I survived."

"I do. They were the temperature and pressure that turned you into forged steel."

She laughed. "Maybe you're right."

They left the restaurant and went back to the hotel. "It's late, Helen. I'll see you around eight for breakfast? Or do you want to eat alone in your room?"

"I think I should be alone."

"Girding your loins?"

She laughed. "Probably. I'll have to look up how one does that."

"Call me. Remember my phone's on. Any time."

"Thank you, Gerard, I'll remember."

❧ ❧ ❧

Helen was up early. She practiced yoga on the mat she had brought from Seattle and then chanted for a half-hour. She ate the room-service breakfast and prepared for her coming hospital visit by putting on the St. John knit suit. Then she went to the lobby to wait for Stewart and the car. She did not see or think about Gerard.

"She's doing pretty well this morning," Stewart said when he entered the lobby and found her. "I thought for a while, two days ago, she wouldn't make it. But she's rallying."

"Maybe I shouldn't have come," said Helen. "I'd hate to think I'm going to have to repeat this in a little while." Then she thought about what she had said and hastily added, "That didn't come out right."

Stewart laughed softly. "No, I don't think it did, but I can understand it. You know, she's always spoken well of you. I think she has great admiration for you."

Now it was Helen who laughed softly. But she did not reply.

They arrived at the hospital, and Stewart went in with her and up to the floor with expensive private rooms where Catherine was ensconced. He told her to call when she was ready to leave. She went to the door of Catherine's room, took a deep breath, and entered.

"Helen, how delightful," said Catherine. She looked, to Helen, remarkably well. Her hair was well cut, clean, and groomed. Her color was good, and Helen even detected make-up.

So much for the "last visit to a dying relative" idea, Helen thought. She sighed in resignation. "Catherine, it's nice to see you looking so well," she said.

"Thank you. I feel better. Perhaps because of the anticipation of this visit."

Helen just smiled.

"Do pull up a chair and come closer. My voice isn't as strong as it once was." She waited while Helen followed instructions.

"Helen, there are some things I need to clear up," Catherine said, and then paused. "Or maybe get clear on, I'm not sure. As you may guess, William's letter, the one Hancock read to us, was a shock to me. I had no idea he thought of you as his legacy. I have no idea what he was talking about when he referred to the Claudius Foundation. What

I *could* tell was that you had a profound influence on him in the last years. I've asked Hancock and Stewart, but all they do is refer me to you. So … come clean, Helen."

"Come clean?" This was an expression she could not fathom having come from her proper Bostonian mother-in-law. It just did not fit. Or not compute, in the modern language.

"What is the Claudius Foundation? Why did William leave you all that money? What did he keep hidden from me?"

It was the last question, Helen suspected, that Catherine really wanted the answer to.

"To answer, I have to go back. About seven years ago, when I lived in Connecticut, I got the idea to create a foundation. I wanted to provide housing to children. Specifically, children in troubled families. Children who were not safe. I thought if they at least had a safe and secure environment they would have a chance. So I bought an old house that was divided into several little apartments. I lived in one of them. Then I looked for children like I had in mind. I found out about them through social workers. Then I'd figure out how to get their parent to move into the building with me. The children usually only had one parent. It was all a little tacky, looking back on it. I was like a benevolent landlord or something and I felt funny about that. Then I moved out of the house, and put some distance between me and the people who lived there and things went better. I wanted to buy a new place." She stopped.

Catherine stared at her. "And …," Catherine said.

"And I thought of William. I was still holding a lot of anger. I blamed him for things that had happened. Me. The twins. Robert. I thought about how he'd destroyed the family—" Catherine started to interrupt, but Helen overrode her. "No, Catherine, I'm talking …," and Catherine closed her mouth. "He destroyed the family, he betrayed me; that's how I felt. It may or may not be true. But, knowing he knew Hamlet so well, I named the foundation Claudius. Then I got in touch with Mr. Hancock and told him about the foundation I'd started. I said I'd be contacting them for money. That was the beginning. I found a couple of places and made William buy them. Then I'd provide housing, based on what people could pay. It sort of grew and grew. When I moved to Seattle,

I kept at it and made it bigger and bigger. Now I have a whole board who works with me. Wonderful people. We help a lot of people now."

"So, you and William were in touch with each other for the past seven years?"

"No, I worked through Hancock. I didn't speak to William at all. In fact, once I had the lawyer in Seattle, I didn't even speak to Hancock. Mr. Pierce, my lawyer, did it."

"Are you telling me you were blackmailing my husband all of this time?"

"No, there was no blackmail. That would require a threat. I never threatened to do anything. I just asked for the funds. And they went to a non-profit. I never used the funds for my personal expenses."

"Why do you think he gave you the money whenever you asked? How much was it anyway?"

"It was about ten million. Why do *you* think he gave it to me?"

"Well … he always liked you."

"Do you keep someone you like locked up in a hospital, drugged, for years?"

"Only if you believe they couldn't bear to face something … then you might."

"Is that what you and William told each other? That I couldn't face it? How long would you have left me there?"

"I want to go back to William. He knew about the money; he had to. Hancock would never pay up without William knowing about it."

"Yes, William knew all about it."

"What did he do?"

"He hired an investigator at some point. He told me about it in a letter he wrote to me when I returned home—"

"Wait … wait … a letter? Returned home from where?"

Helen breathed deeply, lowered her shoulders, centered herself. "When William was in the hospital, he asked me to see him. I did, and we talked. Later, he wrote me a letter. He told me he had followed the Claudius Foundation and found out all about it. He said he had pictures of the properties I'd bought."

"Was he going to sue you or expose you or something? Why did he do that?"

"He did it partly because that's the kind of man he was. He wanted to know and control. That was his thing."

She saw Catherine shaking her head in denial of those words, and Helen dropped it.

"He did it partly because he felt guilty—"

Catherine was shaking her head again.

"Yes, Catherine, he felt guilty. So guilty, in fact, that he needed his whole life to be redeemed. He said that's what I'd done, redeemed him, by using his money and transforming it into something good. That's what he said, Catherine. That's what he believed."

Catherine was quiet. She was looking at the ceiling. She was thinking. And remembering. "Well, the last part is confirmed by the letter he wrote for Hancock to read to us, isn't it? He said you were his legacy, and I wondered what he meant by that. And he mentioned transforming pain, I recall that. But he never said anything about feeling guilty."

Helen just sat. She waited in silence. She was not going to help Catherine find her way through William's words.

Finally Catherine looked at Helen again. "I'm going to ask Hancock to bring me that letter. I need to read it again. And please give me William's letter to you. I want to read it."

"I didn't bring it," Helen said, hoping against hope Catherine would let it drop.

"Get someone in Seattle to go to your home and get it," Catherine said peremptorily. "I'm going to need it, I think."

Helen was quiet.

"You *will* let me read it, surely."

"If he wanted you to read it he would have given you a copy or given a copy to Hancock … or Stewart."

"How do you know he didn't?"

"I don't."

"Well, then. I'll check with them. But if not, I'll want that letter, Helen."

Helen said nothing.

"It's time for my lunch. Come back this afternoon. Maybe three. I'll need to rest after lunch."

Helen thought about not coming. But Catherine was ill. And she was old. And she had nothing else, as far as Helen knew. So ... she simply nodded her acquiescence and left. She called Stewart, and he ordered the car.

"Stewart," Helen said on the way back to the hotel. "Catherine's going to ask you for a copy of a letter William sent me. Do you have it?"

"No, he never said anything about a letter to you."

"What do you think I should do?"

"Depends on what the letter says, I guess. Would it help or hurt Catherine?"

"But what about William? His wishes? Wouldn't he have shared it with her if he thought it was right for her to know?"

"Now I'm out of my depth. William held things close to the chest. He compartmentalized. Sort of a need-to-know mentality going on in his head. So I can't answer."

They reached the hotel, and Helen got out of the car. She pulled her cell phone out of her pocket and called Gerard.

He answered on the first ring. "Hello, Helen."

"I have an issue. Can you talk now?"

"Yes, but I'll go to you. Where are you?"

"Back at the hotel. I have to go back to the hospital at three."

"We'll have lunch. Go to the restaurant there, and I'll join you in less than fifteen minutes." She did as he instructed. Once seated, she ordered a pot of tea. She sat quietly, waiting.

"I'm here," said Gerard, ten minutes later. "I was in the area. So ... want to order lunch?"

"I think so. I only had toast earlier, and I'm hungry, now that you're here. You seem to have that effect on me."

"Glad to hear it. I think. So ... let's order; then you can start talking."

Helen ordered a Caesar salad with grilled salmon. Unfortunately, the waiter intended to create the salad at the table, so they had to wait for the performance art of salad-making to end before they could talk. Finally, the waiter left.

Helen tasted the salad. "Well damn. I wish I could say all of that effort wasn't necessary, but I can't. This salad is fabulous."

"It's always frustrating when you have to admit something like that. My heart goes out to you," Gerard said. She thought the look in his eye might be called twinkling, especially given the appearance of the laugh lines she had seen earlier. She growled at him. He just smiled back and took a bite of his sandwich. They ate for a few minutes.

Then Helen started. "My father-in-law wrote a letter to me shortly before he died. January. He said, 'No eyes but yours and mine will see it,' right in the body of the letter. Another letter he wrote to me was read aloud by the family attorney who handled the will. My mother-in-law was present for the reading of that letter. Now my mother-in-law wants to read the first letter. The one he sent to me in Seattle. My question is: should I let her read it?"

"Is there anything in the letter that would hurt her?"

"I just don't know. It's not about her, and she's not mentioned at all. It's more like a confession, maybe. A lot of it is about me. How the things I've done affected him."

"Why is she so anxious to know what's in it?"

"Because she's trying to understand him, I think. She was totally devoted to him. They always worked as a team, at least where I was concerned. Now she knows he had this area of his life that he wasn't sharing with her. Maybe she's hurt by that. She didn't say."

"My inclination is help her understand him. But a definite case could be made for letting him keep his secrets. The answer to your dilemma might be what you just said. About the letter being somewhat like a confession. If he's Catholic, which I vaguely recall being mentioned, then you could ask his confessor, his priest."

Helen brightened. "You're absolutely right. I should have thought of that. I even know who it is, Father Bodelman. Thank you, Gerard. That's a great idea."

"My pleasure. Anything to help." He said it casually, but she knew he meant it literally.

After they finished lunch, Helen said, "I need to go upstairs, make the call to the priest, and have a rest. Talking to my mother-in-law is exhausting."

"I understand. I'm going back. We're looking at some interesting solutions."

Helen had no idea what he was talking about but was too caught up in her own concerns to ask about it. She tucked the comment into a recess in her mind to follow up on later, and they parted.

❧ ❧ ❧

"Father Bodelman? I'm so grateful you're taking time to talk with me. I'm William and Catherine Prescott's daughter-in-law. I wasn't around when you came to the parish, so we've never met. Now I have a problem related to the Prescotts, and I need your input."

The priest made a neutral throat-clearing sound, which Helen interpreted as permission to forge ahead. So she did.

"William wrote me a letter. In it, he talked about redemption and atonement. He talked about how I used his money to atone for things for both him and me. He said I was originally out for revenge against him, but it got turned into our mutual redemption.

"Catherine is ill, as you probably know, and now she knows about the letter and wants me to show it to her. But in the letter itself, William states that only he and I will see it. So … I have two questions. First, did William discuss this, outside the confessional of course, with you? And second, should I let Catherine see the letter?"

"What would be your intent in showing her the letter?"

"*My* intent?"

"Yes, yours."

"I hadn't thought of it. I guess I'd be tempted to show it to her because she's trying to understand William. To know what he was keeping from her. It might make things easier for her."

"She already suspects he was hiding things from her?"

"She must. Why else would she be tracking his movements over the few years before his death?"

"And will finding out make her months ahead easier?"

"I can't answer that. I have no idea. I know she loved him above everyone. Even above her children."

"What William wrote. Do you believe it was true?"

"I believe *he* believed it was true."

"So, will the letter affect how Catherine feels about you?"

"I can't answer that. William and Catherine were a mystery to me when my husband was alive. To some extent, they still are. I've kept my distance from them for years now."

"Why are you here, then, and why were you here earlier, when it was William in the hospital?"

"Because I feel an obligation. We shared some things. Some very painful things."

"Why the obligation?"

"We're human. We're inextricably tied, one to another. We had some truly awful times. We owe it to one another not to inflict any further unnecessary pain."

"Your answer, then, is before you. Your action will inflict or reduce pain in another human. Do that which reduces it." She knew, from the tone of his voice as much as his words, that she would get nothing more from him.

"Thank you, Father Bodelman."

"You're welcome. Go with God, Helen." The way he said it made her believe he knew of her. Someone, probably William, had told him about her.

Once Helen was off the phone, she called the front desk, then called Alicia on her cell, and gave Alicia instructions. Then she went into the bedroom of the suite, unrolled her yoga mat, practiced postures for thirty minutes. She then sat, crossed her legs, and tried to meditate. As happened so often when she was in turmoil, her mind refused to be calm. Refused to be silent. Refused to move into the emptiness. After forty minutes, she gave it up and went into her breathing exercises.

Stewart met her in the lobby, and they went back to the hospital, arriving just after three. Helen went into Catherine's room. Catherine's eyes were closed. She looked her age, pushing eighty. Every year of it. Then she sensed Helen, opened her eyes, and pulled herself into a sitting position in the bed. She suddenly looked much younger and very much alive.

"Helen, I'm so happy you're here. I was afraid I'd scared you off. That you wouldn't come back."

"Not quite. I don't get scared off so easily these days."

"Yes, I've noticed."

Helen was silent.

Catherine looked at her. "I won't apologize, you know."

"I know that," said Helen. "I don't expect it."

"I did what I thought was right. About everything."

"Yes, I know you did."

They were both silent for several very long minutes.

"But …," said Catherine. Her tone was insistent.

"But your thinking was wrong." Helen said it bluntly, giving no quarter.

"And *you* know what should have been done?"

"I know *now* what should have been done. I don't let children stay in unsafe places. Or with unsafe people. Not when I can change things."

"That's enough, Helen."

They were both silent.

Eventually Catherine spoke again. "Hancock says he knows *nothing* about the letter William sent. Stewart says the same. Are you going to let me see that letter, Helen? Or do you want to punish me some more?"

"I'm not the one punishing you, Catherine. And yes, you can see the letter." She reached into her purse. "I had it faxed to Parker House." She handed the paper to Catherine. "Would you like me to leave while you read it?"

"No, you can stay." Catherine's hands shook a little when she took the paper from Helen. Her voice did, too. She read silently. Slowly. When she got to the bottom, she started again at the top. When she was finished, she closed her eyes. Tears came down her face. Helen rose and got some tissues from a box on the bedside table. She placed them in Catherine's hand. Catherine blotted the tears. Helen sat. She waited. She felt as if she had spent years sitting and waiting. Sitting first beside William's hospital bed, and now Catherine's.

After a time, neither would be able to say how long, Catherine opened her eyes and blotted them gently. "Thank you, Helen. Not for showing me the letter. Thank you for what you did for William. I'll never forget it. Never."

"You're welcome," Helen said quietly. She left, called Stewart, and returned to the hotel.

In her suite, she went into her bedroom and arranged a prayer corner with her cushion and incense. She sat, breathing deeply and quietly and slid into the emptiness of meditation. Gradually a humming vibration entered her lower abdomen. It rose until everything was humming and vibrating inside. She basked in the feeling, floating with it, connecting. A lot of connecting. A lot of spirits or essences moving toward and around her. Touching, retreating, swirling. She was aware of them. She moved with them. They danced. Then they drifted away, slowly. When she returned to the present, it was dark outside the window. It was almost midnight. She climbed into bed and went immediately to sleep.

The next morning, she called Stewart. He had not heard from Catherine, he told her. Helen asked him to arrange the flight home and then called Gerard. He was ready whenever she wished to leave, he told her. She asked if he'd like to come to her suite for breakfast and he agreed. She ordered room service, packed her things, and opened the door for Gerard.

"You look rested," he commented.

"I am. I think I've done everything I was supposed to. I showed her the letter, by the way, after I talked to the priest. It was the right thing to do."

"I'm sure it was," Gerard replied.

Breakfast arrived. Cheese omelets, thick-cut bacon, English muffins. They ate companionably, in near silence. Stewart called to say the plane would be ready very soon, and he was sending the car for them. As they were leaving the hotel, Helen finally asked Gerard some questions.

"Why can you come and go so easily if you're working with people here?"

"Helen, my work can be done anywhere. I can do it at home or in an office or in a lab, in Seattle or Singapore or Sydney. That's what modern communications has done for us."

"But, you really don't have any bosses, do you?"

"No."

"And you don't have to be in Seattle to integrate the new company into yours, do you?"

"No."

"So ... why do you live in Seattle?"

"Now?"

"Yes, now."

"Because that's where you are." He said it very simply.

Helen did not know how to respond. So she did not.

❧ ❧ ❧

On the plane back to Seattle, Helen thought over what she had learned. She had avoided relationships for so long she did not know how to judge them, enter them, manage them, live with them. She was very confused by them as well. She still had not fully understood Gerard's comment in Ocean Shores about arriving at a deeper level of friendship. She was sure she had not arrived because she was sure it would be apparent to her if she had. The journey she was on seemed long, and reaching the destination uncertain. Her thoughts meandered as the plane flew straight.

She mused, half in the present, half in the past. The journey started at the ashram, where the first step was her retreat from the world. The world she left was wrong, and she could not move forward until she first rejected it. That part of the task was very clear and had been from the day she left Riggs Erickson. She mastered the first steps and left the ashram. Then came the Connecticut interlude, which turned out to be a very gradual return. The relocation to Seattle marked a giant step. Alicia barging unbidden into her life, another leap. Then Gerard, the board: those were vast expansions in her new life. And now, a reconciliation of sorts with William and Catherine. She knew, no doubts, the meditation in the hotel in Boston was the key. She had made a breakthrough. She was not sure about a lot of things, but she was sure about that. And she knew her work was critical to her journey. Every building, every tenant, every CASA case. It was all concrete, material, grounded. Very much in the world. All necessary for healing. Eventually the spirit, the mind, and the material would create a seamless integration. Unity. The journey's end.

❧ ❧ ❧

The morning after Helen's return, Alicia came over. "I'm so glad to see you," Helen said as she opened the door.

"Don't be too sure," Alicia replied. Behind her were two men, each with two chairs. "I decided if we had little meetings here, we'd need a couple of more chairs."

"Do we plan to have meetings here?"

"Yes, I think so. Maybe even some that include lunch."

"Well, then, guess I'll need those chairs."

The men came in and put the chairs in the dining room and left. "I need to write you a check, Alicia. The couch, the chairs, the picture. It's too much."

"It's my donation to the foundation. And it's not that much." Alicia dismissed it, so Helen said no more about it.

They sat at the table, and Alicia said, "I want to show you what Ruth found. We can go there if you like, but I made some sketches with Frank's help." She unrolled a tube of paper about two feet wide that turned out to be about four feet long. She held it down on the corners with a teacup, a spoon holder, a salt shaker, and a small bowl, all gathered from the kitchen. They sat side by side at the small table.

"This drawing," she said, pointing to a sketch of a building on a corner of a street, "gives you an idea of location. The building is on a main corner of the town. Down here, you see the various businesses. These windows," pointing to the upper two floors, "show the location of the apartments. They all overlook the two streets. I'm told it's not too noisy since it's not a big town, but it's got to be noisier than a place on a side street would be. And emergency vehicles would surely go down this street, especially at night, to get around town quicker. What do you think?"

"I think you're probably right. One fix would be to replace those windows with triple-pane ones. That can really cut down on noise."

"There are eight apartments, total. Four on each floor. Four have two bedrooms, but she said one of those bedrooms was very small. The others have one, plus a small office-like area without a door or closet. Those are advertised as being a one bedroom with den. Ruth's thinking she'd live in one of the two-bedroom apartments and put tenants in all the others. She also said she could use a room in the mortgage company's office on the ground floor as the foundation office."

Helen studied the picture a moment. "I see two potential problems," she began. "First, living in the same building as the tenants. I did that at the beginning, and it was wearing. I felt odd, having people who paid me rent bumping into me in the halls and at the mailbox and things. Ruth is setting herself up for that. The second issue is the office in the same building. What kind of life would she give herself if she worked and lived in the same space, so to speak? How would she keep balance in her life?"

"Helen, are these your problems? Are you projecting?" Alicia looked at Helen.

Helen looked back and then at the ceiling. "You could be right. Let's ask Ruth."

That settled, Alicia moved on. "Frank sketched out the upper-floor layout. Here," she pointed to another section of the large paper, "the common hallway's in the back wall, which overlooks the alley. The stairs come up in the middle of the hall," and she pointed to that section. "Then the four apartments are lined up on the hall. The two on the ends are longer but narrower. They get windows on two sides. The middle two are wider. All of their windows are on the street. They're the ones with the den instead of a second bedroom. Now ... this sketch," and she pointed to the third drawing on the paper, "has the actual floor plans, one of each apartment type. Notice the layout. The two-bedroom one has a small bathroom attached to the bigger bedroom, but it has only a shower. The small bedroom is across from a second bathroom that has a tub. What Frank and I liked is the idea that the two bedrooms are on opposite sides of the living room so you get separation. Now, in the one-bedroom, notice the location of what they call the den. It's right off the living room, with a big opening, so it really connects to and is part of the living room. We could rent these at market price to a single person, or even to a person with one child. They could share the bedroom and still have this extra space for playing and daytime napping if they wanted."

Helen looked at the floor plans. She thought Frank and Alicia had been right on the money in terms of evaluating the suitability of the layout. And it could work well. The smaller units would be especially suitable for a parent with only one child, whereas the larger one could house two or even three children. Small, but adequate. And far better than an old single-wide trailer house in a bad trailer park, which was often the lot of the semi-rural poor in the northern counties.

"What kind of shape are they in? Do they look nice?"

"I think they're pretty good. We'd want to paint, for sure, and replace the carpets. That'll make a huge difference. I'd like to see new refrigerators. These are those old kind that don't defrost themselves. Geez, how old would that be, anyway? The ranges are fine, though. They don't have dishwashers, but you can't have everything. They have nice double sinks; I liked that. I guess I'd like to see one with new paint and carpet, plus a new fridge, then decide if anything else needs to be done."

"Did Frank make an offer?"

"He did, with a contingency for you to see it if you want. He made it for a week, which runs out in three or four days, I'm not sure which."

Helen thought about it. She knew that, eventually, she wouldn't be able to see every building. This would be the first time if she did not go. She realized she was not quite ready for that step.

"I'll go tomorrow," she said. "I think I'd like a trip to Bellingham anyway. They have a fantastic little art museum. Maybe I'll stop in and look at the current exhibit while I'm there."

"Want someone to go with you? I could, or maybe Gerard."

"No, Gerard was just with me on a quick trip to Boston. I don't want to impose on him again right now."

Alicia hadn't known about Gerard's presence on the trip. She raised her eyebrows, then raised and lowered them again in several repetitions, about to say something.

"Don't go there," Helen said with a smile.

Alicia turned her look into wide-eyed innocence, lips tightly pursed. They both laughed.

"I think I'd like to go on my own. I've been around a lot of people lately. Don't want to overdo it."

They both smiled, remembering Helen's hermitic existence of only a few months earlier.

"What else do we have on our plate?" Helen asked Alicia.

"Well, we have these applications. Kenneth and I screened out the ones with no children involved. There are maybe ten or twelve here. We're filling up the apartments fast. All we have left is one in Fleetwood Arms, two in Sabrina, and maybe three or four in Canal Place. That's it, other than the duplex and the Seventh Street West quad. Kenneth and Rick Cleveland are working the duplex. Shall I send out an e-mail to get more applicants?"

"You could, but let's get Frank wound up again. Get him busy finding some places for us that are tenant-ready. And when I was flying home, looking down at the land, I was struck by the area around Ellensburg. All those farming and ranching operations. I wonder if we should have an office out there. We went north with Ruth and west with the McHales. Maybe we should look east."

"Well, if we go east, we should also be thinking about Walla Walla and Spokane. They're both hubs of pretty large populations. Eventually, we'll need a presence out there."

Helen thought for a few minutes. "Here's an idea. Let's see if we can find people like Ruth in all three places—Ellensburg, Walla Walla, and Spokane. Maybe get several candidates together, interview them as a group. If they create a good dynamic, they could rely on each other a bit. It might save us having to go out there all of the time. So … if you wanted to find these people, where would you look?" She asked it as a rhetorical question and gazed out her dining room window. "Got it," she said after a moment. "We'll ask Ruth how to find other visiting nurses, see if there's an association, maybe an annual meeting or something. We could go to that and meet some people. That's one option. And we could call a couple of people in social work, like Elsa Dutton, see who she knows in that area. Let's try to start with people we know, ask for referrals to other people. That beats just advertising."

"I can do some of that while you're in Bellingham," said Alicia. "We aren't in a hurry, are we?"

"No, we're not. Except I don't want to waste too much time. Next board meeting, we should create a schedule, set some goals, like open four locations per year for four years, something like that. Even if we don't keep to it, at least it provides a guideline for where we're headed."

"Will do. I'll asked Kenneth to put it on the agenda," said Alicia. "Now, shall we look at some of these applications I brought over?"

"Yes, we should."

"Do you mind if I call Oskar? He's at the tea shop, and I said he could help with this if you didn't mind. He hasn't seen any applications yet. He needs to get up to speed on the whole picture."

"Now I know why you bought chairs. Sure, tell him to come over." Alicia made the call while Helen started looking at applications. She stopped at one that was particularly interesting to her. The applicant was a woman with two children. The form had apparently been filled out by a person at a food bank located in a church on Lower Queen Anne. Helen made a call to him since it was the only number given on the application.

"Is a Mr. Lockhart available? … Yes, hello, my name is Helen Smith. I'm with the Claudius Foundation."

"Oh, good. Yeah, I'm the one who helped Dottie fill out the form. What do you need from me?"

"Can you give me some basic information? Who Dottie Haney is, why she needs housing, anything like that?"

"Yeah, I can. She's about twenty-five. She lives in her car, a beat-up old Chevy, I think it is. She parks it in a different place every night, usually somewhere within a mile of here. In the daytime, she moves it to a space that's free for the day in one of the neighborhoods around here. She said she uses a different place each day so the neighbors don't get suspicious. As the day goes on she can slip in and out of public restrooms around here without being noticed. And she tries to bathe the kids from the restroom sink. It's a really bad situation. We give her food when she comes here twice a week. I think she knows where she can get free breakfast and dinner around town. She seems to do all right for food. I don't know how she gets the money to buy gas. Even moving only a mile or so, she'd still need *some* gas. But living in that car … Geez … I just can't see that."

"How old are the children, and how long has she lived in the car?" Helen was conscious of Oskar and Alicia coming back into the apartment after Oskar called and got buzzed in downstairs. They sat across from Helen at the small table, listening in.

"The boys are about two and four, something like that. Both out of diapers. I think she's been living in the car for three or four months. She mentioned she was in Butte, Montana, at Christmas and came here right after that. So maybe since January, say."

"OK, can you hold on a minute?"

"Sure." Helen put the cell phone down in the kitchen and then returned to speak in a low voice. She repeated what Mr. Lockhart had told her. Oskar looked a bit shocked.

"In a car?" he said softly. Helen nodded. "Oh my God, two little kids sleeping in a car on the street. What in the world are we coming to?"

"We need to find out if she's mentally ill or running from the law or what's going on that way." Helen said. "Always keep in mind we have other tenants too. We need to be careful who we put next to them. What if she's running from a gun-happy husband? That's the kind of thing we need to know." Helen retrieved the phone.

"We may be able to help," she said. "But we need to talk to Dottie, find out the story. How do we reach her?"

"I told her to leave me a note on the church bulletin board every day. Tell me where she'd be in case I heard something. Let me go check it, I'm here today doing some financial work for the church." He left the phone and returned shortly. "Yeah, I can find her. She said she'd be wandering around at the International Fountain area. When it gets cold, she'll go to Bartell Drugs and walk around. And her car's in the upper lot near Metropolitan Market. I know where that is. I could probably walk around and find her or leave a note on her car."

"Would she be able to call me? To set up an appointment?"

"Why don't I just do that now; then I'll tell her when and where to be. Will that work?"

"Yes, let me think a minute." Helen turned to Oskar and Alicia. "When and where should we meet her? Mr. Lockhart will get the information to her. She hangs out near her car, I suspect, on Lower Queen Anne."

"Tell her to meet us at the corner of Mercer and Queen Anne at a booth in Kidd Valley, the burger place. Noon tomorrow, we'll buy lunch for her and the kids," Oskar said. Alicia nodded her agreement. Helen passed it on to Mr. Lockhart and then closed her cell.

"Here's what the application looks like," she said to Oskar as she handed him the form. I called the number here and spoke to a guy who is involved with the food bank at the church. He seems to know her, helped her fill this out. I'll be in Bellingham tomorrow to look at the building Ruth Mellon wants us to buy. So you two will be handling this."

"Give me some help here," Oskar said. "She's a new type. She hasn't been screened by somebody like a social worker. So what do we do, exactly, to check her out?"

"First, you'll be seeing her with the kids, so notice how she treats them. That tells you a lot right there. But, expect her to be nervous. Not well groomed; plus she might even smell since she can't take showers every day. Then just get to know her a little. Ask her to tell you how she ended up sleeping in a car. Ask about the kids. Where were they were born? Where else have they lived? What do they like and dislike? The answers aren't so important; watch *how* she answers. Does she seem mentally ill? Is she scared of something? Is she high on drugs? Look at her eyes. Does she seem normal?"

"Do you like her and believe her?" Alicia added. "Could you imagine your daughter ending up in this fix if you had a daughter? Is she a walking disaster, or did she get a bad string of luck? Would you hire her to clean your house or walk your dog or deal with customers?"

"Got it. And, Alicia, you'll be with me, right?"

"Sure, I'll be there. I'll get to the burger joint ten minutes early, just to be sure. She'll be easy to spot, coming in with two little kids."

"Let's talk about where we'd put her if we decide she'd be a good tenant," said Helen. They discussed the pros and cons of each of the available buildings.

"We want a bus line. If it's an old car, it may not last long," Oskar said. "And we'll probably need to get her some furniture. Unless she has it stored somewhere."

"I think Canal Place," said Alicia. "The more modern style might suit her better than the classic buildings. It's right on a bus line. The campus at the college down there is a good place for picnics. And there are ball field; they can watch kids play soccer, maybe find a team for the boys at some point."

"See if there's one with a view of the canal. The little ones could watch boats go in and out," Helen added.

With that, they moved to other applications. Oskar read one and then said, "I think I'd like to make an initial call on this one with you two listening in." They both looked at the application he'd chosen. It was from a counselor in some type of church ministry. The applicant was a single father with a girl aged twelve. Their names were Clifton and Kathy Baskin. Both women nodded, and Oskar took out his cell and called.

"My name is Oskar Lundgren, and I'm calling from the Claudius Foundation. I'd like to speak with Luis Lopez, please … Yes, hello. I'm Oskar Lundgren. I'm calling about Clifton and Kathy Baskin. Can you give me some background, please?" He listened. And listened. And listened. Then, "Just a minute," he said and put the phone in the kitchen as Helen had done earlier.

Oskar returned and related the story. "The mother remarried about two years ago. Her new husband doesn't get along with Kathy, and Kathy doesn't like him either. The parents agreed things would go better if Kathy lived with her father. He was living in a house with two other men and doesn't think he should bring her there. He's employed as a mechanic. Same place for some years. But his hours were reduced over a year ago. The shop owner didn't want to lay anyone off during the recession, so he cut back everybody's hours instead. Clifton makes a decent salary but not enough for a two-bedroom apartment in the area. If he moves way out, he has the problem of not being near enough to be home at a decent hour. He doesn't want to leave Kathy alone for so long after school. The counselor says he's a good guy, devoted to the daughter, clean living, church member for at least ten years. The counselor knows him personally."

Helen did not comment. She waited.

Alicia said, "And what's your conclusion?" to Oskar.

"We take him," Oskar said.

Helen nodded. "You meet him or ask someone else to meet him," Helen said. "Doesn't matter which. If whoever meets him believes he's fine, we take him."

Oskar got the phone back. "When can we meet with Clifton? I think Kathy should be there too since she'll want to see where she might be living." He listened. "Sure, you can come along. We're always happy to have counselors aware of what we offer ... Sounds good. Let me give you my cell phone. Call any time." He repeated his cell number and ended the call.

"He says he'll talk to Clifton and get back to me. It'll be an evening or weekend appointment. I'll take it from here, unless one of you wants to join me?"

"No, you've done this part before, when we had Daniel Fortnuss, remember? You'll be fine on your own," Helen said.

"Yes, I remember. Hard to forget. We really helped that guy. I think of him a lot."

Helen nodded. She knew just how Oskar felt. She thought again of the letter William had written. He had said the work she did constituted *the ideal life*. That was what Oskar was feeling, the ideal life, lived through work that mattered, that made a difference.

※ ※ ※

The next morning Helen got up and ate an early breakfast. She filled a thermos with tea and put it in a bag, then added a tea mug and some fruit. She decided she'd go for a walking retreat. There was an exhibit at the Whatcom County museum she had read about, and she knew there were many scenic areas for a quiet walk and tea break once she got to Bellingham. As she left her apartment, she took her cell phone out of her purse and turned it off. No interruptions, no people except for those in Bellingham she needed to see. A wonderful day.

It rained from the time Helen got on I-5 heading north for almost an hour, until she reached Skagit County. Not the typical light Seattle rain, it was the hard rain, rain you might see in a thunderstorm on the East Coast—buckets and buckets of hard, wind-driven rain crashing on the car windows and roof, waves flying off the pavement and outward, as high as the car windows. This went on for forty minutes or more. Suddenly, when she reached the Skagit Valley, the sun was shining. The blue sky was full of puffy clouds, like the ones small children draw in their early landscapes. The sun bounced off the fields of tulips near La Conner. The peak time for the bulbs was finished, but the faded flowers clung to their youth like an aging beauty queen, giving it their all.

Helen felt as battered by the rain as the car had been. Yet here, just minutes later, it was all in the past. All was forgiven. That was the nature of her Pacific Northwest home. The highway on both sides was bounded by small hills covered mostly with fir trees, though there were some deciduous trees sprinkled about, providing a contrast in color and texture. She was feeling more relaxed now, at one with the calm and peaceful environment. Helen took the exit for Larabee State Park, situated on Samish Bay, just south of Bellingham.

The park was full of wonderful hiking trails with fantastic views of the San Juan Islands. She found a parking place where she could sit and have some hot tea before walking. As she walked through the forest along the beach edge, she looked out at the islands sparkling and shimmering across the water. This, she thought was another of the most beautiful places in the world. She thought that a lot since her move to Washington. Mt. Rainer, Mt. Baker, the Quinault Rain Forest, the Cascades and the Olympics surrounding Seattle with beauty in all directions, even Mt. St. Helen's with her volcanic-blown top missing. She was moved and healed just by breathing in the air around her. Her sense of coming into herself and home to herself was both elevated and grounded by her surroundings. This location, she knew, was the perfect place, a place that nurtured the growing sense of unity she felt within her being. Her work, her board, the properties and the children in them, Gerard, Alicia—they were all part of a new world, one she was just beginning to trust. She sat on a log, closed her eyes, and became one with the space around her. Later, quite a bit later, she slowly opened her eyes. She felt she was smiling from each pore of her body. After a half-hour walking meditation, she was back at the car and drove on to Bellingham.

Once in town, she called the Realtor Frank had arranged to meet her and told him she had arrived. The corner of Railroad Avenue and Holly was in the center of the small picturesque town. The building was just as Frank and Alicia had sketched it on the rolled piece of paper. It looked well suited to its location, substantial and at home. The apartments above the commercial section looked as if they would be safe, part of the life of the town yet high enough above it to afford some privacy.

She introduced herself and was given the tour. The first impression was not good, as the old carpet was stained, matted, worn, and had ripples. The walls were dinged up, gouged, and there was even a large hole in one hallway that looked as if a fist had been driven into it. The bones, however, were nice. The ceilings were nine feet tall, which no one had mentioned. It provided every room with a feeling of spaciousness. The dens were easy to visualize with French doors and were an excellent size for a twin bed or daybed with a bedside table. There was still ample room for a dresser or armoire and even a small desk and chair. She could see how it would have appealed not just to Frank and Alicia, accustomed to seeing beat-up buildings, but also to Ruth. This was, indeed, an excellent property.

"Do you have a nice apartment nearby where our employee could live while this is rehabilitated?" she asked the Realtor. The Realtor took her two blocks away and showed her a newer two-bedroom apartment. It was clean and modern. More than adequate, but without the personality of the older dual-use building. She asked him to hold it long enough for her to get an OK from Ruth and then send the lease to Kenneth so the foundation could secure the space.

Her business done, she walked to the Lightcatcher Building, one of the three buildings used by the Whatcom County Museum.

"Cheech" Marin, of Cheech and Chong fame, was a collector of Chicano art. The museum had on exhibition a group of paintings from his collection, billed as Chiconitas. Each work was sixteen inches square or less, modern, and in several styles and media. The colors, however, screamed the vibrant Mexican and Latin heritage, as did much of the subject matter. Some of the paintings were inspired by street art and murals so popular in Southern California. Others were more personal, portraits, the insides of homes with figures engaged in home life. There were wonderful impressionist gardens and realistic landscapes. Helen spent over two hours looking at and reading about each painting and artist in the exhibit. Two hours of her life, immersed in the emotions and talents of others. It was a gift from her to her, one of the few such gifts she felt she'd earned in the past twenty years.

The drive back to Seattle was similar to the drive out but in reverse. First she was in late sunshine and blue skies. Then, as she left Skagit County, she encountered the same line of dark gray skies and heavy rain. She endured. It let up as she reached the northern edge of the city. She was able to dispense with the windshield wipers just before the Seattle skyline came into view, the sun bouncing off the buildings with enough intensity that Helen needed her sunglasses. She almost laughed. She still could not get used to the mercurial nature of the weather in her newfound home.

※ ※ ※

The next morning Helen was up drinking her tea and eating a peanut-butter-banana sandwich when the phone rang. She glanced at the clock on the microwave as she answered it. Eight. Seemed early for a call.

"Helen, it's Oskar. I wonder if you could meet me at the tea shop at ten this morning. You need to hear a story."

"Of course. I'll be there." She hung up. It must be *some* story if Oskar did not just want to tell her on the phone. Rather than speculating, she followed her own dictum to live in the here and now. She finished her breakfast, read the paper, and cleaned the kitchen, with full concentration on the cleaning. Then she took a shower and put on some jeans, a long-sleeved tee shirt, and a vest. The sun was shining, and the April morning was fresh and clean. As she walked to the tea shop, she was very aware of all of the pots full of blooming flowers. Seattle in spring was so full of blossoms; it was a giant garden. Spring in Seattle, of course, lasted from mid-February to the Fourth of July.

She smiled and said hello to Sonja and then joined Oskar at the rear table. Several other customers in small groups occupied the tables closer to the windows. Oskar rose and held her chair and then sat. He poured her a cup of tea.

"I want to start at the very beginning," said Oskar.

"A very good place to start," replied Helen. He and she both laughed a bit. She thought how nice it was to share a common culture that included a line from an old musical.

"Yesterday, Alicia and I met Dottie Haney and her two little boys at Kidd Valley." Helen nodded, remembering the phone contact with the food-bank worker two days earlier. "The boys are Noah and Carson. They're two and three, almost four. Dottie is their aunt." Helen's eyebrows rose. There must be a story in that. Living in a car with two small nephews.

"First, you were right about her being nervous. Then, before we barely introduced ourselves, she made us promise not to report her to the police or Child Protective Services. So we promised. Then she said the boys' mother and father died in a car crash in Montana last November. Their mother was Dottie's sister Molly. Dottie and Molly's parents are both dead, and Dottie's the only one left. The father was estranged from his family. He was from South Dakota, and that's where his family still lives. So Dottie took the children. They lived in Dottie's little house in Scobey, Montana. But Dottie couldn't take care of the boys and still work. She's totally naïve about social services of any kind. Lived out on the plains her whole life. She may not be aware of public assistance, but she's very savvy. She went to Butte and started looking for work as a live-in maid and housekeeper. It was no-go. No one wanted a live-in maid with two little kids. She finally ran through all her money and all her sister's money. She'd already sold everything that could be sold from both of them, from a television to a sewing machine to kitchen appliances.

"Now you need a little more background. Molly and Dottie spent a lot of their lives in foster care. The father was a farm hand, and he'd work here and there. He never made much. Sometimes he'd go on a bender and disappear. The mom couldn't feed them, so she'd put them in foster care. That way they got fed. Then the parents would get it together, go get the kids, and they'd live together. Then the father would get drunk, run out on them for a month, and the mother would put them back in foster care until Dad came back again. This apparently went on for some years. So ... when it came to Noah and Carson, Dottie refused even to think about giving the boys up to foster care.

"This story was so depressing to me," Oskar continued, "that I thought I'd better check it out. I left Dottie with Alicia and went outside. Used the cell, called Kenneth. He gave me Elsa Dutton's number. I called her while Kenneth started looking on the Internet for confirmation of the car accident and the deaths of Dottie's parents. Elsa Dutton got hold of social services for the county Scobey's in. She got confirmation of the foster parenting Dottie and Molly had. By the way, Dottie's only twenty-two."

"So," Helen concluded, "we know she probably told the truth about everything. And who would live in a car with two little kids if they had any choice? What does she do for cash?" Helen found herself every bit as involved in Dottie's life as if she'd had the interview with her in person.

"Twice a day, for an hour each time, she parks the car where she can see it, leaves the kids locked in it with the window cracked a little, and then panhandles on the left-turn corner onto Leary under the Ballard Bridge. She has a shift there. A couple of guys get the corner in good times; she can have it midmorning and again midafternoon. She makes maybe twenty dollars a day."

"Did you put her in an apartment?" Helen asked.

"Well, that's why I wanted to talk to you. I thought about it. Started to talk about an apartment. But it just wouldn't work. If she applies for any kind of assistance, she might get the kids taken away. And even if we give her the apartment, she can't afford daycare so she can work."

"We could figure something out."

"Well … I know we could. But by then … well …" Oskar was looking around. Not at Helen. He was uncomfortable. "I don't think you're going to like this, but I took her home."

"Home?"

"Yeah, home. We live in the Highlands. The garage has an apartment on top of it for live-in help. We gave up live-in help when our youngest was ten. It spoils them to have their rooms cleaned and laundry all done for them."

"You took Dottie and the boys to your home and put them in the apartment over the garage. How many more potential tenants do you think you can house permanently?" She was smiling at him. "And what did Sonja say?"

"Sonja said hallelujah," said Sonja, who had been eavesdropping on them from her place at the counter.

"Were you in on this?"

"He did call me and tell me about it. Asked how I felt about it. We have three sons at home. So another female around is fine by me."

Helen shook her head. "Oskar, what can I say?"

"That you understand completely how it could happen."

"I understand completely how it could happen."

"Right. I knew you would." Oskar looked relieved to have told Helen everything. He had feared a more explosive reaction.

"Want to hear our plans?" asked Sonja, coming over with a fresh pot of tea.

"I'm not sure. Will it shock me?"

"Not at all. I'll train Dottie in running the tea shop. That way, I'll have flexibility. Plus, you know, when it's slow, I'll have somebody to talk to. There's a great daycare just around the corner. We'll get the kids in there from about ten to three or four every day. So, this will all work out fine. Later, when the kids are a little older, Dottie can think about going to school or training of some kind. She'll be able to support the kids one day, I think."

Helen shook her head slowly. "How do people even begin to get such big hearts? Has it always been in you? Did you get it from your parents? How?"

Sonja and Oskar looked at one another. "We lost two daughters. Both were stillborn. We wouldn't have minded more children." They both had eyes shiny with tears that did not fully form. Helen did, too. She nodded.

"And you should see the little boys," Oskar said, brightening. "They look like little round-headed blond Norwegians, just as ours did. They break your heart. And so sweet. Unbelievable."

Sonja nodded. "It's a gift. A true gift. Thank God it was Oskar who went to meet Dottie. Anybody would have done the same thing, and we'd have missed out. And our boys. This is so good for them. They took to Noah and Carson right off. Even gave them a bath in our upstairs. The little boys loved it. All five of them were in the bathroom together.

The noise! You wouldn't believe it. The room was a wreck afterwards, of course. Water and wet towels all over the place. It was wonderful."

Helen believed her. Sonja really looked and sounded as if not getting to take in the little family would have been a tragedy.

❧ ❧ ❧

Two days later, Helen was returning from her yoga class. As she entered the apartment, she had to rush to the ringing telephone. "Helen, it's Michelle. I have a problem. I think I need you."

"Tell me about it."

"It's a dissolution case. Two little boys, three and four. Mom filed for divorce and moved out with the kids. Temporary parenting plan gives father visitation one day a week, Saturday, noon until four p.m. Mother had asked for the visitation to be supervised, based on what she calls father's 'mental instability.' Father disputed that; mother had no evidence. So the judge gave the half-day unsupervised until the CASA report is in. I assigned a CASA three weeks ago. Yesterday she called me just after she finished her first interview with the father. She told me she couldn't finish the case. Said she had too much on her plate. But I pushed her a little because she sounded strange. She just repeated what she'd said. I asked if she had her notes from the interview, and asked her to fax them to me. They weren't typed up. It just sounds odd, the whole thing. I want you to read her notes and maybe do an interview with the dad right away. And call the mother, as well."

"Yes, I'll do it. Fax the notes to me right now. And give me the names and phone numbers. I'll start now."

"Thanks, Helen. I'm sure glad I have you. The last name is Dixon. Father is Ralph, Mom is Lisa." She read the numbers. "I'll overnight the file right after I send the fax."

Helen waited for the fax with the notes from the previous CASA. She had a funny feeling. Her stomach had suddenly started aching. She was nervous. The fax machine lit up and started spitting paper. Helen grabbed the pages. She could tell that Michelle had taped small pages onto regular typing paper to get it to feed through the fax machine. The notes were originally written in a small notebook. They were cryptic, handwritten, and sprawling. She read:

F is tall strong says mom is a liar says he loves the boys eyes are strange stares while talking to me met mom when they were in high school dated three years married six years ago F is agitated, fidgets when he talks works in a warehouse no college glances around while talking plays with the boys outside a lot run around and chase each other kids eat pb&j drink apple juice toilet trained F bites skin around nails wants more time with sons mom is "bitch" for not letting him see them more she makes mamma's boys values are different no reason for divorce good provider blames mom for keeping kids from him she makes boys scared of him he makes good living good provider watches what I rite wants boys on weekends wants to go camping wants to raise strong boys loves the boys

Helen immediately picked up the phone and called Lisa Dixon. She introduced herself. "I'm taking over the case from the previous CASA. I'd like you to catch me up on the situation. I believe you have primary custody of Wolf and Coyote, right?"

"Yes. I'm so worried. I don't think my husband is stable enough to have the kids with him. It's why I left him. But now, I can't be there to protect them at all when they're with him. This is crazy. Someone has to do something. I called the police, but they said they had no legal cause to interfere. I already have a restraining order so he can't come near me."

"How does he pick up the kids for visitation if he can't come near you? What arrangement do you have?"

"I hired a professional supervisor. She delivers the kids to him and gets them after the visit and brings them home. I don't have the money for this for long. I borrow it from my parents. I don't know what else to do."

"Will he have the kids Saturday?"

"Yes. This will be the fifth visit. And the kids come home worse every time. They're in tears when they get home. The supervisor told me last time they were holding on to each other for dear life, crying, when she got there. She had to pry them apart to get them in the car. Then they spent the whole time trying to reach each other and cried all the way home. And they've started having nightmares."

"I know they're awfully young, but what do they say?"

"They say they're scared. They talk about monsters and getting shot by thieves. And their play is affected. They use their toy soldiers in different ways, saying things like, 'Kill the dude.' Last time, Wolf, the older one, said his daddy put his hands on Coyote's neck and 'hugged his neck.' This is just not normal. But they're little; no one will believe them."

"What time does the supervisor deliver them tomorrow?"

"She'll pick them up here at nine twenty-five. It's only about twenty minutes, but she said she has to be there a little before ten, or he yells at her."

"Got it. I plan to talk to him today if possible. Let me give you my cell. You can call me this weekend if you haven't heard from me before then."

"Can you do anything? I'm really concerned about their safety."

"I'll have to see your husband first. Until I see him, I can't answer your question. With just what I have now I have no basis for making any calls to anyone."

"It's a stupid system when you have to wait until something bad happens before you can keep something bad from happening."

"I couldn't agree more. Well said. I need to get off the phone and see when your husband is available for an interview with me. While I'm doing that, I want you to call your professional visitation supervisor. Get her mobile phone. Then call me back and give me her mobile number. If I'm still on the phone, leave me the number on voice mail. And when you talk to her, make sure she knows to expect a call from me. It's critical that she does not deliver the children to your husband until I talk to her."

She hung up and immediately dialed Ralph Dixon's number. "Hello, my name is Helen Paige. Is this Ralph Dixon?"

Yeah, who are you?"

"I've just inherited your CASA case from the previous volunteer. She is seriously ill. I hate to say it, but I need to start from the top, which means I'll have to interview you myself, even though you were interviewed already. I'm sorry about this. Is today or tonight a good time for you?"

"No, it's not. I got plans. And I don't see why I have to have another meet. It's not my fault she got sick."

"I understand how you feel. It's awful to have to do it twice. I agree with you. I wish I didn't have to ask for another interview."

"Well, yeah."

"I wish I could just move on without having to bother you. I can promise to make it quick, if that would help."

"Well … maybe. But I can't make it today. I got plans."

"How about tomorrow? Would that work?"

"I get the kids tomorrow."

"I need to observe you with the boys. How about I come when they do, and I could do the observation first, then talk to you a bit afterward. That way it would all be done in one visit, and I wouldn't need to bother you again. We'd be all done."

"Yeah … well … let me think … Well, you could come later. They'll be here at ten, you could come at eleven. How about that?"

"That's great. I'll be there at eleven," Helen said. "Can I repeat the address back to you to be sure I have it right?" She did so. "See you at eleven."

Helen's body was humming when she got off the telephone. The vibrations were strong, and she concentrated on them. This, she decided, was not good. She tried to think of a plan. First, she knew she should not be at the home of Ralph Dixon on her own. She now suspected that the previous CASA on the case had sensed something and had been unable to define it but knew it was not good.

The number for Irene McDonald, the visitation supervisor, was on her answering machine. She called and talked to her for a few minutes. Then she called Michelle. "Hi Michelle, it's Helen Paige. I need a way to reach Hilary and you tomorrow, cell phone numbers. I don't have a specific problem, but I'd feel more confident if I had contact." She got the numbers. Then she sat at her computer and made some notes from her call to Lisa Dixon.

Helen knew from personal experience to act on her intuition. She thought about all of the people she knew in Seattle and tried to decide who would be most valuable in a worst case scenario. She decided on Patrick Lowery and Jeff Daniels, two of the tenants at the Lower Queen

Anne complex. She called Jeff, the hospital building engineer, and asked if she could meet with both men at the apartment complex that same night.

"Sure, Patrick's kids come tonight, and we're all getting together for dinner. We're cooking out. Put a grill out in the workshop. Everybody in the building uses it. Why don't you join us for dinner?"

This was so unexpected that Helen had no idea how to respond.

"Oh, come on. It's us and the Hudsons and Carmen Barrios with her two boys. Oh, and the new woman, Liz, with her two kids. It'll be good for you to meet some of the people who owe you big time. It's just burgers and hot dogs with some beans and potato salad. I've no idea what Carmen will bring. She's always the wild card on these deals. 'Course now, we're dealing with Liz too. Maybe something Russian or Asian. That'll be good."

Helen laughed. "Yes, I'd be delighted to join you. I'll need to pull you and Patrick away for a chat so warn him."

"Will do. Come around five thirty if you want. We start gathering around then out in the annex, as we call it."

Helen hung up. She felt much better just for talking to Jeff. It sounded as though the apartment building had more than fulfilled the high hopes she had when she started the foundation. The building itself had become the catalyst for a transformation in the lives of the children.

Later that day, Helen dressed in jeans, a pullover turtleneck with long sleeves, a vest, and a fleece jacket. Even in April, it could get cool in the evenings, and she was not sure how much of the event might take place outside. She parked a block away and walked back to the apartment building. Carmen Barrios with Rodrigo and the younger son was there, as was Christy Hudson with her baby, Lance. Helen joined them.

Rodrigo recognized her. "Mr. Joe bought me a skateboard. Did he tell you that?"

Helen nodded.

"I'm learning everything. This boy named Alex, he might be a teenager, I'm not sure, but he's teaching me. We meet at the skateboard park. I'm getting good."

"Does your mother know him?"

"Si, yes, I meet him. I *met* him. And his mama. They nice, they *are* nice, good for Rodrigo." Helen was pleased that Carmen felt comfortable approaching her. She smiled at Carmen's careful rephrasing and use of English but did not comment upon it.

"How's your job going?"

"Job is good. *The* job is good. The boss, he tell me come to desk ... to *the* desk ... when people need Spanish. I talk with them. Boss gives me raise, one dollar hour."

"She's still taking lessons in English," Christy said. "And now I'm telling her to watch the news every night on television. I heard it was good for learning proper English. Plus, I make her have a conversation with me for an hour every night. And I got her some books from the library, children's books, and she reads to me. I figure sometime, maybe the end of the year, she'll be good enough to go for the desk job full time."

"Hey, ladies, what's up?" Patrick came out from the building with three children. They all said hello. Patrick's daughter went to Christy and held out her arms for Lance. He went to her readily. The boys started playing with Rodrigo and his little brother. They had a soccer ball and were passing it back and forth in a circle.

"Those are my boys," Patrick said, "Jack and Wyatt. And my girl over there," he indicated the child holding Lance, "is Olivia. They love coming over here. I even took them to the Children's Theatre last week. It was great. First play I've seen, and I liked it as much as they did." He looked up, "Hey, partner, who's grillin'?"

Jeff Daniels had appeared with Katie, who went to join Olivia and Lance. "Your turn; I think I did the chicken last."

"You did, indeed, little on the black side, as I recall."

They both laughed, and then the two men pulled a huge gas grill out of the garage area and over to a paved section that was out of any possible wind. While they were getting it ready and cleaning off the grill, Liz arrived with Dato and Tanya. The two children went over to the group of soccer-ball players. The older boys sent the ball in their direction now and then and gave praise when the children managed to kick it back. The adults went in and out of the building, returning with the meat to be grilled, platters to put it on, buns, and cold drinks

Carmen, the men, and Liz each had a beer while the children, Christy, and Helen opted for the homemade lemonade Carmen produced from large pottery pitchers.

Soon they were joined by Ben Hudson carrying a diet soda. The conversation varied from jobs to children to what was going on at the Seattle Center amid a lot of teasing and laughing. Plans were made for a picnic on the grounds near the International Fountain on Sunday. Helen said little. She enjoyed watching the group and thought about how lucky they were to have one another.

Patrick warmed buns on one side of the grill. After the hot dogs and hamburgers were cooked, he nestled them inside the buns, and everyone went back into the building and trooped up to Carmen's apartment. She had put the dining table against the wall, and it was full of condiments and side dishes. Paper plates were stacked at one end. Liz stopped in her apartment and brought back some cheese blintzes and a platter of pot-stickers. Jeff had a large bowl of potato salad he claimed to have made himself, but Patrick was convinced he'd picked it up at Metropolitan Market. Patrick's baked beans, Jeff said, were out of a can and just heated on the stove. Christy Hudson added a green salad, which she loudly proclaimed to have chopped and assembled herself. Carmen had squash and black-bean burrito makings with a choice of four additional toppings. Helen was overwhelmed with the variety and amount of food. By the time they had all helped the children and then gone through the line themselves, however, she noticed that not much was left. It made her realize she had not been around a large group of hungry people in a very long time.

Carmen had placed a very colorful Mexican blanket on the floor in the living room, and the children gathered on it to eat, picnic style. The adults had the furniture in the living room. Folding chairs were brought from a hall closet along with folding tray-tables. It was amazing, but everyone had plenty of room.

As they were putting the used paper plates and napkins into a large trash bag, Jeff pulled Helen aside. "Time to talk?" he asked. When she agreed, he called Patrick over, and three of them went out into the hall, pulling the door closed behind them.

Helen described her problem quickly and told them what she wanted them to do. Then she handed them two pieces of paper. "This one just restates what I've said." She handed one paper to Jeff. "And this one has the names and phone numbers." And she handed over the other one. "Any questions?"

"No … well, yes," said Patrick. "I have a handgun I keep in a safe on the top of my closet. Do you think I should bring it?"

Helen was not sure what to say. If the children were in danger, would a gun help or hurt? Would it cause an escalation?

"I just don't know," she finally admitted aloud. "I guess all I can say is to use your own judgment. Do you have a permit, and would it be legal? I don't even know that. But, for sure, you don't want to do anything that the police would question you about at any time."

"Lots of guys go to ranges to shoot on weekends," Jeff said. "Maybe we could look up some … See if any are around where we'll be. That would at least explain why we'd have a gun in our glove compartment." Helen left it up to the men to decide what to do.

"I've got to work some more this evening. Please tell everyone I said goodbye, and thank you for dinner." She found that, much as she enjoyed the group and seeing all of the children, she was suddenly exhausted. She definitely was not accustomed to a group this size, especially one that included nine happy and lively children.

Saturday morning, Helen drove to the home of Ralph Dixon. Jeff and Patrick followed in Jeff's SUV. They had studied the layout of the surrounding area on Google Maps, the app that used satellite images. The home looked somewhat isolated, situated at the end of a long drive in heavy woods.

Helen arrived at nine-thirty, well before the supervisor with the children could arrive. She knocked on the door and a very large, very unkempt man answered. "Hi, I'm Helen. I'm sorry to be early. I had no idea when I left Seattle that I'd get here so quick. Is this a good time?"

"No, it's not a good time. You're not supposed to show up 'til eleven."

"Well, maybe we could just talk for a bit before the children arrive. Then I'll be out of your hair a lot earlier. You'll have more time to have just the boys to yourself without me around." She smiled at Ralph, hoping it looked natural.

"Well … this isn't … well." He stopped, unable to come up with something to say to make her go away.

"It'll be a quicker this way. I'll be out of your hair a lot sooner. I know it's a bother to have to put up with me." She was praying she could convince him to talk with her.

"OK. I guess. Come on in." She breathed deeply and entered the house. It was a mess. There was a smell of cooked food and rotten food. There was also a strong urine smell, as though untrained dogs or cats might live in the home.

Helen followed Ralph into a living room strewn with newspapers, clothing, and tools of some sort. What looked like an electrical appliance, broken or dismantled, lay on the coffee table. Ralph sat in a chair, and Helen sat on the couch near him. There was a gun rack on the wall with four long guns on it. A display cabinet hanging next to it had several handguns. She got out her notebook and placed it on the table near her. Then she took her cell phone from her pocket, opened it, and put it near her thigh on the couch. She noticed Ralph starting to fidget. He picked at his fingernails. He shook his leg up and down.

"What can you tell me about your children?" she asked.

"What do you mean?"

"Well, what do they like to eat? What do they like to play with? That sort of thing."

"They eat whatever they're given. I don't hold with catering to kids and just giving them what they want. And they play with normal boy stuff when they're here. I have some trucks and cars, a train set, boy stuff. We spend a lot of time outside. That's the problem with them living with their mom mostly. She'll make them into little mamma's boys. Give them whatever they want. Makes them soft. I'm trying to teach them to defend themselves. Stand up for themselves. Make men of them." Ralph's leg was shaking rhythmically, very fast now. He was scratching at his chin as he talked. His eyes were flickering around the room.

"What do you think led to the failure of the marriage?"

"Their mom led to it, that's what. She up and left. We had a good life here. We grow food. I can fish and hunt. Heat the house with the fireplace. We have a pump and a septic system. This is a great place for kids to grow up. Lots of room. Lots of privacy. She liked it fine before the kids came. Then she decided she wanted a city life. Well, fuck that. This is where those boys belong." His voice rose as he spoke, and his breathing rate increased. A vein near his temple stood out, throbbing.

"Are you angry at her for leaving?"

"Hell, yes, what do you expect? Damn whore." By now he was almost shouting at Helen.

"What will you do about that?" she asked.

"I'd kill the bitch, if it was legal. She has no right to take my sons away like this. Those are my flesh and blood. I'd sooner kill them than have them turn into sissies. Goddamn homos." He suddenly stood up as he said this. His voice rose. "And I don't need you asking questions, either! Just another nosy government bitch! You can leave!" He was making full-body gestures with his arms, waving them about as he shouted at her. Helen stood up.

"I'll leave now. Thank you for seeing me." She started for the door.

"So what will you write? Huh? What will you say?" He was shouting as he followed her to the door. She walked to her car, not rushing, got in, and started down the long drive.

She punched a number in her cell. "Jeff? Make the call to Irene McDonald. I'm on my way."

She drove out to the main road, turned, and went to the nearest shopping strip. There was a Wendy's. She pulled up to the rear of the fast-food store and went in. Soon a woman appeared with two small blond boys.

"Hi, I'm Helen Paige," she said, and shook hands with Irene McDonald. It was about ten-thirty. Helen's cell phone rang.

"He's getting into a truck, and he's carrying guns." The message was from Jeff. "We'll follow him." Jeff had been in the trees part-way down Ralph Dixon's drive, watching through binoculars.

Helen dialed Lisa Dixon's cell. "Lisa, get out of your apartment. Don't go to the immediate neighbor. Go across the street or down the block or something. Stay there until you hear from me. Don't worry, Wolf and Coyote are with me and Irene. We're about to buy them a milkshake. Sorry for the junk food; it's the best we can do right now."

Then Helen called the police. Then she called Hilary.

Finally, she turned her attention back to the children. "Hi, my name is Helen," she said to the little boys. Look what I have in my bag." From it, she pulled out two stuffed teddy bears. "I found them. They need a home. Will you take care of them for me?" The boys nodded and took the bears. "This one needs a name," she said. "Do you know what his name should be?"

"Beary, 'cause he's a bear," said Wolf, the older boy.

"Good name. What about this one?" Helen pointed to Coyote's bear.

Wolf looked at it. "Nosy, 'cause it has a nice nose."

"Is that a good name for your teddy bear?" Helen asked Coyote. He nodded very solemnly. "I think these bears want to share a milkshake. Will you share with them?" Both boys nodded. "What kind? Chocolate or vanilla?"

"Chocolate!" they both said. Their voices were soft but excited. Helen nodded to Irene and passed her a twenty-dollar bill.

"And look what else I have," Helen continued and pulled a book out of her bag. "It's called *Go Dog*. This book needs to be read. It hasn't been read enough. See? It looks all new. Books should *not* look new. It means they're not loved. Books are just like little boys. Did you know that? Books are like boys?" They both shook their heads, eyes on Helen's. "Because books need love. And little boys need love. Who loves you?"

"Mommy," said Wolf, and the word was echoed by Coyote.

"That's right. Now, who will love the book?"

"We will!" shouted Wolf.

Helen laughed.

"OK. Now I'll read the book. And look, here are the milkshakes." The boys took the cups and started sucking on the straws. Helen slowly read the book, showing the children the pages. Helen's phone vibrated in her pocket. She handed the book to Irene, who kept reading. The boys were absorbed in their drinks and the book.

Helen stood up and stepped away from them. "Hello, Helen here," she said softly into her phone. She listened. "Oh, God help us. Stay back. And let me know the outcome." Helen called Hilary. "You need to come to the Wendy's I told you about. The cops will want me as soon as I call them. I have Lisa's aunt's phone, and Lisa said she'd tell her to stay home today. Lisa's mother will go there, too. I'll call and tell her."

She called Lisa. "Hi, it's Helen … I know, I heard … Everything is good here. The boys are great. Listen to me." She paused. "Listen to me." Another pause. "This will be the worst day of your life. But the boys are more important than you are. They're much more important. This does not have to be *their* worst day. That's your goal. You *have* to do this. Stay focused. You're not as important today as they are. You do what you have to do. But know, know in your heart, your boys are fine. They know *nothing*. They *will* know nothing. Not until they're older, and this is old news. For now, they're as innocent as they were two years ago. Or two months ago. Or two days ago. This day is your gift to them. It's a fine day for them. Keep it that way. Give them some time to get older. They deserve that, right? Good. Stay tough for them. Just do your job and stay tough. The boys will be with your aunt and your mom. Stay away 'til you can get there without any press. Don't let the cops go there. They don't need to see any cops."

She closed the phone and entered another number, glancing at the card with all of the numbers she had prepared ahead of time. "Mrs. Cardwell? It's Helen Paige. Someone will bring the boys within the hour. Please call your sister and have her there as well. And don't tell anybody. Tell her the same—don't talk to anybody. And don't turn the television on. Or the radio."

Helen sat back down at the table with the boys. She held the teddy bears while they slurped on their milkshakes. When Irene finished the book, Helen took it and started again, from the beginning.

After another half-hour, Hilary Armistead entered the restaurant. She joined the women and children. Helen stood. She introduced the two women. Then she gave the book back to Irene.

"I have to go now. It was so nice to spend time with you. Take very good care of Beary and Nosy, OK?" Both boys nodded. "And don't forget the book. It needs to be read so it can be loved, OK?" They both nodded again, never taking their eyes off her. "I know someone who would like to see you. Your grandma. She needs to hold you because her arms need some love. Will that be good?" They nodded again. Helen touched each of them on the head and then left.

Once outside in her own car, Helen called the police. She told them she would be just off the road at Ralph Dixon's home. Then she drove there and parked. She called Jeff. "What's going on? … So, it's over? … Yeah, you guys can go back home. Thanks so much, Jeff, more than you'll ever know … Right, talk later."

Helen closed the phone, got out to stand beside her car, and breathed. And breathed. And waited for the cops to show up. She called Hilary, who had stayed with Irene and the children. "Are you there? Good. I expect the cops any minute now." She listened. "Yes, I understand," she said. Then she hung up. It was all out of her hands at this point.

The police came and kept Helen at Ralph Dixon's house for some time. She refused to talk to them until Hilary arrived. After talking to Hilary, she started talking to the authorities. She described the inside of the house. They took her inside and had her report the conversation she had with Ralph Dixon. They took her notebook.

Later, they said she needed to go with them to the police station. As they were leaving the house, Hilary insisted they keep her covered. "We need to keep her identity private," said Hilary. "We can't have her name and photo appear together. It's better the press does not even know a CASA was on the premises."

At the station, she told the story again. Hilary sat with her. They gave her paper and had her write the story. She signed her statement as Helen Paige. "What's your name?" asked the lead detective. "We have one on the driver's license, another from your lawyer, you give us another one."

"I have a CASA name, Helen Paige, which is also my maiden name. I have my mother's maiden name I use for everything else, which is Helen Smith. And I have a married name, Helen Prescott, which I seldom use. All are legal. Even the Social Security Administration has all of my names; they're all on the same number."

It was finally over. They had no more questions and she was free to go. During all of that time, she never allowed her picture to be taken.

It was dark when Helen returned to her apartment. She went in, unplugged her landline phone, turned off her cell phone, and went straight to her bedroom. She sat on her cushion. She took care of herself, and she did nothing about getting the drink she so desperately wanted.

The morning newspaper carried a story the next day about a man involved in a stand-off with the police at his wife's apartment. His wife was not home, and neither were her two little boys. No pictures of the family were available. The husband had been shot several times when he turned his gun on the police. He died at the scene.

The same day, shortly after noon, Helen walked down the steep part of Queen Anne Hill. A bright sun glimmered and sparkled on the rain from the night before. The sky was such a clear and bright blue it made Helen's heart hurt just to see it as she walked. She noticed a ferry in the sound moving toward Bainbridge Island. When she got to the bottom of the hill, she entered a coffee shop. Jeff and Patrick were already waiting at a corner table. Both men got to their feet as she joined them. She hugged both of them, surprising all three.

"I wish I hadn't involved you in this," she said quietly. "But I will never, as long as I live, be able to thank you enough." Both men looked at the table, at their feet, around the room. Anywhere but at each other or at Helen. "How much hassle did the police give you? I have a lawyer available for you both. He's just waiting for your call."

"We don't need a lawyer," said Jeff. "The cops never saw us, never talked to us."

"But you were at the scene, weren't you? Didn't they want statements?"

"We knew from the way you talked that it could get hairy, so we talked about it. How to keep from coming to anybody's attention. Even if we didn't do anything wrong, we didn't want our names in the paper or nothing. We do have kids to watch out for, you know. We both watch law-and-order type shows on TV. Believe it or not, we both read books. Wasn't hard to figure out," Patrick concluded.

"When we followed him," added Jeff, "we stayed well back. He parked so we went on down the street. Parked in a different area. Then we walked along to a coffee shop on the corner nearest the apartment house. We just sat and had coffee. The place was full of people doing the same thing. As soon as we saw cops, we milled around like everyone else. When it was over, we walked real casual back to the SUV and left. No reason anyone would even notice us."

"What about the call to Irene? What if they trace it?"

"Won't do any good. We bought the cell in a crowded shop in Bellevue. It was a throwaway. Right after we made the call, we wiped it off and threw it out the window several miles from where we made the call."

"Amazing. I guess I found the right men to help me out."

"You going to get in any trouble, Helen?"

"I don't think so. I had a lawyer with me. They asked a lot of questions, but I think it's a closed case already. They're calling it a 'suicide by cop' incident, off the record."

"How about the kids?"

"They're good. They're just little guys. They won't know about it until the mom starts leaking it out a little at a time. By the time they're really curious, they'll be twelve or more, I expect. With any kind of luck at all, their lives will be so far away from this and so much better, it won't leave permanent scars. Time will tell." She thanked the men and went back up the hill to her apartment.

Shortly thereafter, Gerard called. "Want to go back to Cloud Mountain? I can take you there." She thought about it. It was tempting. But she felt she could get through this experience on her own. She wanted to try.

"I'm going on retreat in my own bedroom," she told Gerard. "But dinner tonight would be a treat."

"Six fifteen, then," he said.

"Yes, six fifteen," she replied.

❧ ❧ ❧

They walked to Moorage in near silence.

"Gerard," she started when they were seated at what was now their table having soup, "there's a lot you haven't told me, isn't there?"

"There always is."

"Why haven't you told me more?"

"When you're ready to hear more, you'll ask. You always do."

"You meditate, don't you?"

"I do."

"For a long time."

"For a long time."

"When you look at me, what do you see?"

"You're asking about the non-material plane, aren't you?"

"Yes."

"I see your aura."

"What color?"

"Violet."

"I don't know anything about auras. I've just heard about them."

"You don't need to know about them. You don't even need to see them," Gerard said. "Typically, for a person who sees them, they only confirm what was already known through other means."

"So, what did you know through other means that was confirmed by seeing the aura?"

"In your case, I actually saw the aura, and then went about confirming. I saw the aura at the first AA meeting when you walked in. It was immensely powerful, even from across the room."

Helen felt very strange hearing this. Especially from Gerard. She thought of him, engineer and inventor, as a very grounded person. She was, in almost every respect, a very grounded person. Especially now, with her work. More so now, in fact, than ever before in her life. Apartments are very grounded objects. Looking at them and filling them, very grounded. Remodeling them, very grounded. Writing reports for CASA cases, very grounded. She was grounded. Except, of course, in her meditation, where she tried to escape being grounded. And where the other really important work happened.

"What does the violet tell you?"

"You're inspirational. Visionary. And you have a goal of saving people. See ... I didn't need to see the aura. Anyone around you for very long would see the 'meaning of Helen' without seeing the aura."

Helen did not know what to think. She started to argue with him about it. But she could not argue with all of it. Not the part about trying to save people. And it *had* been inspiring to start the Claudius Foundation. She recalled the inspiration to do so had arrived during a meditation session. So … maybe she would let the argument pass her by, think about it later.

"Why does an engineer know about auras?" she asked instead.

"I'm a physicist. The engineer piece is just a means to accomplish tasks. The physicist is interested in energy. All sorts of energy. Auras are just energy. It all fits."

Somehow, when Gerard said it, it *did* fit. It was almost too simple.

"Helen," he said, after the silence had extended for two or three minutes, "it's time for you to speak about what you haven't told me. You've arrived, you know."

Helen thought about it. She knew he was right, of course. She started talking. "My husband, Robert, was deep in a depression, the low point of his roller coaster of ups and downs. I'd been confined to Riggs Erickson for over a year by then. My in-laws were talking to the staff there, making sure I was under a partial sedation at all times. They feared if I got truly healthy I'd see how ill Robert was, and I'd leave him. They didn't want that. They watched over the twins to some extent and had a full-time governess on the premises. But Robert and the twins lived in a separate house on the estate. It was the governess's day off, and the children were home from school for a partial holiday. Robert put the twins in the back seat of the car, had them buckle up. Then he drove out to Gloucester. He knew the road well. We vacationed there several times a year. There's a place where a highway goes straight to the ocean, crossing over another major road to do it. Once across that road it's straight out to the bluff overlooking the ocean. It's a steep drop, all big granite boulders. He was going over one hundred miles an hour, the highway patrol said. He sailed off the cliff. My twins were seven years old. Their names were Franklin and Stephen."

# Book Club Questions

1. Transformations occur throughout the book, including the transformation William Prescott acknowledges in his letter to Helen and that of James Butler as he moves from the house his parents purchased for him to the Lenora Apartments. What other examples of transformation did you notice in the book?

2. Helen goes on retreats to a yoga center and the Cloud Mountain Retreat Center. What function in her life do the retreats serve?

3. How does the relationship between Alicia and George affect Helen? Why does this occur?

4. In what way does the work of the foundation affect each of the board members?

5. What is Helen's role in the death of her children? Does she take any responsibility for what happened to them?

6. How does the work of the New Life Institute reflect the issues Helen sees in her own life story?

7. How does the author use physical objects, such as art and furniture, to show transformation in Helen's life?

8. What is the role of houses and apartments within the book? What does housing represent for some of the adult characters in the novel? Why does Helen focus on apartments as a solution to the problems of children?

9. Is Helen acting in an ethical way in combining her work for CASA with her foundation work?

10. What is Helen's role and responsibility in the death of Martin Larch near the end of the book? Do you believe she deliberately goaded him into taking the action he did?